YELLOW BIRD

YELLOW BIRD

A DOC ADAMS MYSTERY

RICK BOYER

FAWCETT COLUMBINE ▾ NEW YORK

A Fawcett Columbine Book
Published by Ballantine Books
Copyright © 1991 by Richard L. Boyer

LIBRARY OF CONGRESS CATALOGING-IN-PUBLICATION DATA
Boyer, Rick.
Yellow bird / Rick Boyer.—1st ed.
   p. cm.
ISBN 0-449-90506-3
I. Title.
  PS3552.0895Y4 1991
  813'.54—dc20   91-70537
                                                       CIP

Text design by Beth Tondrean Design/Jane Treuhaft
Manufactured in the United States of America
First Edition: October 1991
10 9 8 7 6 5 4 3 2 1

FOR MY OLDEST AND
CLOSEST FRIEND

MIKE CRAMER

ACKNOWLEDGMENTS

Thanks are in order to the following people for helping me in this book: Paul Tescione, D.D.S., and Robert Scully, M.D., for helping me with the intricacies of dentistry and oral surgery. Thanks also to my critical readers: Bruce and John Boyer, Pat McAfee, and Bill Tapply, for all their help and suggestions. For Detective Don Babb, who has provided a lot of help on police matters. For Major William Rawls, U.S. Army Special Forces (Ret.), and Jeannie Ye, for their expertise in weaponry, mayhem, and the deadly arts.

Finally, thanks to the best editor in the business: Leona Nevler, Vice-President of Fawcett Books.

YELLOW BIRD

ONE

t was an unexpected phone call that came one cold evening in the middle of January to our house in Concord. It jerked me twenty-five years back into the past. A time warp over the wire.

"Is this Charles Adams, the famous medical diagnostician from Chicago?" came a vaguely familiar voice. My throat tightened.

"Uh . . . yes. Who is this?"

"You can't tell by my voice? Why it's me, Jonathan Randolph, yore old med-school sidekick. Now don't say you don't remember, Adams!"

Jonathan Randolph, whom I had met at Northwestern University Medical School in the sixties and hadn't seen since, did sound familiar. But his voice had taken on a southern drawl. Where the hell had he been? What had he been up to? And did I really care? Did I really want to relive all this?

"I've retired, sold my practice in Houston, and moved to Osterville, down on Cape Cod. Do you know Osterville, Adams? Lovely place."

Since Mary and I own a cottage on the Cape, I did know Osterville, Mass. It was lovely indeed, and very pricey too. All of New England is on the pricey side, but Osterville, like Weston, Belmont, Manchester, Chestnut Hill, Dover, Lincoln, and

Marblehead (and maybe six or seven other towns) was approaching astronomical. Come to think of it, they're not exactly giving away Concord these days, either.

Jonathan Randolph, a pretty good friend and drinking buddy back in those frenzied, sleepless, and strung-out days of medical school, was not, if recollection proved correct, a particularly good student. I wasn't outstanding, but good enough to land a residency at my first choice of hospitals: Mass General. Which is how this hayseed from the Midwest made his move to the East, and married an Italian girl from Schenectady.

Randolph, again if memory served, finally settled on his fifth-place choice somewhere in Arkansas. Was it Pine Bluff or Bull Shoals?

"Listen, Adams, c'mon down and see us. We're having an open house this Saturday. Saturday the twenty-first. How's your calendar look?"

"I think it's full, but I'll have to ask Mary," I lied, wanting the option to attend, but the choice to decline as well. Who wouldn't under these rushed circumstances?

"Mary, I take it, is your better half?"

"Yes, she's my wife."

"Any kids?"

"Uh-huh. Two boys. Jack is now, jeez, twenty-three, and Tony's twenty-one."

"Time marches on. Hey, if those kids of yours are even a little like you were back in Chicago, I bet they're really something—"

I got a sinking feeling in my gut. Leave it to Jonathan Randolph to relate all our wild misdeeds as young med students in front of Mary. And if I remembered him correctly, he'd elaborate the sleazy parts and make me out to be the chief instigator. I decided to myself the calendar was definitely full. No need to consult Mary.

"You still there, Adams?"

"Kind of . . ."

"This Mary. If I know you, she's a looker, right?"

"I think so." Well, he got that right, anyway.

"If she's a sport, she won't mind us reliving some of those wild old days, hey?"

Mary is a sport, but there are limits. Randolph obviously didn't know her.

"Okay, here's the deal: we've made some fast friends here already. Christ Almighty, are we glad to get out of Houston! Anyway, the open house starts at two, but I thought maybe you'd like to mosey on down here a little early, say about noon-ish?"

Mosey on down. Well, sure, podnah, we'll jes' mosey on daown. . . . He'd been in Texas awhile, that was for sure.

"All right, Randy, give me directions, but I still cain't *gaarn-*tee it."

"Haw, haw! Adams, y'always was a stitch! And whudduyah know, you even remembered my nickname!"

Dammit! So I had. The years fell away. The Hindus are correct; time is meaningless . . . it doesn't exist.

"Okay, Randy, we'll try to make it. Now give me directions."

As Saturday approached and I remembered the unexpected, almost eerie invitation from Randolph, I hoped Mary would decline interest in the jaunt and have me call and cancel. But to my surprise she said she was delighted.

"I can't wait to visit Osterville again, Charlie. Those houses along the shore are just too much."

"Uh-huh—too much money."

"You know, now that the kids are almost out of school, we could think about buying one of those, and sell the Breakers."

"Aw, c'mon, Mare. I like our cottage because it's a *cottage*, a three-bedroom, cozy house. If we bought one of those fourteen-room monstrosities, it wouldn't be a hideaway; it would be a money pit."

"Still, I want to go and look. What's Jonathan Randolph like?"

"Well, back in the mid-sixties he was a blond-haired, beefy kid from Philadelphia right out of Penn. He wore dark-framed glasses and polo shirts with madras pants. Your typical preppie, if that word is still around."

"Did he marry anybody you know?"

"I have no idea. If my memories of Randy are correct, he's probably on his third wife by now."

"Oh really? What makes you say that?"

"I don't know," I said, after thinking about it for a few seconds, "it's just a feeling I have. C'mon; it's almost ten."

Traffic to the Cape is almost nonexistent in January, and the drive down was fast and pleasant. The farther south and east we got, the more the sky brightened and the less snow we saw on the ground. In less than ninety minutes we were rolling along Bay Shore Drive in Osterville, looking for number 34. Mary was oohing and ahing at the mansions that lined the road, whipping her head back and forth like a tennis spectator as we rolled along, trying to see over dense hedges, through high iron gates.

Number 34 was a contemporary house overlooking the sea with a wide cantilevered deck along the oceanside, high glass walls with stone pillars, and a big, tapering stone fireplace on the far side. The roof was gently sloping wooden shakes. I couldn't even imagine what it had cost. And then I got an inkling of why Randy had invited me down: to show off his obvious success in medicine.

"Gee willikers!" said Mary, eyeing the place as we oozed up the drive in Mary's Audi. The car was a 5000, now almost five years old. This was fine with me; I could handle it. But would the Conspicuous Consumption Division of the Osterville PD have it towed away?

"I guess old Randy did quite well for himself in Houston," I whispered. I spoke low because I didn't want to wake the Old Money.

"Is he in oral surgery too?"

"I doubt it. Randy and I both trained for general medicine. I don't think he knows about my leaving general practice to become an oral surgeon. I suspect he specialized in something lucrative, like radiology or perhaps neurosurgery."

Gee, I thought, I'd sure hate to have Jonathan Randolph operating on my CNS. Why was I thinking this? Was it fair to good old Randy?

A man wearing cream-yellow pants and a white pullover slipped out of the glass doors and onto the deck in the gathering sunshine. He was red-faced, almost bald, and thick around the waist and butt. He went to the side-deck railing, waving down at us.

"Is that him?" Mary asked, opening the passenger door.

"I guess so. Wow, he sure looks older."

"That's reality, Charlie. But those thick glasses you mentioned are gone; he probably wears contacts now."

We got out of the car and walked around the house to the deck. Randolph leaned over the rail for a closer look at his guests.

"Well, Adams! Good to see ya, fella! How ya been? God, you look young! What the hell you do, boy? Have yourself frozen each night, or what? And—whooooeee!—hold the phone! Who's that with you? Ohh, my *Lord*!"

Mary gave him a quick grin, but she wasn't impressed by his male flattery. For one thing, it's routine with her. Second, like most women, she isn't excited by the premature and obvious compliment. We walked up the deck stairs and then inside, with Randy leading the way. The place was done in contemporary Beverly Hills. White suede couches twelve feet long. High pile, beige carpeting over thick foam pads; you could do a trampoline act on it. Oversized prints of irises and lilies in transparent glass containers on a black background—you know the ones I mean. In the fireplace, which was walk-in size, a log fire purred and snapped. A young woman with a sequin sheath lavender dress rose to meet us. Long, honey-colored hair. Shiny, high-heel shoes that were too high to be polite—the nasty kind with no backs. I could put up with them. Pretty green eyes. Something wasn't right with them. They weren't quite focused. Too soft . . .

"This is my wife, Michelle," said Randy. She took my hand in hers; it was cold and wet. She and Mary exchanged greetings with thin smiles and eyes that didn't smile. I sensed instant reserve, almost antagonism. Or was it mutual fear?

We sat in front of the fire and sipped Bloody Marys while Dr. Jonathan Randolph gave us a capsule summary of his past twenty years as a radiologist. I'd guessed that one on the button. He'd done very well in suburban Houston, which, he half admitted, wasn't all that difficult in the oil-and-gas-boom days of the seventies and early eighties when the whole region was awash in depletion-allowance cash. He'd invested in real estate and had the good sense, or perhaps luck, to bail out of it and cash in before the crunch hit.

"And you should see Houston now," he said, refilling his tumbler from the big iced pitcher on the glass table. "It's got a forty-percent vacancy rate downtown, a crime problem that rivals Miami's, and a climate we got sick of real fast, right, hon-bun?"

"Ohh, yeah. And Ah'm from Dallas m'self," Michelle drawled with a slow smile. Despite her calm demeanor, the glass trembled in her hand. I couldn't see it, but it was there; I heard the ice cubes chatter.

"Michelle was a Kilgore Rangerette, as if you couldn't guess from her body," Randy continued. "Anyhooo, we decided to pack up from Houston and move somewhere with a little sanity. We got one of those almanac books that tells you where the best places to live are? Well, the Cape was right up there with the best, so here we are."

"Do you ever regret leaving medicine so soon?" Mary asked, setting down her tumbler and declining a refill. "I mean, it's obvious you've done very well, but do you ever feel that the medical field needs you?"

Mary is a registered nurse, and the question reflected her honest concern.

"Tell you the truth, Mary, hell no. Medicine is a hard, hard life. Several of my close friends died of heart attacks before they reached forty-five." He leaned over the table and helped himself to some garlic cream-cheese spread, which he smeared over a Ritz cracker and popped the whole thing in his mouth. Besides the yellow pants, he wore canvas boat shoes without socks and a white terrycloth pullover half-unbuttoned. Around his neck was a gold chain as thick as a pencil. The gold looked real; I had a hunch it was. He wore a gold Rolex on his left wrist. "Nope, I sold my practice for a tidy sum, liquidated my real-estate holdings, and split the scene, as they say. So far, I haven't regretted it. So what about you, Adams? Hell, I woulda called you earlier but I didn't know you were anywhere around these parts. I expected you to settle in Illinois or Iowa—one of those god-awful flat states that begin with vowels—"

"How long have you been here, Randy?" I asked.

"Almost three months. Came here just before Thanksgiving. Hey, hell of a winter they've got here, though, eh?"

"We like the cold winters," Mary said. "But it's nice today, isn't it? They said on the radio it was almost forty down here, and the sun's coming out."

Randolph then asked me about my practice and was surprised to learn that I'd left internal medicine within two years after my residency. I explained that I found internal medicine too stressful and became a surgeon because I discovered I was good with my hands.

"More than one of your dates told me that. Haw! Haw! Pardon me, Mary. Just kidding," he said, laying his hand on her knee. She flinched. "But seriously, Adams, you were the best diagnostician they ever had at school; I remember three professors saying that—"

"I know, but straight medicine just wasn't for me. I'm happy where I am."

I did not tell Randolph the whole story of why I'd bailed out of medicine so quickly. The truth was that one of my very first patients, my six-year-old nephew Peter Brindelli, died as a result of medication I recommended for him. The medication was the proper one, in all but one out of twenty thousand instances. I was not the only physician to recommend it, either. But it was a horrendous blow to me and the family. There isn't a person on earth I like more than Mary's brother, Joe. His son's death, partially at my hands, came way too soon in my nascent practice. Frankly, I'm still not completely over that grim episode. Mary, sensing my stress at the subject and perhaps fearful of further, more probing questions, stood up and asked Michelle if there was anything she could do to help in the kitchen.

"No, hon. Everything's fahn," she said, heading for the kitchen. The phone rang, and Randy jumped up to get it. After talking briefly in hushed tones, he cupped his hand over the receiver and looked back at the two of us.

"Hey, you guys, looks like I'll be awhile on this one. Long distance from the Lone Star State. I'll make it as quick as I can—"

"I swayuh, that man's got so many business deals a goin', it just drives me crazy," Michelle said, opening the oven door and peering inside. Out wafted the pleasant aroma of seafood and popovers. She looked up at us and grinned. "Crabmeat puffs. We just love 'em to death. They'll be ready right quick."

"I thought your husband got out of real estate," Mary said.

"Oh, most of it. But, Lord, he's still got his fingers in all sorts of pies."

She pronounded it "pahs."

"He's always on the phone, and spends a lot of time out of town. I gave up trying to keep track of him. Why, I nevah even knew him when he was a doctor."

"Oh, really?" said Mary. "How long have the two of you been married?"

"Almost two years. As you might have guessed, Ah'm not the first Mrs. Randolph." She grinned and winked slowly at us. "Fact is, Ah'm number *fowah*."

Randy cupped the phone again and leaned back toward us. "Hey, Adams! If you want, you and Mary might like to take a stroll up the beach for a few minutes. The weather's great, and some of the houses along this stretch are really something. Just an idea—the others won't be here for another forty minutes."

Mary and I looked at each other. Just a glance told me that fresh air was just what we needed. We had our coats on in a wink and headed for the back door that opened onto the deck.

"The best views are up that way," Randy pointed. "To your

left at the bottom of the stairs. Don't get lost now!"

We said we'd be back in a half hour or so, in time for the crab puffs, and escaped out into the cool air and sunshine, walking down the deck stairs and onto the beach.

"Well, Charlie, you *are* a master diagnostician. Twenty-five years pass, you can still read Jonathan Randolph like an open book. He *is* a radiologist, or was. And he's on his fourth wife."

"Wrong there; I guessed third."

"Doesn't surprise me. Boy, I'm glad to get out of there. What's she on, anyway?"

"I'd guess downers—maybe Quaaludes if they were still around—but who knows? Randy doesn't seem all there, either. Maybe it's just the passage of time, or his living in Texas. I don't know."

"You said you liked Texas."

"I do, but it's a different culture. Houston is a long way from New England, in every sense of the word."

We walked along the hard-packed sand of the water's edge. The wind was cold but it wasn't constant, and the sun, though low in the sky in January, was warm. It was hazy-bright, the sky above a glowing metallic silver of scattered clouds. The gulls cried and the surf boomed.

"What are you thinking, Charlie?"

"I'm thinking, quite honestly, that I don't wish to become friendly with the Randolphs. Let's put our time in at the open house and scoot back to Concord. And let's not mention the fact that we have a house here on the Cape, just up the road. If he finds out, they'll be bugging us all summer."

She squeezed my hand. "I'm so glad you said that."

The houses—if such they can be called—stood in silent ranks of grandeur along Bay Shore Road. Mostly wooden and built during the twenties, they were multi-storied and wide, with sweeping pillared porches, round Queen Anne towers with dome roofs, and immaculate lawns that stretched like lazy putting greens to the beach grass and sand. There was no snow on the Cape that day. It seemed as if spring was just around the corner.

We had been walking scarcely ten minutes when the sound of a muffled explosion reached us. We turned in silence and stared at the blue-gray wooden house opposite us.

"What was that?"

"It sounded like a shot," I said.

"Uh huh. But from where? Inside that house?"

"I don't think so; the place looks closed up for the winter. Look around; do any of these places seem occupied now?"

We scanned the row of mansions. All were perfectly kept up, but there was no sign of human habitation among them. Silent and empty.

"I think they're all vacant, Charlie. Maybe Randolph's place is the only one inhabited."

"I think you're right. Randolph is New Money; he only has one house, spectacular though it might be. These belong to Old Money. Their owners are down in Boca Raton or Palm Beach, or the islands, for the winter."

"If this house is empty, then what made that noise?"

I shrugged my shoulders. "Bursting water pipe? I bet the heat's off. Car backfiring on the road behind the house?"

"Let's go look," she said, walking toward the house. I followed her; we went up to the big white door that was set several feet into the house and flanked by enormous brass carriage lamps. Rang the bell. No answer, but we didn't exactly expect James the Butler to appear in his tux and white gloves. In fact we couldn't even hear the doorbell chime inside: the house was too big and the crash of the waves too loud. Mary went to the nearest window and peered inside, holding her hands around her face to cut the glare of sunlight.

"Gosh . . ." she said. "You'd think God lives here . . ."

"Don't, Mary; we'll get arrested."

"Nobody's home."

"Maybe. But you can bet these places are wired to the hilt with security devices. Even as we speak, lights are probably flashing on a panel at Lloyds of London. Pretty soon a black van will pull up and they'll unleash the rottweilers, foaming at the mouth . . ."

"Oh, c'mon, Charlie. I'm going around to the other side."

"That's a dumb idea."

"You don't have to come . . . chicken."

I followed her around to the other side of the mansion—I am given to understand they actually call these places "cottages"— and watched her ring the bell at the rear door. As a joke, Mary and I named our little beach house—a true cottage in every sense—The Breakers after the fabulous Vanderbilt mansion in Newport. We were just kidding, but this place was no joke. She backed up and peered at the windows on the second and third floors.

"Put your ear up against the glass of that window," she said, "and I'll ring again. Tell me if you hear anything."

Half expecting a fatal dose of current, I went to the window and stuck my head against it. Mary jabbed at the wall, and from deep within I heard the sonorous, mellow sound of chimes.

"Well?" she asked.

"Remember that Sunday in Venice when they rang the bells at San Marco for two hours?"

"Uh huh."

I jerked my thumb at the window. "Better," I said. "Now let's go." I walked back toward the beach, but Mary skipped quickly up the walk, through the open gate of the high stockade fence, and out to the road.

"A car and a truck down the road a ways, but nothing behind the house," she reported as we resumed out walk. "So it wasn't a car backfiring."

"Cars don't backfire when they're parked; a car cruising along probably backfired as it passed the house."

"Oh."

We walked another ten minutes. The houses gradually diminished in grandeur, but were still impressive. Up the beach a man was throwing a Frisbee for his golden retriever, who jumped and barked and dove into the water. Gave me the chills just to watch. On the way back, Mary stopped and stared at the teal-colored house again. It was done in the Federal style, with a big fan window over the front door. All the windows on the first and second floors had fan tops on them. Those on the third floor were gabled and smaller. All the windowpanes reflected brilliant light back at us.

"Couldn't see in if we tried," she said. "Still, I think the sound came from inside, and maybe from the second floor. A sound from the road would be more of an echo. What we heard was close, but muffled."

"I'm not so sure of that," I said.

"I am. Your ears are going, Charlie. Too much pistol shooting."

I looked at my watch and said we'd better get back to the party. So we hiked back, although neither of us were too keen on it. The house was full when we returned, and so was the parking area, full of what we'd expected: Jags, Beemers, Mercedes, Lincoln Town Cars, Caddy Eldos, and so on. There was even a Lotus, bright magenta red, and maybe three feet high at the roof. Made Mary's poor little five-year-old Audi look out of place. I loved it all the more. There were twelve or fifteen couples inside, all overdressed and laughing hysterically at each other. They wore designer lounging outfits, with lots of gold and expensive accessories. The conversations mostly revolved around the best shops, vacation resorts, golf courses, imported cars, and investment plans. Mary and I later agreed on one thing: nowhere, in any of the conversations we heard, did the subject or interest level transcend the materialistic, status-seeking, ego-enlarging preoccupations of what has sadly become Mainstream America.

It wasn't a total loss. The crab puffs were good; they had imported beer and played Keith Jarrett, George Winston, and Scott Hamilton on the stereo. I drank two bottles of Becks and one of Amstel, and stuffed myself. Mary did likewise. Sometime during our wanderings from couple to couple, we mentioned to Randy that we'd heard a sound like a shot from one of the beach mansions.

"Really? No kidding?" he said with alcohol-induced intensity. "Listen: I'll call the police and report it."

"No, I don't think so," Mary said. "I mean, we're not sure

about the noise, and nobody was home, anyway. We think it might have been a car."

"It wouldn't be any trouble."

"Let's wait and see what happens."

"Fine. Here's Michelle to say good-bye."

She oozed up and clutched him around the middle. Her eyes were bright, her gait unsteady. Say good-bye, Michelle . . .

"G'bye, y'all. Hope to see you again soon. Great meetin' yah—"

We left at four thirty, and were home just after six. It was cold and dark in Concord. We built a fire in the kitchen wood stove and ate a late night snack of cheese fondue and frozen-baked French bread. I kept thinking about that magenta Lotus parked outside Randolph's house. We huddled together and watched Masterpiece Theatre, then we went up to bed to watch a late movie and cuddle in the cold. We do like the cold winters in New England.

It never occurred to us that we'd already forgotten about the noise in the deserted house on the beach.

hree weeks later I was standing with Mary's brother, Detective Lieutenant Joe Brindelli, out on the rooftop garden of his penthouse apartment on Pinckney Street in Boston's fashionable Beacon Hill section. It was dusk; a blizzard was moving in off the ocean, pelting us with heavy wet snow and wind as we stood outside in the gathering darkness, right in the teeth of the winter storm.

Joe was looking at his pigeons. We were standing in the coop he'd built two years ago. He was really getting into pigeons when he married Marty Higgins, his old girlfriend from police headquarters he met way back when. But she hadn't been in the Beacon Hill apartment two weeks before she put the heavy kibosh on the pigeon thing, saying that they were ugly, noisy, dirty, and disgusting. Joe was disappointed, but Mary and I agreed with Marty. Mary thinks her brother got into pigeons because he was lonely, living by himself in that big apartment all those years. Frankly, I'm convinced it was some sort of homage to Marlon Brando. But Joe denies it.

Joe loves to show off his roof garden, even in a blizzard, and even to his relatives who've seen it lots of times. But I can't blame him for being proud of the apartment. He bought it in '72, right after he moved to Boston from Schenectady, before real-estate prices in Boston went through the stratosphere. It was a run-down apartment in a seedy old building on Pinckney Street. *Then*. But he'd fixed it up, little by little, knocking out walls, adding a skylight or two, renovating the three fireplaces, and so on. In '83, new management re-did the entire building, making it a deluxe cooperative. Joe now had a primo Boston penthouse apartment. Since he'd married and settled down, Mary and I were coming into town from Concord more and more often to visit Joe and Marty.

Joe was filling ceramic cups with pigeon feed, which he placed up on a board shelf near the perches.

"Marty's letting me keep these last three, Doc. Until summertime. Then it's sayonara for all of 'em, and the coop gets torn down. Hey, did I tell you that pigeon-keeping dates from the Middle Ages?"

"No. And also I don't care. It's getting cold and dark out here, despite the view. Let's go inside."

"It's true. It started in Italy."

"Where else?"

He ignored me, looking up at the perch in the far inside corner of the coop, up in the dark there, where now only three birds remained, warbling and cooing, their feathers ruffed up to fight the cold, staring out of their dark refuge. Thin, bubble-gum-colored membranes flicked over their frightened yellow eyes. I could live without them. They reminded me how cold I was getting. I raised the cut-crystal tumbler and took another swallow of the Talisker single-malt whiskey. Thank God for the antifreeze.

"It was a war game that began in northern Italy, near Florence. Noblemen would fly their flocks in hopes of capturing their rival's birds."

"Capturing other birds? You mean their pigeons went out and captured other pigeons? How the hell they do that?"

"Pigeons have a strong flocking instinct, as well as a homing instinct. A large flock of birds can surround a small one and lure the birds back to a new coop. Then your rival's gotta pay you to get his birds back. It's like holding them for ransom."

"Beginning to sound Italian—"

Still no rise from him. I stamped my feet and blew a big cloud of steam. Behind us, beyond the sliding thermo-glass kitchen doors, our wives were preparing Friday-night dinner. I couldn't wait to go in.

"Why don't you let these guys out and see what happens?" I asked, looking out over the railing at the Charles River basin, five stories below.

The river was bluish gray in the dusk. Maybe it would freeze over again. *Brrr!* The February wind and cold were fierce out there. I looked down at the rooftops of historic Beacon Hill, the oldest part of America's oldest major city. The slate roofs were steep, with tall chimney pots that stood all crooked. The copper gutters were pool-table green with age. Beyond those rooftops you could see the Museum of Science, the mouth of the Charles River, and the deep bluish gray of the North Atlantic beyond that. Directly across the river from us were the severe, cubistic buildings of M.I.T. What a great school. It's not tweedy; it doesn't have the class and panache of Harvard, a few miles upriver. Harvard has buildings with names like Eliot House, Dunster House, and "The Widener." M.I.T.'s buildings have names like E-12 and H-4. Figures. But M.I.T. is the primary reason for Boston's economic rebirth. We owe our dominant position in high-tech R & D to the graduates of M.I.T. who stayed in the area and founded the small, pacesetting firms that line Highway 128, and sprout in little towns like Randolph and Wilmington and Burlington. They pump billions into the economy of Beantown and the Bay State. We owe a lot to that cluster of stark, angular buildings, sans ivy, that compose Massachusetts Institute of Technology.

Up close was the intersection of Charles and Cambridge streets, the commercial hub of the Beacon Hill district, with its raised footbridge that loops up and over the street. In the falling light I could see bundled-up people scurrying over the small bridge, blowing clouds of vapor. They were hurrying home to get warm.

"Let them out? Now?"

"Why not? Marty wants them gone."

"The little dummies will starve."

"I doubt it. I've never noticed a scarcity of pigeons in this city. Or alley cats."

Not waiting for his answer, I opened the wire door to the coop and held it open. The pigeons sat, twitching their necks and snapping their heads around nervously, like snakes. Get 'em out of here, I thought.

Joe followed me out of the coop, leaving its door propped open. We walked over to the edge and put our glasses on the wooden rail cap of the brick wall that surrounds the rooftop garden at chest height. It was now almost dark. The cold wet wind stung my face.

"I heard on the radio it's snowing like crazy west of 128," Joe said. "Concord and Lexington will get at least a foot of snow, maybe more."

"Swell. Makes me glad Mary and I are staying here tonight. If I only had somebody to shovel my walks."

Joe and Marty had invited Mary and me into town for the weekend. This was to pay us back for the seventeen hundred and ninety-one times Joe had spent weekends with us in Concord before he was married.

I smelled sizzling fat, replete with all its vessel-clogging cholesterol and carcinogenic carbon. What I needed. I turned and looked through the big double sliding glass doors that led to the kitchen. I saw the two women inside, Mary with her dark Calabrian complexion and almost black hair, and Marty, with her light brown hair a little gone to gray, and her blue eyes and light skin. Mary was basting the boned leg of lamb on the Jenn-Air grill. Marty doesn't eat meat, but the rest of us sure do. I saw her watching patiently as Mary centered the big black hunk of meat over the broiler grate and basted it with the marinade. The marinade was a mixture of olive oil, crushed garlic, basil, red wine, lemon juice, and teriyaki sauce. We would have white beans with butter and garlic and hot French bread with the meat. I would make my Greco-Romaine salad as an accompaniment. A couple of bottles of vintage claret to round it all out, and we'd cap the feast with an English trifle and cappuccino.

To keep warm in the meantime, Joe and I were sipping single-malt Talisker with a splash of soda, no ice.

Joe had lost thirty-seven pounds since his marriage, thanks mostly to Martha Higgins and his new motivation to get healthy and stay thin. He was still on his diet, but tonight he was breaking it a wee bit. Joe looked terrific. If an Italian man can stay thin and keep his hair (odds are against both), he's probably handsome. Now, damned if Joe *didn't* look like Marcello Mastroianni. Mary's always claimed this, but I was an unbeliever—until I saw the proof.

Wings fluttered and snapped behind us. There was just enough light coming through the kitchen doors to illuminate the three pigeons as they made their break. They flew up twenty feet, took off over the railing, and banked sharply to the right, then swung down toward Charles Street.

"There's loyalty for you," Joe grunted.

"Here's hoping they don't return," I said, raising my glass.

"Listen, Doc, the real reason I wanted you to come out here with me is, uh . . . there's an urgent request for your professional services at headquarters. In fact, I'd planned to ask you tonight if you'd mind slipping over to Ten Ten Commonwealth Avenue with me for an hour or so tomorrow morning."

"Are you serious? C'mon, Joe; this was supposed to be a totally fun weekend. Marty and Mary are going shopping; you've got two great seats for the Celtics game . . . now you're saying you want me to look inside some dead guy's mouth all morning?"

For the past couple of years, I have been doing part-time oral forensic work for the Commonwealth of Massachusetts, Department of Public Safety: the state police, for whom Joe is a detective lieutenant.

"I know it kind of screws things up. But this is pretty important. We've got a John Doe who's been out in the cold for a week, maybe more. We need to get a fix on him. Problem is, he was found in a vacant house belonging to a big shot. We're kind of under pressure."

"This guy's been out in the cold for over a week? Then he's

good and ripe. Holy Christ, that sounds as bad as a floater."

The term *floater* describes a drowning victim or murder victim disposed of in water. The body sinks initially, but rises and floats after a week or so, when the putrescent gases of decomposition form inside the gut and lift it to the surface like a grotesque, bloated bathysphere. Most of the time you can't even tell they're people. And as you might suppose, they don't smell good. The job of working with a gooey mass like this is so disgusting I actually quit a part-time job as forensic pathologist for Barnstable County, Cape Cod. This was two summers ago, and my strong opinions about working with floaters, or other ripened cadavers, remains fixed. *No way, Jo-sé.*

"This guy is very well preserved, Doc. No odor. I know, because I saw him down in the morgue at Ten Ten. It was cold in that house; kept just above freezing so the pipes wouldn't freeze. Now, it'll only take an hour or so, and we'd really appreciate it. Since it's Saturday, you'll get double time as well. Shit, I wish the rest of us got hiked rates for weekends and nights."

We heard a pounding noise behind us and turned to see Mary knocking on the glass kitchen doors. She leaned close to the glass and peered out into the dark to see us. She rapped again impatiently, holding up a copy of the evening *Globe*. She folded back the front page and was pointing to a photo on page two. I couldn't see what the photo was.

"What time do they want me down there?"

"I told them around ten."

"So you already accepted for me, eh? How nice. C'mon, let's go in before we freeze our asses off. Mary wants to show me something in the paper."

"Yeah, it's that big house down in Osterville where they found the stiff."

My hand stopped, barely touching the cold metal handle of the door frame. I stood there, riveted, while faint chimes sounded in my head.

"Osterville? A house on the beach, perhaps?"

"Yep," said Joe matter-of-factly. "If you could call a mansion like that a house."

The chimes in my memory were familiar. Then I knew them: the chimes inside the house Mary and I stopped at three weeks ago. I slid open the door and walked into the warm kitchen. The aroma of garlic and hot meat hit me, but I scarcely noticed. Mary came at me, holding the paper up.

"Charlie! This is the house! Remember?"

She put the newspaper down on the butcher-block kitchen table and spread it out with her hands, pointing at the photograph in the bottom right-hand corner of the page.

"The very same," I said softly.

"There was a body found there yesterday, Charlie."

Joe came up behind us, unaware of what his sister was saying. "This is big news at headquarters," he said, tapping the picture with his finger. "Like I said, the place was closed up for the winter. Two or three months . . . No heat, just enough to keep the plumbing from bursting. That's what kept the body in such good shape. The M.E.'s office is having a bitch of a time making a fix on time of death—"

"Oh yeah?" I said. "Well, your sister and I can give you a real good fix on the time of death. Like down to the exact minute, can't we, Mary?"

"What are you guys talking about?" asked Marty, coming up beside her husband and peering down at the paper.

"So that *was* a gunshot we heard," said Mary. "It wasn't any car backfiring. It was a shot. I just knew it—"

"Would you two *please* tell me what's going on?" said Joe.

"Sit down, Joey. You too, Marty," said Mary. She briefly related the events of January 21. She did a great job of relating the story, including some details I'd forgotten. While she talked I opened a bottle of red for all of us, poured four glasses, and took mine and paced around Joe's kitchen. It was a tall, sky-lighted room with a wine rack that covered an entire wall, rows of gleaming copper pans and skillets, a stainless-steel work island and cooking area, and everything else you'd want, including the vented range-top grill where the leg of lamb sizzled. As smoke rose from the meat it was sucked into a small vent and disappeared. The rest of the apartment was equally well furnished, with the previously mentioned skylights and working fireplaces, three bedrooms, and three baths—one with a Jacuzzi.

How does a state cop afford all this? He doesn't; it just so happens that Joe and Mary's family made a nice pile of change in the building business in Schenectady, where they grew up. As Mary finished the story I glanced back at Joe and Marty, both sitting there stunned.

Joe looked at his sister, then at me. "January twenty-first, eh?" he said, flipping through his pocket diary. "Three weeks go by, you don't tell me?"

"Why tell you?" I said. "How did we know what we heard was really a gunshot?"

"No, Joey," said Mary, "we heard the shot."

"Heard it, eh? You're walking along the beach and you heard it? From inside this house, second floor? With the windows all closed up tight for the winter?"

"Uh-huh," she said. "We heard it plainly. A shot. But we couldn't tell what floor it came from."

"How'd you know it was a shot?"

"Well, it sure sounded like—"

"We weren't sure, Joe," I said. "I remember telling her that it could have been a car backfiring on the road. Remember me saying that, Mary?"

"Well, obviously, Charlie, now that we know a body was found there, we can assume it was a shot. Are you retarded or something?"

Joe stubbed out his cigarette in the ashtray on the table, leaving it broken and smoldering. Smelled terrific. "What time of day was this, and who is this doctor friend of yours you were visiting? I never heard his name before."

"It was just about one-thirty. Jonathan Randolph was an old med-school buddy; I hadn't seen him in twenty-five years. Frankly, I don't care if I ever see him or his ditzy wife again."

"Hear, hear," said Mary, taking a swig of red. "Here, Charlie, read the article." She slid the paper to me and I bent over and read it.

Osterville—The body of an unidentified man was discovered in this seaside home of Northrop F. Chesterton, a retired investment banker who has spent the past eight weeks vacationing in Jamaica, where he has a winter home. The discovery was made by Owen Lightner, an employee of Mr. Chesterton's. The cause of death was a gunshot wound to the chest, an apparent suicide.

Mr. Chesterton, who made no comment on the incident when reached in Jamaica, said he plans to return to Boston early in the week to aid in the investigation.

"Yeah, safe to assume you heard a shot," said Joe. "Except the M.E. makes the TOD to be between twelve and fifteen days previous, not three weeks ago."

"Thought you said they were having a tough time fixing the time of death," Mary said.

"They are. See, when a well-preserved body like this is more than a week old, fixing even a rough TOD is a bitch. They examine the concentration of various chemicals in the blood and tissues. You might know more about it, Doc."

"I deal with live patients, not dead ones. And as a jaw-and-mouth guy, I get more removed from general medicine each year. I know death dating is a specialized branch of forensic pathology. I think serum urea and potassium are two of the things they look at, but I'm not sure."

Marty came and sat down next to Mary, her bright blue Irish eyes scanning the article.

"If I remember, Joe," she said in her husky voice, "when that much time has elapsed, they usually use the aqueous humor, the eye fluid, to measure the potassium concentration. I think that's right but I'm not sure; I only worked in medical records two months, and that was seventeen years ago."

"You worked in medical records? I always thought you just worked in forensics and personnel."

"That's when you arrived. You keep forgetting I was working at headquarters at Ten Ten two years before you even showed up."

She ran her finger along the column in the paper. Joe, standing over her, ran his big brown hand, with fingers the size of bananas, gently down the center of her back, and she smiled a big smile. Right then I got a little tic, a tightening in my throat, and had to blink a few times. I'm not particularly an emotional man. Perhaps no man likes to admit he is. But thinking about what Joe went through fifteen years before, losing his wife and two children, and all the hell and loneliness that followed— well, seeing him happily married again in his own place made me feel like a million bucks.

"What I heard," continued Joe, "this stiff was found in an upstairs room of this locked and sealed house that was very clean and cold. Still, Mary, the M.E. is making the TOD at just about two weeks."

"Wrong," said Mary. "Three weeks. But remember, he was just about frozen."

"They take that into account," said her brother, walking to the wall phone and punching in a number.

He waited on the line a few seconds, then mumbled into the receiver. I caught the words *aqueous humor*. . . . I helped the women set the table while we waited for Joe. We poured the wine, and he was still talking. We lit the candles. We carved the lamb. . . . We said the blessing. . . .

Joe sat down, helping himself to the food without a word. Bad sign; usually the Brindellis are so gabby you can't fit a word in with a pry bar. Especially at mealtime. He jabbed his finger at Mary and me. "Lucky you're staying in town tonight. They want us all at Ten Ten Comm. Ave. tomorrow morning."

"What?" said Mary, her face falling. She frowned and put her head on her hands. "C'mon, Joey! Marty and I were going shopping tomorrow. This is the first weekend in ages I've stayed in town. We were going to Newbury Street and then up to Copley Square—"

"I know, I know," he said, waving her off. "But this is really important. Really. Doc already got his bad news out on the roof before we came inside. He's got to do an oral forensic on the guy."

"The guy they found in the mansion? Why so soon?"

"Because Chesterton, the owner of the house, is a big shot. You've probably heard of him, and read his name in the papers before."

"Didn't he play a big part in the redevelopment of downtown?" I asked.

"Yep, and this doesn't make him look too good. So we gotta move on it. I'll take both of you over first thing after breakfast. Doc, you can work in the lab while we grill Mary."

Mary threw her napkin down fast and frowned. She was pissed.

"What do you want to ask us, Joey?"

"All about what you saw on that walk you took on the beach three weeks ago. All you saw and heard."

"That'll be easy," Mary said, winking at Marty. "We can still shop when it's over."

"I doubt it. After the preliminaries in the office, they want me to take you down the Cape and walk through the whole thing, start to finish. Oh, and another thing. Why I was waiting, I wanted to hear the latest from the M.E.'s lab. They refixed the TOD. They now put it at three weeks, on the nose. So maybe you *did* hear a shot."

"I told you," said Mary.

"Trouble is, that means that the killer might have seen both of you as you walked along the beach. . . ."

It took a second or two for this to sink in. I put my fork down and stared at the plate. The animal juices were mixing with the bean broth, making zillions and zillions of tiny green, blue, and yellow lights.

"Say that again?" said Mary.

"The murderer, up in the second-floor bedroom. He might have glanced out the window. He might have seen the two of you. Maybe there's even a chance he thinks you saw him, too. You say you couldn't see in because of the sun's reflection, but maybe he doesn't know that."

"There was no killer, Joey. The paper says it was suicide."

Her brother shook his head. "No. Made to look like a suicide.

I have just been informed by the lab that it was most definitely *not* a suicide."

A slight pause.

"Didn't you say that after you heard the noise, you went up and looked at the house?"

Mary's face was frozen. Then she spoke.

"Hell, Joey, we went up to the house and looked in the downstairs windows."

Joe's eyebrows flickered.

"Uh-huh," I added, noticing an increasingly heavy feeling in my gut that I didn't think was the food. "Not only that, we went up and rang the bell, just to see if everything was all right."

There was silence then. A lot of it, if you know what I mean.

"Then what?" asked Marty. Her low, husky voice was hushed in expectancy. She leaned over her plate, wide-eyed. Strands of her fine, blondish-gray hair wafted around in the faint air currents.

"Nothing happened. Nobody answered the door; we couldn't see anybody inside; the place was locked up. So we just left. Didn't we, Charlie? Just continued our walk down the beach," said Mary. "We went about a half mile more, then turned around and came back."

"But we stopped on the way back, remember? Stopped and looked around again briefly."

"Uh-huh, we—wait a second, Joey! How are they so sure it wasn't a suicide? How do they know there was a murderer up there?"

Her brother chewed a slice of meat reflectively, then frowned. "The investigators thought it was suicide at first because the revolver was at the scene lying next to the body, one round fired, and there was no sign of violence. Also, the doors were all locked, with no sign of forced entry. But that's an old ruse, and even after they tell the press the obvious, they make further checks. On the phone just now, I heard about something weird that Karl Pirsch and his men in the lab discovered. Turns out this corpse had heavy powder burns on the torso, indicating a close-range shot."

"So he could have killed himself—"

"But no powder burns on the shirt. All the shirt had was a hole no bullet could have made."

"You mean somebody killed this guy, took off his shirt, then put another shirt on him?" I asked.

"Well, it'd be damn hard for the *victim* to do it, wouldn't it? So it's a homicide. Either the killer switched clothes on the guy, or else he was bare-chested, or even nude, when he was shot, and the murderer dressed him afterward."

"In January? In an unheated house?" Mary asked the question leaning way over the table, right in her brother's face.

"I know it's strange. The killer tried to make it look like a suicide. The gun, a Smith model nineteen, was left next to the victim. It was wiped clean, except for a set of the victim's prints—just one set, right hand—neatly and conveniently found on the stocks and frame. It never happens this way in real life, so it was a setup. But it's also interesting that the gun's serial numbers were filed off, so we're thinking it's a pro hit. When doing a hit, it's always safer to leave the murder weapon at the scene than get caught with it later. All IDs were removed from the corpse. A pro hit, I'd say. A weird one, but still a professional job."

Joe resumed chewing, slowly. Then he stopped, frozen, his face staring far away. He pushed his plate away and stood up. Oh-oh. When Joe Brindelli puts the chompers in neutral, it's generally not an auspicious sign.

He went back to the phone again. More big silence, the kind you can cut with a knife. Joe returned. I wish I could say his face was jovial.

"The DA's office wants to see us first thing tomorrow," he said. "We go there first, then to headquarters at Ten Ten, *then* down the Cape."

"Oh, dammit all . . ." sighed Mary, putting her fork down. That made two Brindellis not eating. *Bad—*

"That's the whole day, Joey. Marty and I were gonna have fun this weekend, shopping on Newbury Street, then lunch at the Westin. What's the big deal, huh?"

"The big deal is, first of all, the neighborhood it happened in. These are heavy hitters down in Osterville, Mary. They want answers, and fast. Also, like I said, Chesterton's a big shot. Carries a lot of clout down the Cape and up here. Big-time financier. Also—and this is just rumor—he may be connected."

"*Connected?*" said Mary. "Oh, great. You're saying maybe we witnessed a mob hit?"

"I didn't say that; you yourself said you didn't see anybody."

"But what if he *thinks* we did?" I said.

"There's always that chance," he said, walking to the glass doors and looking out, vacant-eyed.

"What are you thinking about, dear?" asked Marty, going over to him and putting her hands on his wide back.

"About my birds," he said. "I wonder if they're coming back."

THREE

Next morning the pigeons woke me at six.

Pigeons?

What the hell was this? I thought they left. . . .

It was jet black outside and our room was cold because we had the window open, which is how we always sleep, winter and summer. Mary was snuggled up against me in the queen-size bed. I sure didn't want to get up, but the racket wouldn't let me sleep. Our bedroom was in the rear of the apartment and opened onto the roof garden. Hadn't the damn birds departed last night just before dinner? Or did you dream it, Adams? Was it some sort of wish fulfillment acted out in your sleep? I hate to admit it, but this was happening with increasing frequency lately: not being able to remember what had happened or what I *thought* had happened. Uh-oh. Was it advancing age? Senility? Alzheimer's? Schizophrenia?

All of the above?

One thing for sure: the noise outside my window was real. Annoyed, I threw on a robe and went out into the hallway, then through the kitchen and opened the sliding glass doors. A blast of icy air hit me. And pigeon sounds. The cooing, the gurgly murmur, the quick flutter and flap of the filthy critters.

Joe's birds had come home. And brought all their low-down street friends too. Every pigeon from Beacon Hill was in that coop, slurping up the pigeon food that Joe had set out the previous evening. Maybe he was right. Maybe pigeons could steal other birds and bring them back to their home coop.

Thing is, who the hell needs it?

A light went on behind me. "Oh no!" said a weary voice. I turned to see Marty standing in the kitchen, right in the path of the cold air, clutching her bathrobe around her.

"I agree entirely," I said, going outside, bare feet and all, and into the coop. I shooed the birds away and grabbed the ceramic food cups Joe had filled, taking them indoors and throwing their contents into the trash. Then I returned outside with a broom and swung it around inside the wire cage until the last of the birds fled. I shut the door and staggered back inside, shivering, and returned to bed. But Marty and I had made a secret, unspoken pact then and there. We kept mum about these early-morning deeds, and Joe never found out that his birds had returned.

"You're welcome to come with us," Joe told her over breakfast coffee and croissants an hour later.

"No, Joe. I'm going to look for material for the living-room drapes, remember? Sorry, Mary."

"I am too. But if we get back in time, we'll go for a short stroll down Newbury Street anyway."

At 8:45, the three of us emerged from Joe's apartment lobby onto Pinckney Street and began the short walk to Ashburton Place and the DA's office. Joe said that for them to see us on the weekend was special in itself. Great. I was simply thrilled. We fought the wind and the cold all the way there, which was less than ten minutes on foot.

In L.A., you can't survive without a car. In Boston, cars are death. This is because our streets, which originated in the early 1600s, began as cow paths, not roads. Most lead to or from the "Common," which was a common pastureland for all the cows of the city. Now Boston Common is a city park—the nation's oldest public city park. But the streets haven't changed; they're still cow paths: narrow, crooked, and hilly. If that's not bad enough, these "streets" change names every few blocks.

Just for laughs, of course.

I can't count the number of times I've seen a tourist standing beside his car in tears, or perhaps foaming at the mouth, kicking the fenders and screaming, having totally lost it because finding one's way around in Boston requires a registered guide.

Traffic? You haven't seen a tie-up until you've been in Beantown at 5:00 P.M. We've raised gridlock to an art form.

Since you can walk across town in twenty minutes, it's easy to see why most residents keep their cars stowed by the month in underground garages, at a cost that's only slightly greater than a private hospital room.

Why put up with all this? Because when you're on Beacon Hill, the heart of old Boston, you're not in twentieth-century America. Walking along the cobblestone streets, past the old-fashioned gas lamps that lean at funny angles and the ancient brick buildings with tiny-paned windows, you could be in London town. Every time I walk on Beacon Hill, I half expect to see the Artful Dodger and his band of street urchins come around a corner. Or perhaps hear the clip-clop of a lone horse and see a hansom cab halt along the high granite curbside, an angular man with an opera cape and deerstalker hat emerging, agitated, muttering, "Quick, Watson, the game is afoot!"

"Something wrong, Charlie? You're deep in thought."

"Just thinking how much I like Beacon Hill," I answered, "even in the winter."

"It looks pretty in the snowfall," said Mary, gripping my forearm as we walked up the hill. She'd made the best of it, and her mood was buoyant again. As we departed Marty told us she was going to make a big kettle of New England boiled dinner for us when we returned.

One Ashburton Place is the headquarters of the district attorney of Suffolk County. He wasn't in, which was no surprise. We were shown into the office of one of his assistants. I knew the man behind the desk; he was Bernie Kirk, a rather short fellow with blond hair and a very wide upper body. Bernie had an iron pumper's physique; he worked out regularly at the old BYMCU, the workingman's gym at the corner of Boylston and

Tremont, where I go to work out occasionally, and brush up on my self-defense moves with Laitis Roantis. Bernie was a pal of Roantis, too. It may not be the best thing to be a pal of Laitis Roantis. On the other hand, it's definitely not good to be his enemy. So take your pick. When Bernie checked in at the front desk of the gym, I noticed the little Walther .380 auto affixed to his belt in a DeSantis "Hi-ride" holster over his right kidney. Working for the Boston DA's office can be a bit dicey.

We sat down in leather chairs in Bernie's office. Outside, the snowfall was picking up; big wet clumps of flakes were hitting the windowpanes with a sound like a jazz drummer working brushes on the skins. The bells of Park Street Church were pealing nine o'clock. It was nasty out; but warm and cozy in the second-floor office of One Ashburton Place. I smelled the leather of the chairs, the lemon oil on the ancient furniture, and the old dust in the Persian rugs. I snuggled deeper into the armchair and was about to doze off.

"Why is the state so hot to trot on this thing, Bernie?" asked Joe.

"Mafia ties," Bernie answered, leaning back in the leather chair, his hands locked behind his head. Big biceps popped up like baseballs under his white shirt. "If the evidence shows this killing's mob-related, that might fuel further investigations into Chesterton's affairs. The thing could mushroom. . . ."

"You trying to put him away? After all his help on the redevelopment downtown?"

Bernie smiled. "No, Joe, we're not trying to put him away. We're trying to help him out, you wanna know the truth. Frankly, I think Bud Chesterton's a helluva guy. But I only met him once. What we'd like is a quick and thorough investigation that turns up a blank slate. Clear him of any implications with organized crime once and for all. In fact, our office is under heavy pressure from, uh . . . community leaders . . . to do just that."

"What's Chesterton say?"

"He's shocked, upset. Swears he's got no idea what's behind this. That's why he's flying up here Monday. Wants to cooperate fully, clear his name. Your testimony could be crucial, Doc. Yours and your wife's. Seeing as how you're a physician, it's no secret that your testimony on Chesterton's behalf would—"

"Hold it, Bernie," said Joe. "Hold it right there. No way are we going to—"

"Wait, Joe. I don't mean for Doc and Mary to whitewash this thing. I'm just saying that eyewitnesses—"

"*Ear* witnesses," said Mary. "We didn't see; we heard."

"Okay. Witnesses as unimpeachable as these two . . . well, it wouldn't do us any harm, if you follow."

"Uh-huh. But what if it turns out that what they heard and saw goes against Chesterton? What then?"

"Then we let the chips fall where they may," said Bernie, rapping an unsharpened pencil against his desktop.

"How would it be crucial?" asked Mary. "All we did was happen to hear a shot as we walked by. We didn't see anything."

I thought this was a good question.

"They heard *a* shot," said Joe, lighting a cigarette. "We don't know if it was *the* shot. We don't know if indeed it was a shot, or maybe a car backfiring on the road in front of the house."

"I know, I know," said Bernie. "But we've talked to Major Mahaffey at your headquarters, and we all think it'd be just great if you and Doc and Mary could go down there and walk through the thing." He turned to us. "Is this okay with you two?"

We nodded.

"Good. There will be a photographer with you, from Ten Ten. Joe, it's your friend, Herbert Sams. He'll take some pictures of the house from where you were standing when you heard the noise. Walk around the place, you know. Maybe some other things, little details in the back of your mind, will come back to you. For starters, I assume you saw nobody in or around the house?"

We shook our heads.

"Did you see any vehicles?"

I shook my head.

"Yes," said Mary. "I remember there's a fence in front. A high wooden fence made of stakes."

"A picket fence?" asked Bernie.

"No. The kind you can't see through."

"A stockade fence?"

"Right. I saw a car out in the road, in front, about, oh, thirty or forty yards down."

Bernie put his pen down and leaned forward. "I thought you said you couldn't see through the fence."

"I couldn't; I stepped out onto the street for a second and looked around."

"Doc? You see this?"

"No," I said sheepishly. "I stayed on the property."

"Mary, what did this vehicle look like? Sedan?"

"A car's a sedan, right? It's hard to tell; cars all look so much alike now. I don't think it was Japanese. I believe it was a GM car. Red. A Pontiac or Oldsmobile, I think. But I'm not sure. It was facing away from us, on the other side of the street. I took a mental note of it because of what Charlie once told me about rich neighborhoods. He knows about rich neighborhoods; he grew up in one."

"Not rich, Mare. Well-to-do."

"*Pah*-don me."

"You were saying? Rich neighborhoods?"

"Charlie says that in rich neighborhoods, any car you see parked on the street is visiting, since the houses all have their own driveways."

"Makes sense," said Bernie. Joe rolled his eyes and tapped his fingers irritably on the edge of Bernie's desk. "And you're sure it was red?"

"Red. And the first three digits of the plate were nine-eight-nine. I remembered that because of the year: 1989."

Bernie and Joe exchanged glances. "You sure about that?" asked Joe.

"Positive."

"Nine-eight-nine is a rental-car prefix," said Bernie, stroking his chin. "Good going, Mrs. Adams."

"Thanks, Bernie. My name's Mary. You have no idea what this accolade means to a poor housewife who mostly does dishes and floors."

Bernie looked crestfallen. Joe was grinning. I thought I might be sick.

"There was another vehicle further down the road," Mary continued. "It was some kind of truck with a white tank on the back."

"Like an oil truck?" asked Bernie.

"Kind of, only different. The tank was smaller and rounder, like a pressure tank? Or maybe one of those gas trucks, you know, the kind that have the big white tank?"

"You mean a propane truck?"

"Yeah. Not a gasoline truck, a propane gas truck. It was there when we went around the house to ring the front doorbell. But when we came back, maybe a half hour later, it wasn't there. And the red sedan was gone too."

"Any people?"

"Not that I remember," I said.

"Yes," said Mary.

I sighed and leaned back in my chair, shutting my eyes. They say memory is the first to go. . . .

"There was a man with a golden retriever up the beach. He was throwing a stick in the water for the dog to retrieve it."

"I think he means relevant, important people, Mary."

"We mean everybody, Doc," said Bernie. "Continue, Mary, this is most helpful."

So she described the man exercising his dog, even though it was another quarter mile up the beach. Then Bernie asked us how far apart the houses were. We said far apart; forty or fifty yards, minimum.

"Going on this, then, would it be likely that the neighbors inside their houses would have heard anything?"

"Very unlikely," I answered. "And you're assuming they

were home. Frankly, most of those big houses looked deserted to me, vacant and closed up for the winter."

"But you two, walking along the beach, heard it clearly?"

We nodded.

"Isn't that kind of strange?"

I shrugged my shoulders. "Maybe. But we heard it clearly. It was close by, but muffled."

"So then it occurred just as you were passing the house, correct?"

"Yep. Just about eighty or ninety feet away from the backdoor."

Bernie took out a manila folder and rapped it with his index finger. He turned to Joe.

"I'd come along, Lieutenant, but there's a lot of stuff coming down here right now. Doc, see you at the Union Club. Mary, we appreciate it. Joe, let us know all developments, including especially the ID of the victim."

"So far, nothing on that. Ran his prints through R and I. Nothing."

"Something will bounce. We'll run his postmortem photo in all the papers if we have to. Happy landings. What's wrong, Doc?"

"Nothing," I lied. I was trying to think of the exact saying about the memory being the first to go.

Trouble was, I couldn't remember it.

FOUR

There I was again, down in one of those cold little basement cubicles at Ten Ten Commonwealth Avenue, the head-quarters building for the Department of Public Safety, Commonwealth of Massachusetts. The room was colder than ever on this winter morning. I hated to think what it was going to be like walking on the beach later in the afternoon.

The John Doe, the corpse whose identity was yet undiscovered, lay in front of me on a stainless-steel gurney. His head was draped, as per my unyielding request. The white cloth extended over his head and face and ended just below the nose. It was wrapped around his head and fastened in back so it wouldn't slip off as I pried, cut, chiseled, and gouged at his mouth. The rest of him was draped as well, since he had undergone a stan-dard autopsy already. I knew he had a huge, Y-shaped scar running down the center of his body. The major organs had been removed. The M.E.'s report was sitting on my desktop, along with my tools. These consisted of a series of retractors and neoprene wedges to force the mandible down and keep the mouth open, a number-four set of probes, a six-millimeter Meyerding Bone Gouge, scalpels for excising soft tissue, a Lowe Breck cartilage knife, a Virchow postmortem knife, and a Coun-cilman postmortem bone chisel.

What a swell set of toys. Fun weekend, indeed!

I had to get that mouth open. In a live patient, it's hard enough. You'd be surprised at how many simply clamp up out of fear. But a dead patient is much tougher. The congealing blood leaves not only the dark discoloration called lividity, or *livor mortis* on the skin, but inside the body causes *trismis* of the muscles, a thick stiffening of the muscle fibers that resembles the infamous rigor mortis but remains long after this temporary rigidity leaves the corpse.

I knew I was going to have to stretch and cut to get that mandible down far enough to work inside. But before I even began, there was another problem to overcome. The smell.

There is an odor to a dead body that I cannot get accustomed to. This is why I vastly prefer to work with bones—the skulls and teeth of long-dead victims—rather than with cadavers. From med school on, I haven't gotten used to it. Never will. Therefore, I took out my primary tool for this unpleasant task: an H. Upmann Corona Imperial cigar. These are so strong you need a prescription and proof of age to buy them.

I lighted the nasty monster, letting the smoke hit me the way it does from a fine cigar: high, light, dry, pungent, right in the upper nose—just below my eyes. The stinging, aromatic smoke went through my head like a Spanish saber. Soon my dismal cubicle was full of the rich smoke and the odor of the corpse and the lab chemicals all but gone.

I read over the autopsy report. In a nutshell, and skipping the technical jargon, the M.E. found the cause of death of this male Caucasian—probable age forty-six to fifty-two—to be a gunshot wound to the chest by a .38-caliber, 125-grain lead bullet, fired from a distance of not less than three feet. Right there was proof positive it was not a suicide. More interesting to me, however, was the report on the various organs, notably the liver and pancreas. The former was forty-percent above-normal size and showed duct blockage and fibration. Additionally, the deceased seemed to suffer from pancreatitis. Both of these are hallmarks of chronic alcoholism, and either of them alone can be fatal. These observations, coupled with the findings of the M.E. that the man was underweight and showed signs of severe malnutrition, lead to the diagnosis that the man was very sick and was probably not more than six months away from death, barring his murder.

I knew that in his last days, this man could not be feeling well physically, probably suffering from constant abdominal pain and nausea. No doubt he was also in the deep despair and near psychosis that accompany prolonged alcohol addiction. Therefore, he had good reason to take his own life.

But it seemed that somebody else in that deserted house did the favor for him. . . .

I sighed, put down the report, and inserted the Seldin retractors into the sides of Mr. Dead's mouth. These retract the cheeks and lips of the patient. Soon his lips parted into a wide and eerie grin that wasn't in the least humorous. I noticed immediately the sores in the corners of the mouth, the commissure of the mouth where the upper and lower lips meet. A sign of malnutrition, particularly a niacin deficiency, these sores came as no surprise. Next, using the Werk pry bar, I opened the mouth a little at a time, pushing the neoprene mouth props farther and farther back into the juncture of the teeth as I went. It was slow going; the mouth that had been closed for three weeks in death didn't want to open easily. I made two incisions into the soft tissue and cartilage just above the condyles of the mandible, the hinge joint itself, and it went easier.

My impressions of the mouth supported the conclusions of the medical examiner. I saw advanced periodontal disease, with severe erosion of the gum line and cervical decalcification of most of the teeth. Taking the Hu-Friedy forceps, I tested the second molars and found them both loose. I also noted a missing upper bicuspid, left side, and a missing second molar lower right. If he had remained alive, I doubt he would have had half his teeth left three years hence. Never had I seen a more neglected mouth. Evidence of a poor diet was everywhere, from the surface of his tongue to the edges of his soft palate. My probes revealed pus pockets in the bucchal (cheek side) mucosa of his two lower third molars (commonly called wisdom teeth), both of which had erupted mal-occluded and must have been painful even notwithstanding the draining abscesses the pus pockets revealed. I knew an X ray would reveal inflammation and decay of the root canals of these massive teeth. Finally, there were many untreated caries, chipped and cracked teeth, and missing fillings typical of a mouth totally ignored.

And then the surprising part: Mr. Dead showed flawless dental work on his six-year molars. The full gold crowns still retained their satin texture and their original luster. I have never seen better crowns anywhere. The gold fillings that hadn't fallen out were equally impressive. Therefore, in his youth, this man had been privileged to receive the very best dental care money could buy. I made an inference then and there: he was born rich, but had died a drunken pauper. What was the untold tragedy of his life?

Something else was registering in my head, a series of observations that led me to scribble a short notation on my pad: *UK?*

From the number and placement of fillings, the superb gold work, and other minute variations in this oral history, I had a hunch the man was originally from Britain. Twenty percent of the residents of Concord are British. Therefore, so is a sizable portion of my clientele. Even if they have resided in the United States for years, I can still see certain telltale signs that often point to an English background. It doesn't always work, of course. One reason is that New England's resemblance to the mother country is more than nominal. Besides the fact that people read a lot in both places, for example, they also share certain dietary and social habits that have medical implications: namely high per capita intakes of sugar, animal fat, and alcohol. Perhaps a major reason for this is climatic. The intake of fats and alcohol generally increases the farther one goes from the equator. In any event, I scribbled the notation almost automatically.

But all of these observations were trivial compared with the one thing in this man's mouth that caused me to pause and put down my dental probe with a hand that was almost trembling.

There, clinging to the roof of his mouth just where the soft palate began, was a pale spider of malignant tissue.

I had seen one just like it the previous year in the mouth of a high-school kid, one of the star students and athletes at Concord-Carlisle High School. The one in the boy's mouth was located on the bucchal mucosa instead of the roof of the mouth. But it was the same monster. I knew it well and painfully by now, because I was the one who referred the boy to an oncologist friend of mine and was the first to hear the bad news that the boy was doomed.

Kaposi's sarcoma, a malignant tumor most often found on the neck, upper back, or inside the mouth, is the most obvious and dramatic hallmark of the HIV virus. It is a sure sign of advanced AIDS.

I reached for the phone on my desk and called General Pathology, telling the assistant there what I'd found and requested that the senior pathologist, Zack Robinson, a part-timer from Mass General and therefore my counterpart, be notified. He replied that he was in the building and would be down soon to excise the growth, microtome it, and confirm or refute my rough visual diagnosis.

I turned out the exam light, left the small room, and paced to and fro in the dark hallway, hearing my feet echo as I walked, puffing the cigar. Within ten minutes, pathologist Zack Robinson was inside the room removing the growth. Next Joe came down, brimming with questions. I knew a normal murder victim would never have excited this much attention.

"AIDS, huh? You sure, Doc?"

"Pretty sure; we'll know soon enough."

"Well, we're all ready to go down the Cape. Mary and Herbie Sams are waiting for us in the lobby. Mahaffey thinks Kevin should come along too. He says another pair of eyes always helps."

"Fine. Let me wash up and we'll be off."

"Oh, and another thing. Try and get in touch with that old doctor buddy of yours before we start; I'd like to interview him as long as we're in the neighborhood."

I made the call, but the Randolphs weren't home. All I got was their answering machine.

We all got into Joe's cruiser, Joe and I riding in front because of our long legs. In back Mary rode with Herbie and Joe's partner, Kevin O'Hearn. We entered the Southeast Expressway and headed for the Cape. The Southeast Expressway is usually a nightmare of traffic. On a Saturday in February, however, it was quite light. Light enough for Joe to turn halfway around in the driver's seat just as we were passing the Jordan Marsh warehouse. "Let's recap a few things," he said. "One: this guy you haven't heard from in twenty-five years just happens to call you up and ask you down to his house. Right?"

"Right," I said.

"Two: you accept and go down there. Within an hour's time, you and Mary just happen to take a walk up the beach. This is largely the result of his suggestion to pass the time. Right?"

"Right," said Mary.

"Three: as you walk past the house of Northrop Chesterton—a guy who is very important right at this moment, and also in pretty hot water—you just happen to hear a noise you think could be a gunshot. Right?"

"Right."

Joe drove in silence for a while, drumming his massive fingers on the steering wheel. "You don't think that's strange?"

"A little," said Mary.

"That's what Mahaffey says too. When we get down there, I'd like you to try calling Jonathan Randolph again. Maybe you can catch him in this time. The more I turn this business around in my head, the more I want to talk with him."

Mary suggested we go to the Randolph house first, leave the cruiser there, and reenact our walk up the beach. We all thought it was a great idea. Nobody was at home at the Randolphs'. A glance inside the window of the locked two-car garage revealed a pale blue Jaguar inside.

"If they've got two cars, then maybe they're using the other one," said Kevin. "Seems to me, though, that they've been gone awhile."

"How do you know?" I asked him.

"Just the general look of the place, Doc. A sixth sense you pick up after years in the business."

A yellow Toyota wagon pulled into the driveway and a young blonde woman got out. She was wearing a red parka and blue jeans and carrying a strange-looking tool kit with trowels and sprayers in it. "Hi. Are you looking for the Randolphs?" she asked as she drew out a ring of keys and started looking through them. Joe explained our mission.

"Well, gee, I don't think I can help you. I'll leave Michelle— that's Mrs. Randolph—a note on the counter. I'm just here to water the plants and clean the house."

"Do you know how long they'll be gone?"

"They said two weeks. They went to Texas, but didn't leave a number. They said they'd call in now and then."

Joe took her name and phone number and we started walking up the beach, leaning into the wind and cold and hollering at each other over the crashing waves. Joe, Mary, and I were out in front, just a few feet from the surf, looking at the darkening sky near the horizon. The storm had passed, but another was on its way. The water was seething with whitecaps, and a lot of the spray was reaching us. We were bundled in down parkas, which made it almost bearable. Behind us, Herbie Sams walked with Kevin. Joe brought up the rear, turning around and walking backward every so often, staring at the Randolph house and frowning, as if it might be the home of the Wicked Witch of the West. Kevin spotted the bluish-gray mansion up ahead and pointed.

"Yeah, that's it, all right," yelled Joe, turning around, his hair blowing in the wind. "Hard to miss; big as a damn college dorm."

The Chesterton "summer place" hadn't changed since we'd visited it three weeks earlier: same flat dark gray paint, with a hint of teal blue in it. Attractive in a reserved, understated way and set off the house's gleaming brass lights and fixtures.

Mary stopped walking, stamping her feet in place as if to mark a spot on the icy sand. "We were just about here when we heard it," she said. Herbie Sams came up and snapped away.

"You said earlier it was right before two o'clock . . . just before the party, right?" yelled Joe, trying to read his notebook with the pages flipping around in the wind. We nodded at him. "So it was just about an hour later in the day. Except that three weeks ago, the sun would be lower in the sky. So I say the sun would be about in the same position. What do you think?"

He squinted into the sun, his hand to his brow. It looked the same to us. Turning to face the big house again, we all saw that the windows were bright with the sun's reflection. No way to see inside from where we were.

"You couldn't see inside—"

"No way," said Mary. "Even if a guy was standing right behind the glass, up close, doing jumping jacks, we couldn't have seen him. Not from here."

"Umm. But he could see out."

Herbie took a few more frames and we moved on. They told us to walk up to the house just as we had done earlier. So we moved up, with Sams behind us snapping pictures as we walked. A man in a trench coat came out of the house and stood on the rear terrace, the wind whipping at his coattails. Paul Keegan was the state detective lieutenant for Barnstable County, which is Cape Cod. Mary and I had met him a couple summers earlier under trying circumstances, when our older son, Jack, was a suspect in a murder. Turns out he was innocent, which hardly surprised us. Keegan was professional, competent, and all business, with a reputation for being a bit of a hard-ass.

"Hello, everybody," Paul said in a clipped voice, stamping his feet. Same crew cut. Same steely-blue eyes. Same wide neck with no fat. Keegan could give Bernie Kirk a run for his money in the fitness department. Or maybe the other way around.

"Hey, Paul," said Mary, entering the house as he held the door for her. "Good to see you again, especially when it's not, uh, family business."

He chuckled softly and shook hands with me as I walked inside.

"Need me in there?" asked Sams, calling to Joe and Kevin. When they shook their heads, he ambled off to take exterior shots of the house and road. He said he'd wait for us in Joe's cruiser.

We were standing in a lofty atrium. Off to the right was a deep dining room with two enormous brass candle chandeliers. To the left was a large parlor room. The furnishings were a mixture of Federal, Queen Anne, and the neo-Chinese that's so popular now. Beige carpeting, oil paintings of ancestors and sailing ships. Chinese porcelains. Didn't look like a beach house to me.

Keegan led us to the side of the house that faced the road. I saw Joe look through the windows of the front door and make a mental note of the high stockade fence at the property's edge. Verifying his sister's powers of observation and recall. What every good detective does. I saw him grin to himself.

"Did she pass?" I asked.

"Haw! Can't stop her, Doc. Got eyes and a mind like a steel trap. You couldn't choose a better witness."

Back inside, we ascended a curved staircase with delicate white spindles under a thick oak banister. Upstairs we went along a wide hallway to its center, then through a double door into what had to be—with the exception of the châteaux I'd visited in Europe—the biggest bedroom I'd ever been in. Three tall fan windows opened out onto the ocean. In front of the one farthest to the right and closest to the bed stood a tripod with a telescope on it, facing toward the sea. A massive, king-size four-poster bed was set against the near wall. The center of the room was sealed off with the state's plastic ribbon.

"Who's he?" whispered Mary, pointing to the end of the room. On a couch at the far wall sat a young man of about twenty. He was handsome, with dark skin and bright bottle-green eyes. He wore his dark woolly hair in a short ponytail. He had the Michael Jackson look even down to the strands of hair falling down around the face. He rose anxiously and walked up to us.

"This is Owen Lightner," said Keegan. "He's the houseboy who discovered the body."

He shook hands with all of us, plainly nervous, yet composed, even dignified.

"Owen arrived here Thursday night from Jamaica," continued Keegan. "He found everything normal until he walked into this room. He found the body right there, lying in the center of the room. Except for the dead man shot in the chest, there were no signs of a struggle; everything was just the way you see it now: picture perfect. Right out of *House and Garden*."

"What about the doors? They locked, jimmied, or what?" asked Joe.

"No sign of forced entry," said Keegan. "Whoever came inside had a key, apparently. That's also why none of the alarms went off. As you might have guessed, this place is wired to the hilt."

We looked at Owen Lightner, who shrugged, palms up.

"Gentlemen, what more can I say? I came here from Logan Airport late Thursday night, in a taxicab. I unlock the door, I look around . . . everything is fine. So I say, tomorrow I will do the housecleaning, take care of everything on Mr. Chesterton's list, then go into Boston to watch the Celtics game this weekend. Fine."

He paused and walked to the edge of the ribbon in the center of the big room, pointing at the floor. "So what do I see when

I come upstairs? A dead man, in Mr. Chesterton's own bed-room, lying right *there*."

"On the bare floor?" asked Kevin.

"No; there was a rug. A blue rug. Chinese, I think. It had blood on it; the police took it away for examination in the laboratory." He pronounced it *lab-OR-itry*. Veddy British.

"And you called the police immediately?" asked Joe.

"Yes, sah. The officer came and saw it, and then he called the other police. Later that night I answered a lot of questions, during which time men worked here under very bright lights for many hours. It was not until early Friday morning that I was able to retire."

"Where is your room, Owen?" asked Kevin.

"Upstairs, on the third floor. In back, which is really the front of the house. That is, the side away from the beach."

"And you stay here alone when Mr. Chesterton and his family are in Jamaica?"

"Actually, sah, I am usually with Mr. Chesterton, wherever he is staying. But when he is on the island, during these winter months, he has me fly to Boston two or three times to check up on things. Each visit, I stay a week or so, cleaning the house and making my occupancy quite visible, for security reasons."

"You mean, to make the house appear lived in, rather than vacated for the winter?"

"Exactly. And I clean the place thoroughly. In the summer-time we have a cleaning service that comes twice weekly. But in the winter I do it all, since the house is closed."

"What about the mail?"

"It is delivered to the box at the head of the driveway, you see. It is collected daily by the people from Alert Systems. They keep it for us until I, or Mr. Chesterton, returns."

"Alert is a local security firm," said Keegan. "They do a drive-by each day, collecting newspapers and mail, checking the grounds and all doors and windows on the first level. At night they come by at least once, usually twice. The alarms are all connected to their office in Hyannis. To all appearances, everything was normal here since Owen's last visit in the middle of January."

"So the killer and his victim entered this house three weeks ago," said Joe, his eyes darting around the big room. "They used a key, or else they were expert enough to pick the lock and bypass all the systems."

"I think that's unlikely, frankly," said Keegan, looking at the floor and moving his feet nervously. "I favor the key, which of course means an inside connection."

Owen Lightner, upon hearing this, began pacing the floor in a small circle slowly, looking up at the ceiling and running his hands through his long hair.

"They came up to this room," continued Joe. "Since there was no sign of a struggle, I assume the murder took place almost immediately. So I say the victim was lured up here on a pretext, then shot."

Keegan nodded.

"Then the killer was in this room when Doc and Mary came up to the house," said Kevin, running his hand over his many chins. "They rang the bell, looked around, and called out to see if anyone was home. He waited in here and watched them leave and resume their walk up the beach. He could even have used that telescope there to watch them—"

"Funny you should say that, Kevin," said Paul. "We found that scope completely clean of prints, which suggests that it was wiped down, much as the gun was. So there's a chance the killer did use it."

"Okay," continued O'Hearn. "When he saw that Doc and Mary were safely away, he went back outside, got in his car, and drove off."

Keegan nodded again.

"You guys are assuming a lot." Joe rocked up and down on his toes. The policeman's stationary dance step. Comes from too much standing around. "Owen, was any other part of the house disturbed? Anything valuable taken? Anything disturbed in the kitchen or bathrooms?"

"No, sah. Nothing I could see. The police officers who were here earlier asked me those same questions, and they inspected the entire residence most thoroughly."

He talked in that musical, singsong cadence peculiar to the Caribbean islands colonized by the English. He sounded erudite, and conscientious too. But that could be my bias; I hear a British accent and automatically think the speaker is a gentleman who knows his stuff, a person in whom you can entrust your life. David Niven movies did that for me.

"Who else comes in here regularly?" asked Joe.

"During the off-season, only I. But when Mr. Chesterton returns here, which is generally in April, early or late depending on the weather, the rest of the staff comes with him. First, there is Reginald Westley. He is the gardener, both here and at Shooter's Hill Plantation."

"Shooter's Hill Plantation? That the name of Chesterton's estate down in Jamaica?"

"Yes, sah. Near the town of Buff Bay. A lovely place. Much bigger than this. The staff he brings include Reginald, Maria Townsend, who is the cook, and Anne Rawlings, who is the maid. But she no longer works for Mr. Chesterton, you see, because she is also the attendant of Mrs. Chesterton, and they are no longer together."

Joe looked at Paul Keegan. Kevin was looking at both of them with his watery blue eyes.

"Divorce," said Paul. "Imminent. And bound to be messy. At least that's my guess based on what Owen's told me."

"There will be difficulties, yes, sah. But please, don't let it be known that I spoke about this."

"From what I gather, the missus caught old Northrop Chesterton fooling around one too many times and called it quits," said Keegan. "The problem is aggravated by the fact that she's going to try to take him for as much as she can in the settlement."

"Where's she staying now, Owen?"

He shrugged his muscular shoulders. "Maybe the French Riviera, maybe Mexico. Maybe Nevada, or perhaps Palm

Springs. I believe you can ask Mr. Chesterton himself when he arrives here tomorrow. I hope you will not detain me much longer, gentlemen; I have a lot to do before then."

"Go ahead, Owen, and thanks. Can we look around the house again briefly?"

"Certainly. Call if you need me."

We toured the rest of the upstairs, with its four bedrooms, study, sitting room, four bathrooms, and a second-floor parlor. The third floor, which was much smaller due to the slope of the roof, was reserved for the help. We ducked into Owen's quarters first, the largest of the four, which was really a two-room suite with private bath. It had garret-style windows and was carpeted, with a big bed and dresser set in the bedroom and bookcases, a desk, a television, stereo, and a lot of personal items in the living room. Scuba and soccer gear was stacked in corners. There were several photo posters of women in bathing suits. They were tasteful, and nice to look at. It was a first-class place to live. Apparently Northrop Chesterton took good care of his hired people. I noticed a chauffeur's style hat hanging on a peg next to a big mirror. Evidently, Owen Lightner doubled as a driver for Northrop Chesterton. All in all, the room was conservative and tastefully furnished.

The maid's and cook's rooms were somewhat smaller, elegantly furnished in the feminine counterpart of Owen's, and entirely shipshape. However, the one formerly reserved for Anne Rawlings, Mrs. Chesterton's maid, was devoid of personal effects; all that remained was the furniture and carpeting. Nestled between the two bedrooms was a bath the women shared. This cluster of rooms occupied the east end of the big house.

We went into Reginald Westley's quarters last. The gardener lived in one big room that was directly over the master bedroom downstairs, though not nearly as large. It had its own adjoining bathroom. The view was spectacular. This room was not as conservatively furnished as Lightner's. Reginald had posters on his walls too, but they weren't of women. They were singers, most of whom wore their hair long, in the thick, ropy dreadlocks common to the Rastafarian reggae singers. I read their names on the posters: Bob Marley, Jimmy Cliff, Ziggy Marley, Peter Tosh, and Maxi Priest.

"Is Westley black too?" Kevin asked Keegan.

"Yes, sah," came a voice behind us. "We're all colored."

Looking over my shoulder, I saw Owen leaning into the room, his right hand holding on to the doorjamb behind him, his left on the doorknob. He walked into the room, a smile on his handsome face. But the smile had a strained look.

"Reginald is, as you say, black," he said quietly. "As I am. Even though my father is English and my mother"—he paused and seemed to smile to himself—"and my mother is one quarter Dutch. That is always the question the white people are obsessed with: is he colored?"

"He was asking for the sake of identification," said Joe wearily.

"Certainly. To answer your question, all the domestic staff are . . . as I am, somewhat dark-skinned."

Mary was looking at him. Her face impassive. After Lightner left the room, O'Hearn said: "Cocky."

"Trouble—" Joe added.

"He's right though," observed Mary. "He does have a point, you guys. Charlie, when Tony gets tan in the summer, is he as dark as Owen?"

"Oh no," I said, reflecting on our second son, who picked up his mother's Calabrian coloring. "Tony's darker. Darker by far."

"Uh-huh. But nobody calls him black."

A Kodak carousel slide projector sat on Reginald Westley's desk, with its big circular slide trays stacked nearby. I looked around for the screen, but couldn't see it. Didn't see a camera either, but assumed he had it with him. Since I also like to take pictures, I reached down and took out a slide. Holding it up to the light, I saw that it was a shot of leaves, taken from under the tree. The sunlight shone down through the leaves. I picked another slide. Same subject. The next one was also the same. Not the same shot, but a very similar one. I picked out the next slide and saw that it was a blank, a piece of opaque cardboard that would block the light from the projector lamp. The next three slides were also blanks. Then another picture, this one of a gorgeous red sunset. Corny as some people think them, I still love sunset pictures. The next one was another sunset, as was the next . . . and the next. Then four more blanks. Then came a shot of clear sky. No clouds, no birdies, just sky. Another just like it. And another—

"Hey, Doc, what are you doing?" said Kevin.

I turned to see all three police staring at me. They weren't pleased.

"Better not touch that stuff," said Paul. "Bad enough if we did it in the absence of the occupant. Know what I mean? Also, it may be evidence—"

I murmured an apology and replaced the slides in the trays, then locked down the metal collar that held them in. Mary and I followed the cops around the room and back into the modest third-floor hallway. There on the wall I noticed a color photograph of the Chestertons and the household staff. Owen was standing next to Chesterton. A tall, skinny kid with delicate features was standing on the side of the picture. This was obviously Reginald Westley, the gardener. Mrs. Margaret Chesterton was a tall and handsome woman, with auburn hair, light creamy skin, green eyes, and fine bones in her face. Looked like a vintage model out of *Vogue*. A dark, slender woman standing at her side was probably Anne Rawlings. She too was pretty. Maria Townsend, the cook, stood in front. She was lighter skinned than the others and rather plump.

Northrop Chesterton, standing center in back, dominated the picture, as he no doubt dominated most people and situations. Tall and powerfully built, with white hair and a ruddy complexion that looked to me almost unhealthy, he towered above the rest, beaming with pride and confidence. I had the feeling that if I ever met him, my feelings would not be neutral. I would either like him a lot or hate him.

We followed the back stairway all the way to the ground floor, bypassing the main staircase, and found ourselves standing in a small vestibule near a side door that led outside. This,

Keegan explained, was the servants' entrance. We examined it, a wooden door with glass panels on top. Dead-bolt lock connected to the alarm.

"Are the keys to this the same as the ones for the main doors?" asked Mary.

"Yes," said Paul. "Owen told me that Chesterton figured it was simpler that way. Why have two sets of keys if either one can gain access to the entire house?"

"That means that his ex could have a key—" said Mary.

"Yep; I've been thinking the same thing," said Joe.

"So what?" I asked.

"So what? C'mon, Charlie, think about it. They're going through a divorce; she wants to make him look bad. She arranges to have a killing take place right in his house. This arouses the rumors of his mob ties. Makes him look like a monster . . ."

"Hey, maybe he did arrange it," I said.

"Nah," said Joe.

"Who asked you?" I said.

"I asked me. I think you're all wrong; I think somebody swiped a key and did the hit here because it was a good place to do a hit, *period*. Locked and empty house. Wintertime, doors and windows closed. Neighbors gone or far away in closed-up houses, so they wouldn't hear the shot. Paul, you remember that homicide over in Fall River two years ago? Same situation: big summer house on the water closed up for the winter months. Guy lured the victim into the house on the pretext of pulling a joint burglary. Waited till they'd cleaned the place out, then nailed him. We didn't even know there was a killing until the weather turned and things got . . . aromatic."

"This wasn't a routine murder, Joe; it was carefully planned," said Kevin. "The murderer had a key. He knew the house would be vacant. Therefore he had to be familiar with—"

"That's what we think too, Kevin," said Paul, leading us back into the main hallway. "We think the killer even knew about the security service and all the other household routines. Everything points to an inside job here."

"So what about the help?" asked Joe as we exited the front door. "Are they accounted for?"

"All except one," said Keegan. "All the household staff, except Owen Lightner, have been working at Shooter's Hill Plantation during the past six weeks, never absent for more than twelve or fourteen hours."

"And where was Owen?"

"He says he went to Florida to visit some friends in college."

"When was that?" asked Kevin.

"Third week in January."

We all looked at each other.

"Can he verify?" asked Joe.

"He claims he can; we're waiting on it," said Keegan.

"How about the wife?" asked Mary.

We turned and looked at her. "Where was Margaret Chesterton?"

"Obviously not at the plantation, since they separated shortly after Christmas. We don't know her whereabouts."

"I'd talk to her; she needs a look," said Mary.

We stood there for a while underneath the fancy brass lamp that hung down by a big chain. Then we walked outside to the road. Mary showed us the spot where she saw the red car and pointed in the direction where she saw the truck with the white tank. Keegan asked her to describe the car again, and she did. Joe told him they were running down the plate prefix.

Just before we started our walk back down the beach to the Randolph place, I saw Joe kneeling down at the front door. He gave a low whistle. He motioned me over, and I knelt down and saw the massive brass-and-steel locks set in the heavy hardwood door. The locks looked different from any I had ever seen. Could have been used to lock a castle.

"These are made by Chubbs of England," he said. "They're cut backward, the way post-office box keys are. This assures that they cannot be duplicated, except at Chubbs's offices. That means making a casual duplicate is out of the question."

Joe should know; he's a master locksmith. If Joe were a crook, he could be skinning in and out of those Beacon Hill flats in a wink, taking all kinds of loot. In fact, if I ever find some loose ice or pearls in his place, I'll go straight to Major Mahaffey and turn him in.

Unless he gives me a cut, of course.

It was cold as hell walking back to Randolph's. We skipped and ran most of the way to keep warm. Tried the doorbell. Nobody home. The only sound was the wind and the waves. We got into the cruiser and headed back to Boston.

At Ten Ten Comm. Ave., I returned to the basement where Zack Robinson had taken the growth from our dead patient. In our absence, and no doubt to make his job easier, he had undraped the face. I didn't know this until he called me over to the bank of large steel drawers in the mini-morgue around the corner from the autopsy labs.

"Let's take a look at this lesion, Doc," he muttered, rolling out the drawer, which rode on double bearings and hummed out just like a giant filing cabinet, while I flicked on the powerful overhead lights. They keep them off whenever possible because they heat the place up. I walked over to drawer number seven, looked down into the dead man's face, and almost fainted.

"Doc? You okay?"

I was turned away, standing bent over, hands on knees, breathing deep. I was trying to tell myself I hadn't really seen what I thought I'd seen.

"Doc?"

I straightened up, turned, and looked again.

"Holy Jesus—" I blurted.

"What is it?"

"*I know this man.* I knew him. I'm almost positive."

"You knew him? You mean personally? As a friend?"

I pointed down at the undraped face, colored almost bluish

black by *livor mortis*. I nodded. "His name was George Brenner. Mary and I knew him briefly in Concord five or six years ago. I could almost swear to it."

"You didn't say anything before."

"I couldn't see his face; I had it draped. Let's call Mary down from upstairs and see what she says. Don't prep her in any way; just call her down here with Joe and have her take a glance at this guy."

Five minutes later Mary, Joe, and Kevin were all standing in front of the bank of drawers in the chilly, tile-walled room. I stood behind her, not saying a thing. Zack wheeled the drawer open. Mary took one look and said: "Oh my God, Charlie! It's George!"

Kevin and Zack and I were staring at each other. Joe was pacing back and forth, his heels echoing in the chilly room. Joe turned fast and ran his fingers through his hair.

"Okay, Doc; that's number four. Remember what I was saying in the car? This thing sounding like a setup? So now it turns out you and Mary know this guy, for chrissakes. Are we still supposed to believe it's all coincidence?"

"No," I said. "They say that once is happenstance, twice is coincidence, but three times is enemy action. This is the fourth bad penny in a row."

"You and Mary are in the center of this," said Kevin. "You may not know how or why, but you are."

"It's him," Mary said, leaning over close. "But boy, is he dark."

"The skin discolors after death," said Robinson. "*Livor mortis* does it. Congealing blood. Turns purplish brown."

"I know what lividity is, Zack; I'm a nurse. But I've never seen it this pronounced before."

"You've never seen a corpse this old before," I answered.

"I say that's him, Charlie. What do you say?"

"I agree. But we haven't seen him in a while. I'm trying to remember his jawline and profile."

A white-smocked attendant came in the room. "Joe?"

"What is it, Henry?" asked Joe, drumming his fingers on the steel cabinet, making a sound like an idling engine.

"Karl Pirsch wants to see you upstairs in the lab."

"Okay. It'll be a second, though. We've just had a new wrinkle on this thing."

"Can we get one of you to sign a statement of identification?" asked Henry the attendant. "It's just temporary, but it's better than nothing until we get a next-of-kin or a positive medical fix."

"I'll sign it," said Mary. "And his wife's name is Sarah, if it's any help. But we haven't seen her in a long time, either. Did they get divorced, Charlie?"

"I don't know; I think he just left her. We can ask around when we get back home."

"So the name would be Sarah Brenner?" asked the attendant, pencil poised over clipboard.

"Yes, but she doesn't live in Concord anymore."

"Do you recall the address in Concord?"

"It was a big farm out on Lowell Road about two miles from Concord Center. I don't know the number—"

"Thanks; we'll get it." He snapped the cover down on the clipboard and moved to shove the drawer back into the refrigerated unit. I told him to wait one second while Mary and I took one last look. Even allowing for the lapse of years and the discoloration of the skin, the corpse in the cabinet couldn't be anybody but George Brenner. There was the same golden-blond hair, the heavily lidded eyes, and delicate, almost feminine features that reminded us so much of Peter O'Toole.

We'd known him for about two years, seeing him at dinner parties and other social gatherings around town. Whatever else could or couldn't be said about the late George Brenner, he was a charmer. We never discovered his occupation, although I remember him telling us he worked in "finance." Mary and I took that to mean he had family money, since hard work didn't seem to fit him. He and Sarah lived in a large rambling wooden farmhouse that included, if memory served, sixty or eighty acres of meadowland. A nice spread that was well tended by landscapers on the outside and housekeepers within.

I remembered one dinner party especially. It was at George and Sarah's farm and centered around the pool in back. George had hired a caterer to roast a lamb over coals, a Turko-Greek (if such a possibility exists) band to provide music, and a voluptuous belly dancer to wriggle around the pool deck, stuffing dollar bills from appreciative viewers into her cleavage and down her waistband. After her second dance, she allowed her fans—all males, for some strange reason—to stuff the bills for her. I think it was so she could keep moving her arms in time to the music. The men loved the show and clapped for two encores. I think a few wallets emptied, but mine wasn't one of them. Whenever her wriggling form drew near us, I saw Mary looking at me out of the corner of her eye. The look said: Just you try it, buster. . . .

We found out later that the wives weren't so keen on the show. In fact, rumors of domestic altercations pervaded the community for some time.

A little later on that same evening, around 11:30, after more than his share of the booze, George bumped into me just as I'd left his pool. He made a couple of fast two-steps to catch his balance, wiped his shirt off, grinned at me, and said: "Well, if it isn't Florence Chadwick in drag." George never did things halfway. Where was Sarah Brenner now?

"Want more time, Charlie?" asked Mary.

"Hmm? Oh . . . no; wheel him back in." I watched the drawer slide back into the bank. *Ka-thunk.* Night-night, George. Sleep tight.

"Doc?"

"Hmm?"

"You okay?"

"Yeah. Just trying to think who his dentist is. Was."

"We can find out when we get home. C'mon, honey," said Mary, taking me by the hand. She has much less trouble with death than I do. As a registered nurse who still works part-time, she sees it on a regular basis. As an oral surgeon, the most serious thing I generally see is impacted molars. Sure, I've done my share of removing carcinomas and sarcomas of the mouth, and done the follow-up reconstructive procedures afterward. And there was that terrible discovery of Kaposi's sarcoma in the mouth of that high-school star, but the actual checking out, the cashing in the chips, the handing in the old dinner pail—that I don't see often.

Mary and I walked to the bank of elevators with Joe. Kevin was waiting there for us, holding the door open. Inside the car, I saw him punch the "5" button.

"Aren't we gonna stop in the office first?" asked Joe.

"You kiddin'?" said Kevin, checking his watch. "Karl wants us up in the lab . . . and we're *late!*"

"**D**r. Adams . . . Mrs. Adams . . . ah, how nice to see you!" said Karl Pirsch in his clipped, Schleswig-Holstein accent. He bowed to Mary, who smiled back at him. I heard Pirsch's heels click gently together as he lowered his head.

"Karl, before we start, there's been a new element added to this case," said Joe. "It appears that Doc and Mary were friends of the deceased."

For once, Karl Pirsch seemed at a loss for words. His perennial rigidity seemed to soften. He slumped a bit; it was the first time I'd ever seen him not standing at attention. He looked at Mary and me.

"This is true?"

"We think so," I answered. "Unless it's later refuted by laboratory evidence. George Brenner was a friend who lived in Concord five years ago. We're trying to locate his estranged wife, Sarah, and searching for medical records too. But it looks like it's him."

We then proceeded to fill him in on the details, during which time he sought a chair and sank down into it. Finally he sighed and clapped his palms down on his knees. "And you heard the shot too? This is correct?"

We nodded at the seated lab chief, who scratched his bald head in wonder.

"Then don't you think it's more than mere chance that—"

"Yes, we do, Karl," said Joe. "We think it's some kind of setup, but we haven't made the connection yet."

Pirsch sighed. "Well, then perhaps what I have found will be even more interesting to all of you. Follow me, please."

Karl walked double time to his desk at the rear of the laboratory. His lab coat flew outward as he walked, but he grabbed the lapels and fastened the coat severely around his pencil-thin form. We practically had to run to keep up with him.

The crime lab is on the top floor of the headquarters building so that the various chemical vapors—primarily caustic acid fumes—can be vented quickly. It's big, brightly lit, full of interesting equipment and specimens, and very, *very* neat. We hurried past rows of glassware, stone-topped counters, blue flames, bubbling vats, and a dozen or so technicians who worked furiously in silence.

Karl marched us over to his desk, where he hurled himself into his chair and attacked a sheaf of papers. Without looking up, he gestured for us to take seats around the front of his desk. He peered through his wire-rim glasses at the papers as he shuffled them, his beaky face in mute concentration. He held up his forefinger, as if calling class to attention.

"First, the autopsy report. Cause of death: gunshot wound to the chest. Thirty-eight-caliber, semijacketed hollow-point bullet of one hundred twenty-five grains, which destroyed the entire left side of the heart and most of the left lung, lodging against the spine."

He looked up.

"You have all read this report, yes?" We nodded.

"We have the bullet, and there is something interesting about it. Come look."

We followed him over to one of the long, marble-topped counters. The workers in the lab all parted before us and dispersed. Pirsch leaned over a stereoscopic microscope and turned on the bright light inside it, peering into the twin eyepieces. He fiddled with the focus knobs, then stood aside, motioning us to take turns looking. When mine came, I peered in and saw several fuzzy fibers of different colors: black, yellow, orange, and bright blue.

"Joe told you about the switching of the shirts?" Karl asked.

"He said that the shirt found on the body wasn't the one the bullet went through," I answered.

"Quite right. Your friend was found dressed in a beige cotton dress shirt. The shirt was a Manhattan, size fifteen, thirty-four. That is not a large size, and yet the shirt was too big for him. The bullet hole, however, which appears to have been made by a small knife, was the giveaway. That and the fact that the victim's chest showed evidence of powder burns, while the shirt did not."

He paused, then continued. "Also, we know the man was wearing a leather jacket when he was shot. This is one reason the fatal bullet did not exit the body. We surmise this because in addition to these fibers you see, there were particles of cowhide, thick, and dyed black on one side. It is a special chromium tanning process done almost exclusively in England."

I remembered the dental work in George's mouth and marking the letters *UK* on my notepad. Karl's mention of England sent a small flag waving in my head.

"So what about these fibers?" Joe asked, peering through the microscope again.

"A rayon and polyester blend," said Pirsch. "Such fibers are commonly found on women's blouses, dresses, and men's tropical shirts."

"You mean those brightly colored Hawaiian jobs?" I asked. "The kind my crazy friend Moe Abramson wears?"

"Exactly."

"Any reason for the switch?" asked Kevin, swiveling back and forth in his chair.

"There is obviously a reason, but we don't know it," Pirsch answered. Then, after a few seconds, he added: "We were thinking there was a possibility that the victim could have been wearing some kind of women's clothing, perhaps a blouse.

Since you knew him, you may judge whether or not this theory is worth pursuing."

"No, I don't think so. Right, Charlie?"

"I'd say so too, except for something I found on the roof of his mouth." I then explained the malignancy that Zack Robinson had confirmed was Kaposi's sarcoma.

"So he had AIDS as well," mused Pirsch, stroking his sharp chin with his slender fingers. "It may be premature to make sweeping generalizations, but the possibility that your late friend had, let us say, a double life, presents itself."

Mary shook her head. "C'mon! We knew George, Karl. He wasn't homosexual."

"Don't be too sure," said Joe. "A lot of people lead secret lives, especially gay men. We cops find this pattern a lot more often than you might think."

"Well, I find it hard to believe," said Mary. "George sure came across as the man about town."

"But if it were true," I said, "maybe that could explain the marriage breakup."

"It could explain a lot of things," said Joe. "How's the fix for TOD, Karl? Consistent with Doc and Mary's testimony?"

"Perfect. We relied mostly on analysis of the aqueous humor."

"So I heard."

"It's very stable. Serum concentrations of certain elements, such as potassium, change at predictable rates after death and continue to do so for some time. From these data, I say that the Adamses' testimony is genuine."

Pirsch stood still for a few seconds, putting his thin finger up against his temple. Then he paced the floor, looking like a giant stork wading in a lily pond. "And perhaps it will help explain the other curious thing. . . ."

He walked over to another counter and pulled open a drawer beneath it. He took out a cardboard box, sliding it along the counter until it was in front of us. He opened it, revealing a revolver that looked like a standard police-issue Smith & Wesson.

"Here is the murder weapon," he said. "A Smith Model Nineteen, a .357 Magnum. The serial number, located at the juncture of the crane arm here"—he pointed with his pencil, not touching the weapon—"and on the bottom strap of the frame handle, has been ground off with a wheel, making it impossible to trace. A typical professional weapon, which is usually left at the scene so the killer won't be apprehended with it in his possession."

"Three-fifty-seven Magnum?" said Mary. "I thought you said the bullet that killed George was a .38."

"It was. The bore diameter for the .38 and .357 Magnum is the same, as are the bullets they shoot; it's the cartridge cases that are different. The Magnum has a longer case with more powder capacity. In essence, the .357 is simply an oversized, hot-loaded .38."

"Oh—"

"The curious thing about this weapon is that upon recovering it, we discovered that the cylinder was misaligned."

"Out of the frame?" said Joe.

"No. It was in the frame, but not aligned properly in the frame. The fired round's empty case wasn't where it should have been."

"You mean that it wasn't under the hammer?" said Joe.

"Correct. The gun was found with the empty cartridge case just to the right of the barrel, which means that after the shot was fired, the piece was opened, then closed again. We think there was an assumption on the part of the killer that the cylinder rotates to the right, which it doesn't. Colt revolvers have cylinders that rotate to the right; Smith and Wesson revolvers rotate to the left. Furthermore, since a revolver is not an automatic weapon, the just-fired case remains underneath the hammer, in line with the barrel, until the trigger is pulled again. You follow?"

We all nodded. Mary nodded too, but tentatively.

There were a few seconds of silence. I had to ask the obvious question.

"Why did the killer swing the cylinder out and back in the first place, Karl?"

"To reload the weapon."

"But you just said the spent case was to the right—"

"Yes," Pirsch hissed, "that is correct, but only half the story: upon further investigation, we discovered that this gun fired two rounds, not one. I know this because the revolver was thoroughly cleaned before the job. Cleaned with nitro solvent and wiped down, with no gun oil applied. This was done to remove all fingerprints and other evidence. As you know by now, the victim's prints were found on this gun, but we are all but certain they were put there by the killer, using the dead man's hand."

"So how do you know two shots were fired?" asked Mary.

"The piece was clean enough so that when we examined the cylinder chambers, we found that not one, but two, showed signs of firing."

All of us were now leaning closer and closer to the counter, our faces crowding together over the revolver that lay in its cardboard sarcophagus, a wondrous relic. . . .

"The killer fired two shots, not one?" said Kevin, leaning over the counter with a keen gaze in his eyes.

"That is exactly what I said."

"Okay, Karl," said Joe. "We're just double-checking."

"Two of the cylinder-chamber lips showed the powder residues and oxides that can only be produced when a round is fired in the chamber. These two chambers were next to one another. All the other chambers were spotless."

"So what's the scenario, Karl?" asked Joe. "How do you read it?"

"Here's what I think happened: the killer shoots the victim in the chest at close range. For some reason, he removes the dead man's leather jacket and the blouse—or whatever garment it was—and puts on the beige dress shirt. So far, I think, only one round has been fired. But before he leaves the scene, for some unexplained reason, he discharges a second round."

"Where? How?" I asked. "Was there any sign of another bullet in the bedroom?"

"No," answered Karl. "But I will take another look at the room, and the entire house as well. Now, let us return to the killer. He has just fired a second shot, but wishes to give the appearance of only having fired a single shot. The reason for this is obvious: what suicide is going to shoot himself *twice* through the chest, *hein*? So he must hide evidence of the second shot. What does he do? He swings out the cylinder and removes one of the spent cases and puts it in his pocket, inserting a fresh cartridge in its place. He then swings the cylinder back into the frame. But in doing so puts the cylinder back incorrectly, leaving a live round under the hammer, which arouses our curiosity in the first place."

"So what does it all mean?" asked Mary, brushing back long strands of her hair that had fallen in front of her face.

"It means we go now to look at the room sketch."

The room sketch, drawn by the lab team, was sitting on a light board, which illuminated it from behind. It was a simple pencil sketch on graph paper that gave the room's dimensions and showed the placement of furniture, doors, windows, and of course, the body. Pirsch began pointing out the salient features with his pencil.

"We cannot tell where the murderer was standing when the shot was fired, since the body was obviously moved to change the clothing," he began. "But we do think we know something that the killer did in the room besides commit murder," he said, tapping the sketch with his pencil. He pointed at the east window, drawing the fine point of his pencil along it.

"Standing in front of this window, sitting on a tripod, was a telescope."

"It's still there; we saw it at the house," said Mary. "I bet they use it to look at passing ships."

"The scope was wiped clean; the team worked over every inch of it to find latent fingerprints."

"So Paul told us, Karl," said Joe. "He thinks, therefore, the killer used it."

"I think that is a good assumption," said Pirsch, holding his finger up again to emphasize the point. "A good assumption, yesss, because what do you suppose we found on the scope instead of prints?"

"We have no idea, Karl," said Kevin wearily, shifting his feet, "so why don't you just tell us, hmm?"

"Traces of gun solvent," whispered Pirsch, a triumphant smile on his lips. "The solvent is Hoppes Number Nine, and matches perfectly the solvent on the murder weapon."

"Hoppes Number Nine's the most popular solvent," said Kevin. "Still, I see your point. If the killer wore gloves to ensure leaving a weapon clean of his own prints, which he would in wintertime anyway, they would pick up traces of solvent from the revolver. Therefore, if he touched the scope, then wiped it down, he'd leave some solvent there too."

"Yes, exactly! But it's the implication of this action that I find interesting. I think—"

Karl Pirsch froze again, suspended in concentration. I could almost see his brain working, see those Wagnerian scenarios flipping across his cerebral movie screen. . . .

"Which side of the house did you approach from?" he snapped, glaring at me.

"The east."

"The scope was facing out the east window. Therefore, if the killer was looking out that window at the opportune time, he could see you and Mary walking toward the house. Correct?"

I nodded, but slowly. I was being dragged into an inquisition here. I felt the monstrous grip of Teutonic logic licking out at me. . . .

Karl shifted his steely gaze now, staring at Mary.

"Using the telescope, he could also have seen you a long time before you got to the house, correct?"

"Sure," Mary answered, turning to me. "A good chance, anyway, right, Charlie?"

I nodded, trying to see what he was getting at.

"So, the fact that he knew we were coming," I offered, "that he knew we were on our way past the Chesterton place, makes it very strange that he would wait and shoot—"

"Yes—you heard the shot when you were just opposite the house. Therefore he *intended* for you and Mrs. Adams to hear it."

"Why?" asked Mary.

Karl Pirsch shrugged, turning his thin hands palms up.

"You knew this guy, George Brenner," said Joe. "That's the connection."

"But he wasn't the killer, Joey; he was the victim."

"So? Who's to say that the killer didn't also know you?" said Kevin. "What about this? Suppose that before the hit, the killer and your friend George are walking around the room, talking. The killer is getting ready to take out the revolver. George, unaware of what's about to come down, plays with the scope, spots the two of you walking up the beach, and says hey, I know this couple. . . . Let's see, ah . . . then the *killer*—"

"Nah," said Joe. "Too complicated. But I like the idea of the deliberate murder shot. I like it because it's strange, and strange always provides a lead."

"I don't believe the shot Doc and Mary heard was the murder shot," said Pirsch, leaving the room and stalking back to his desk. We followed him and gathered round. "What they heard was the *second* shot, fired after the victim was dead. The shot he intended them to hear. And then he attempted to hide it by placing the fresh cartridge into the chamber. Good day, gentlemen."

I took this to mean that we were excused. We went down to Joe and Kevin's office for a few minutes. But that place is so squalid and depressing, with its bent and twisted metal window shades, strong fluorescent lighting (hell is lighted with banks of fluorescent lights—trust me), and dented gray metal furniture on tired linoleum, that I just can't stand it. How a man with Joe's education and taste—a guy with a beautifully furnished home, a guy who collects original art—could remain there for an hour straight was beyond me. Mary, sharing my discomfort, gave her brother a subtle hint.

"Joey, this place smells like a vacuum-cleaner bag," she said, heading for the hall. "If I hang around another second, I'm gonna get the dry heaves. Let's go now, huh?"

So we did, leaving poor Kevin to talk with Major Mahaffey.

Outside, it was almost dark. It was snowing even harder now, and cold as hell. We reached Joe's car and snuggled inside, shivering. The snow was already two inches deep, and wet. Great driving out tomorrow. Great.

"I dunno," mused Joe at the wheel as we headed back Commonwealth Avenue toward Beacon Hill, "maybe Karl's onto something."

"You think he's right?" said Mary, leaning over between us from the backseat. "You think the hit man killed George, waited until we were near the house, then fired another shot so we'd notice?"

"Like I say, I don't know. But it sounds interesting. Whatever happened, you two are in this thing now, whether you choose to be or not. Whatever goes around, comes around."

"So what's coming around, Joey?"

"Your past, Mare. A little hunk of your past is spinning around back at you, like a boomerang."

I thought of poor George Brenner, the urbane charmer, lying in drawer number seven. I pictured him four years earlier, martini glass in hand, leaning against his mantel, laughing and regaling his guests with wit and humor. But he'd come to a bad end, murdered in a vacant mansion.

One thing for sure: this boomerang had a sharp edge.

SEVEN

The following day, Sunday, after identifying the body of her late and former husband, Sarah Brenner accompanied us back to Joe's apartment on the hill. She needed a rest and somebody to talk to, so we invited her for Sunday supper. It was nice to see her again, despite the circumstances. She was still the attractive, strawberry blonde of regal height. I put her at five-ten anyway. Hair pulled back in a modified ponytail, wool suit, and ruffled silk blouse. She looked businesslike. There were lines around her eyes, from sadness as well as age, I thought. A nice, solid woman—that's how both Mary and I recollected her. Although not the flamboyant half of the Brenner couple, she was the sensible one—the one we all felt seemed to keep George in line, as much as possible, that is.

She sat on the big cream-white sofa in Joe's living room, wiping her eyes now and then with a delicate hanky. She was by no means grief-stricken. But she was sad, perhaps for the loss of potential as much as anything else. The fact that a man with the wit and charm of George Willis Brenner should end up an alcoholic, derelict murder victim to lie unclaimed for almost a month was universally depressing.

"I'm not so surprised after all, Mary," she said, shifting herself on the couch and accepting a mug of hot tea from Marty, which she did with a nod and a sincere smile. "I hadn't heard a thing from him in two years. Not a thing from him or about him."

"Did he usually stay in touch?" asked Marty, sitting down next to her.

"Yes, pretty regularly at first. After he moved out, he always either wrote or called me every two or three months. He always said in his letters that if I needed anything, to call him."

"Where was he living then?" asked Joe, blowing on a hot cup. He was eyeing the big stack of oatmeal cookies on the tray. But he hadn't taken one. Not a nibble. I think he knew that if he did, he couldn't stop until he'd eaten all of them.

"At first, he bought a small condo up in Gloucester, right on the ocean. But then, about two years ago, he wrote and said he was moving into town. Somewhere on Marlboro Street. That's the last I heard from him."

"Would that be Sixty-seven Marlboro Street?" asked Joe.

"Why yes. That's the number. Did you look it up?"

"Nope," he said softly, his legs stretched out straight at a long angle to the floor. His ankles were crossed, and his shoes flipped together and back, making a flapping sound like a wet halibut in the bottom of a boat. "Didn't have to."

We all looked at Joe, but he remained silent, sipping his tea.

"Why he moved, I think," said Sarah, "was that he lost a lot of money, or suffered some sort of financial reversal and could no longer afford the condo. So he moved in with another guy . . . or maybe there were two of them, who had this apartment in Back Bay."

"And you think the move was financially motivated? No other reason?" asked Joe.

"I think so, yes. Because when he last wrote me, he said he regretted it, but he could no longer help me financially if I needed it."

"Did he loan you money on a regular basis?"

"No," she admitted. "But when we separated, he gave me fifty thousand in cash, plus the equity in the house in Concord, which was twice that. Considering we had no children or other dependents, he left me in good shape, Mr. Brindelli."

More foot flapping from Joe. I heard the high rasp of beard stubble as he stroked his chin in thought.

"This is painful, but I have to ask: who would want to kill your former husband?"

She stared at the tea tray awhile before answering.

"I have no idea," she said finally. "But I'm coming to realize that there was a lot about George I didn't know. He was very private about his past. All he told me was he had a poor child-hood with a mean, drunken father. His mother died when he was a baby."

"Where was this?"

She shrugged her shoulders.

"Did he have any brothers or sisters? Uncles? Aunts?"

Another shrug.

"What was his occupation?"

"Ah, that I know. He was an investment counselor. He had his own firm in town, near Copley Square. I've kept one of his cards—"

She rummaged in her purse and drew out a dog-eared and yellowed business card. She passed it around. The center of the card read:

GEORGE W. BRENNER
President & Founder
New England Investment Services

On the lower left corner was an address on Boylston Street right near Copley Square. The lower right corner had a phone number. Joe excused himself briefly, then returned to his easy chair.

"Doc, c'mon in the kitchen and help me with the meal. We'll let the women catch up, okay?"

I followed him down the long hall into the tall, brightly lit kitchen. His first act was to reach up high and extract two bottles of Grenache rosé from the wine rack. These he placed in the refrigerator. Then he put a twenty-inch cast-iron skillet over a medium flame. When it was warm, he dropped a stick of margarine into it, frowning as he watched it slide around and dissolve.

"Butter is so much better," he growled. "But that's one of Marty's rules. That and the pigeons."

"You miss them?"

"Nah. Actually, they were a pain in the ass. We're getting a cat next week."

He unwrapped six fresh Cornish game hens and cut them right down the middle with a giant butcher knife. Then he dusted them with flour and preheated the oven. We browned the bird halves in the skillet, then placed them on a rack and slid them into the oven, saving the margarine and drippings in the skillet.

"Why I left the room was to put George's name and the name of his company out on the wire," he said, turning on the FM radio. A flute concerto that sounded like Mozart came out. Good sounds and aromas in the kitchen. "We'll see what that yields, if anything. But Sarah's down, Doc."

"Mary suggested we invite her out to the country for a week or so. And maybe, while she's there, we can get hold of something, maybe just an offhand comment or allusion that will help us get a handle on this thing."

"You didn't tell her about our feeling that it's not a coincidence, you and Mary being there on the beach?"

"No."

"Maybe it's better just to let her recollect things her own way," Joe said. He plugged in the rice cooker and dumped in his own special mixture of wild rice, brown rice, and Cajun "popcorn" rice. We went back into the living room, where we saw Sarah silently crying into her wadded-up handkerchief. Mary and Marty huddled close on either side of her.

"I know it's silly," she wept, "but I still love him. I suppose now I love his memory. And even though I hadn't seen him in so long . . . going there today to identify him was hard. And he . . . he looked so *awful* in that drawer—"

It was some time before she composed herself. "I scarcely recognized him at first—"

"That's to be expected," said Joe softly. "It's not a pleasant thing to have to do. And you did it well, Sarah. You've been admirable through this thing. You should know that your ID is important. It's invaluable. *And*," he added with emphasis, "it's *over*."

Mary put her hand on Sarah's and made the invitation for her to come out to Concord with us for a few days and escape her loneliness. Sarah brightened immediately.

"That's great of you, Mary. Doc, you won't mind?"

" 'Course not. There's plenty of room . . . going to waste now that Joe's settled down."

"Not going to waste as much as you think," said Marty. "We're both coming out next weekend. Mary and I decided this morning."

Joe and I returned to the kitchen, now heavy with the aroma of roasting fowl, and popped one of the bottles of wine. "You've got to test the stuff," Joe said, "it's part of the host's responsibility."

Joe added some reduced chicken stock to the skillet. When the birds were done baking, he took the pan of drippings and added them too. Then he grated the rinds of two oranges into the mixture and added his own touch: two heaping tablespoons of orange marmalade. Then a few drops of white vinegar, some lemon juice, some Oriental brown sauce and thickener, and finally, three shots of cognac. The orange sauce smelled terrific, and we let it simmer and thicken. We served the game hens and orange sauce over the rice, having the wine as an accompaniment. It was plenty. Sarah visibly cheered during the meal. Then Mary put her in a cab for her apartment in Brighton, saying we'd be by after the Patriots game to pick her up and take her out to Concord.

At five, we ransomed Mary's Audi from a private garage, picked up our houseguest, and drove out Storrow Drive to Route 2, and Concord. The slush and wet snow had frozen into ice.

▼ ▼ ▼

Monday morning, just after my third patient departed, I got a call from Joe.

"Doc? Joe. I'm at the office. Is Sarah still out there with you?"

"Was when I left. She and Mary are seeing old haunts around town. You'd think that reliving those years in Concord would only depress her further, but apparently it's what she wanted to do."

"If I were to tell you that we checked on Brenner's firm, New England Investment Services, and found that it was entirely bogus, would that surprise you?"

I thought for a second. "A week ago, yes. Now it doesn't."

"There's no office at the address, for one thing. It's a letter drop, nothing more. A service from a company that specializes in providing addresses that sound legit. The phone number is an answering service."

"So New England Investments doesn't exist?"

"Hard to say. I guess anybody can hang out a shingle, print some stationery, and call himself an investment counselor. Maybe the late George Brenner did give some investment advice now and then. But the pattern that's emerging suggests that if he did, the investments would be shady at best. Probably outright scams."

"No wonder he was so guarded about his private life."

"Yep. And his past. That's another interesting thing. The people on the fourth floor at headquarters, in R and I, have been running his name through data banks. Hardly anything for the past nine or ten years. Then, *zip*. Absolutely nothing prior to about seventy-eight or seventy-nine. Before that, it appears that George W. Brenner did not exist."

"He changed identities?"

"We're pretty sure he stole one that matched up. R and I just buzzed me; they finally got a hit on the wire. There are a hundred possibles, but this one sounds like a good bet. Get this: there's a George Willis Brenner who was born in Joplin, Missouri, in 1938. He died in 1959."

"Born in thirty-eight would be a good match for the age," I said. "So it seems our late friend, whoever he really is, got hold of this birth certificate and social security number. . . ."

"And created George Brenner, respectable investment counselor."

"I bet Sarah's going to be glad to hear that."

"Overjoyed."

"Do we have to tell her now? Do we have to lay all this bad stuff on her all at once?"

"I don't see any way out, Doc. But the icing is this: right in the middle of trying to lay our noses to Brenner's trail, who should pop in to pay a visit but the DEA. . . ."

It was fitting together now. All those pieces floating weightless began locking up, clicking together like pieces in a puzzle or a construction game. Dovetails, hooks and eyes, lap joints, snaps, buttons. *Click click*—

"They tell us they've been watching Brenner for two years. Never told us, or any other agency. They do this sometimes— lie low and keep watching and waiting til they get lots of big fish in the net. That's why there was no record on George Brenner and why his prints aren't on file anywhere."

"A drug hauler. That explains his high living and the bogus business in town."

"Yep. That's why he needed the fake career in the first place: to explain his absences and odd hours. Whoever checks up on an investment counselor? And if anybody he knew asked for advice, or an appointment, he could always turn them down, saying he had a full slate."

"How close were they? When were they going to move on him?"

"Sometime this spring. But some rival got to him first. The guys from DEA are pissed because if they'd gotten to him when he was vulnerable, they're sure he would've turned state's evidence on some big-timers."

"Maybe whoever killed him saw it coming—knew that George was about to be picked up and that he'd turn. So they took him out."

"Doc, for once you are a hundred-percent right. I told all of you it was a pro hit, and a pro hit it was. One more thing we've got to do: we need to dust his apartment on Marlboro Street. Especially his bedroom, that's where most of his prints will be found. If we match them to those on the corpse, that'll be proof that the body we found was indeed Sarah's former husband. But I guess we'll never find out his true identity before he assumed the persona of George Brenner."

"Are you still trying to get ahold of Jonathan Randolph?"

"Yes, and he's still not in. I just stuck his name on the wire this afternoon. Oh, and another thing: Bernie Kirk just called and said that Northrop Chesterton's coming to town tomorrow. Wants to cooperate fully and all that sort of thing. Since you and Sis are the lead witnesses, I'd like you on tap, so to speak."

"C'mon, Joe; we've jumped through enough hoops for you guys the past two days. Except for the tag number on the rental car, what Mary and I saw and heard at the Chesterton house three weeks ago isn't crucial right now. Let's wait to see what else Karl turns up, if anything. Meantime, what do I tell Sarah Brenner?"

"Nothing. That's my job."

"She'll be here tonight. You want to come out and talk to her personally?"

"What's for dinner?"

I sighed to myself. Joe's subtlety can be overwhelming.

"Joe, I thought that was done with now. You're married; you have your own home; you're *thin*—"

"I'll bring veal scallopini and fresh-baked Italian bread."

Instant saliva rush in my mouth. Quivering of taste buds. I fought it.

"We don't eat veal anymore. You know how they raise veal? You know what happens to the little calves?"

"I don't want to hear it."

"If I told you, you'd never touch it again."

"Try me."

"I'll see you at Ten Ten tomorrow, late afternoon."

"I'll see you tonight, Doc, at your place. I'll bring fresh sea-food and Marty."

He did. Bluepoint oysters in the shell, giant shrimp, scallops, and swordfish steaks. I could stand it. Best of all, all five of us were in the kitchen, talking, laughing, drinking beer, and kidding one another. The wood stove was purring, Luigi Boccherini was on the stereo, snow was pelting the windowpanes, and good smells were everywhere. It was doing Sarah worlds of good. She helped Mary and Marty wrap the scallops in bacon and skewer them with toothpicks; we put them on the grill with the monster shrimp, which we basted with an Oriental-style barbecue sauce. Joe made a dill-and-green-peppercorn sauce for the swordfish steaks. Looked a little bit like guacamole sauce, but stronger. We had the oysters as a pick-me-up while we were preparing the main dishes. Then came the scallops and bacon, dipped into melted butter and lemon juice, with hot bread on the side. The steaks and prawns we had with Chinese rice, the doughy, clumpy kind that tastes great. Washed it all down with iced Coors. Every now and then you have to treat yourself to a feast like this. It's one of the perks of living in Boston. Not too often, though.

Twice a week, *max*.

After dinner, over cappuccino, Mary and Sarah filled the rest of us in where they had gone in Concord, including, as I suspected, the farm out on Lowell Road where the Brenners lived once upon a time.

"Did you know it's for sale again?" said Sarah. "We got there as it was getting dark, but tomorrow, if I can talk Mary into it, we'll go back and look around."

"You sure that's a good idea, Sarah?"

"It's okay, Doc. I really want to go back, just for a little while. I feel it's something I have to do one more time."

"Mind if we all tag along?" Joe asked. Sarah and Mary shook

their heads. Sensing the relaxed atmosphere, Joe asked Sarah if she'd mind if they talked privately a few minutes in my study. Sarah went readily enough, but I think she suspected Joe had some interesting news about George.

"Joe told me he talked to you earlier today about what they've discovered," said Marty, leaning over to me and speaking in her husky whisper. "How do you think she'll take it?"

I shrugged, and we waited.

Although we pretended to ignore the tête-à-tête in the next room, we all waited nervously until Joe and Sarah came back out of the study. She had been crying, that was certain. But the smile she wore was genuine. It was the smile of relief, the result of some kind of purge.

"Ohhhh, God, Mary! I feel so much better—" she said, collapsing into my chair and placing her palms on her knees. "A woman always has to know why. For these three years, I didn't. Until just now. Now I know why he left and why he stayed away. I feel so relieved to know it wasn't just *me*."

She looked much better now; her eyes had taken on a sparkle that belonged to the Sarah Brenner we'd known before. Mary and Marty hovered around her for a few minutes, performing those female strengthening moves. Then they regrouped and tagged Joe as a fourth for bridge. It's no mystery why I wasn't chosen. For me, bridge has always been slightly more complex than general relativity, so I avoid it. And people who like the game avoid me, after only a few hands. I was left to retreat into my study with a recent issue of *Smithsonian* and a Mexican cigar.

Smithsonian always comes through for me; this issue had an article on the history of windmills, complete with technical diagrams reminiscent of Eric Sloan, and color photos of some of the ones still in use. It had not the remotest connection with my job, my family and loved ones, or the unpleasant business we had been thrust into. In short, just what I needed.

After an hour and a half, around eleven, Mary stuck her head into the room. "Right after breakfast we're all going to look around the farm. When's your first patient?"

"Ten."

"Good, plenty of time."

"Why does she want to do this?"

"Try to dig up some old memories. Maybe she can remember some link, some person who hated George."

"Did Joe put her up to this?"

"A little."

"Well," I said, getting out pad and pencil, "it looks like another one of those busy days. I better pencil in my schedule."

"I guess you'd better," she said, and went back to join her friends.

By 8:30 next morning, we were tramping around the innards of the old farmhouse on Lowell Road that Sarah and George Brenner had owned a few years previous. Joe had gotten the key from the realtor, having called her the night before. When she discovered our errand was investigatory instead of commercial, she declined to go with us, especially at such an early hour. The place was empty and cold. The electricity was off, but the sunlight, reflecting brilliantly off the deep snow outside, flooded the house, enabling us to see the rooms clearly. It was a fine old place, but to my mind, a deserted house without furnishings is dismal. We walked and talked, with Sarah leading us through each room recollecting this and that. Still, she failed to come up with any connection with the past that might prove enlightening.

But I did.

In the butler's pantry, I found myself stopped in front of the glass doors of the built-in china cabinets. I froze without knowing why, but as I stared at the wiggly reflections in the old glass, images from the past flashed into my head with remarkable clarity. A mental videotape started playing my own private movie, complete with sounds and aromas, and snatches of perfectly remembered conversation, from a dinner party long ago:

George is uncorking a bottle of bubbly in this very room—the bottle resting on this same countertop, his hands working on the cork, back and forth, the cork squeaking: *eeek, eeek*. Mary,

Sarah, and the other guests are in the dining room, talking and laughing, the clink of silverware on plates, the melodic tinkle of ice cubes in crystal goblets. A loud howl of laughter from Jim DeGroot. George and I are alone in the little pantry. He leans over. "Hey, Doc," he says in a half whisper, "I read somewhere that oral surgeons can change faces. Is it true?" Yes, I answer, of course. Surgery of the facial bones, the realignment of the mandible and maxillary, can drastically alter the face. Far more than the most extensive plastic surgery, which only involves the soft tissues. . . .

The cork flies out with a pop, thumps off the ceiling. Hoots and cheers from the next room. Bring it in, George, we're dry!

"How much does it cost?" he asks, wiping the foam with a towel. A lot, I answer, between five and fifteen thousand, depending . . .

Then he's gone, bearing the foaming bottle to the table. I proceed in the other direction, on my original mission to the bathroom. The incident, lasting perhaps ten seconds, is so insignificant I forget it; it is filed away in the dark recesses of my brain with millions of other trivia.

Until now.

"Charlie?"

"Hi, honey."

"What are you doing staring at the sink in here?"

Joe, Marty, and Sarah followed her in. We were all packed into the little room that, when I last stood there, served as a wet bar. I told them all the snatch of sub-rosa conversation I'd had with George that had jumped into my memory upon entering the room again.

"Listen, Doc! I remember something about that," said Sarah, leaning against the countertop and crossing her arms. She looked down and studied her feet patiently, trying to recall. "George had an article from some magazine . . . or maybe it was a pamphlet from a hospital or doctor's office. There were photographs of men and women, before and after these operations. You couldn't tell it was the same person afterward."

"Right. But these people in the 'before' pictures—I assume

they had some kind of facial deformity. Mandible excess, prognatia, cross-bite, maxillary excess, microgenia, and so on . . ."

"Microgenia? What's that?"

"Dwarf chin. What I'm getting at is, people with no problem don't seek maxillofacial surgery. It's not like having a tooth pulled; it's major, major surgery of an extremely important part of your body."

"And if anybody was not facially deformed," said Mary, "it was George. He reminded us of Peter O'Toole. Why, he was so handsome he—"

She looked down at the floor, shocked. Sarah Brenner had collapsed, face buried in hands, sobbing to beat the band.

"George!" she called, her voice muffled and wet. "Oh, George!"

EIGHT

After Mary and Marty got Sarah into the car, Joe and I stood in the side yard, knee-deep in snow, looking around in the brilliant sunshine. The snow had stopped falling, but powder was blowing all over. It stung my cheeks in a pleasant way. We watched Mary's Audi plow through the drifts to Lowell Road, then walked back to the farmhouse. Snow was clumped on all the branches of all the trees. So bright out it killed your eyes.

"I say we hang around a little longer," he said, thumping up the front steps onto the porch and stamping his feet hard on the floorboards. Caked snow came off his pants in avalanches. "I mean, hey, you got lucky in the butler's pantry. Sort of like Marcel Proust, ya know? Stare at the sink, think of George opening the champagne bottle, and *pow*! You're back there in time. What was it that set Proust off?"

"The madeleine biscuit, I think. Seeing one of them made him remember dipping it in tea when he was a kid. So he retired to his sickroom in Paris, lying down on his chaise-longue with his mentholated cigarettes, and batted out the entire seven or whatever volumes of *A la Recherche du temps perdu.*"

"You ever read it?" he asked.

"You kidding?"

"Let's go inside and—what are you staring at, Doc?"

"George's old radio tower. It's still here."

"That big tall thing? Hell, it must be fifty feet high."

"Sixty. He removed the antenna wires, but the tower . . . well, I guess he knew he couldn't take it with him to the condo in Gloucester. And the subsequent owner didn't bother to take it down."

The tower was made of aluminum tubing, triangular in cross section, and was steadied by three guy wires from its top to anchors in the ground. Now one side of it was white with clinging snow.

"He must have been a real shortwave nut. He the one who hooked you with the bug?"

"Uh-huh. He got me started, but my enthusiasm never approached his."

"Did he just listen, or did he transmit too?"

"He never told me he sent. But considering what we've discovered about George, there's no telling. Who knows? Maybe he talked to Moscow every night. . . ."

We went inside and stood around the living room.

"Where'd he keep the radio?"

"Upstairs in a spare bedroom that was his study. The antenna ran from there over to the barn along the roof ridge, then up the mast."

"And he could hear all over the world?"

"Oh, you bet. So can I, on my ICOM. Europe, Russia, the Far East . . . Africa . . . Australia . . ."

"Well, I was just wondering. If he was a drug smuggler, a shortwave that he could call anywhere would be a real—"

Eeeeeep! Eeeeeep! Eeeeeep!

Joe's beeper was piping a blast of shrill noise, telling us he had to call headquarters. He reached around and silenced the device on his belt. Since there was no phone in the empty house, he went back outside to his cruiser to call in. While he was gone I went upstairs and found the room that George had converted into a study. *Study* was a strange word to call a room reserved for George Brenner, I thought as I stood in the doorway, since I never saw him sit still long enough to crack a book. And yet he was obviously well informed. Not in the classics especially, but he showed a keen grasp of current events and world politics and also had an acute mind for financial matters—especially in the making of deals; I caught enough of his comments and conversational asides to know this. Although never an intimate friend, I recalled, he was perhaps as close to Mary and me as anybody. I was beginning to realize the truth about George Brenner: he was not a man who made close associations or commitments. He was just passing through. This was true even of his relations with his wife.

Standing in that spare bedroom, I remembered the German-made Grundig radio that sat, complex and illuminated, on the small desk right under the window I was now looking through. I remembered George sitting in front of the machine, fiddling with all those arcane and wondrous gizmos found on premium world-band receivers: frequency-band selectors, RF gain controls, bandwidth filters, noise blanker switches, notch adjustment, pass-band tuning buttons, entry keyboards, beat frequency oscillators, preamp bypass, mode switches, and so on. Fascinating. And all the bells and whistles to go with it. Can't forget them! I love the bells and whistles. Anything that has them, I buy. They ought to call me Bells and Whistles Adams. Mary came close; last summer she stuck an F.A.O. Schwartz sign on my study door, saying I've got more toys than *them*.

But world-band radio is terrific. It's the telegraph wire through the swamp. On shortwave, you can hear everything: BBC newscasts, Balinese temple music, a funeral in Kyoto, Czech art lectures, Scots pipe bands, tugboat captains in the Baltic, the call to prayer in Jidda, Bible thumpers in L.A., steamer pilots on the Ganges, Australian rugby matches, Welsh drinking songs, a polo match in Berks County, and so on. And on and on and on. With thousands of frequencies broadcasting from hundreds of global stations, the primary problem of the radio nut is choosing one frequency among the hundreds coming to him at any given minute.

All major countries have a government-sponsored world-service radio station. Ours is Voice of America. My favorite is the BBC World Service. Radio Moscow is interesting. George had a fondness for two in particular: Schweizer Radio International, the world radio service of Switzerland, and Deutsche Welle, the Voice of Germany. These he listened to diligently, both in English and German, in which he was fluent. Perhaps this helped explain his preference for the Grundig radio over the less expensive Japanese brands. Brenner was a German name—ah, but that wasn't his *real* name. . . .

Where was George Brenner from? What were his origins? We'd probably never know. But one thing was for sure: Sarah still loved him. Her collapse minutes before had shown us that. Poor thing. Joe's car honked outside; I returned downstairs, locking the front door behind me as per the instructions of the realty agent, and joined Joe in the cruiser. We went back to our house, the car moving along the snowy roads with that silence peculiar to winter days.

"It was Kevin who paged me. He says Karl struck pay dirt down in Osterville. He didn't say what it was, but I'm heading back to town. I don't know if Marty's coming with me or not. What about you? Can you take the afternoon off?"

"I've got patients till late afternoon. Tomorrow morning's free, though. If Marty wants to stay here with Mary and Sarah, maybe I could stay in town with you. Boys' night out?"

"Great idea." He grinned. "Let's go back to your place and look at today's *Globe*. Kevin says there's a big article on Northrop Chesterton's return to the beach house."

The women were sitting around the wood stove in the kitchen having coffee. I did not like the expression on Sarah's face. It was totally relaxed, but the eyes were dull and unfocused. She was hysterical, or in shock, or maybe both. Apparently, the sense of relief after Joe's little conference with her the night before had been only a temporary reprieve from her grief and anger. I took her aside, and she promptly let her head fall on my shoulder and cried.

"He left me," she wailed. "He left me twice. Only now, the second time, he can't ever come back."

"And you never had any indication that he feared for his life, that he had enemies?"

"Oh, he always used to tell me his favorite saying whenever I asked him about his business deals, or his past. He said a famous baseball player told it the first time. He'd say, 'I never look back; something might be gaining on me.' "

"Yeah. I think that was Satchel Paige. One of his rules for longevity."

"Well, it obviously didn't work for George."

"You're not totally surprised that he was involved in illegal dealings, notably drug smuggling?"

She wiped her eyes and stared blankly ahead, shaking her head. "No. The older you get, the less things surprise you. I know now, looking back, that I should have suspected something wasn't right. The way he never talked about his job . . . the late-night phone calls and meetings . . . the two-week absences when he never left me a destination or a number where he could be reached—"

"You think he could have been out of the country?"

"Doc, that man could go anywhere. You remember him; you remember what a free spirit he was."

There was silence, then she continued.

"The thing that hurts the most is knowing that I was never that important to him. And I thought I was. Now events have proven that I was one of many things in his life; I was never the center of his life. And God, I wanted to be!"

"Please don't take offense, but I'm going to ask you a question I want you to think about carefully before answering, okay?"

She nodded.

"There's a chance—maybe only a slight chance—that George was bisexual. Does that surprise you?"

She turned to face me.

"Yes, it does surprise me. And no, I don't believe it. He was too good a lover. Good in bed, good to me whenever we were together. He loved me, Doc. And he loved me as a woman. A woman knows. I don't know much about homosexuality, but one article I read said that bisexuality is pretty rare. Men are either gay or straight, it said, at least in the vast majority of cases. A lot of men who admit they're bisexual are really gay and are just trying to hide it."

"And you are convinced George wasn't one of those?"

"Well, he was sure full of surprises, wasn't he? But I'm pretty sure, yes. We were married a little over eight years. Before George, I was married—miserably so—for fourteen years to a man I finally had the nerve to divorce. Now, if you told me that he was gay, why it wouldn't have surprised me at all. But not George. Who says he was gay anyway? Why would anybody say that?"

I explained to her the clinical evidence. The switched shirt was sketchy at best—any theorizing there would be based on stereotypes and preconceptions. But there was no arguing with the evidence of AIDS found in his mouth. She winced at all of this, replying that there was still no absolute proof of his sexual preference. I couldn't help but agree.

"And another thing, Doc. The house was cold, wasn't it? So where was his overcoat? Wouldn't he have worn a coat in the middle of winter?"

"He was apparently wearing a British-made leather jacket when he was shot, but the jacket is missing."

"Well, this whole thing is difficult enough for me to deal with . . . but it's also strange. The shirt isn't necessarily sexually connected. This man, this Karl Pirsch, is he sexually uptight?"

"Words cannot adequately define his character," I offered, hoping this would suffice.

"Well, couldn't the shirt have some significance besides sex? I mean, maybe the shirt George had on when the killer shot him would have offered a clue."

"You mean, helped us to identify the murderer?"

"Sure. Why else would he go to all the trouble to remove it?"

"Well, we all assumed that part, yes—"

"Then I sure hope you stay involved in this, Doc. Because, besides maybe Joe, you're the only one who seems to have half a brain."

She rose from the living-room couch and started back to the kitchen.

"Please. Please, Doc. You and Mary and Joe and Marty have all been so great to me. I have to know how it happened, and why. I guess in my heart of hearts I always suspected that George was engaged in things . . . less than totally legal. I'd have been a total fool if it never crossed my mind. But I'm a pretty good judge of character. George wasn't mean. There wasn't a vicious bone in his body. Everybody who knew him was crazy about him. You included."

"I never knew him that closely, but—"

"Nobody did. That was part of the mystique. He could have been in a movie with Marlene Dietrich. But you know what I'm talking about. He didn't deserve this. He didn't deserve to be shot to death and left like that. Please tell me you'll—"

"Sarah, we'll do what we can. As it turns out, Mary and I are involved whether we want to be or not."

"Thank you, Doc. It means a lot to me."

It wasn't until half-past six that I entered the lobby of the state-police headquarters at Ten Ten Comm. Ave. I walked over to the bank of elevators and punched the "up" button. Soon the doors opened to reveal a large mattress. Two men held it upright. One of them was Karl Pirsch.

"*Güten nacht*, Herr Pirsch," I piped. He looked back at me with his beaky stork face and his merry blue eyes. He tried to smile, couldn't. He patted the mattress and grinned.

"*That's* your prize from the Chesterton mansion?" I asked.

"Remember I told you there was another shot fired, Doc?"

"Uh-huh. And you went down the Cape looking for evidence of it."

"Here it is. Are you on your way to see Joe?"

I nodded.

"Come up to the lab with me; we'll buzz down for him. He should see this."

NINE

Ten minutes later Joe and I were examining the mattress that Karl had retrieved from the Chesterton place. It was lying on a stainless-steel table, positioned exactly as on a set of box springs. Karl pointed with a sharpened pencil at a tiny hole in the center of its lower end, on the side edge of the mattress under which the feet would rest. We had to get very close before we even saw it.

"Hah! You see?"

"Bullet hole?" asked Joe. Karl nodded, grinning.

"Entrance hole," he said. "And no powder burns. The shot was fired from some distance away." He motioned us around to the opposite end with waves of his hand. There, at the lower left side of the head end of the mattress, was an ugly eruption of ripped cloth, a disembowelment of cotton stuffing and springs the size of a softball.

"Exit hole," I said. They stared at me, amazed at my brilliance.

"So?" said Joe.

Another wave of Karl's bony fingers, motioning us forward. We went over to another table, upon which lay a bundle of cloth. Karl unfolded it.

"This is the bedding," he said, smoothing it out. "Mattress pad, sheets, light blanket, and bedspread. Notice that the foot end is untouched; there are no holes or marks whatsoever. Now, as we unfold the head end, what do you see?"

"One sheet, I guess it's the bottom sheet that was tucked around the mattress, has a big hole in it. Okay, Karl, a shot was fired through the mattress."

"Ah, but several things are interesting, not the least of which is the act itself. First, it is obvious that the bedding at the foot end of the bed was pulled up over the mattress before the shot was fired, then replaced afterward to hide the entrance hole."

"Whoever fired the shot wished it kept secret," I said. "But why was the shot fired in the first place?"

Karl held up a finger. Uh-oh.

"The killer wished to keep the shot secret *after* the fact only, not during the fact. As I mentioned, there are no powder residues at the entrance hole in the mattress; therefore, the shot was fired from a distance. If whoever fired the shot wished to muffle the noise, he would simply press the muzzle into the mattress, thus eliminating most of the blast, you see?"

"But he didn't," added Joe. "So he wanted the noise. He wanted the sound of the shot, but not evidence of it."

"Precisely. This mattress confirms my earlier thinking, all of which started by noticing that the revolver's cylinder was replaced in the frame incorrectly. Doc: I think this is the shot you and your wife heard from the beach outside. This shot was fired deliberately—I think after the victim was dead—to arouse your attention and suspicions."

"But *why*? That's the strangest—"

"I don't know why. And it is strange. I believe Kevin O'Hearn is correct when he says that it will provide us a lead. Sooner or later, it will prove pivotal in the case."

Ignoring Pirsch's withering glare, Joe lighted a cigarette. He walked over to Karl's immaculate desk and the corner windows and looked outside into the wintertime darkness. Both Eastern Mountain Sports across the street, and the Greek's at the corner, were illuminated by bright signs. "So, taking it from the top, let's try to reconstruct this thing," he said, sitting in the chair facing the desk. Karl seated himself behind it and I drew up another chair next to Joe.

"Okay, the two guys go into the house, using a key. The murderer shoots the victim, one George Brenner, real name unknown. Then he sees Doc and Mary walking up the beach. For some reason, he wishes to get their attention. He does this by firing a second shot, the evidence of which he conceals by lifting up the bed covers, shooting through the length of the mattress, and then letting the covers fall back down over the foot of the mattress. To further obliterate this mysterious second shot, he removes one of the spent shells from the revolver and replaces it with a fresh round. Karl, I assume you recovered the second slug, and that it matches the one in the body."

"*Certainly.*"

"Just asking."

"I still have a problem with this scenario," I said. "First: we must either assume the murderer knows us, or that just before his unforeseen death, our friend George told his killer he knew us. In either case, the firing of the second shot to alert us makes no sense. Another possibility is that George was dead before the plan for the second shot was even germinating in the killer's mind. In which case, the fact that we knew George—and knew him pretty well, as it turns out—is entirely coincidence. This I can't believe."

"Why are we all so sure that the murder shot was fired first?" asked Joe. "What if the bogus shot through the mattress came before the lethal one?"

This was a good question. I could tell it was a good question because there were no quick rebuttals. We all sat for a few minutes and pondered it. Then Joe spoke: "Suppose he fired the mattress shot first. He and George are in the room. Somehow, he tells George—hey, *that's it!*"

"What's it?" I asked.

"Don't you see? The killer wanted to test the safety of his plan. He wanted to see if a shot inside the house could be heard. So he shot the first round through the mattress."

"So then we heard this round, or the round that killed George?" I asked. Joe shrugged.

"That doesn't make sense, Joe," said Karl. "Because if he was so careful about the noise, and felt the need to test it, then why would he be so careless as to actually shoot his victim with two people right outside the windows, *hein*?"

I had an idea. "How about this: the killer comes to the house alone a day or so before the hit. During this initial visit, he checks out the house, the alarm system, the grounds, walks around the house looking for the ideal room to do the killing. He selects the bedroom as perfect and shoots a secret round through the mattress, leaving immediately. He watches from a safe place. When nobody comes running to the house, he knows he can do the hit there safely. He returns later with George."

I sat back in the chair, arms folded across my chest.

"Not bad, Doc," said Joe. "I think that could be it. What do you say, Karl?"

The gaunt man shook his head slowly, making little clucking noises in his throat. "I don't think so," he said finally. "The reason is the revolver. Would a man do the test shot, then return a day or more later and do the killing without reloading the weapon?"

"No, he would not," I admitted, seeing my theory go down in flames. "He would have a full cylinder going back into the house the second time. For sure."

"So there we are again," said Joe. "Weirdest damn thing I've seen in some time. I don't think we'll ever make sense of it."

"We must continue to try, and we will," said Karl sternly, glaring at the mattress across the room. "That is what they pay us for. Good day, gentlemen."

Back down in Joe's office, a slip of paper was waiting for him on his desk. It was a torn-off sheet of computer printing paper. The Wire speaketh. . . .

Joe read it and gave a low whistle. Then he waved the paper up and down as if fanning himself.

"This is it, Doc. This is the lead we've been waiting for!"

"It explains the mysterious second shot?"

"Hmm. Maybe. Listen to this: your old friend from medical school, Jonathan Randolph? Maybe you wondered why he retired early?"

"He said he was sick of the stress of medicine and had made some money in real estate."

"Wrong, pal. It seems the medical community asked him to leave. Guess why? Charged with possession of cocaine in eighty-seven."

"No."

"Yes. Possession with intent to distribute. They let him off with six months in camp and a year's probation, due to his 'standing in the community.' That means he paid somebody, in case you didn't know."

"And they bounced him out of the profession. That's no surprise."

"Are you making the obvious connection, Doc?"

"Between Randy's drugs and George's drugs, you mean?"

Joe nodded, tapping the eraser end of a pencil on his desktop. "I say George Brenner and Jonathan Randolph were in business together. Somehow, somewhere, they met. Somehow, somewhere, your name came up in conversation, Doc. The mutual friend."

"Which is why Randy just happened to invite me down to walk on his beach the day George was killed in the Chesterton mansion."

"Yep. Problem is, we still can't find Randolph."

"Maybe he's back in Houston setting up more deals."

"Maybe. And maybe he and George turned out to be rivals in business, which is why George was killed."

"But why would Randolph have George killed in such a strange way? And one that would certainly drag him into it?"

"I don't know." He shrugged. "Maybe to establish an alibi. He *was* in his own house, throwing a party, when you heard the shot."

I thought about this. "You mean he killed George, or had him killed, then had some accomplice fire the shot as we passed the house?"

"Could be. Hey, try this: he could have killed George elsewhere. When you passed the house, there was probably no body inside, just the accomplice with the gun. See? That way, if the cops did arrive, they wouldn't find anything."

"So when did he put the body in the bedroom?"

"Who knows? Remember, he had three weeks to do that."

"Joe, there have got to be ninety-seven easier ways to kill a guy than that."

"I guess you're right. But you've got to admit, we've got a couple live wires here. I say we can splice them together somehow."

"Are you going to visit George's apartment on Marlboro Street? That might give you more to go on."

"Yeah, I've called his apartment mate, a guy named James Howland, and set up a visit for tomorrow morning. Since you say your day is clear, you can come along."

"You want me to?"

"Yes. In fact, I insist. You knew George Brenner much better than I ever did."

"Okay; count me in."

"Good, now where to?"

"To eat? Not the Greek's, I hope. Not for Boys' Night Out dinner in Beantown. Joe Tecce's?"

"Naw. Did him last week. Scotch n' Sirloin?"

"Nah. The Marliav?"

"Naw. Nix on wop, Doc. Had it up to here." He held his hand up to his forehead.

"Locke Ober's?"

"How about the Union Oyster House?"

"There ya go!"

Joe didn't feel like driving his cruiser, so he left it there. Since I had no car, I was wondering how we were going to get all the way to Dock Square.

"Cab," he said, walking around the building.

"How you going to find a cab back here? What's wrong with the street?"

"Ah, here's one. And reasonable too," he said, heading for a dark green sedan that was moving slowly along the curb. He grabbed my sleeve and hustled me up to it. He opened the backdoor and we jumped in.

"Hey, Lieutenant," said the young man at the wheel. He was dark, rather Hispanic looking, and wore a gray flannel sport coat. Looked sharp, with military written all over him. Master sergeant was my guess. Maybe the marines. He turned around and grinned at Joe.

"Hi, John. Call me Joe; that's my name. This is my brother-in-law, Doc Adams. Doc, John Gutierrez."

We shook hands. John had a Boston accent.

"You want the meter running, Joe?"

"Better the meter than the friggin' blue light. You going uptown?"

"Just as far as B.U. We'll have to do the pony express; I'll call McNally," John said, reaching for the radio microphone. We drove on for a minute or two, then the cruiser's radio squawked. "Anybody seen Brindelli?" a voice cackled. John grabbed the mike and reported our position, our destination, and estimated arrival time.

"Somebody wants to see us," Joe said, snuggling back into the seat. "I wonder who?"

At Boston University Joe slid out of the Commonwealth Avenue traffic and in front of a burgundy sedan that sat at idle, huffing clouds in the cold. We said our good-byes and Joe prodded me out. "Fresh horses," he said as we slipped and skidded our way over the packed snow to the red car. We got in back and Sgt. Lonnie McNally drove us all the way to Dock Square, and that crazy, slant-roofed, ancient emporium with a whole lot of miles on it: Boston's Union Oyster House.

We thanked Lonnie and headed for the door.

"You travel like that often?" I asked.

"Often as I can. You're buying."

I don't know of any eatery that's more Boston than the Union Oyster House. Except maybe Durgin Park, another famous restaurant and watering hole. It's not far away from the Union. In that place, the waitresses generally have names like Moira, Kathleen, and Sheila, and throw forks at you if you sass them.

We entered the noisy, low-ceilinged, dark, aromatic, cozy joint. First thing you see is the bar. Not the booze bar—the oyster bar. This solid end-grain wooden bar is rounded and gouged in smooth canyons by a century and a half of oyster knives and scaly shells, patrons' elbows, thumping beer mugs, and general abuse. The bar and surroundings behind it are packed with shaved ice and bushels and bushels of the crusty, tan-gray, oblate shells of that noble mollusk.

Seeing them stacked up like that reminded me of a little ditty I'd read in *Smithsonian* about oysters. How did it go? *The oyster lives between two shells, his inner life he never tells. . . .*

"You got room upstairs?" Joe asked one of the waiters. He shot a thumb skyward.

"Oh yeah. Whole lawta room up theah. Nobody's out tonight."

In philosophic calm he dwells. The Oyster.

We trundled up the narrow dark oak stairway, past old ship models stuck against the yellow walls. Harpoons, cable, blocks, more old ships . . . nautical lights . . .

For no selfish, shellfish girl, he makes a grain of sand a pearl. His heart is never set a-twirl. The Oyster.

"This okay with you, Doc?" said Joe, sliding into a booth. I followed. He grabbed a menu. "What say, Doc; two chowders to start with?"

"No. Two silver bullets to start with. Then the chowder."

"Right."

When ice surrounds him on a plate, and lemon and Tabasco wait, he coolly contemplates his fate. The Oyster.

"Hey," he asked, "you okay?"

"Fine. Just thinking about a silly poem. After the chowder, I'm having the stuffed flounder. Or maybe the bacon-wrapped fillet . . . can't decide."

"I better be good and stick to broiled sole, no sauce, twitch of margarine."

The waiter came and we ordered our drinks. Made with Boodle's. Up; twist. I rubbed my hands together, sniffing the heavy aroma of baked and fried fish, sizzling meat, and that semimetallic, briny smell of fresh oysters. My drink came and I took a hefty sip, letting it slide down and warm me up, slashing through my interior like Captain Kidd's cutlass.

Joe squinted and leaned forward, trying to see something across the room. Through the smoke haze and dim light, he seemed to recognize a face. "Well, son of a bitch, Doc. You won't believe who's coming up the stairs."

"Who?"

"Owen Lightner, the Jamaican houseboy. And that big guy with him must be none other than Northrop Chesterton."

"That's some coincidence, Joe."

"I don't think so, Doc. If what I hear about him is true, he's the one who was calling the dispatcher at headquarters, trying to get a fix on our position."

TEN

The big red hand came out, and down, to meet mine.

"Lightner," called Chesterton, tipping his jaw back, speaking over his shoulder but keeping his eyes on me as he pumped my hand in an iron grip, "is this the doctor you spoke of? The man with the pretty wife?"

Then his mouth flashed into a wide grin, revealing big, perfect teeth. Northrop Chesterton was waiting for me to smile back and laugh. I didn't. He turned to Joe, who stood toe to toe with him, looking him level in the eye. That made Chesterton a solid six-three. The two of them moved off a few paces, near a vacant table, and bowed their heads together, talking in low tones. Chesterton had snowy-white hair, very tan skin with a lot of red in it, and a thick, rugged face. He wore a navy-blue suit of worsted wool, three-piece. He was doing his damnedest to look Old Money. But his manner betrayed him; he was too aggressive for Old Money. And way, way too familiar. He had made his own fortune, that was for sure. Salesman, hustler, daring wheeler-dealer. It was written all over him in twenty different ways. Northrop Chesterton—if that indeed was the name he was born with—was new money. So new the ink on the bills wasn't dry.

But there was something underneath it all I couldn't help liking. And what it was, I think, was the nouveau riche itself.

Maybe the shred of attraction I felt for him was that he *wasn't* an old-line Yankee. And here I am, with the quintessential New England Yankee name. *The* surname in these parts. But I come mostly from the farming stock of the Midwest, and have more German, Huguenot, Swede, and Scot in me than anything else. The longer I remain in my adopted home of New England, the more I realize that the "proper Bostonian" thing isn't its strong suit.

New England's strong suit is a social and political climate that allows you to be your own person and say and do whatever you like so long as you don't hurt anyone. Absent is the Teutonic regimentation of the Midwest. The Anglo-Scots macho gallantry of the Old South is gone, too. So is the West Coast's frenzied and schizophrenic hedonism. Here you can be yourself without fear of reprimand. Only New England could have produced Henry David Thoreau. Or tolerated him.

Joe and Chesterton continued discussing the case sotto voce. I could tell it was about the murder because I caught several key words now and then—one of which was my name. Several paces behind Chesterton I could see Owen Lightner, impeccably decked out in gray flannel pants and navy blazer with some kind of crest in gold braid embroidered over the breast pocket. A closer inspection revealed it to be the Buff Bay Polo Club. This somewhat surprised me, since I assumed that private clubs, particularly polo clubs, would exclude servants. But what did I know?

Owen looked good in the outfit, no doubt about it. It fit him, in every sense of the word. More and more I was getting the feeling that Mr. Lightner was much more than a houseboy. It seemed that Northrop Chesterton had great expectations for the lad.

Behind me and to my left, a voice said: "Doc Adams. Aren't you a friend of Brady Coyne's?"

I turned to see a heavy man in a winter trench coat and large-brimmed safari hat with thin horn-rim glasses. Looked about my age. He held out his hand.

"Yeah, you're the infamous Doc Adams."

"Guess so. And you are?"

"Anton Bradshaw, Bud's attorney."

"He goes by Bud?"

"Sure. How would you like to be called Northrop? I heard about you from Brady; he's always telling me how you're getting him into trouble."

"Brady said that? Listen: I was doing fine until I started hanging around with him."

"Where is he now?" Bradshaw asked.

"Down in Belize, fly-fishing for tarpon. Last week, just before he took off, he asked me to go with him. Now I wish I had."

"And miss out on this nasty business?"

"Just how nasty is it for Mr. Chesterton?" I asked in a low voice.

"Bad enough. It's what he really doesn't need right now, with his political plans going into high gear."

"Political plans? Hadn't heard about them."

"Not for public consumption right now; I may have already said too much, but since you're a close friend of Brady's, and he speaks well of you, I think maybe I can trust—"

"Oh, sure. I'll keep mum. How do you feel about this?"

"Well, I'm sure my client didn't do it, if that's what you mean. He's been down in Jamaica at his plantation the whole time."

"Nobody disputes that; the question is: could he have paid to have it done?"

"Yeah, well, that won't hold up; there are no connections between this murdered man and Bud, that's for sure. But way I hear it, Doc, there are connections between him and you."

"So it seems." I sighed, draining the last of my Boodle's. I could use another. Like hell I could. I snagged a waitress and ordered a beer for me and one for Bradshaw.

"Who's the big guy with Bud?" Bradshaw asked as we slid back into the booth Joe and I had occupied. I told him the big guy was my brother-in-law, who was also the investigative lieutenant on the case. Bradshaw stiffened when he heard this and quickly slipped out of the booth, interposing himself between Joe and his client, obviously fearful that Chesterton might let slip something incriminating, even damning. But Bud reassured him with a slap on the shoulder.

"C'mon, Bradshaw, I've got to talk with this man sooner or later. What he tells me, I've already faced down the bad guy, right, Joe?"

"Who might that be?" asked Bradshaw, nervously pumping up and down on his toes.

"Paul Keegan, according to Lieutenant Brindelli," said Chesterton, smiling broadly, enjoying himself immensely. "According to Joe, if I can talk to Keegan, I can talk to anyone."

"You want to have dinner with us?" I asked the three of them.

"Of course we do!" said Chesterton, beaming again. "Took you long enough to ask, Adams—"

So the four old guys shared the booth, with the immaculate Owen Lightner sitting at the head of the table in a chair drawn up for him.

"You play polo, Owen?" asked Bradshaw. He was smiling, as if he'd made a wisecrack.

"A little," Owen replied, and returned to his soup. I noticed he dipped the wide spoon in from the back, and sipped from it politely, pausing now and then to daub his mouth softly with the white linen napkin. Amy Vanderbilt would have approved.

"Mr. Lightner took three trophies at the club last year," said Chesterton softly. "I was the only member to take more," he continued, "but I have full expectations that in a few years, Lightner will surpass everyone."

"If they continue to let me on the field," said Lightner, sliding his empty soup bowl three inches away.

"They'll let you play." Chesterton continued to speak softly, but now there was a hard edge to his voice that showed determination. "I built that club single-handed; they bloody well better let you play."

There was silence again until our main courses arrived.

"Okay, so who killed Mr. Brenner in your house, and how did they get in there?" asked Joe. It was the question we all were waiting for; Joe apparently thought he might as well get it out of the way.

"Easy answers," said Chesterton. "Don't know, and don't know. Lightner and I have been discussing it ad nauseam, and can make neither head nor tail of it."

It hit me then: the British patter. Chesterton was either British by birth and had learned American, or else he'd spent a whole lot of time in Jamaica. The accent was American, but the patter and the intonation had Oxford Street written all over them.

"The dead man is unknown to us, for starters. And none of the family or staff were at the cottage at the time."

Yeah, it's a cottage, I thought, like a sixty-foot Hinckley is a sailboat.

"There's a possibility that Owen was there," Joe said. His words slammed across the length of the table like a ball of shot. Everybody looked at him.

"I wasn't, sah," said Owen.

"I think so too. I was speaking *pro curiae* only; you cannot establish your alibi yet."

"He will," interjected Chesterton. "And even if he doesn't; I can assure all of you—place my reputation and net worth on it in fact—that he wasn't."

"I believe you," said Joe with a totally deadpan face. His voice was low and level and gravelly now, a Bogart voice. His face and demeanor commanded respect. Knowing him as a relative and friend, I usually forget Joe the cop and am continually amazed at how great a cop he is—how thoroughly professional, managing to ooze authority and compassion both at once.

"I believe you most of all, I think, because I want to. But you see what we could be up against. A lot of community leaders want to clear this thing. So do we. Best thing to do, I think, is to talk about it right here and now."

"No," said Bradshaw.

"Yes," said Chesterton. "We have nothing to hide. And I want to help; that's why I came up here a few months early."

The talk lasted almost ninety minutes. At the conclusion of it and our meal, I realized we hadn't answered any of the important questions. Chesterton turned to me.

"Frankly, I have to think that Doc is the key person. I'm certainly not, no matter what anyone might like to think. Doc was there when it happened, and he knew the dead man."

"I know I'm the most personally involved, but I think Joe wants to know why it took place at your house."

"Happenstance," snapped Chesterton. "Pure happenstance. Somebody wants to do a killing in a house to conceal the deed and the body," he said, as if there should be no questioning his version of the events, slicing his hand down in the air as he emphasized each point. A salesman. And it was working.

"That's what I said," said Joe, finishing up the remnants of my stuffed flounder. He was reaching over me to get at the food. I heard his heavy breathing. "But now I'm not so sure. And you, young man," he said, pointing his fork at Owen Lightner, sitting straight in his chair with an impeccable sport coat on, like a kid at an English boarding school, "you had better get some good witnesses to shore up that alibi. Events show you weren't at Shooter's Hill. They also show you *were* in the U.S. All I'm saying."

"I'll back him, Joe," said Chesterton, looking into his glass as he swirled the dying ice cubes around and around in it, making a sound like a Tibetan music bowl. "I'll back him to the hilt."

He snagged the chit from the table and handed it to the waitress, topping the bill with a gold Barclay's Bank card. He threw on his overcoat, a showy number in tan cashmere with a very wide fur collar around it. Too much fur, I thought, especially for Boston. It was a coat Henry VIII might have worn. We worked our way through the noisy babble of patrons, down the rickety dark oak stairway of the old oyster house, and out into the cold.

ELEVEN

Bud insisted on driving us to Joe's apartment. He offered to take his lawyer, Bradshaw, as well, but Bradshaw declined, snagging a cab on Congress Street and heading off to his condo on the waterfront. We watched the cab depart, diving out into that maelstrom of nighttime Boston traffic. It swung and half slid out of Dock Square. There might be worse drivers in Rio, but I doubt it.

"Well, hell." Bud sighed, his arm on Lightner's shoulder. "With him gone, maybe we can relax a little." We got into his car, a racing green Jaguar XJS, and fought that same Boston traffic. We went fast, drifting around corners on the hard-packed snow that made the car feel like a speedboat. During the ride Bud continually leaned out his open window, pointing skyward into the darkness with one hand while attempting to steer with the other. Unnerving, especially in Boston in the snow.

"There! There's a prime property. Government lease will run out next January, and I've got an option to buy."

Frigid air swept into the plush car. Cars honked at us, and Chesterton, with a barely concealed show of annoyance, stopped his running guided tour of his real-estate empire long enough to avoid collisions.

"See that six-story? Only three in this whole area. Joe, did you know that?" Joe shook his head, bundling his overcoat up around his neck to cut the chill.

"Wish that son of bitch would sell that warehouse. See it over there, behind that billboard? Prime location, I'm telling you. Prime."

Knowing downtown better than cops working the beat, Bud wheeled the big green Jag up in front of Joe's doorway in no time flat. Out of courtesy we asked them inside for a nightcap.

"Why certainly. We'd like that, wouldn't we, Lightner?"

The boy nodded mechanically, looking absently out the side window. I thought he looked homesick. "Well, let's get cracking, then!" said Bud, swinging the car over to the curb and cutting the engine.

"Better not park there," cautioned Joe. "It's a no parking zone."

"Not for me," he said with confidence. "City Hall knows the tag number." He led us out of the vehicle, oblivious of the fact that he was accompanied by the police. The snow had started up again. We all made a beeline for Joe's lobby. Once Joe opened the door, Chesterton bounded up the stairs ahead of us with more speed and grace than I would have expected. We found him waiting on the top landing, not breathing hard at all.

I caught myself wondering how he had known which floor Joe lived on. Maybe just a lucky guess.

Once inside, he took one sweeping glance at the prints and paintings on the walls, the furnishings, and the size of the place, and held up his hands in mock surrender.

"Okay, Brindelli, I won't even ask."

"Ask what?"

"What you had to do to get this place. No, don't tell me. I'd rather not know. But this certainly isn't standard issue for a state detective—I'm not that naive, you know."

"Numbers . . . hookers . . . protection . . . drugs . . . the whole schmear . . ." whispered Joe, gliding into the wide hallway that joined the living room in front to the kitchen in back, with three bedrooms opening off it. He made his way to an alcove and flipped a light switch. Tiny track-style spotlights illuminated a well-stocked bar. It was compact and simple, and held only the best. Lighted the way it was, it resembled the bars in Italian hotels and fine restaurants. Joe swept his hand in front of it with a flourish. "Help yourselves, gentlemen," he said.

Lightner made a gin and bitters for Bud, who took it with scarcely an acknowledgment, then poured himself a large tumbler of tonic, no gin. I opened the refrigerator under the bar and drew out Labatt's for Joe and me. We followed Joe down the long hall, illuminated only by the small shaded lamps over prints and paintings, and entered Joe's study, which was the first of the three bedrooms. This dim haven, with its tufted leather chairs and deep burgundy carpet, walnut veneer walls, and a Dutch-style tile fireplace, was the perfect place to be after the cold and wet of outdoors. Joe set the fireplace in motion with a long match as we sat down. I saw that Chesterton's eyes were fastened on the lighted gun cabinet against the far wall. In it were fourteen double shotguns, standing in two rows of seven. He rose, as if hypnotized, and went over to it.

"You hunt, or shoot?" he asked.

"Used to shoot quite a bit. Skeet mostly. Did pretty well in competition. Gave it up when I became a cop."

"Busman's holiday?"

"You got it."

"Damn fine guns, Joe."

"Thanks. Mostly Italian and Belgian. Perazzi, Beretta, Piotti, Berardelli, and so on. Two German: a Merkel and a Krieghoff. I keep them only because I know how fast they're appreciating."

"Think you'll ever shoot again?"

"Doubt it."

"Not if you come down to Jamaica. We've got bird hunting that will amaze you."

Bud left the gun cabinet and settled back in a chair in front of the fire.

"Can we talk about your wife?" asked Joe. Chesterton glanced at him with a weary eye. He put his fingertips together nervously and flexed his fingers.

"Of course. If we must."

"My sister, wife of the eminent doctor here, and no slouch when it comes to human nature, says she should be discussed."

Chesterton seemed to slump deeper into the chair and bowed his head in thought. Gone in an instant was the boyish enthusiasm, the self-confidence, and the extraordinary energy. He gained fifteen years in a twinkling. He sighed. A long drawn-out sigh of regret, which reminded me of a song by Edith Piaf.

"I hurt Margaret terribly," he said at last, making a face as though he might cry. "I can never forgive myself for what I did. It was stupid and impulsive. And very, very ephemeral, I assure you. It's the stupidity of the thing that's most disgraceful. An affair out of love or desperation is bad enough; one out of pure momentary lust is totally beyond the bounds. She found out and was wounded too deeply for reconciliation."

"You've tried reconciliation?" I asked.

"My God, I've been on the phone twenty—a hundred times in the past three months! I've sent messengers to her. Mutual friends, concerned relatives. I've tried everything."

"Where is she now?" Joe asked.

"I'll tell you, but I want it to remain confidential. I know where Margaret is, or was until last week, anyway. I know through informants; she doesn't know they exist. Her last address was in Mexico City. But she may have left there already, now that word of this killing has spread."

"Well, we can find out where she is even if you can't. And we may subpoena her if there's enough evidence to warrant it."

"No . . ." Chesterton said in a tired voice. "She didn't do it, or have it done. If you're worried about motive, gentlemen, she's an obvious candidate. And I'm a personal witness to the old saying that 'hell hath no fury like woman scorned.' But as angry and bitter as she is, Margaret wouldn't kill. She'll try to skin me in court, and may succeed. That's all."

"Well, then, as to motive," I said, "it seems that it must be drug-related, wouldn't you say, Joe?"

"That's our best guess now, since the DEA people had fingered Brenner a while ago and were waiting to pounce. We think other members of the ring knew this and killed Brenner so he wouldn't cop a plea and put them away. Another thing, Bud: Keegan just informed me that there are several drug rings operating around the Cape. One is big-time, and has been around for years. It imports high-grade marijuana from Jamaica. It's known in drug circles as the Purple Gang because the enforcers carry sawed-off shotguns, .45s, and tommy guns— the old Chicago Typewriter as it used to be called."

"Good Lord. And you think this Purple Gang killed the man in my house?"

"Quite possibly. And perhaps with some inside help from somebody in your employ. Anyway, Paul says he's not letting go until he interviews the rest of your staff when they arrive here. Maybe you'd like to tell us a little about them."

"I doubt there's any connection," said Chesterton. "Certainly none of them were directly involved, since they were all in Jamaica during the murder."

"Then how did the killer get the key?"

Chesterton shook his head impatiently. "That I don't know. Lightner and I have talked about it frequently. Duplicating the keys is impossible. I don't know if you were told that."

"I recognized the Chubbs locks."

"Ah, you know locks, then. I had the Chubbs locks installed on all the doors. These take left-handed keys. Here, let me show you—"

He stood up and retrieved a ring of keys from his pocket. A big brass one stood out. He held it up under the table lamp alongside a standard one. Joe leaned over and ran his finger along the blade.

"I've seen these in school," said Joe. "I attended locksmithing classes now and then. Hobby of mine. See, Doc, the left-handed cuts? See the groove underneath the flat side? No blanks available. Therefore, they can't be copied."

"Exactly, unless you send away to Chubbs for the blanks," said Bud. "And they've got to know you, personally, or it's no go."

"So this means that nobody could have lifted a key from the

staff and rushed down to the local hardware store for a copy," I said.

"Correct," said Bud. "The only way in would be to pick the lock or else make a wax impression. But even the impression would be useless without the proper blank, and the locks are electronically rigged to sense all but the most delicate and precise tampering."

"So it remains a mystery," said Joe. "But it does tell me something."

"What's that?"

"That the murder in your beach house was not by chance, as you said before, but the result of careful planning, and the procurement of one of your special Chubbs keys."

Bud sat down again, chin on his hands in thought.

"You're right, dammit. Hadn't thought of that."

"And Margaret had such a key," Joe continued. "More than one, in all probability."

"Then perhaps you'd better speak to her after all," said Bud, getting up and pacing the small confines of the dark study. Outside, I heard the wind moan and sigh through the neighboring chimney pots. The fire snapped, the room glowing on and off with the flames.

"Is there anything else we should know about the household staff at this point? What about this Reginald Westley?"

Bud and Owen exchanged glances. After a second or two Bud shrugged his shoulders. "Tell them, Lightner."

Owen looked up at Joe. "He's a nancy boy, sah."

"A what?"

"A sissy. You know. Gay."

Joe sat and thought for a minute, trying to shift this new piece of information into a meaningful position. The cop's perennial job. I guess I was doing it too, because when making any sort of diagnosis, that is also the physician's job.

"You knew this when you hired him?"

"What difference does it make? I knew he was a damned good gardener; he came most highly recommended. Am I supposed to have some built-in bias against gays?"

"No."

We let the issue drop. I saw Owen staring at the floor.

"Is there anything you wish to say, Owen?" asked Joe.

"No, sah."

"Well, we'd better be going," said Bud, heading for the hallway. "It's past eleven, and we've got a full day with the police and the press tomorrow."

"You going all the way back down the Cape tonight?"

"No; we've got a suite at the Ritz for the next two days. Hopefully, the bulk of this business will be behind us by then."

"When do you plan to come up here for the summer?" I asked.

"Generally in time for Patriots' Day."

Patriots' Day, celebrated only in Massachusetts and Maine, commemorates that spring day in April, 1775 when the Concord minutemen opened fire on the British forces at Old North Bridge and started the American Revolution.

"Will we be seeing you before then?" Joe asked. He put the question as a polite inquiry, but there was professional business behind it.

Chesterton shrugged again. "I suppose that depends on what develops. Getting back to Reggie Westley, we've all noticed that he seems quite down in the dumps right now. It seems his longtime boyfriend has given him the heave-ho . . . taken off with somebody else. So he's spent a lot of time moping around the grounds at Shooter's Hill during the day and hitting the pubs at night. Hitting them hard, if you know what I mean."

"You plan to dismiss him?" asked Joe, lighting a cigarette and waving out the match.

"No. I'm loyal to my staff, and they, in turn, are loyal to me. Lightner, fetch my coat please."

The boy left on the double.

"There's a chance, and it's only conjecture at this point, that George Brenner might have been homosexual as well," said Joe, exhaling a cloud of blue smoke and leaning back in his chair.

"So? I still don't see any connection," said Bud, carefully placing his empty glass back on the cork coaster. "But when I see Reggie next week, I'll ask if he loaned out any keys. Of course, if he did, I'm certain he'd deny it; I've made it very clear that the loaning out of any of the special Chubbs keys, for either Shooter's Hill or the beach house here, is strictly forbidden and can result in dismissal."

"How about the two women? The cook and the maid?"

"The cook, Maria Townsend, is a fairly recent addition. However, so far she has proved trustworthy, and I have no reason to suspect her. As with the rest of my staff, she is well paid and housed and receives benefits and privileges that far outshine anything she could expect in Jamaica. Lightner would wholeheartedly agree, if you care to ask him."

"From what we saw at your house," said Joe, "I have no trouble believing it."

"The maid, Anne Rawlings, is another matter entirely. She's left my employ to be with Margaret. She is to her what Lightner is to me: an utterly faithful servant and confidant. Where Margaret goes, Anne goes."

"And we can assume that in this discord, her sympathies lie with your wife."

"Without question."

"She's been with your wife for how long?"

"Years and years. From before I even met Margaret. She left when Margaret did," he said, wincing. "On September twenty-sixth."

"And she had a key?" I asked.

"Of course."

"But since the two of them are now in Mexico, then neither one of them needs a key, correct?"

He nodded. "Where the hell is Lightner?"

"So that's a possible source for the key that let in the killer and the victim," said Joe.

"Anne might have done it on her own, you know," Bud said reflectively. "She sees me as the source of all her lady's misery. Sad to say, there's some truth to it. It may have been she who gave the key away. But the question remains: to whom? And why?"

"To make you look bad," said Joe. "To resurrect the old rumor that you're connected."

"Ah, yes. *That*. Joe, you're an Italian-American who happens to be in law enforcement. I am aware of the hatred that only you can feel for the mob."

Chesterton paused, running his big fingers around the rim of the empty whiskey glass. He looked at both of us keenly awhile. Then, as if satisfied with what he read in our faces, he continued.

"The origin of that rumor lies in the fact that when I was starting out in real estate here in the early sixties, I secured a loan from a very connected person. Since I was practically penniless, he was the only person I could find who was willing to back me. The interest on the loan was minimal, the repayment schedule generous and flexible. However, he took a percentage of equity as a silent partner. I paid the loan off within six years, but to this day, he remains a silent partner in these few properties. I have tried to buy him out, but he won't budge. Obviously, he sees this toehold as a source for possible future influence, should I decide to run for the governorship."

"So you're seeking the statehouse," I said. "That's what the fuss at One Ashburton Place is all about."

"Yes, Doc. And there could be some white water ahead. That's why this tragedy and the domestic estrangement comes at a particularly delicate time. I'd appreciate it if you'd keep this to yourself."

"Who else knows?"

"Some important people on both sides of the fence, including one or two at Ashburton Place and city hall."

"And they want you to run?" asked Joe.

"Oh yes. Most of them, anyway. The rebirth of Copley Square and the South End are the primary reasons. We proved that private capital and commercial enterprise far surpass federal programs in giving cities new life. That goes against the grain in Massachusetts, as both of you surely know. So yes, certain parties would love to see me run and make a turnabout in this state. Of course the state bureaucrats in the Saltonstall

Building, and a lot of people at the statehouse, would hate to see this and are eager to see me stumble in scandal. Excuse me," he said, looking irritably at his watch.

He left the room, looking for his manservant. Soon Joe and I heard stern words from the hallway. Joe rose from his chair, motioning me over with his hand. We stood near the door, necks craned out, eavesdropping on them.

"You'll do as I *say*, Lightner. No matter what your personal feelings might be. You are bound to me, and there's no escaping it. Some things you must simply accept."

After what we thought was a decent interval, Joe and I left the study and joined our two guests in the hallway. It was obvious Owen Lightner had been crying. When they were bundled up against the cold, we said good-bye and watched them walk down the carpeted stairway. Now I was positive the fur collar on Bud's overcoat was way too wide. The building was quiet as a tomb. When we went back inside the apartment, I noticed that one of them had left behind a cashmere scarf. As I picked it up, noticing its quality, I realized that it could belong to either one of them: the master or the servant. Somehow, the scarf seemed to embody this strange relationship.

But that was not nearly so strange as what happened next. I took the scarf and hustled down the stairway to return it. Although I was moving fast, my feet made no noise on the thick wool carpeting. I caught up with them in the lobby, but stopped dead in my tracks. They were standing in the lobby alone and did not see me coming. I ducked back around behind the corner, then peeked back out. Bud and Owen Lightner were embracing, hugging each other. Bud stroked the boy's head, kissed him on the cheek, and murmured something into his ear. The boy kept crying, shaking with sobs, as the older man comforted him. I crept back up the stairs in amazement, the elegant scarf draped around my neck.

I was thinking: Lots of luck running for the statehouse, Bud, old boy. . . .

TWELVE

I didn't tell Joe until next morning at breakfast. I wanted to sleep on it so I could be more objective.

"You *serious*, Doc?" he whispered over his croissant and cappuccino. "So our friend Bud's a—what did they call it?—a nancy boy?"

"I didn't say that. I merely told you what I saw."

"You don't think that's enough? Hey, c'mon; I'm as open-minded as anybody. I'd be the last one to start a rumor. But hell . . ."

"But hell, nothing. We can interpret the relationship in any number of ways. As a medical man, I know the danger of forming a diagnosis too quickly."

"Yeah. Cops can jump to conclusions too. And I know the danger of that. Still, it's a possibility, Doc. A strong one."

"I agree. A definite possibility."

"It seems this case has several threads dealing directly or indirectly with gay men. Reginald Westley, the late and mysterious George Brenner, and now this—"

"George is still in question, Joe. AIDS is not sexually selective; he could have contracted it many ways. Besides, Mary and I and Sarah have strong doubts George was gay."

"You're right. But still, it keeps appearing in this business.

We should consider it; it could provide a motive . . . the strongest of motives."

"Okay, leaving that issue aside, what do you think of Bud Chesterton?"

"I like him. A lot. I didn't think I would. Maybe this will change it; I don't know. But for all the guy has done, he seemed remarkably candid and down to earth, didn't you think?"

"Exactly. I found the guy very appealing. Now I can't help thinking this is unfortunate. I guess that's prejudice."

"Oh hell, I don't know, Doc. It seems everything you say nowadays pisses off one group or another. Marty's always giving me shit about what I say. Does Mary do that?"

"Not too much. Mary's pretty much the complete modern woman, you ask me. She doesn't go after the rhetoric much. I think women with lots of self-confidence aren't rabid about it."

"Well, she's got the self-confidence, that's for sure."

"Yep. Did you know Roantis is a little afraid of her?"

"Your pit-bulldog buddy? The guy who shits grenades? No, it doesn't surprise me. I got a confession to make: when we were little she used to beat me up."

"Must have been when you were really small."

"Eighth grade? Fourteen years old?"

"She was, or you?"

"*I* was. Beat the living piss out of me on our family-room couch in Schenectady. In front of my friends, for chrissakes! You believe it? Know what that does to the ego of an Italian male? Took her Bobby Rydell album and hid it. Told her I broke it. *Mistake*."

"Did your dad ever find out?"

"*Pop?* Ohhh . . . thank God, no. If Pop ever knew, he'd make me change my name. How tall is Mary anyway? Five-nine?"

"Five-seven-and-a-half."

"You sure? Seems taller. How big?"

"One-thirty-one."

"Looks heavier to me."

"She isn't. Looks it because of her frontal development."

"It's not her size that's fearsome, Doc; it's her passion."

"You don't have to tell me, but let's return to Mr. Chesterton and his paid companion."

Joe thought a second.

"You know, that's really what he is, isn't he? And the kid is what, eighteen? And we thought slavery was dead."

He took a bite of his croissant—just a dab of margarine, no more gobs of butter—and a sip of coffee.

"I wonder if the kid even had a choice, you know? Maybe not; maybe our friend Bud went to some famine-ridden village on one of those islands and bought Owen Lightner for more money than his poor mother ever saw, when he was like ten or twelve. . . ."

"C'mon, Joe, you're letting your imagination go crazy. We don't know anything at this stage."

"I know one thing: I've made up my mind about how I feel about this setup. I see lots of sick things in my line of work; I'm supposed to have built up a tolerance. But I tell you: this stinks. Maybe it's because Owen Lightner looks too damn much like Tony, Doc. No, I've decided I don't like Mr. Chesterton. Not at all."

After we shared more coffee, a smoke, and the paper, Joe called his office, saying he was going directly to the Marlboro Street residence of the late George Brenner to interview his apartment mate and would come into headquarters later in the day.

Then he went over to the cappuccino machine for another cup. He stopped cold, frozen in thought.

"Hey," I said, "you okay?"

"That's it, Doc! That *is* the motive! And it explains the scene of the crime too. It wraps it all up—all the unanswered questions."

"Are you suggesting the killing was a lovers' triangle instead of a professional hit?"

"Sure! All the strange stuff that didn't fit was out of place because we—I—made the wrong assumption at the start. If it had been a straight pro hit by some rival drug gang, they'd just nail the guy and put the body in a Dumpster. But no: it was made to look like a suicide. They changed the guy's clothes. Strange clothes too. This also explains Brenner's mysterious double life. He was a closet queen, and so erased his past. Everything now points to a jealousy murder, carefully planned and acted out with personal hatred and vengeance. Follow?"

I was skeptical. "I have to admit it explains some things, Joe, but not all. What about Mary's and my connection with it? And how about the shot fired into the mattress—the shot intended to draw our attention? And if what you say is true, then who was in the gay triangle? Bud, Lightner, and George Brenner? Or did it involve Reginald Westley?"

"We don't know at this point," he said, waving me off impatiently. "The details are unimportant. Thing is, we're on the right track now; I feel we're on the path that will lead us to an arrest."

"Roger."

"We'll go into the interview this morning, and follow all the rest of the leads, with this new motivation in mind. You watch: now all the details will click into place quick as a wink. Just you wait."

He called James Howland, George Brenner's housemate, to let him know we were on our way, and we left. During the ride, he was silent for three blocks, then he said: "Any predictions on this housemate?"

"Why?"

"I'm just thinking, this guy who shares his house, he could have it too."

"AIDS?"

"Could be. They're probably more than roommates, you know."

"Why would I know? How do you know?"

"This neighborhood. Seventy percent gay."

"So what do we do, Joe? Retreat to headquarters? Call John Wayne?"

"Just, uh, think of good questions," he said.

We had to park two blocks away, and illegally at that. Joe

wasn't worried about a ticket; his cruiser's make, model, and tag number were instantly recognizable by any patrolling squad car. Perhaps almost as recognizable as Chesterton's infamous green Jag. But just in case some rookie traffic cop wasn't wise, Joe flipped the driver's visor down so that his badge certificate was visible through the windshield. Parking's always murder in Back Bay, but the snow had made things much worse; cars were buried under it, skewed in and out of parking places like crooked dominoes. We trudged and skidded our way along the sidewalk, then up the ornate Georgian-style stoop to the black-enameled door of number 67. Joe paced around nervously on the icy stoop.

James Howland answered the door.

"Hello there, Lieutenant Brindelli? C'mon in and have some coffee, gentlemen. I'm expecting company momentarily, but I'll give you all the time you need."

He was over six feet tall, dressed in a wool crewneck sweater, chino slacks, argyle socks, and old brown loafers. He had a trim brown mustache and short brown hair. If it weren't for Joe's cautionary words, I would have thought Jim Howland to be perfectly straight. We sat on the couch in a giant living room that was, to my mind, very conservatively furnished.

"You've got to know from the start that this came as a complete shock to me," Howland said matter-of-factly as he brought out the coffeepot. "I have no idea why anyone would want to kill George Brenner."

"Well, we're hoping that something you recollect will help us find a lead," said Joe, taking one of the thick navy mugs Howland placed on the table. I like coffee out of those white porcelain mugs. Only way to drink it, and I told Howland so.

"I started with navy mugs when I was aboard the S.S. *Iwo Jima* in the South China Sea," he said, handing me one. The coffee smelled strong and rich as he poured it.

"You were in Vietnam?" Joe asked him, somewhat puzzled.

Howland nodded. "Captain in the marine corps. But getting back to George, I don't think I can help you guys much. See,

I really didn't know him all that well. Do you think I was involved, or what?"

"Were you?" asked Joe, looking him dead in the eye.

"No, I wasn't. In fact, I was out of town when he was killed; I travel a lot in my job. I'm afraid I can't be much help. See, George and I had a strange sort of relationship. . . ."

Here it comes, I thought.

"After my divorce two years ago, I relocated to Boston—"

"You were married?" Joe blurted.

Howland gave him a slightly pained expression. "One usually has to be married, Lieutenant, before one can be divorced. At least, that's what I've always assumed. Anyway, I work for a Seattle-based firm. My ex and my two sons still live there. When Jean and I split, things were painful enough so that I accepted this post for the New England region. But business takes me back to the Pacific Northwest constantly. As I just mentioned, I was in Seattle when George disappeared. Anyway, I didn't even know he was gone until I returned, and even then I didn't suspect anything was wrong."

"Why not?" asked Joe, his notebook on his knee.

"Because George kept an erratic schedule. He'd disappear sometimes for two, even three weeks on end. He'd just say he was away on business. He never volunteered more, and I never asked."

"How did you two meet?"

"As I said, I moved here two years ago after my divorce. I wanted to stay in town, and these old buildings are fabulous. Fabulous, but very expensive to rent. I was about to give up and buy a small condo in the suburbs when the realtor mentioned that another guy was interested in this house but thought it was too steep for him, and too big. He arranged a meeting, and George and I both decided to give it a try. Since we're both out of town a lot, we figured that we wouldn't get in each other's way. This turned out to be true, and also was beneficial because when one of us was gone, the other was usually around, which was good for security. I'm sure you're aware, Lieutenant, of the high burglary rate in this fashionable town, especially here in Back Bay."

"When was the first you heard of George's death?"

"Hell, just a few days ago, when I read in the *Globe* they'd identified the body."

"You have no idea who might have done it?"

"No. But I didn't know much about George Brenner. I got the feeling nobody did."

"So you didn't, uh, know him that well. You weren't, uh, very close."

Howland shook his head. Joe fidgeted, drumming his fingers on his knee. I felt it was time to rescue him.

"Mr. Howland—"

"Call me Jim. Why not?"

"Jim, there is a possibility that the late George Brenner was homosexual. Since this might bear on the motive for his murder, we have to ask if you have any knowledge of this, firsthand or otherwise. Of course, you may decline to answer."

He stared at us, dumbstruck.

"Bullshit," he said. "George wasn't gay. I'm not gay. You think we were a couple? Is that it?"

"We don't think anything," said Joe. "We just have to check out the possibilities."

"First of all, how do you know he was gay?"

We explained the chain of evidence, sketchy as it was. Through it all, Jim Howland sat with his elbows on his knees, shaking his head wearily back and forth.

"I don't believe it," he said. "Now, this neighborhood's full of gays, that's for sure. But that doesn't mean that everyone who lives here is."

"We never said that."

"Listen: I think I knew George well enough to admit that he was a little mysterious, but I'm also practically positive he was not gay. In fact, I met two of his girlfriends. One's name was Henrietta. I forgot the other one."

Joe looked dumbfounded. The doorbell rang and Jim Howland got up to let in the company that he had mentioned upon our arrival. He came back with an extremely attractive brunette on his arm. Dark eyes, hair, skin. Black sheath dress and white silk scarf. Heels. In the snow, yet. Three-inch heels. As Mary would say: where are the clothes police when you need them? But I'm glad they weren't around. I just love high heels. I'm convinced that what makes the contestants in the Miss America contest look so great isn't the bathing suits; it's the heels. The woman before us looked to be a very young thirty-seven or -eight.

"Hi, guys!"

Big smile, gorgeous teeth, flashing eyes. Good sense of humor. Sign me up.

"Lieutenant Brindelli, Dr. Adams, this is Louise, my fiancée."

She sat down with us and Jim poured her a mug. We told them the details. I saw Louise blanch when Joe mentioned that George Brenner had AIDS. But Howland's composure was enough to convince me that he wasn't worried in the slightest and had no reason to be. But again came the headshake.

"Nahhhh," he said despondently, lowering his head, "I still don't believe it. I really don't. Louise? You saw him three or four times. Did he strike you as gay?"

"Oh, not at all. In fact, I thought he was a knockout. A real charmer."

"A lot of gay men are good-looking," said Joe.

"So what?" said Louise. "As soon as you sense they're gay, and most women pick right up on it, you lose interest and think, What a waste."

"And you never got that feeling with George?" Joe asked.

"Never. In fact, I thought he was just about the sexiest guy alive," she said, then paused, looking at Howland. "Except for what's-his-name here." She moved closer to him on the sofa, reaching her hand around behind him and pinching him on the butt. "Hey, what's your name?" she said with a wide grin. Then she winked at me. Right at me. *Only* me.

Show me the dotted line. . . .

Joe slapped his notebook shut and muttered something under

his breath. It probably wasn't *son of a gun*.

"Think we got the wrong guy, eh? Great. Except that both Doc here and his wife, who happens to be my sister, ID'd the victim as George Brenner. So did his wife. And so did you, by the postmortem photo."

"I know I did. I know George when I see him. But the AIDS part doesn't fit."

"Well, you can get AIDS any number of ways," Joe said. "Incidentally, the mysterious business that George was in was the drug business. There was no evidence on the corpse that he used a needle, but he could have, occasionally."

Joe paused in thought, sipped coffee, and added: "Or he could indeed have been gay and kept that part of his life very secret. Anyway, as I told you over the phone, Mr. Howland, the lab team will be here tomorrow to confirm the ID when they dust for prints in his bedroom. Where is that?"

"Upstairs. He had the two bedrooms up there and used that bath. I had the downstairs bedroom and the den. We shared the rest."

"Did you go upstairs often?"

"Lieutenant, I don't think I've been up there more than seven or eight times in the past two years. There's no need to. If the light was on in the hallway, I assumed he was up there, but I never bothered him. We never ate together except sometimes for breakfast."

"So we can assume that if they dust for prints up there, that the ones they get will be mostly his, correct?"

"Yep." Howland nodded, looking up the handsome staircase.

"Good. So if those prints match those on the body, then that body belongs to George W. Brenner. Do you object if we go up for a look?"

Howland replied absolutely not. Upstairs, checking out the bathroom on the way down the hall, Joe said, "Guess I had Howland pegged wrong. I mean, if he's gay, Clint Eastwood's gay."

"That's what I was thinking too."

"But I feel a strong possibility is what I've been suspecting all along: George Brenner was a closet homosexual, or perhaps a bisexual, who kept his gay side well under wraps. Look at that mirror; the guys ought to get some good prints off that. Let's go into the study."

The study was the upstairs spare bedroom. I told Joe that I figured a lot could be learned by going through the desk and small file cabinet next to it, but he disagreed.

"I doubt it. Crooks love to keep bogus files around, full of real innocent stuff, you know? Old electric bills. Appliance-repair receipts. Warranty cards. Invitations to high-school reunions. Shit like that. The cops go through it, they figure the guy's legit. The stuff we need, the information he needed to do his illegal dealing, he either kept in his head or someplace secret. We won't find it here."

"Yeah, but we may find something like an invitation to a high-school reunion."

"So what?"

"What I'm getting at is, maybe that could give us a clue as to his previous ID or his gay love life."

"Uh-huh. I'm sure I'll have a chance to go over it in due time. But Jesus, this guy was cagey; that becomes more and more apparent."

The bedroom was nondescript, nicely furnished, and excruciatingly neat. Although dust had gathered on the furniture, the place was spotless. Two clean hairbrushes, looking almost new, were arranged neatly parallel on the top of the dresser atop a crisply ironed linen cloth. The bed was unmade, as if its occupant was called out early and left without time to make it. I saw Joe staring at an impressive-looking radio on the bedside table. A thick coaxial cable snaked from it, through the window frame, and outside.

"Shortwave, right?"

"Uh-huh. A Grundig. Is that his old Grundig or a newer model? I can't remember."

"And those are top-of-the-line?"

"Grundig is to shortwave receivers what Leica is to cameras."

"This thing only receives? It doesn't transmit?"

"It receives only. Look outside."

I stood behind him and pointed out the window to the "sloper" antenna, a double-wired cable of unique configuration fastened to the outside window frame and sloping down at a forty-five-degree angle to a post in the small garden yard in back. This configuration is designed to optimize worldwide reception in a broad range of frequency bands. Joe recognized it as similar to the one I had connected to my ICOM receiver in Concord.

"How much do these go for, Doc?"

"For this model, the Satellit 650, around a grand. It's known for its ability to haul in distant stations, and for its superb audio tone," I said, reaching for the set. Joe grabbed my hand, warning me about disturbing prints. We studied the upstairs for another twenty minutes before returning downstairs. Jim Howland and Louise were washing dishes in the kitchen.

"We'll be going now," said Joe. "Sorry for the inconvenience. Everything will settle down after the lab team leaves. I'll probably come back after they leave to look around again, then we'll leave you alone."

"No problem," he said, putting a stack of dishes in the cabinet. "I hope you can figure out what happened. Did you see anything up there that helped?"

"Just his shortwave."

"Oh yeah. That damn radio. He had it on almost every night he was home. I got real sick of hearing German. It wasn't too bad most of the time, though—he kept the door closed."

"Was that the only radio he had? Did you ever see any other electronic equipment up there?"

"Nope. But like I said, I was only up there briefly a few times."

"Was George always neat and clean?" I asked.

Louise laughed, and Howland grinned.

"Hell yes. That's one of the reasons he was a good apartment mate. He kept a low profile and always cleaned up after himself."

"Unlike this guy," said Louise, pointing with a hitchhiker's thumb at Howland. "What we're doing now is cleaning up last night's dishes. After dinner we got, uh, sidetracked."

"Did you have a professional cleaner or housekeeper?" I persisted.

"No," said Howland. "And you know what? That very thing was probably the only point of contention between us. He wanted one; I didn't care enough to spend the money. Know what they charge? Christ! But what finally happened just after Christmas, George talked me into a one-shot, top-to-bottom cleaning job on this place by one of those professional, four-man teams. He told me he simply couldn't stand it anymore. Place looked okay to me, but I finally agreed to split the cost with him. I figured it wouldn't be a bad idea once or twice a year. Well, they were here *two days*. When they left, they gave us a bill for nine hundred bucks!"

Joe whistled.

"Yeah. They did all the windows inside and out. Washed the walls, took up the rugs and had them cleaned, wiped down the woodwork, cleaned the floors and double-waxed them. Cleaned the oven and the refrigerator inside and out. The works. But I won't do that again. Not for a long, long time."

"I think," said Louise, "he's expecting his new roommate to do it all. Well, Jim, I've got news for you. . . ."

We said good-bye, leaving them in the kitchen and letting ourselves out. As we walked along the slippery walk toward the car three blocks away, Joe asked me what my thoughts were. I replied that it seemed that Jim Howland was straight and aboveboard. If George had some secret life, Jim had no knowledge of it. Also, I added, Howland was probably not connected with the killing in any way.

"I agree, Doc. But we'll check his Seattle alibi to make sure. What we've got to do now is try to reconstruct as much of George's secret life as possible, because I'm still convinced the motive in this murder was personal, not professional. And I—"

Hearing him stop in mid-sentence, I looked up from the icy patches I was avoiding and saw Joe staring across the street. Following his gaze, I saw a bar half a block down a side street.

I did not remember seeing it before. Above the doorway was a picture of a naked Greek youth with a shield and sword. Underneath it was one word, done in bright green letters: HEROES.

"What's that, a restaurant?"

"A bar," he said, checking his watch. "It's quarter-past eleven. You ready for lunch?"

"No. You know I don't eat lunch, Joe. Keeps me fit and trim."

"Do tell. I don't eat much of it myself nowadays, in case you haven't noticed. Still, I think we might find this place interesting. Maybe we can find out something important."

"Is it a gay bar?"

"Is it ever. Just opened last fall. John Gutierrez says it caters to the yuppie professional class."

"What's he doing going into gay bars?" I asked.

"Cops go into all kinds of bars, Doc. Hell, bars are the greatest neighborhood grapevines ever. Come on—"

"I'd rather not go, if you don't mind."

"I'd rather not, either. But duty calls, and I *do* mind. Now, let's go."

So I followed him across the intersection, slipping and sliding all the way, and not at all crazy about the idea. We reached the place, walked up three steps, and Joe swung open the brightly varnished door. He swept his hand graciously in front of me in an arc.

"After you, Alphonse."

I stared at him. "This is another fine mess you've gotten us into."

THIRTEEN

The bare wooden floors were well varnished; white rosettes of reflected lamp glow came up at us as we walked to the bar. It too was varnished, with conical green glass shades that lighted the perimeter of the place. Banker's lamps set in heavy brass fixtures. No fuchsia, chartreuse, or hot pink so far. No flocked velvet on the walls yet. But hey, watch out; we haven't seen the back room yet. . . .

There were three men in the place: the barkeep and two drinkers. They all stared as we walked in and sat down on the high stools at the front end of the bar. I noticed that the floor behind the bar, under the wooden "duckboards," was white hexagonal tile. Spotless. The lower walls were oak wainscoting. Above this heavy dark paneling was a green wallpaper with tiny gold designs in diagonal print embossed on it. Overhead, wide, four-bladed fans swirled slowly without a sound. The tops of the front windows were stained glass. Art nouveau, I thought, the kind with translucent glass in muted pastels. Each one was a stylized narcissus flower. Tastefully done, and not what I expected.

I heard low voices coming from the next room and the muted click and thump of a pool table. Looked just like a standard Boston men's club to me, and I told Joe so in a low voice as we leaned over the lustrous, mahogany bar. "Yeah," he answered in a deep whisper, "until you get a good look at those photos on the wall behind you."

I turned and looked, and saw a series of tastefully framed photographs on the wall opposite the bar. The pictures weren't large, perhaps ten-by-fourteen inches. They were of naked men in various poses. They were all races, all colors and body types. The pictures weren't large enough to be prominent, yet there was no mistaking their intent. They were not subtle. There were also posters on the walls, maybe five or six of them, depicting heroes: Superman, Captain Marvel, Conan the Barbarian, and so on. All the guys in these posters were built to the hilt and wearing exotic costumes.

So this was definitely a gay bar. A masculine gay bar. An upscale, tastefully furnished gay bar that catered to monied professionals. It was an education of sorts for us.

The barkeeper, talking with the patron at the far end of the bar, made no move toward us. The near patron, a man in a gray windbreaker-type jacket and stone-washed blue jeans, sipped his beer and looked straight ahead. He had dark blond hair combed back wet, a prominent, sharp nose and chin, and hard eyes. He resembled Kirk Douglas a little. His face was lined and reddish, showing a lot of miles. I guessed he was around forty.

"They're ignoring us," said Joe softly. "Standard procedure when they know you're straight."

"How do they know?"

"They know. And they're not rude; they just don't acknowledge your existence."

"How many gay bars have you been in?"

"Not any more than I have to. But enough to know that that's the drill."

"And your colleague Gutierrez comes in here often?"

"Well, he's got the Back Bay beat. He comes in enough to keep up with all the latest news."

"What branch of the service was he in?"

"Army paratroopers. How'd you guess?"

"It's written on him. Why does he know so much about all these bars?"

"Like I said, bars are the greatest source of neighborhood gossip there is. Especially late at night when the patrons are oiled up and ready to talk about stuff they swore they'd never divulge."

I looked back along the bar. The bartender, a small, beefy guy with a baby face, was still talking to the solitary drinker at the far end. I saw him put his hand on the guy's forearm and squeeze it. As far as he was concerned, Joe and I might as well have been on Mars. "Well, it doesn't look like we're here at the right time, then."

"May we have a beer?" Joe bellowed. Three sets of eyes came to rest on us. Apparently, the men were amazed to see us . . . and even more surprised that we actually wanted something to *drink* in this place. The barkeep flung his counter rag down behind the bar in a snit and began to walk up to us. Very slowly, like those young black guys who walk in front of my car, scarcely moving their feet, taking thirty seconds to stroll past so I have to wait on them, just like they've had to wait on everybody else for the past several hundred years, their eyes lifted off into the distance, pretending your car isn't even in the same state.

He came up to us, not making eye contact. His skin was pale, which didn't go with his dark brown eyes. His black hair was thinning and kinky, and he wore it parted right down the middle. He wore a mustache too, a faint one. He had fat cheeks and a pudgy neck.

"Yes," he said in a small voice. Joe ordered two drafts, and when the guy brought them back, Joe already had his shield out on the counter. The man, who was about thirty, looked at it and then nervously up at Joe. He began pulling at the corner of his mustache.

"Sorry to keep you waiting. What it is, see, we have a policy. . . ."

"Forget that. How long have you worked here?"

"Since last September."

"And your name is . . . ?"

"Ken."

"You work just days, or nights too?"

"Both." He giggled. "It seems I live here."

Joe slid the postmortem photo of George Brenner across the bar. "You ever see him in here?"

The man nodded. He nodded right away, without even having to think. "But for a short time only," he added quickly. "Like, only about five or six times."

"When was that?"

"A month or two ago, I think."

"And how often did he come in?"

"I told you, four or five times."

"Once a week? Twice?"

"No. He came in like every night for a week, then he was gone." He looked at the picture again. "He's dead, isn't he?"

Joe nodded.

"Was he sick? You know . . . infected?"

Joe nodded again, and I saw the bartender bite his lip.

"I thought he looked sick when he was here. What did he do wrong?"

"He was murdered. We're not sure what he did wrong. We think he dealt drugs, but we're not positive. We're hoping you, or maybe somebody else in here, can help us out."

"I don't think so. Like I said, he came regularly for a week, maybe longer. Then we didn't see him anymore. I thought he was maybe traveling through."

"You say we. Who's we?"

"You know, the guys who come here."

"Any of those guys here now?"

He shook his head. The near drinker, the Kirk Douglas lookalike, continued to stare into the mirror over the bar. The guy at the far end of the bar—who was no more than a kid—set down his empty mug and picked up a full shot glass, which he put to his lips and drained in one slow, steady toss. Hitting it a wee bit hard for the middle of the day, I thought.

"Did he tell you his name?" Joe asked.

"Nope. Liked those rum drinks and watching TV. Didn't say too much. I think he was from England."

There it was: the U.K. connection a third time. The flag started waving in my brain again. Undoubtedly the Union Jack.

"England?" said Joe, raising his gigantic eyebrows. How he does this without hydraulic assistance is beyond me.

"The way he talked. Sounded like he was from England."

The sharp-featured man sitting at the bar next to us came to life. He looked at the barkeep and said: "Wait a second, Ken. He could have been an actor. Lots of theater people come in here. If you've studied Shakespeare, then you talk like that."

"Did you ever see him in here?" asked Joe, sliding the photo over to the hawk-faced man. The man nodded.

"We shot a couple of games of pool together. He said he was staying with a friend up the street."

"And that's the last you saw of him?"

The man nodded again, raised his empty mug at Ken, fished out a pack of cigarettes from his gray windbreaker, and lit one.

"May I have your name, sir, just in case?"

"I'd rather not."

Joe shrugged sympathetically, then handed the man his card. As he was putting it into his jacket the stranger said what the hell, and gave his name, address, phone number, job number, everything but his blood type. Sometimes I forget just how good Joe is. He could have pushed the guy, threatened him, and gotten nowhere. But his soft manner, his quiet acquiescence, had opened the guy up. Joe asked both men if George had ever talked drugs. The reply was no.

"Did he mention anybody he was going to meet, or do business with?"

"No," said Ken. "He just said he was staying with a friend up the street."

"What was the friend's name?"

"Didn't say. And we didn't want to . . . pry."

"I understand. What was *his* name? Did he tell you?"

"Our mutual friend? If you didn't know that, how could you be asking us all this?"

"I want to know what he told you."

"I can't remember."

"Was it Jim?"

"I can't remember."

"How about Bill? William?"

"Can't remember."

"George?"

"I can't . . ." said Ken, closing his little brown eyes and squinting up at the ceiling fan directly above.

"Was it George?"

"It might have been. Don?"

"Yeah. I think that was it: George."

"But you're not sure?"

They shook their heads. Joe looked down at the solitary drinker at the far end of the bar. "What about him? Was he here when George was coming in?"

"No," whispered Ken, wiping the wet rag quickly along the bar groove with nervous hands. "He's new in town. Came here to die."

"What?"

"He's from Binghamton. Got diagnosed as HIV positive week before last. His family kicked him out; said they never wanted to see him again. So he came here to wait it out. We're his . . . new family."

He managed a short grin. For a millisecond, the little dull eyes lit up with enthusiasm and warmth. Then went dead again, as if a brief and powerful current had passed through them, then died.

Joe handed Ken a card, and said thanks, and that he could expect more visits. We buttoned our coats and left, stepping out into the cold, bright air. Whenever I go in a bar and have anything to drink, I automatically assume it will be dark outside. The bright daylight startled me. As Joe and I walked back to the car, neither of us spoke. I was certain Joe was also thinking about the poor kid at the end of the bar. And I was thinking that if there's a malaprop of malaprops in this era, it is the word *gay*.

Then I thought of something. I spun around and walked back to Heroes. I heard Joe's powerful footsteps right behind me. I leaned inside the door and called to the men.

"Hey, you guys: what kind of shirt was George wearing?" I asked. "Quick, without thinking—just picture him in your head. What color?"

"Black!" shouted Don.

"And what was painted on it?" I asked quickly.

"Flowers!" shouted Ken, his balding head shiny under the brass lamps. "Ooooo, no, I'm wrong—"

"No, you're right!" I said, pointing at him.

"There was something else on it too," said Don, becoming increasingly animated. He pounded his palm quickly on the bar, moving it so fast it blurred, clutching the top of his head with his other hand, shutting his eyes tight in thought. "It was the name of a place. . . . Ohhhh, shit! What *was* it?"

"Hell if I know," said Ken, shrugging his shoulders as he wrung out the bar rag. "I sure can't remember."

"Jamaica?" The question boomed out behind me. I turned to see Joe, hands stuck in his coat pockets, flapping his lapels hopefully.

"Nope," said Don, stroking his chin and looking at the floor. "Wasn't that . . ."

"If you remember, either of you, can you give us a call?" Joe said, and we went back out the door.

FOURTEEN

"I got to hand it to you, Doc; I had completely forgotten that shirt."

"I wasn't sure George ever wore it to the bar," I said, climbing into the cruiser. "It was just a lucky shot."

"Wish they could remember what it said on that shirt; it could be important."

"You mean, like the reason somebody removed it after George was killed?"

He nodded, and we drove on for another quarter hour until we were out on Commonwealth Avenue near the town of Brookline. We swerved into the parking lot behind Ten Ten and rode up to Joe's office. What a treat. His first act was to dispatch the lab team to the apartment on Marlboro Street to dust for prints and look for any additional evidence. Then he sat with his elbows on the desk, chin on fists.

"Nothing on George Brenner earlier than eighty-one, Doc. Not a damn thing."

"How can you tell?"

"Nothing on the INLETS wire. We've tapped every crime data bank available, and we get no hits on G. Brenner. *Nada*. Zip." He sighed. "Of course, there's a chance he wasn't into crime then—that he just took it up as a lark in recent years."

"You don't believe this."

"Not for a second. From what we're getting from the DEA, Brenner had all the hallmarks of the professional criminal. And I'd bet my last paycheck, skinny as it is, that if we only knew the correct alias, we'd get printout after printout of this guy's past history."

"So? What good would that do?"

"Help us find the killer, and get Chesterton off the hook."

"You don't think Chesterton was involved, do you? Directly or indirectly?"

"As I said earlier, I don't like the guy now. I liked him fine until you told me about him and the kid. But to answer your question, no, I don't think he's involved, and I think you feel the same way. So the guy's a closet fruit. Doesn't make him a killer, especially in his own house."

"But we've just seen how a so-called closet fruit leads a secret life. George Brenner was apparently the straightest guy in the world to his straight roommate, Jim Howland."

Joe thought a minute. "Don't you think it's strange that George went to Heroes right before he disappeared?"

"And not earlier, you mean?"

"Right. And he told them he was visiting a friend up the street, that he was just passing through."

"If you were gay and wanted it kept a secret, I doubt you would patronize a local gay bar," I said. "What you'd do, you'd go to one across town, or even in another city."

"Hey, that's a good point, Doc. You sure you don't wanna be a cop?"

"I am, of sorts. Remember?"

"But you're right: if he wanted his gay life kept secret, why did he choose to go to Heroes, just a hop and a skip down the street?"

"Who knows? Maybe he just wanted to check it out, make a contact."

"Yeah, maybe. And he'd know Howland wouldn't go in there, so his secret was safe. Speaking of Howland, I better call and tell him the lab team's on its way."

"While you've got him on the phone ask him about George's

black T-shirt. See if he can remember what the hell it said on it."

"Hey, right! The name of a *place* . . . isn't that what they said?"

"Uh-huh. Tell me, how do you trace missing persons, anyway?"

He leaned back in his swivel chair and locked his fingers behind his head, grinning.

"I could tell you that I go all through this big, mean city, interviewing people who knew the person—old girlfriends and wives, creditors, employers, friends—and then I go to some flophouse, or gin mill, gun drawn, and find him dismembered in a filthy bathtub. I could say that."

"But you won't, because that's not how it's done."

"Uh-uh, not anymore. What we do is punch a whole lot of computer keys and gain access to these data banks. Most of them aren't even connected to law enforcement. We get the DSS, check out the Social Security number. What's his status? Does he receive benefits? If so, where does he live? The IRS is usually a big help. Only thing they're good for, you ask me. We contact utilities. Did he pay a gas or electric bill? To which known address? How about bank and checking accounts? CDs? Securities? Real estate? Phone bills? And of course, the police have immediate access to post-office-box numbers and letter drops. You see? You cannot go through life in twentieth-century America without leaving tracks all over the place, no matter how hard you try."

"But prior to 1981, George Brenner left no tracks. So you think he switched identities sometime around there."

"Positive."

"How does one do this?"

"Fake ID is tough. A driver's license won't cut it. Basically, there are only two airtight documents: birth certificate and passport. Both can be had for a price. Going rate on either of these is two to five grand. Once you've got, say, a fake birth certificate, filling in the rest of the blanks is easy. Driver's license, library card, credit cards, even Social Security number aren't that tough. And once you have fake ID, you hang on to it. Store it someplace secret so you can pop back into that old identity if things get hot. So what I think is this: somewhere, perhaps even in a secret place in that apartment—*not* the file cabinet—is George Brenner's old ID. If and when we find this name, we can punch it in and come up with *beaucoup* leads. Follow?"

"You mean find something in his past that will point the finger?"

"Yep. It's all we've got, it seems. Unless you find something else inside his mouth."

"I've gone over his mouth as much as I can. The only thread—faint as it is—that keeps reappearing is the connection with England."

"Yeah," Joe recalled, leaning forward and shaking a Benson & Hedges out of an almost empty pack, "even Ken the bartender noticed the British accent. So you think that George was born in England and came here in his twenties, or maybe thirties?"

"It's a possibility."

"You didn't know him prior to eighty-one?"

I shook my head.

"Then maybe he was in England before that time; that's why he's got a blank slate over here."

"Bingo!" I said, and watched Joe contact the main desk in the wire room and ask for overseas assistance. After he put in this request, he was beaming. But soon the glow faded; he leaned forward again and massaged his ever-present stubble, shaking his head slowly.

"Well, then explain this to me, Doc: why didn't he ever talk that way in front of you, Mary, or his wife, Sarah, hmm?" He lighted the cigarette and shook out the match, a faint smirk on his face.

"I have no idea," I admitted. "I don't recall his having any sort of accent. He certainly didn't have the Boston regional speech."

"Thank *Gaawwwd*," Joe mimicked. "Well, why do you think he spoke like a Brit in the bar, but like an American to you and Mary?"

"I don't know. I also don't know why he was fluent in German. And finally, AIDS or no AIDS, I have no idea why he let his diet and personal care go down the drain."

"I can guess," Joe said, making an imaginary glass with his right hand and tipping it up to his mouth. "Alcohol, the greatest solvent after water. It dissolves marriages, families, jobs, health. . . ."

"I forgot about the booze. Yes, that could explain it."

"I'll interview Sarah again in light of this new evidence, Doc. Meanwhile, the lab team should finish up at George's apartment by the end of the day, and maybe something will shake loose from that. Why do you have that funny look on your face?"

"I keep getting the feeling that there were two George Brenners. One was the guy Sarah was married to, the guy we knew in Concord. He was mysterious, yes, and maybe a trifle shady, but the transition from this witty, charming guy in his country estate to the beat-up old drunk lying in a deserted mansion with a bullet through his chest . . . well, that's a big transition in just three or four years."

"Being a cop, know what I say to that?"

"What?"

"I say that you're right: there *were* two George Brenners. All along there was the outward George, the guy you knew, and the secret, inner George. The inner self he was too ashamed to show, and that finally caught up with him."

"Just the same, if you're going to talk with Sarah again, maybe you could ask her, and Howland too, about George's drinking habits and his personal hygiene."

"I'm going to talk to Sarah again, don't worry. And Howland, and the guys down at Heroes. But . . . the guy I really want to see, we can't find."

"Who's that?"

"Your old med-school buddy Jonathan Randolph."

I sat down in Kevin's beat-up old swivel chair. Fake leather seat torn, and old gummy grayish-brown foam rubber dribbling out of it all the time. Ugly? It makes Old Sparky, the Florida pen's famous electric chair, look handsome. Stink? The odor was old spilled coffee, old cigarette smoke, Juicy Fruit gum, cheap cigar smoke, you name it.

"You okay, Doc?"

"No. I can't stand this office, Joe. I can't believe you're the same guy with the wonderful apartment on the Hill."

"You'd rather go elsewhere?"

"Yes. Anywhere. This office is my version of Dante's eighth circle of hell."

He suggested we go over to the Greek's for lunch. He didn't have to twist my arm; as a rule I don't eat lunch, but I love good subs.

"So what's your thinking on my old schoolmate Jonathan Randolph?" I asked him between bites of my Italian cold-cuts sub with lettuce, provolone cheese, hot peppers, oil, vinegar, tomatoes, feta cheese, and spices. The sub was their giant size, but still not big enough. If I did this every day, I would weigh two hundred instead of one hundred seventy-four. Can't resist those subs. Joe was having a large steak and cheese, with similar fixings. In and around Boston, the word large is pronounced *lahge*. (The word *lodge*, denoting a rooming house, is therefore pronounced *lawdge*.) Anyway, what struck me then as we sat in the Greek's, was that I was having a bigger sandwich than Joe. What next?

"I think this about your old school chum," Joe said, trying to eat and talk at the same time, "I say that you and Mary being on the beach when your erstwhile friend George Brenner, a drug dealer, was killed in a nearby house is more than coincidence."

"We're all agreed on that," I said, pulling a piece of pepperoni skin from between my teeth, "but I thought you were leaning more toward the gay-lover-triangle thing. I think that's a better bet, especially considering what we've learned about Reggie Westley, Bud Chesterton, and Owen Lightner."

"You watch: any day now we'll discover that Jonathan Randolph is gay too."

"Yeah. If we ever find him."

Joe chewed thoughtfully, then sipped at the steaming cup of coffee. His hand slammed down on the table with a thump that startled me. Everybody in the joint stared at us.

"Got it! We go back to Heroes and show them photos of Bud and Owen Lightner. See what the story is there. Maybe even take a copy of that picture in the hallway of Chesterton's house . . . you know, the one that shows the entire staff, and Mrs. Chesterton too? Then maybe bring Owen Lightner in there and—"

"You shaking that jar of bugs again?"

"Huh?"

"Mary told me that when you were a kid, you liked to collect a whole bunch of different bugs in a jelly jar. Put the cap on and shake it, watch all the bugs go nuts and try and eat each other—"

He looked hurt, and pointed his big brown hand at his breast. "*Moi?*"

I threw my empty cup in the trash along with the sub wrapper and eight grease-soaked napkins. I swear: you get more waste from a sub lunch than you do from thoracic surgery. "Let's get out of here."

"And go back to my office?"

"Hell no. Back to your apartment and call Concord. See what the women are up to."

"Sounds good to me. After you, Alphonse."

"You said that last time."

"Excuse me. After you, Gaston."

FIFTEEN

Two months passed. Except for the matching of the finger-prints on George's corpse with those found in his upstairs bedroom—thus confirming the ID we were all but certain of anyway—nothing else turned up. It was now Saturday, April 15, and out in Concord—birthplace of the American Revolution—the town was hanging out its red, white, and blue bunting in anticipation of Patriots' Day.

As I mentioned before, that was on April 19, 1775, the day when civilian sharpshooters from Concord and Lexington broke all the rules of war and played a dirty trick on King George's redcoats. Instead of standing up in wide lines facing the enemy and offering themselves as targets—as the British were taught—they cheated and crouched down behind trees and stone walls and sniped at the redcoats from distance and safety, killing and wounding a lot of them. This unsportsman-like conduct sent the army that had conquered the world lurch-ing, limping, and bleeding back to Boston.

So now the local "minutemen," some of them descendants of those original rabble-rousers who'd humiliated the Crown, donned their tricorns, coats, and buckle shoes, shouldered their replica muskets, and marched around the village common to the accompaniment of fife and drum bands playing "Yankee Doo-dle."

When they do that, I leave. "Yankee Doodle" is a neat tune, and I'm as patriotic as the next guy. But enough is enough. After the five millionth time, you're ready to take the feather out of Yankee Doodle's hat and shove it up his nose.

To escape all this prehoopla hoopla, I made a slight detour from downtown—which we call "Concord Center"—and drove out Walden Street, across Route 2, and out along Walden Pond. I was going to pay a visit to that modern-day version of Thoreau: Dr. Morris Abramson.

Because if you thought Henry David was a little strange, you ought to see Moe Abramson. . . .

"Happiness, of course, is not a psychological state," he said, looking up from his paperback and peering at me over the tops of his silver granny glasses. We were sitting in lawn chairs right outside the door of his ancient Airstream trailer, watching the Nubian goats in the corral. They were chewing on the thick wire of the fence, making a sound like an old, out-of-tune banjo.

"Happiness is not an emotion we feel," he continued. "That's *contentment*. Contentment and happiness are not the same thing. Mortimer Adler correctly identifies this mistaken notion of happiness as one of the ten philosophical mistakes of our age."

"So then, what is happiness?"

"It's an ethical, rather than emotional state; it is the natural, and inevitable, result of a life well lived."

"Well lived? You're the last guy in the world to talk about living well, Moe. You and your 1957 trailer. Your dried figs and blue milk—"

"That's not what I mean; that's the opposite of what I mean—"

"—your puffed grass and bean sprouts . . . and your voluntary celibacy."

"I didn't mean living well in the sense of living it up. I meant living well by doing the right thing."

"And what's the right thing?"

"Ha. You could start by asking Socrates, Plato, Aristotle, the Bible, and the Talmud. Even then you couldn't know. But you'd have a *clue*. . . ."

"Well, anyway, however we define happiness, it's plain that Sarah Brenner doesn't have any right now. You could say she's miserable."

He stroked his chin; his eyes lost focus as his thoughts turned inward. "I know."

"How many sessions have you had with her, Moe?"

"You know these matters are strictly confidential between doctor and patient. Six."

"Well?"

"As you say, she isn't happy. She asked me to confer with you about her progress, or lack of it. Apparently, she is spending a lot of time with the two of you."

"Right. Like every weekend."

"And you don't mind it?"

"As you say: 'what's to mind?' It's for a good cause."

"I think that whatever improvement she shows is due as much to you and Mary as to me."

"Well? Is her unhappiness the result of a life that wasn't well lived?"

"Maybe the result of a life that she *perceives* that way, yes. Perhaps she sees her marriage to George as a tragic mistake which has ruined her life."

"Well, guess what? Northrop Chesterton is back on the Cape now, for the summer season. His whole staff is here with him too, and he's invited Mary and me to go down there for the weekend."

"So?"

"So I was thinking of asking Sarah to come along with us."

"What?"

"She thinks that going down to the scene of George's death will help her."

"It won't. It's a dumb idea and I advise strongly against it. If you and Mary go down there to visit that rich guy, go yourselves, and leave Sarah at your house. Give her something to do, something that will let her think she's paying you back for your hospitality. At the same time it'll keep her mind busy."

"That's your final advice?"

"Yes. Ten bucks, please."

"Get serious."

"I am," he said, leaving his chair and reaching his arm around through the doorway of the trailer. It came back holding an oatmeal carton, which he shook in front of my face. It had a slot cut in the top and I could hear coins rattling around inside.

"The farm for runaways is finished, Moe; your dream is realized. I should know; I gave you the farm, for crying out loud."

"Ethiopia."

I crinkled up a bill and stuffed it down the chute. You don't even get a tax receipt with Moe.

"Dat's not a ten. Dat was a five."

"Consider yourself lucky, pal. And if you want to come over for a bite later on, you're welcome."

"I better not; Sarah Brenner has designs on me."

"Oh really. How do you know?"

"It happens; it's part of psychotherapy. You should remember that, Doc, from your psychiatric residency."

"You mean transference? When the patient sees the physician as a father-protector symbol and then—"

"Yep," he said, rocking slightly side to side in the chair. "Yep, that's what happens."

I could tell this made him nervous. "And you never get tempted to, uh . . . follow through in any of these situations?"

" 'Course not. Unprofessional."

"Even with the knockouts?"

"Absolutely not. I'm surprised at you, Doc."

"Old John Winthrop's got nothing on you, Moe."

He got up and carried the oatmeal carton back inside the tiny trailer, placing it back on the shelf right above the picture of Albert Einstein. He brushed off his pants and said, "Tell Mary I'm not coming over for supper. She'll know why, but tell her thanks."

"Do you want to come with just the two of us down the Cape and see the Chesterton mansion?"

"What a silly question."

This didn't surprise me. Moe, who leads the life of a religious ascetic, is hardly into the life-styles of the Rich and Famous.

Next day Mary and I got down to Osterville by two o'clock. I didn't tell Moe, but I had a feeling this wasn't just a social visit engineered by Chesterton, bon vivant that he was. I had a hunch it had something to do with the murder investigation and his desire to clear himself. The fact that Joe was also invited added to this suspicion, and when we pulled the car up outside the mansion and saw Paul Keegan's cruiser parked there next to Joe's, I knew.

"No, Doc, the DA's office has failed to indict, and every other agency has failed to clear," Keegan said, his foot propped upon the lower rung of the deck railing. We were standing on a small balcony deck that extended off Bud's first-floor "study." Inside, Mary sat with Joe and Bud on tufted suede sofas beneath a small French crystal chandelier, sipping champagne punch. Luncheon, consisting of creamed chicken Dijon crepes, was imminent. The sea was choppy under low scudding clouds. Wisps of fog rolled up over the sand toward us. The air was cool, but not cold, and had a damp, balmy feel to it. I like this weather, and the Cape has a lot of it between March and June. I drained my coffee mug and knocked out my pipe, letting the ashes fall on the sand below.

"You met Reggie yet?" Keegan asked. I shook my head.

"You've got a treat ahead."

"Can't wait. He that bad?"

"Nah. A nice kid, it seems. A bit soft around the wrists, but a nice—there he is now, staring at you."

I turned to see a slender youth, hedge clippers in hand, peering at us from the far edge of the house. He raised one hand and gave us a quick wave, then returned to the hedge. He was darker than Owen, and a little too skinny, with longish Rastafarian hair that seemed deliberately, desperately unkempt. I turned back to face Paul, who was looking over my shoulder.

"He's still looking at you, Doc."

"Me, or us?"

"You."

"Oh goody; hey, let's go in and have some lunch. Smell that chicken?"

After the meal we all sat around the living room with Bud. Owen Lightner was there, the only one of the staff present in the room. He sat in a chair off in the corner, dressed in white ducks and a cotton sweater. Sometimes he sat leaning back with his hands clasped behind his head, his feet stuck out straight. At other times he scribbled in a pocket notebook. He seemed self-assured, almost bored, confident of his place in the hierarchy of Chesterton's life.

"What are you going to do about your wife's comment to the press last week?" asked Joe. "The one in which she practically accused you of being a henchman for the mob?"

"I expected something like that," he said, waving it off with his hand. "Fact is, I'm quite surprised she's said nothing until now. I expect it'll die down in time. However, I am anxious for some statement from the authorities that lets me off the hook a bit, if you get my drift." He inclined his head to Joe and Paul as he said this. The two men stared back impassively.

Getting no response, Bud fiddled with some cookies on a plate and cleared his throat with a little noise.

"Mr. Lightner," said Paul. "We have just made a rather interesting discovery. You weren't in Gainesville on the night of January twentieth, the night before the murder of George Brenner, were you?"

The boy looked up, startled.

"Not only were you not down in Florida visiting your college buddies, but you were, in fact, up in Boston."

We all sat in stony silence. Bud was looking at Owen; he had stopped chewing. I saw fear in his big, red face.

"You were in Boston, staying at the Copley Plaza Hotel."

The young man reached for a cookie, the polite kind served at teas, and took a wee bite. His hands were steady. He chewed with detached self-assurance. I had to admire him. Mary was staring at the kid so hard I thought her gaze would melt him. On her face was a look of horror.

"We know it was you there at the hotel that night," Joe said softly. "The employees identified your picture, not to mention your signature on the room receipt. By the way, Bud, the credit card he used was an American Express Gold card. It's in your name. I assume you know about this. In fact, we assume you knew about it all along."

"I must tell you all that this is a personal matter, and none of the state's business. Neither I nor Lightner will say more."

"It is the state's business now. Your employee, using your credit card, obtained and stayed in a room in a leading hotel in Boston the night prior to the murder of a man in your oceanside house an hour's drive away. All evidence points to a premeditated killing in which the killer used his keys to this house and his knowledge of the grounds and the neighborhood to pull it off. Don't tell us it's none of the state's business."

The boy stirred in his chair. "It was a personal visit—"

"*Lightner!* Don't say another word. Promise me you will not say one single word until we've had a chance to talk with Bradshaw. Is that clear?"

"Yes, sah."

"Now, gentlemen, if you'll take my word that this visit to Boston was a strictly personal affair on the part of Lightner, we can go on to this business of Margaret and her—"

"Excuse me, Mr. Chesterton," said Paul in a dry voice, "but we cannot take anyone's word for anything. That's not a procedure we can follow in our line of work." He pointed at me. "Two years ago I had to pursue a murder investigation involving Doc's son Jack. I knew Doc's reputation through Joe. If there was anybody whose word I could trust, it was his, and Doc's. But I couldn't. I trust you appreciate this. So if you want to be, as you say, 'off the hook,' then the best thing to do is cooperate fully, and have Mr. Lightner do the same."

"I see your point, but it's quite impossible right now, for reasons I can't reveal. You'll just have to take my word that

Lightner was not involved in this killing; he couldn't have been."

"Owen, do you wish to say anything?" asked Joe. The boy shook his head. "Owen, you could be in a lot of trouble. You have the right to speak in your own defense. I advise you to do so."

"I already told you," said Bud through his gritted teeth, "that Lightner doesn't wish to say anything at this—"

"You're not in Jamaica now, Bud," snapped Joe. "This is a serious charge we're talking about. He's in a lot of trouble and so are you. It's about time you stopped operating under the assumption that your money sets you outside the law. You want to get off the hook, fine. But you've both got to come clean, and *soon*. I don't care what the personal relationship between you and the boy—"

"What personal relationship? We have no personal relationship, and it's none of your bloody business."

I saw Owen lower his head and blink back tears. Joe slammed down his glass, got up, and stalked off. Mary got up and followed her brother. But before she left the room, she shot Chesterton a withering glare. Calabrians call it *il malocchio*. The evil eye. Beware.

It seemed our fashionable luncheon was ending up like a Sam Peckinpah movie. I was glad that neither Sarah nor Marty was with us to see the shambles. Bud's face was purple with rage, but faded gradually to cherry red, then the glowing, brownish pink that was his natural Englishman-in-the-tropics hue. He played with his spoon nervously, making it clink on the parchment-thin china plate that had gold around the border. Probably one of those K Mart brands like Limoges or Haviland.

"It's, uh . . . awkward," he said softly, running his big palms over his face. "There are circumstances which prohibit us from saying more."

Keegan folded his napkin. I could tell he was about to get up and join Joe and Mary in the hallway.

"*At this time . . .*" Chesterton continued lamely. But it didn't ring true, to my ears, anyway. I'd heard the same drill so many

times from big shots caught with their pants down in public.
It all sounds the same after a while. I was angry; I was boiling
mad at the hold Bud had over this boy. Joe was right: the two
of them were living proof that slavery was alive and well.

Paul got up and motioned at me to follow him. We left the
big room, went out through Bud's study, and stood together on
the small deck. The tide was rushing in now, and the booming
of the surf and the crying of the gulls made me feel better.
There is no tonic like the ocean.

"I think Joe and I better back off, Doc. The more we push,
the more he'll stall."

"Should the kid get a lawyer?"

"He hasn't been charged with anything yet. And won't be."

"Did Joe tell you about what I saw in the lobby of his apartment?"

"Yeah," he said, nodding shortly. "Makes me sick. Not the
relationship—the master-servant thing."

"Mary doesn't know about it," I said. "If she did, she
might—"

Something I saw made me stop in mid-sentence. Paul stared
at me, then turned around to follow my stare, which was di-
rected up the beach about a quarter of a mile.

"What is it?" he asked.

"Up there. A guy with a dog. Looks like a golden retriever."

"So?"

"Don't you remember? Mary saw a guy with a golden retriever when we walked past here the day of the murder. You
and Joe spent a month trying to find him for an interview, but
you couldn't. Well, there he is."

He turned back to me, bored. "Not the same guy, Doc. If he
lived here, we'da found him. There are lots of golden retrievers
around. Reason we never found him was because he didn't live
here; he was passing through. Happened to be here the day you
were taking your walk, then left the Cape. I'd bet my salary on
it. Joe says the same."

"It's him. You never saw him, but I did. See him throwing
that Frisbee? See the way he tucks it back down underneath his

arm to throw it? I remember that from last time. He doesn't cock his arm across his body the way most people do; he flips it out from the same side. See?"

He turned and watched. The dog came running back to the man. We heard a faint laugh from the man, borne along to us in the shore breeze. The man stooped over and petted the dog, then looked in our direction

"Want to talk to him?" asked Paul. "Beats staying here, witnessing real, live slave trade in the Commonwealth of Massachusetts. Supposedly the most civilized state in the union."

"The most civilized state in the union is Iowa. But yes, let's go up and see him. Ask him where he's been these eleven weeks since he was last seen here—the day George was shot."

So we took off, walking gingerly up the beach in the direction of the man and dog. But as we walked the man hurled the plastic saucer up the beach repeatedly, running after it with the dog. Paul shouted, then whistled, but the man did not turn his head. All we could see was his long brown hair, which hung down almost to his shoulders in back and bounced a bit as he ran. His jacket was tan corduroy, unzipped in front and flapping in the breeze. The next thing I knew we were running.

And then, so were the man and the dog, the Frisbee toy long forgotten. I'm a runner, and I know Paul's in fantastic shape. I know because I tried to fight him once.

But try as we might, we couldn't touch that guy with the dog. He was long gone before we knew it, and as we stood there, hunched over cussing, and puffing and blowing like two surfacing whales, I knew it would be a while before we saw him again.

If ever.

SIXTEEN

The gardener's long, thin hand came up to the windshield, spread out like a giant spider, and lay there in front of my eyes, pressing against the glass as if trying to get in.

"Please, please, sah! Dr. Adams!"

I rolled the window down.

"What is it, Reggie?"

He looked to and fro quickly, then licked his lips and talked fast. "I must see you! There is something I must tell you. Please—"

Mary and I were rolling out of the Chesterton driveway in her Audi. I was driving, having recovered from our abortive run to catch the man with the dog. We'd gone back to the mansion, where Paul had told Joe about the incident. Then they called an all-points bulletin. Then we decided things were chilly enough around the mansion that we'd better hightail it. So Mary and I were going up to our cottage in North Eastham for the night. Just the two of us. But once the car was on the other side of the giant hedge and the tall fence, and thus concealed from the house, out had jumped Reggie, full of agitation and his desperate demand to see me.

"What is it, Reggie? Tell me now; I'm engaged in something important. If it's urgent, tell me right now."

"I can't do it, mon. Not now . . ."

"Why not?"

He inclined his woolly head quickly in the direction of the house.

"Owen?"

Headshake.

"Chesterton?"

Headshake.

"*Who*, for chrissakes?"

"The man killed," he wailed, tears forming in the corners of his eyes. His pathetically thin body was shaking. "Was . . . was my lover!"

"Oh Jesus—" whispered Mary.

The boy doubled up in grief. At the same instant I heard Chesterton calling for him.

"Listen," I said, "do you know where the Eastham windmill is?"

Headshake.

"You know Eastham? Up on the Outer Cape, near Wellfleet?"

"On the way to Provincetown? I know P-Town."

You would, I thought. "Yes, on the way. Meet me at the windmill in Eastham at . . . when?"

"After eleven. My absence may be noticed before that time."

"Okay, between eleven and midnight."

"Will you tell the police?"

"Only my family," I said, knowing it included Joe. He slid away from the car, wiping his eyes and stifling his sobs, then darted through the bushes sideways and was gone.

"Oh my God," said Mary.

"You can say that again."

"Oh my God."

An hour later Mary and I were out on the little screened porch that juts off the back of our cottage, the Breakers. The compact beach house sits on a bluff overlooking Sunken Meadow Beach in North Eastham. A wide deck extends all along the rear of the house, and the porch is at the kitchen end. I leaned forward in the Adirondack-style chair and peered through the screen at the ocean, now dark gray in the twilight. The waves were choppy in the shallow bay, and clouds of dusky gulls wove about in the air, flying low and screaming at each other. They always remind me of people.

Mary lighted the hurricane lamp on the driftwood table while I filled her balloon goblet with white zinfandel. I lighted a tiny Jamaican cheroot and let the heavy smoke sting my nose. I love the Breakers. I love the screened porch where you can watch the storms at close range, or play poker or read all night in the cool rush of sea wind. I love the low-beamed kitchen, with its old-time wooden settle against the far wall, its work island with copper pots hanging over it. I love the study corner of the living room, with its brass student's lamp and illuminated globe. . . . It's a splendid little pied-à-terre less than two hours from home.

I had been listening to world-band radio on my little Magnavox portable. Reception is really great on the Cape. In fact, it was the station at Nauset Beach, just across the neck of the Cape from our cottage, that was a receptor of Marconi's first transatlantic transmissions back in the early 1900s. I ran through the nineteen-meter band, picking up the BBC and other notables from across the ocean. Later on in the evening, the lower frequencies of the forty-nine- and thirty-one-meter bands would become clear, and I could pick up Radio Japan, Radio Beijing, Radio Prague, and hundreds of other stations.

Aromas drifted from the kitchen. We were going to have garlic mussels over linguini with hot French bread. Then coffee and cheesecake, and liqueur. And then sex. I knew it. I could tell by the way she was sitting and talking. The way she was smiling to herself and tilting her head. The way she touched her neck when she talked to me. We were going to screw our brains out later on. Life can be sweet. . . .

"Not a very happy household, is it?"

"Huh?" I said, turning to look at her.

"The Chesterton domain. What do you think Reggie wants with you tonight?"

Oh God! For a few delicious minutes I had forgotten about the late-night appointment. Now it loomed up and shattered my reverie. No loving tonight. A bad scene was ahead, I thought, and wrecked the mood. Damn! I needed a night alone with Mary. She did too. Away from phones and relatives, patients and confused widows. Away especially from miserable people.

"I hope it's not your body," she said.

"Nope. He wants to talk about George. Hoo boy. Why did I ever say I'd go meet him, Mary? Why?"

"Because you're a caring person, Charlie. You can't stand to see people suffering or in trouble. Same with Joey. Same with Moe."

"I'm a sap, that's what, from hanging around Moe too much. I think I'll call the Chesterton place and cancel."

"You won't. I know you won't. But don't worry, Charlie; I'm going with you."

"Really?"

"Why not? It's only a ten-minute drive, and Reggie may need somebody like me to talk to."

I told her not to bother, but she insisted. Inwardly, I was glad she was coming along. I went into the kitchen and helped her put the scallions, parsley, garlic, and lemon juice into the hot olive oil while we sautéed the mussels. I don't understand why they're not more of a hit in America; all of Europe loves them. But it's just as well for us; with the demand low, they're dirt cheap. We added a little wine at the end, some of the white zin we'd been drinking, and then cooked most of it off before pouring the contents of the skillet over two mounds of linguini.

It was dark by the time we ate. We had the cappuccino and liqueurs by the single flame of the hurricane lamp. Then Mary snuggled onto my lap as a light rain began to fall. It made a snare-drum noise on the roof above. This, along with the booming of the surf, made me feel relaxed. Mary leaned over and blew out the light, then snuggled back into me.

Somewhere in the middle of all this we had taken off our shorts and moved onto the sea-grass rug on the floor. . . .

"Charlie, you just kill me," she said, biting softly into my shoulder.

"How come?"

"You're so damn cute. And I just love your buns," she whispered, clasping me from behind and digging her nails into my posterior. "Your ass is as big as a postage stamp—"

I kissed her hard on the mouth to shut her up.

"**W**hy are we parking so far away?"

"I don't want to draw attention to where we're meeting, Mare. People always meet here. I just hope it's not popular at night—"

"Can't see a crowd from here," she said, squinting into the darkness ahead. Occasional cars still swept by on the road, which was no surprise. Route 6 is *the* highway on the Cape, and on weekends it still has some traffic, even in the off-season. "I say we invite Reggie back to the cottage to talk. What do you think?"

"Okay with me, but let's see what he has to say first."

We approached the old restored windmill that sits just west of the highway, right near First Encounter Beach. It's authentic even down to the carved wooden gearworks inside that mesh the power of the turning horizontal shaft to the ancient granite grindstones of the mill. But the door to the inside room was shut and locked now, since the place closes at dark.

"I don't see him," she whispered.

"Why are you whispering? Nobody's going to overhear us."

"I always whisper in the dark," she said. "Where can we sit and wait?"

"There are benches all around. See?"

"Let's sit at the one over there, near the bushes. That way we can see whoever comes into the park."

So we went over to the far edge of the grass and sat on the backless bench, which was so uncomfortable it made me wish doubly that we were back at the Breakers.

"What time is it?" asked Mary.

"Eleven-ten. We'll wait till twelve-ten, give him ten minutes on the outside."

"Maybe we could leave a note," she said. "Go to the car and get some paper and stick it on the windmill—"

"Believe me, kid, I'd like to. But we'd better wait an hour and see what comes down."

Twenty minutes after we sat down in the dark a couple walked by the old windmill. We didn't know where they'd come from or where they were headed. They walked around the place briefly, making a few comments we couldn't hear, then walked on. Ten minutes after that a sedan pulled into the park. We saw the powerful, pencil-thin beam of a spotlight play on the windmill and the surrounding grounds. Then the beam snaked around farther and farther from the old windmill, in widening concentric circles. It swept across us, stopped, came back. Stayed. We held our hands up to our eyes to fight the glare. I heard a door open, then slam shut. Footsteps approached us, making a grating noise on the gravel. We were still caught in the bright light, and it made me uneasy.

"Charlie!" Mary hissed in terror. "They'll shoot!"

Suddenly I knew she was right. Our meeting with Reggie had been discovered, and whoever was after him was going to kill us. I grabbed her and started to run toward the bushes.

"Stay where you are, please. This is the sheriff's office," said a voice. No way was I staying put. We kept running, and were just into the bushes when I heard a sound that made me hesitate; it was the crackling and hissing, the staccato pop, of a two-way radio. The image of a police cruiser jumped into my head. Maybe it was true; maybe the guy was a cop.

"Barnstable County Sheriff," said the voice again. "I'm Sergeant Little. If you'll just give me a second of your time." A man with a DI hat approached us with a flashlight. Behind him, the bright beam of the cruiser's spotlight shot through the brush. I heard the throaty idle of his modified engine. "Sorry to frighten you folks; we just like to check this place regularly at night, especially on weekends. You live around here?"

I said yes and gave our names, explaining that we lived in

North Eastham and were just visiting the windmill.

"At this time of night?" said the officer. He was a blond kid, big and strong, but still covered with a layer of baby fat.

"Well, we were really waiting to meet somebody," said Mary.

I flinched. Swell, Mary.

"Oh? This late?"

"It's kind of, uh, confidential," she said, scarcely stopping to catch her breath. The deputy stood there in silence, looking at us.

"Can you please tell me what this person looks like?"

"Officer, I don't think we have to tell you," I said.

"You're right, Dr. Adams. But there's been an incident up the road, and we're checking this area pretty thoroughly in response to it. That's why I came in and shined the light in first place."

"What happened? Car wreck?"

"Would you mind describing this person you were to meet?"

Mary looked in my direction and I nodded.

"He's a tall, skinny black kid. Nice looking in a sort of delicate way. A Jamaican. He wears his hair kind of long."

"Would you come with me, please?" said the deputy, and we followed him up to his cruiser while he got inside and held the mike up to his mouth. He asked where our car was, and we told him we'd left it up the road. He asked us to describe the Audi. We did. He let his gaze linger on us.

"Would you mind if I drove you to your car now?" he asked.

"I'm afraid we'd better wait here a little longer," I said. "We said we'd wait until twelve."

"I hate to be nosy, but would you mind giving me the boy's name?"

"His name's Reginald Westley," said Mary, "and he works for Northrop Chesterton. You ever heard of Northrop Chesterton? Anyway, he's his gardener—"

"He doesn't need all that, Mary," I blurted, trying to interrupt her before she told him her life story, my life story, our hobbies, etc.

"How long have you known Mr. Westley?"

"We just met him today," I answered.

"Would you mind getting in the back?" he said, opening the door for us. We got in and he pulled out of the park and onto Route 6, heading south. After about five minutes I saw faint winking blue lights up ahead. When we were abreast of them, Sergeant Little pulled off onto the shoulder, easing the car slowly along the sandy grass until it was right behind two other squad cars and an ambulance. As he killed the engine another uniformed man had opened our door and was escorting us out and toward the ambulance. I heard the sound of running engines. I saw a hundred blue lights winking around me. It was a bad dream. Mary's frightened face, lighted up in shots of blue, was pathetic.

I got an unmistakable and familiar feeling. The feeling that Yours Truly was once again about to step off the end of the dock and up to his ass in alligators.

We walked with the deputies to a blanket-covered litter. There was no mistaking the recumbent shape beneath it. After the initial jolt of seeing it, the same old thought flashed through my head: Thank God it isn't Jack or Tony! Then I hated myself for thinking it. The brushed aluminum of the litter glowed in the flashing light.

"Dr. Adams, would you come forward, please?" said Sergeant Little as he knelt down by the head of the litter and prepared to raise the blanket.

"Come on, Mare, let's both look," I said, motioning her forward.

Sergeant Little lifted the blanket and shone his flashlight down on the body.

Reggie Westley stared into it, dull-eyed.

"Was he hit by a car?" asked Mary in a whisper.

"No, ma'am. By a shotgun." Sergeant Little pulled the blanket down. Reggie's gray sweatshirt was blood-soaked. "Looks like double-ought buckshot to me." He replaced the blanket and we stood up, surrounded by the law.

"And you tell us you were meeting this young man? May I ask why?" asked Little.

"We don't know. He was going to tell us when we met," I said.

"Would it have anything to do with the murder there a while ago?"

"Probably."

"And what's your involvement in this thing?"

"More than I'd like," I said, taking Mary's arm. "But if you know Paul Keegan, and my wife's brother, Joe Brindelli, they can help fill you in."

Yep, I thought, looking at the blanket-covered body of poor Reggie Westley and the sea of winking blue lights, the throng of uniformed lawmen all around us, *up to your ass in alligators*.

SEVENTEEN

"How do you do it, Doc?" asked an amazed Brian H. Hannon, chief of police in Concord, Mass. "How *do* you do it?"

"Shut up, Brian."

"Don't tell me to shut up; I'm the chief of police in this town."

"Ex-*cuuuse* me."

"It's a title worthy of respect."

"Then how did you get it?"

He pretended not to hear this. Instead, he flipped and shook the newspaper in front of his face. It was the Sunday *Boston Globe*, always a hefty chunk of news pulp to handle. But this particular one had a lot of news in it about the murder of Reginald Westley, employee of Northrop Chesterton. It also had quite a bit about Dr. and Mrs. Charles Adams, mysterious couple who were found waiting to meet the murder victim near the old windmill in Eastham. My patients were going to love that. Just eat it up.

"Do they need oral surgeons in the French Foreign Legion?"

"Hmm? What were you saying, Doc?"

"Forget it. Where's Mary?"

"At the front door, trying to keep the press away. They interviewed her for television earlier. Taped her with a video camera right on your front-door stoop while you were upstairs taking your sauna bath. Feel better?"

"I do not. I think perhaps a small drink might help."

"At ten in the morning, I think perhaps it won't. Trust me."

I trusted him; Brian was a fifteen-year veteran of AA.

"Then what, pray tell, might make me feel better?"

"How about a trip to Jamaica?" he said.

"Not funny, pal."

"Have you heard from Joe yet?"

"Uh-huh; he's down at the Chesterton mansion, or supposed to be. That's what he told me last night. He's going to line up the entire staff, Chesterton included, and give them a grilling right out of the Spanish Inquisition. See if he and Paul Keegan can't shake something loose."

Just then the phone rang. It was Joe, calling from Osterville. "*Qué pasa?*" he said.

"You've been hanging around with that whazzizname Latin cop too long, Joe."

"Gutierrez? Yeah, well, I teach him wop and he teaches me spic. You'll never guess what's come down."

"Bud confessed to the whole thing."

"Nope."

"Bud's wife Margaret confessed."

"Nope."

"What is this, twenty questions? Okay, the kid Owen Lightner confessed."

"Close."

"Oh, bullshit. He didn't do it, Joe. Trust me. He didn't kill either one. I'm pretty sure about this. So is your sister."

"That makes three of us. Still, we could be wrong. But that's not the issue. What happened was, at four-thirty this morning, Bud and the boy took off for Jamaica from the New Bedford airport. Chartered plane."

"You're kidding."

"Nope. They just skipped town. They heard about the Westley boy's death at one. Paul was down here by two-thirty, waking up everyone and doing preliminary interviews. Bud and

Lightner begged off, saying they'd continue in the morning after breakfast, so Keegan let them go back upstairs to bed. He shows up early today and gets the news that the two of them left in the wee hours for the airstrip at New Bedford, then flew down to Jamaica. Even as we speak they're probably ensconced in the plantation house at Shooter's Hill."

I whistled under my breath. Brian was glaring at me, feeling left out. "Well?" he demanded. "What the hell's up?"

"What are you doing now?" I asked Joe.

"Minding the fort down here. Paul Keegan's at home, trying to catch a little shut-eye; he was up all night. I'm sitting here watching lab guys go over everything in Reggie's old room on the third floor. You remember, the one opposite Lightner's?"

"Yep. Find anything interesting?"

"Yes, we did. That's why I want you to come down here as soon as possible. Bring Mary and Marty, too. That way we can go back up to the Breakers and spend the night together."

"Last time we tried that we ran into some rum luck. Just remind me not to ask anybody to meet us at the Eastham Windmill. . . ."

"Hurry on down. There's a photograph we found that you'll find interesting."

"Really? Of what?"

"You'll see. *Arrivederla.*"

"Well? What's happening?" Brian asked.

"Oh nothing, Brian." I yawned. "Nothing that directly concerns you, anyway."

It set him off; I knew it would.

An hour later the three of us—Mary, Marty, and I—drove back down to the Cape and the Chesterton house. I noticed the sky was thickening over the ocean. I thought how nice it would be to spend the night up at the Breakers again, sitting in the study corner with a book, with the sound of the rain and wind outside, the fireplace roaring, Mary cooking something great in the beamed kitchen. . . .

We found Joe up in Reggie's third-floor room, watching the lab technicians work the room in silence. The two women excused themselves for a walk on the beach. Joe told me Keegan wouldn't be back for another hour. He went over and retrieved a small snapshot from the dresser top. "Here's the photo I mentioned. We found it in the dresser drawer under a bunch of clothes."

I took the color print and saw Reggie with his lover, George Brenner. They were seated together at a small table in a large, dark room with rum drinks in front of them. From the background I assumed the photo had been taken inside a bar or nightclub. But, as is typical of flash pictures taken in low light, the near objects were brilliantly illuminated while distant ones were dark. I managed to discern a brightly colored sarong a few feet behind the men, with a very tan arm hanging down next to it. Girl on a dance floor, probably. I examined the two men closely, and found myself wishing that the shot of George had been taken more in profile instead of head-on. "Are you sure this is really George?" I asked, studying the face, trying to get some feel for the jawline. "He looks different from when we knew him."

"Looks the same to me. Exactly. But I never knew him before. A lot can happen in four or five years, Doc, especially with the life this guy must have led. But the main thing is the shirt he's wearing. Check it out."

George wore a shiny black T-shirt. On it was a brightly painted tropical scene showing a deep purplish-blue lagoon surrounded by giant green leaves. A yellow parrot perched in the foreground. Underneath the picture were two words. The second one was BIRD. I couldn't see all the first word because of wrinkles in the shirt as George twisted his torso.

"Low bird? Is that it?"

"Try 'Yellow Bird,' Doc. It's what we came up with. The Y-E-L are hidden. Also, there's a big yellow parrot in the middle of the thing, in case you haven't noticed."

"Where's a phone?"

"Why?"

"Don't you think we should call our friend Ken the bartender at Heroes bar?"

"Hey, why didn't I think of that?" He looked at his watch. "We should find him there; Sunday afternoon's the best bar day in Boston. I'll call and you listen in from the hall phone."

Joe took out his notebook and got the number; I was on the other line as soon as the phone began to ring. Joe made contact and reintroduced him. Ken remembered, but seemed hesitant, guarded.

"I just want to try to jog your memory about the shirt that our late friend was wearing when he came into your bar," Joe said. "I'm going to say a word, and then you say the one you think would be next, okay?"

"Well, I guess. . . ."

"Yellow."

"*Bird*!" answered the barkeep without hesitation. Joe thanked him and hung up.

"Good," he said when I came back into Reggie's room. He was sitting on the bed, rubbing his hands together. "Question is, what does it mean? What's the Yellow Bird?"

"We should find out, because whoever killed George thought it was important enough to hide so that he removed that shirt and dressed him in one of his own. Do you think the same person who killed George killed Reggie?"

He shrugged. "Hey, wait. The guy with the dog. The guy you and Paul couldn't catch yesterday."

"The Frisbee thrower with the golden retriever?"

"Right. He was on the beach the day you heard the shot, right?"

I nodded. "And he was there yesterday. The day that Reggie was killed. You think he did it? Because he could not have killed George; he was a quarter mile up the beach when that gun went off inside the house."

"I know, but think about it: you and Mary see this guy on the beach after you hear the shot. Afterward, searching for leads, Paul and I bust our ass trying to locate him. No luck. Then, the very day of the next killing, there he is again with the dog. What are the odds of that?"

"Maybe he's a lookout."

"I say he's the front man for the killer. But lookout's as good a term as any."

I looked around the room, at the two silent men who were sifting through personal belongings wearing pale gray cotton gloves, photographing this and that, placing objects into ziplock baggies. Placing shreds of clothing and fiber into same. I looked again at the carousel slide projector sitting on the desk. Looked around for a screen or camera, didn't see either. Asked Joe what he thought.

"I don't think it's that important right now, Doc, you wanna know the truth."

"It's curious. It's singular, as Sherlock Holmes might say. Slide projector full of slides. Spare slide trays packed with more slides. No camera. No screen. What gives?"

He eased himself around and stared at the projector and shrugged. "Who knows? Maybe he was into porno slides. Stan, you guys find anything so far that's unexplainable?"

"We found a lot of dirty magazines. Just guys in 'em, doing each other. No broads."

Joe and I briefly examined the six publications the team had put into a cardboard box. Explicit homosexual sex. Somehow, to my eye, the gay pornography seemed infinitely more pornographic than the "straight" variety. But perhaps that was in the eye of the beholder. We tossed the material back into the box, and Joe sat back down on the edge of the bed, rubbing his big brown fingers over his beard stubble. He had quite a crop growing there. A knock came at the door, and Marty and Mary came in. Mary was holding one of her sneakers in her hand and asked if she could dump the sand out of it into the wastebasket. Joe sent her down the hall.

"Have you guys looked at the sky?" Marty asked. "Storm's getting close. Mary wants to get a bunch of good stuff for dinner and head back to the Breakers in time for us to watch it from the porch while the food's cooking."

"Sounds good to me, hon," said Joe absently. I looked at his eyes and could tell he was tired. "What shall we get? Steaks? Flounder fillets? Lobster? I think we can—what the hell's *that?*"

Stan was holding a rolled piece of translucent plastic. It looked rather like a window shade, except it would not block out much light.

"Here's another, just like it," said Stan's helper, taking the rolled material out of the closet. He let it drop, holding on to one edge. The stiff plastic sheet was about two and a half feet wide by perhaps four feet long.

"It's a window shade," said Marty, walking over to it. "See, it's even got two holes at the top to hang it up with."

"But there are already shades on these windows," I said.

"Well, stack 'em in the corner," said Joe. "Marty, take a look at this picture. It shows the famous shirt that George was wearing when he was shot."

Mary came back in and sat next to the two of them on the bed. She asked me what I was fiddling with.

"A window shade that isn't one. Why did he keep these rolled up in the closet? And if there are two holes at the top of each one, where are the hooks?"

"Here they are, up on the window frames underneath the roller shades," said Stan, who was kneeling on Reggie's desk, pulling the drapes and shades away, looking up underneath them.

"Do you think that was his screen, Charlie? To show his slides?"

"Maybe so; there doesn't seem to be any other screen around. Or even a camera."

"Let's call the cook, Maria Townsend, up here," said Joe, and left the room. He came back in less than a minute with Ms. Townsend, the pleasant-looking woman we had all seen earlier in the staff photo in the upstairs hallway. She had café au lait skin and some freckles on her face. I guessed she was in her early fifties. She now wore the black-and-white maid's uniform, explaining to us that in the absence of Anne Rawlings, the former maid who had left with Mrs. Chesterton, she was having to do double duty. She listened patiently to Joe's questions about the strange window shades we found in Reggie's closet. She said she had never seen them before.

"Not even when you cleaned his room?"

"Oh, but I never clean the room. No, Master Reggie, he always said do not disturb his private things, just sweep the floor and dust, and clean the lavatory."

"Did he take a lot of pictures?"

"No, sah. Not that I saw."

"Did he have a camera?"

She held up her palms, shrugging at the same time. A strange, helpless smile formed on her face, and I could see that her left incisor was covered with gold.

"You never saw Reggie taking pictures?"

"Oh, maybe. I don't know," she said with a giggle. She was a little scared.

"Maria, did you ever come into this room and see these plastic shades hanging from the two center windows?"

"No. Never."

We thanked her, and she went back downstairs.

"Well, well, well, well, *well* . . ." I heard Stan say as he removed the central desk drawer and began removing its contents, laying them neatly on the desktop.

"Well well *what*?" asked Joe.

In reply, Stan flipped the empty drawer over. Taped to its underside was a map. Actually, it was a nautical chart, a navigation aid prepared by the government. We keep an identical one aboard our boat, *Ella Hatton*. The chart showed the south shore of Cape Cod, from Woods Hole to Chatham.

"Now, why would he keep it there, Charlie?"

"Offhand, Mary, I'd say it was to keep it from being discovered."

"But it's just a chart; we've got one like it, don't we?"

"Yep, but without those color codes," I said, pointing to small circles of blue, red, green, and yellow drawn in with colored pencil or crayon along the beaches.

"So for that he's got to keep it hidden?" she asked.

"I think," said Joe, looking over my shoulder at the chart, "that Reggie would have been wiser to hide this chart the way the Arabs do it: in the light of day."

"You mean out in the open?"

"Yes. On the wall, for instance, where people would scarcely notice it."

"Like 'The Purloined Letter,' you mean?"

"Exactly. But by hiding it underneath his desk drawer—a trick so old it's pathetic—all Reggie's done is show us that he had something to hide. . . ." Joe took the chart and ran his eyes along it.

"I see groups of colors spaced along the shore. . . ." he said, half under his breath. "We've got yellow, red, and green . . . blue, red, and green . . . red, black, and blue . . . green, black, and green. . . ."

"Can you do this later, Joe?" asked Marty, shifting impatiently from one foot to the next. "Mary and I want to get the stuff for dinner now, and we'd like all of us to go up to Eastham together."

"I've got a few more things to do here."

"But you've been here since eight this morning, and this is Paul's turf anyway."

Stan chimed in that he could handle things until Paul returned, so the four of us left Osterville and headed up to the fresh-seafood market at Wellfleet, then back to the cottage. We had a nice cocktail hour, watching the storm approach from the screened porch. Then we cooked and set the table in the kitchen, with the tiny wood stove purring and tinking next to us. But somewhere in the middle of the garlic scallops and snow peas, or maybe it was the lobster subgum guru (Mary's own invention), I stood up from the table and strolled out onto the deck, squinting into the dying sun, which had emerged, tired and gray, in the wake of the spring squall. The chatter behind me ceased. I didn't know it then; Mary told me later.

"Charlie?"

I spun around, rubbing my eyes.

"Reggie smuggled drugs," I said to her. "George was his partner. Joe! Let's go back down to the beach house."

A grunt and a shuffle came to me from behind the screen. Then Joe came out. "How are you so sure?"

"I'll show you when we get there."

"Can't it wait until we finish dinner?"

"I'd like to get there before they disturb anything else in that room," I said.

"I'll call first, let them know we're coming."

"Use the radio while we drive, okay?"

"You can wait a *second*, Charlie, for crying out loud," said a voice behind us. It was Mary, putting on her windbreaker. Marty stood behind her with hers already on.

EIGHTEEN

By nine o'clock we were back in Osterville, standing in Reggie's bedroom again. Maria Townsend had just brought us up a big silver pot of Blue Mountain coffee, the nine-bucks-a-pound stuff grown only in Jamaica. We watched Paul Keegan holding the phone up to his ear with a hunched shoulder while he moved the slide projector on Reggie's desk. He was on the phone to Stan, the lab man who'd dusted the place just hours earlier. He wanted to make certain we weren't screwing things up as we moved the objects around. Because we all knew who was head of the crime lab and what would happen if Karl Pirsch ever found out we messed up one of his scenes. The Eastern Front for sure. Maybe worse.

"Okay," Paul said, nodding into the phone, "we won't touch anything else but those crazy shades, unless we call first . . . right . . . yeah, bye."

"Is that the way you want it, Doc?"

"No; it has to go over on the bureau, much farther from the window."

Paul carried the machine over to the chest of drawers and set it so that the projecting lens was facing the windows in back. It looked just right to me. I could tell because the elevation screw on the bottom of the machine had been set so that on the bureau, the machine would project a picture smack dab on the center of the double windows. What added to my feeling that we were on the right track was the fact that there was no outlet near the bureau to plug the projector into. But somebody had rigged an extension cord to the bureau from another outlet, and the cord's socket end had no other plugs in it.

While Joe and Paul hung the plastic sheets on the windows I turned on the machine. The plastic shades on the windows remained dark; the first slide was blank cardboard, as I had remembered from my earlier examination of the slide tray. I pushed the automatic button; the big slide cartridge on top of the projector began turning with metallic clanks while picture after picture appeared on the window screens: sunset, sunset, dark, ocean, ocean, dark, sunlight through leaves, sunlight through leaves, bright white (no slide), sunset. . . . It would keep going like this, around and around, while the automatic mode was set.

We all left the room and went down the stairway past the second floor, down to ground level, then out the back door that was really the front door and out onto the beach. It was cold, dark, and blowing loud out there. We turned and looked up at the darkened mansion. The two windows in the second gable from the end flashed out bright red. Then, for a second, it was dark again up there. Then red, then dark, then blue.

"What a signal—" said Joe above the surf and wind. "That high up, and that big and bright, you could see it five miles out. Maybe ten."

Then we all just stood out there in the blowing dark, listening to the ocean crash behind us, watching those giant flashes of bright color and light and dark. RED, RED, BLUE, BLUE, GREEN, GREEN, WHITE . . . RED, RED, BLUE, BLUE, GREEN, GREEN, WHITE . . .

It wasn't until we were walking back to the house that Marty, who'd had her back turned and was looking out over the dark water said, almost as a joke: "You think that's weird, you guys. How about that boat out on the water there, *flashing back*?"

arly the following morning, Joe, Paul, and I were out on the
terrace of the Chesterton house, drinking more of that Blue
Mountain coffee that Maria Townsend brought out to us in
the nice silver-plate service. I was going to stay in this thing
for the coffee, if nothing else. They were leaning over the chart
that the late Reggie Westley had taped to the bottom of his desk
drawer: NOAA Chart #13237—Nantucket Sound and Ap-
proaches. It was weighted down on its corners and sides with
smooth beach rocks. Still, the paper rattled in the sea wind. I
was standing on a chair, sweeping the clear horizon with my
Steiner marine glasses, noting that whoever had been out there
last night had moved on. Surprise, surprise.

"You really didn't think we'd run into them over on Succonnesset Point?" Paul said to Joe, leaning over the chart. He
was referring to a small spit of sand a couple miles down the
beach, to the west, where Reggie had drawn in the double red,
double blue, double green circles with colored pencil. Since
they matched the pattern of the light show we'd put on the
previous night, we'd all hopped into Joe's cruiser as soon as
we'd seen the flashing out at sea and scurried over there in the
dead of night to the point. There we'd hidden behind a low rise
of sand covered with dune grass, hunkered down in the cold,
blowing dark, waiting. Mary and Marty knelt on the cold sand

in the faint moonlight, rubbing themselves in the chill wind, speculating excitedly about the imminent arrest that they'd be part of. Well, nobody showed up. No boat from the ocean, not even an outboard runabout. No "low rider" hoodlum car with hollow rocker panels to hide the stash and a threesome of uglies to guard it. Nobody at all.

"If we're assuming the boat was out there waiting for Reggie's signal, that means that whoever's out there doesn't know he's been murdered."

"That's right," said Joe.

"Well," I said, jumping down off the chair and joining them at the table, "that means that his drug partners didn't murder him; somebody else did."

"Well, it wasn't Owen Lightner," Paul said. "Or Northrop Chesterton, either. They were both inside the house until they got word of the killing. I know because I'm the one who broke the news, within an hour of the event. And Maria Townsend verifies."

"She would, of course," said Joe. "That's part of her job. As far as we know, she could have been in on it."

"I doubt it; I called the home earlier for some questions and found everybody there."

"But still, Doc's got a point. If Reggie's partners knew, they wouldn't be offshore in a holding pattern, waiting to bring a load in."

"How do we know we had the right place?" said Paul, peering at the chart again. He tapped his finger on it right near the black X on the paper in the form of a crude Maltese cross, which marked the location of the Chesterton mansion on Wianno Beach—the stretch of sand we were now looking at, and which Mary and I walked the day of the shooting that now seemed forever ago. He traced his thick fingers along the shoreline to the cluster of colored dots near the point.

"Let's go over there again after Pirsch shows up," said Joe.

"Didn't see much the first time," said Paul.

"That's why we should go again. We couldn't see a lot in the dark."

We had to drive; little Cotuit Bay intrudes into the shoreline in between Wianno Beach and Succonnesset Point. We saw the same thing when we got out and walked around: from the point to the edge of the beach further east, where it looked as if a boat would have the best chance of running ashore, there was nothing at all on the beach, and only shore scrub and grass and a scattering of houses farther back. We walked around the houses this time, examining each one from all angles. They were all still vacant.

"We're getting a list of owners," said Paul. "As soon as we have it we can call them. Bet a lot of the calls will be long-distance to Florida or the Sea Islands."

"Maybe we had the right place but the wrong night," Joe said. "Maybe they'll come tonight."

"You mean the signal is for a drop the *following* night?" I asked.

"Could be."

"I'd be surprised," Paul said. "If you've got a shipload of ganja, the longer you cruise around offshore the more chance you'll get caught."

"I see two lines in the sand," said Joe, squinting into the distance. "Or is it two and a half? Is that the remnants of the tracks of three men, whose tracks crossed one another's?"

"Looks too smooth to be tracks," I said.

"The wind's been blowing enough to smooth them out," said Paul, and then he and Joe were walking toward the roughly parallel lines that ran from the shore brush to the water. I sighted along the direction of the tracks, looking landward. Up on a rise, past the brush and weeds, dune grass, and stubby little scrub-oak seedlings, was a cottage. It was smaller than the others, and almost dilapidated. Then I noticed it had plywood over the lower windows. I walked to it. Soon I heard them coming up behind me.

It was a small, squarish building with two floors and a sloped, shingled roof. They were asphalt, not cedar shake. It had been sided with aluminum a long time ago. Clearly, this summer house was not of the same caliber as others in the area. Perhaps it was a guest house, a satellite of one of the bigger, older homes farther up the hill. It was not in good repair, and obviously had not been lived in in some time. Front door padlocked. Back door padlocked. Couldn't see in anywhere because of the plywood. Joe rattled the big brass locks.

"They look newer than the hasp."

"Brand, spanking new, you ask me," said Keegan. "Let's get your ring of keys and try some."

Joe went to the trunk of the cruiser and returned with his old gray metal toolbox. He sat it down on the empty front porch and opened the lid, revealing rows and rows of special connected trays that came up and out with the lid, just like a tackle box. When the thing was fully opened, it looked like the Harvard Bowl with eight rows of bleachers on each side. Lock picks, tension bars, electronic safecracking devices, debuggers, electric lock picks that resembled electric toothbrushes, manufacturers' brochures for locks, alarm systems, and safes. Finally, two huge steel rings fully laden with keys. Joe squinted at the lock and read something off its bottom. Then he discarded one of the big rings of keys.

"Iberia Model 881," Joe muttered to himself, flipping through the keys on the big ring. There must have been two hundred of them. Many of them were color-coded. I saw circular white cardboard name tags—the kind as big as a quarter and rimmed with metal between the keys here and there. They had scribbles and codes with Joe's handwriting on them.

Joe is quite a key-and-lock man. The only guy better is Jimmy Hoolihan in Theft.

And the hundred or so top Boston pros on the other side of the wire, of course.

Snink!

The big brass padlock snapped open. Joe removed it from the hasp and swung the hasp arm back. Then he replaced his giant key ring and snapped up the metal case. I saw Paul take his handkerchief and drop it lightly on the doorknob, then put his hand over it, touching it only with the tips of his strong fingers, and twist it gingerly, pushing the door in with his elbow. The door swung open.

Empty house. We walked in.

Stacked against the walls were large, blocky bundles piled like cinder blocks. They were wrapped in black plastic that resembled plastic lawn bags. I was conscious of a faint, sappy odor. The sweet, leafy tang of marijuana.

But we noticed these only later, after we had finished gaping at what was in the center of the room. There were two men on the floor, lying on their backs in a pool of congealed blood. One white and one black. Their throats had been cut.

The black one had long woolly hair spewed out in dreadlocks. The eyes were open too, giving that blank, doleful, dull-eyed stare that tells you something is very wrong. It wasn't pretty.

But it was the other dead man that I was staring at. Joe and Paul didn't recognize him. But I did, having seen him fairly recently. The same pink face, the almost bald head. A little thick in the waist and butt. But the difference was that ugly smile-shaped gash around the base of his neck, that brownish-red crescent of dried blood.

"Well, Joe, you've been wanting to see Jonathan Randolph . . . there he is. But it seems we're a tad late—"

"Holy Christ," said Joe, leaning over the sprawled form. "So tell me he wasn't involved, Doc. Tell me it was just a coincidence."

"Yeah," said Keegan, "and how about this?"

He was pointing at the shirt the Rastafarian wore. It was a black T-shirt. Even his blood didn't hide the picture and the words. Same parrot, same scene in the background. Same words too.

Yellow Bird.

picked at my pasta salad. Behind me, through the doorway that led to the back hall of our cottage, came the *tink*, *tink*, *tink* of the heater in the sauna bath. In a half hour it would be ready for me to go in and bake out some of my frustrations. I had just run a loping nine and a half miles along the hard-packed sand of Sunken Meadow Beach, where our cottage, the Breakers, sits.

This mess about George Brenner was growing "curiouser and curiouser," as Lewis Carroll said in *Alice in Wonderland*. Some recent items, largely provided by my brother-in-law:

1. The stash in the empty house weighed in at just over seventeen hundred pounds of high-grade Jamaican ganja, the buds (not the stems, leaves, or seeds) of the *cannibis sativa* plant picked at the peak of their resin content and then compressed into bundles the size of hay bales and covered with plastic. This grade of marijuana is usually referred to stateside as *sensimilia*. The best there is. Estimated street value: one to two million, depending on local markets and demand.

2. My late med-school chum Jonathan Randolph was part of the ring, perhaps even its head. Why he was killed was uncertain, but what is certain is that this kind of violence goes with the drug trade. I had to admit that being found with one's throat cut in a room piled high with two million bucks' worth of

smuggled grass, next to a murdered Jamaican "mule" wearing a now infamous T-shirt . . . well, it tends to implicate one.

3. Almost as strange, nobody could turn up Michelle Randolph, the former Kilgore Rangerette and drugged-out bimbo we'd seen way back when this mess first got under way. State police headquarters at Ten Ten Commonwealth Ave. had been in contact with the Houston police and the Texas state agencies too. Perhaps even the redoubtable Texas Rangers were in on the hunt. But neither they nor any local cops, nor the FBI, could find a trace of her. Joe told me the odds were heavy that she'd been killed as well, probably by the same people who'd killed her husband. According to Joe, the "smart money" at Ten Ten was saying the Purple Gang looked really good for it.

4. The demise of the extraordinarily upwardly mobile Randolphs led Mary to ask this somewhat rhetorical question: "Charlie? How many of these so-called beautiful people who seem to have everything, at least on the external front, don't really have diddly-shit? Hmm? How many of them with great educations, super professions, imported cars, and spare houses, are really skating on thin ice?" "I dunno," I answered after some thought. "Maybe thirty or forty percent." Which didn't, I reflected, put America on very solid footing.

5. In light of the above, it now seemed certain that my late acquaintance George Brenner, who smuggled drugs, and my late school chum Jonathan Randolph, who took a lot of drugs and also probably smuggled them, were in some nefarious way connected, most likely via the Jamaicans who worked in the Chesterton household and who manned the boats that brought the ganja inshore.

6. And also in light of the above, Dr. Charles Adams, as a common link—perhaps *the* common link (italics not mine)—between the two dope smugglers, was *in the soup* (italics mine).

Hence my picking at the pasta salad, and awaiting the soothing, cleansing, mind-purifying heat of a sauna bath.

"Are you going to practice sweating, Charlie?" asked Mary. "You know, practicing for when the fuzz takes you into the dark room with the hot light to sweat the truth out of you?"

"Not funny. And this salad is below par."

"Of course it is; I didn't make it. Janice DeGroot made it. You remember Janice, love. The one with the amazing tush you're always trying to grab."

"That was a long time ago, love. I've matured since then, if you haven't noticed. And what are you trying to do, make things worse?"

"Nope. Joey's here to do that; he just pulled up."

I lifted the edge of the gingham curtain and saw him getting out of the cruiser in the light rain that had begun to fall since I returned from the beach. He came in and poured himself a big mug of coffee and sat down opposite me at the kitchen table. Next to his sister.

"We're not getting any recent makes on your doctor buddy Randolph. We've run his mug past all the local savvies in the drug business, and nobody recognized him. He must have been really careful."

"Disagree," I said. "If he were really careful, we wouldn't have found him with his throat cut under a ton of dope."

"True . . . true . . . Which brings us to the second point. The motive for the killings."

"A double cross, don't you think?"

"Uh-huh. The obvious guess. Maria Townsend told Paul Keegan that the cut throats of the victims may have special meaning."

"You mean other than as a silent means of killing them?"

"Uh-huh. She says in Jamaica, and in a lot of Latin America as well, the slit throat is a sign of a turncoat."

"Then it was some kind of revenge killing," Mary said. "But you guys have figured out that it wasn't the same bunch who killed Reggie Westley, right?"

"Right," said Joe. ". . . I *think*."

"You know," I said, "maybe George never smuggled drugs. Maybe he just happened to fall in love with this Reggie Westley who was part of it. Somehow he found out too much and they had to kill him. I mean, his murder in Chesterton's mansion has *got* to be in some way connected to Reggie."

"Doc, why do you seem to gravitate toward the center of all this shit?"

Joe Brindelli was looking at me slow and steady. A Humphrey Bogart look.

"I have no idea. Really and truly. I hadn't seen Jonathan in years and years."

"But despite your mysterious connections to this case, Doc, your leads haven't been worth much. About as much as a free pass to Heritage, U.S.A. If it weren't for Mary, who happens to have a steel-trap mind, we wouldn't have two of our biggest leads."

"Which are?"

"The rental car on the road outside the Chesterton house and the man with the golden retriever. Both were recalled by Mary, if you recall. Which you probably don't because you—"

"I take it this steel-trap mind runs in the family, Joe?"

"Of course."

Joe got up and went to the john. When he came back, he said, almost as an afterthought: "We're bringing Owen Lightner back from Buff Bay and booking him."

"Joey!"

"Hey. Facts are facts. He was the only one here when Brenner was killed; he was here when Reggie was murdered. He can't, or won't, give us an alibi for either one. Finally, he took off when things got hot; that's never a good sign."

"Why, Joey? Where's his motive?"

"We don't know. Yet."

"Oh, bullshit. Owen didn't do anything bad. Trust me."

"Like to, but we can't. The commonwealth has wired Kingston; we've got a working relationship with Jamaica. I feel confident that we can get him back there," Joe intoned in his official police voice, ignoring the withering glare his sister was shooting him. I must confess I was none too pleased, either. This was the first I'd heard about extraditing the kid.

"I bet Chesterton can block it," I said.

"Yeah, I thought of that too. So did Paul. We say he'll cooperate, give us the kid to save his ass."

"Joey, c'mon! Don't dump on Bud too. I thought you guys liked him."

"We do, but—"

"But what?"

"Tell her, Doc."

"No, you."

"No you."

"You."

"You."

"Shut up, for chrissake! Charlie: *spill*!"

So I did. Told her I'd caught Northrop Chesterton hugging and kissing his manservant in the lobby of Joe and Marty's apartment.

Well, she hit the roof. And to say that she can cuss is like saying Tyson can fight. "That filthy son of a bitch!" was how she started out. It got much worse real fast. And her body motions—the jumping around the kitchen pulling her hair, the rebounding off the refrigerator, the standing-with-fists-clenched-and-shrieking routine—added quite a bit as well. I really had not seen the Old Spouse so steamed up since the North Carolina reunion of the Daisy Ducks.

When she heard about that caper, she could have powered several generators, let me tell you.

"Mary! Mary!" wailed Joe, about to depart for the deck, drizzle or no. "Settle down, will ya?"

"If he ever touches that boy again, I'll—"

"Hold it, Mare. The kid might be, you know . . . same way—"

"Bullshit! I know. A woman knows. That poor boy is a modern-day slave."

And so on, and on.

I never did get my sauna.

TWENTY-ONE

We didn't see the plane until it burst from beneath the mucky gray clouds over the tiny New Bedford airfield. It banked sharply, a glowing white fire bird against a stormy sky, and came in, making that fluffy, fluty blowing sound that props planes make. I had missed that sound; it also forced the realization on me that jets were no longer the new mode of travel; they were standard. Propeller planes, like Doc Adams, were survivors of a bygone era.

"Well, he kept his word. I'll give him that much," growled Paul Keegan, tucking his neck down further into his overcoat.

"Had to," said Joe, blowing big clouds of steam and stamping his feet. "The adverse publicity if he didn't would be too much. As it is, the papers are going to go nuts."

"Do they know about the . . . uh . . . other aspects of this case?" Mary asked, frowning at Chesterton's big green Jaguar as it sat idling behind us in the parking lot. Her silk scarf was blowing around under her chin.

"I don't think so. Nobody knows but Doc and us, as far as I can tell," said her brother.

"Well, if it gets out, then the papers and the TV stations will *really* go nuts. And I hope it does. I want them to find out that Mr. Northrop Chesterton, with aspirations for the governorship and God knows what else, is keeping a boy. I've a good mind to tell them myself."

"Don't," I said. "They're in enough hot water already."

She growled that she supposed I had a point. There were only two passengers in the little Beech commuter, which came as no surprise. Northrop Chesterton and Owen Lightner walked down the little boarding ladder with their heads down, collars up, fighting the cold sea breeze. Neither looked happy. The Jag XJS came up and snapped to a stop, the driver exiting and opening the back door for the two men. I had not seen this man before. Obviously, since Owen Lightner was the usual chauffeur, he had been brought in very recently. Perhaps he was simply hired for the time being. They slid into the car and the driver shut the doors, got behind the wheel, and guided the big car off the tarmac. The pilot in the private commuter airliner revved his engines again and the Beech turned, pivoting on her locked starboard wheel, and faced into the cold, wet wind.

Mary and I were heading toward her Audi when the big car came alongside. The window oozed down, and Bud Chesterton stuck his head out, inclining it to us in a half bow. He looked at Mary.

"Yes, you are indeed beautiful, Mrs. Adams," he said in a voice dripping with honey. He extended his hand to her. She looked at it, didn't take it.

"We've returned entirely voluntarily," he said, switching his gaze to my direction. "There will be a hearing in Boston tomorrow afternoon. I'm not sure of the exact time and place, but Joe and Lieutenant Keegan will know. I'd like to see you there. Both of you." He looked at her again, but she didn't meet his gaze. The window slid up, and the car purred off.

"Asshole," she said under her breath. "Thinks he owns the whole goddamn world."

"I take it, then, you're not going to the hearing?"

"Hell no. I'm not giving him or his kind any encouragement. The more people follow these types around, ogling and ahing at their wealth, the more they get off on it. You're not going, are you?"

"Wouldn't miss it for the world."

She turned and walked to her car in silence. But I had a hunch what she was thinking.

I turned to see the commuter plane roaring along the tarmac. Its tail lifted, then lowered again almost to the ground as the plane rotated on its wings and lifted off, thrumming into the dark, stormy sky.

"**T**wo o'clock, third floor at One Ashburton Place. You coming?" said Joe over the phone from his office. I answered that I sure was, but his sister wasn't.

"C'mon; tell her Marty's coming."

So I did, and Mary changed her mind, saying that she reserved the right to stand up in that crowded courtroom and tell everybody what she thought of Northrop Chesterton.

"I don't think you'll need to do that, Mary; as this story unfolds he'll be in enough trouble."

We got into the chambers early, and it was a good thing, because everybody and her brother wanted to see the mighty brought low. That, on top of a triple murder—the press was busy, as always, making connections on dubious grounds and claiming that all three killings, Brenner, Westley, and Randolph were related—made the large courtroom in the heart of Boston the place to be, its immeasurably tall ceiling, carved columns of dark varnished wood, and the tall, imposing judge's bench the perfect setting for the courtroom drama about to unfold.

"Has this sex-slave business come out yet?" Mary hissed in my ear as we sat down in the third row. Kevin O'Hearn, sitting to her right, leaned over and raised his bushy, sandy-colored eyebrows.

"No, dammit, so keep mum."

"I will *not*!"

"Joe can't make it," said O'Hearn.

"Why not?"

"Got a call to go to Brenner's old apartment on Marlboro Street—the place you visited with him, Doc. Seems there was an attempted burglary there last night. Joe and Major Mahaffey thought there might be some connection, so off he went."

"That means Marty's not coming, either?"

"Guess not. Sorry, Mary."

She slid down in her seat, pouting. "Only reason I decided to come," she muttered.

"Oyez, oyez, oyez," said the bailiff, and we were under way. Bud Chesterton, Owen Lightner, and Anton Bradshaw sat at the table for the defense. At the plaintiff's table sat our old pal Bernie Kirk, looking snappy indeed in his dark blue pinstripe worsted with vest and watch chain. After opening statements, in which each side made it clear to the judge and the grand jury that their side of the story was the correct one, things got under way in earnest.

I won't go into all the details; I assume you have seen enough *Perry Mason* reruns to get the gist of this hearing and trial stuff. A lot of reporters there, though—even more than we expected. It was the kind of human-interest story coupled with murder that the press dotes on. Rather like the Von Bülow trial. The reporters stood along the walls, cameras and strobe lights dangling across their chests. But the thing that got me, about twenty minutes into the fight, was that Bernie Kirk was feeding the opposition straight lines. Bernie, supposedly on the other side, was casting his bread upon the waters so that Bradshaw and Chesterton and Lightner could scoop up the pieces and eat them. The harder Bernie and the DA's office worked, the easier it was for the accused. Setup; I could smell it a mile away. I had not the slightest doubt that the two sides had conversed thoroughly before this show and had the scenario all worked out, down to the last line and double take. The performance was as spontaneous as a professional wrestling bout.

It came down basically to the most damning thing against Owen Lightner: that he was not, as he had claimed, in Gainesville, Florida, the night before the murder, visiting friends at the university. Instead he was in Boston, in a deluxe room at the Copley Plaza Hotel. And therefore, he could have easily gone down to the house in Osterville, barely an hour away in the sparse wintertime traffic, and killed George Brenner in the bedroom of his employer's deserted mansion. This was circumstantial, of course, but since Lightner was the only member of the household staff off the island during this time, and since he deliberately lied about his whereabouts when first questioned, and since he had a key to the house as well as a familiarity with the locale . . .

Throughout these proceedings, the threesome at the defense table said nothing. Under cross-examination, Lightner refused to explain his presence in Boston on the night in question. This did not look good for Owen, despite poor Bernie Kirk's best efforts to throw the other side easy questions, or those that would elicit favorable or sympathetic responses.

Then, just as it seemed the jaws of justice were about to clamp themselves around the kid in a death grip, Anton Bradshaw rose from the defense table, approached the bench, and asked to call an unscheduled witness. The judge motioned him up to the bench and they conferred in private for a few seconds. Then the judge nodded, Bradshaw walked back down in front again, and said in a loud voice: "*Your Honor, the defense requests the presence of Miss Charlena Eames!*"

Silence in the big room then. I heard a hundred people sigh with anticipation.

Charlena Eames? Not *the* Charlena Eames . . .

"Charlie!" whispered Mary, beside herself. "Do you think he means Charlena Eames the singer? *Do* you?"

Charlena Eames was a rock singer and contemporary of another Katie-Bar-the-Door vocalist: Tina Turner. But Charlena, from what I'd read about her and from hearing some of her songs, was more into reggae than rock. Reggae . . . could it be?

"Who the hell's Charlena whazitz?" whispered Kevin to Mary. She didn't respond, her eyes glued to the back of the courtroom. A tall woman with a hat and veil was sidestepping her way across the seats, heading for the center aisle. Even all dressed up as she was, there was no mistaking that majestic carriage, that stage presence. I heard ooh's and ahh's in the audience.

"Well, what do you know?" I whispered into Mary's ear. "Surprise witness for the defense. Aren't you glad now you decided to come?"

"Shh!"

"Who the hell is she?" asked Kevin again, convinced there was some kind of conspiracy of silence against him.

"Shh!"

Kevin frowned and settled back in his seat, flipping his big fat fingers around, convinced now of the conspiracy.

Whap! Whap! Whap!

"Order. Order in this courtroom, please!" said the judge, setting his gavel down as the tall woman walked up before the bailiff. "Are you Miss Charlena Eames?"

"Yes, Your Honor."

"And your business before the court?"

"If it please the court, Your Honor," said Bradshaw, "Miss Eames would like to explain why it is impossible that Owen Lightner could have committed the murder in question."

"This witness will establish an alibi?"

"Yes, Your Honor."

"Very well. Bailiff, swear in the witness." He did. Charlena Eames took the oath and entered the witness stand. Gray wool suit and cream-white blouse with a big bow in front. She removed her hat and veil. A lot of her hair seemed to cascade down when she did it. I remembered seeing that radiant face on television not six months previous. I think it was a benefit concert for South Africans or something. Same throaty voice, same high, wide cheekbones and Arabic nose that reminded me of Tina. The big chamber buzzed with soft voices.

"Miss Eames," said Anton Bradshaw in his most practiced courtroom voice, "would you please explain the events of the night of January fourteenth, the night before the murder took place in the summer home of Mr. Northrop Chesterton?"

"Certainly. Mr. Owen Lightner was in Boston the entire

time. He came up here especially to see me. I was doing a concert at Hynes Auditorium that night and met him at the hotel after I was finished."

Murmurs in the courtroom now. Murmurs of amazement and possibly outrage. What was this woman, pushing fifty (though she could probably pass for late thirties) doing shacking up with this boy from Jamaica?

"Now, Miss Eames," continued Bradshaw. "Would you kindly explain the reason for your meeting Mr. Lightner?"

She hesitated. Buzzes and whispers everywhere. Owen Lightner leaning forward over the defense table, eyes lighting up. Intense, handsome, about to cry . . . Chesterton with his head bowed, staring at the veneer of the tabletop inches from his face. Mary leaning forward too, starting to rise up from her seat . . .

"I don't see that it matters," Charlena Eames said, raising her head and speaking in a rich, throaty contralto.

O'Hearn whispering: "I still don't know who the hell she *is*—"

Bradshaw looking at the judge now, the judge looking at the dark beauty on the witness stand. The judge looking back at Bradshaw again, the lawyer turning to his witness and saying: "Miss Eames, it would help to establish your credibility as a witness if you could indicate the . . . eh . . . nature of the relationship between yourself and Mr. Lightner."

A lot of whispers and buzzing again. *Whap! Whap! Whap!*

"Owen Lightner is my son."

"Charlie!" squealed Mary.

"He sees me regularly, five or six times a year. On the night in question, we had made arrangements to meet at the hotel room his father reserved for us."

"His father?" said the amazed Bradshaw.

"Yes. His father always foots the bill. I'll give him that much." She was looking down at her hands now, which were in her lap. She looked wonderful sad. It tugged at my heart.

"Was his father in that same hotel room with you? Perhaps his word together with your own testimony—"

"No. He wasn't. But he's here now, in this room."

She raised her head and stared out at the packed room. The

crowd was growing riotous. I couldn't hear myself think. Cameras began to go off; strobe flashes were bouncing around everywhere.

Whap! Whap! Whap!

That died away too. Charlena Eames stared straight ahead. Her eyes were wet and glistening. The strobe flashes made them sparkle. Two shiny streaks covered her cheeks.

"Ohhhhh!" said the crowd.

"What is it, Charlie? I can't see, dammit!"

"She some kind of singer, besides being his mom? Is that it?" said O'Hearn, leaning over between us. Mary pushed him back.

A tall man was making his way up to the bench, with Owen Lightner close behind. When he got up to the witness stand, he kissed Charlena Eames, and she grabbed him hard and held him. Then he turned and hugged his son.

Bud Chesterton hugged Owen Lightner exactly the way I saw him do it in the lobby of Joe's apartment. The boy was crying for real now. Everybody was crying. Most especially Mary.

"Oh Charlie, look! Look! We were so wrong about him!"

"Hey, how about that!" said O'Hearn. "How about that, huh?"

Cheering now from the audience. Standing ovation. Flashes everywhere. Stomping of feet.

Curtain.

TWENTY-TWO

Joe was butting into the line, fighting his way toward the crabmeat dip. Marty tugged gently at the tails of his sport coat from behind.

"Remember, dear: Marcello Mastroianni."

"Huh? Oh, yeah. Just a couple hits, okay?"

He dived in there with the subtlety and grace of a bull elephant in rut. Marty smiled at him. I looked over to the corner of the immense living room of Bud Chesterton's suite on the sixth floor of Boston's Ritz Carlton. He and Mary were talking low and close together in front of the roaring, snapping wood fire. She sure had done a turnabout regarding him. Maybe you could slip a piece of tissue paper between them. If you worked real hard at it and were lucky.

It was early afternoon of the day following the hearing, the hearing that cleared Owen Lightner of any implications in the murder at the beach house and also publicly established him as Northrop Chesterton's son. Not a bad day's work for the lad, I thought. As I looked out the window at Boston Garden several stories below I felt a gentle hand touch my forearm and close around it. Charlena Eames. *The* Charlena Eames, touching Yours Truly. Maybe this whole mess was worth it. . . .

"Dr. Adams, Owen has spoken most highly of you and your lovely wife. May we sit down and chat for a minute?"

May we sit down, she says. Gee, let me think about it for an hour or so, Charlena, then I'll send you a postcard.

"Whoa! Hey, there's no hurry, doctor," she said, following me over to the love seat. Okay, I guess I was pulling her along a little. . . .

She had shucked off her courtroom clothes and now was wearing a tan silk pant suit, large gold earrings the size of bracelets, and had her hair done up in a West African–style cloth turban. We talked about her childhood in Jamaica, her early singing career there, first in all-black nightclubs, then the big-city clubs, then the ritzy white hotels, then finally, her move to America and the Big Time.

"I met Pinky in Jamaica right before I started singing in America," she said, sipping her champagne.

"*Pinky*?"

"Oh!" She laughed. "You call him Bud. Other friends call him Bud. I always called him Pinky because of his face. Europeans in the tropics usually have a bright pink face. Anyway, Pinky was very generous in helping me launch my career here; he's an influential man, and has the means as well."

"And Owen just happened?"

She nodded. "In the way children always do." Her face was buoyant; she showed not the slightest trace of remorse. It reminded me of the Edith Piaf song "Je ne regrette rien."

"Have you and, uh, Pinky always stayed in touch?"

"Oh yes. But I used this circumstance to force him out into the open. Not for my sake," she said, turning her head and looking at Lightner, who was busy serving drinks to some young friends of his, wearing a huge smile, "but for our son."

"Some people can't help but think he didn't come forward soon enough."

"And you are one of those?"

"I guess so. Of course, it would be difficult, being married."

"Yes; now that Margaret's out of the picture, I figured he would respond to pressure. But you should know, Dr. Adams, that I do owe almost everything to Pinky; I wouldn't have made it without him. Also, I never told him I was pregnant; I was his girlfriend, but because of the color issue, we never discussed marriage. A mixed marriage is not easy now; you can imagine how it was twenty years ago. I kept the pregnancy a secret, which was easy to do, since we saw each other sometimes only once or twice a year then, when I was starting out touring."

"So you went and had the baby without his knowing about it?"

"He didn't know he had a son until Owen was almost two."

"And what happened then, when he found out?"

"I thought he would be furious; that's why I was careful to keep it a secret. As soon as he saw his son he fell totally in love with him. He was angry at me for keeping him a secret, you see, but only because he discovered Owen so late."

"Has he other children?"

"None. None but that beautiful boy over there."

"When did he start living with his father?"

"It happened gradually, from the time he was about eight. Pinky and I realized that the road was no place to raise a boy. Since my career was going well, we decided that Owen would spend increasing amounts of time on the island with his father. There was still the color issue to consider. And where did this eight-year-old boy materialize from? Since Pinky had been married in the meantime—to a thorough bitch, I might add—he thought it best not to reveal Owen's true identity. So the natural thing was for Owen to assume the duties of a houseboy on Pinky's staff."

"So you gave the boy the surname Lightner."

"Exactly."

"He didn't seem to mind."

"I think it bothered him a lot, down deep. But Owen's always been such a good boy. Really and truly."

"So what happens now?" I asked, engrossed in this family saga that seemed right out of daytime television, or maybe a show like *Dallas* or *Falcon Crest*.

"First, I believe we'll see some fireworks from the direction of Margaret. If nothing else, she will be furious at being upstaged. She must always be the center of attention, you know.

Once that dies down, things will settle down into a normal routine. At least, as normal as things can be, considering."

I wished her well, and she leaned forward and kissed me on the cheek.

CLACK-szzzzzt! CLACK-szzzzt! The photographer from the *Herald American* backed off with a smirk. He'd caught us in the act, and no doubt my mug would appear in the next morning's paper. Charlena—obviously used to this stuff—showed no reaction. I figured if she could stand it I could, and watched the photographer move over across the room to take pix of Mary and Chesterton.

When the crowd began to thin out, Joe collared me and told me about the incident at 67 Marlboro Street.

"Attempted burglary. Jim Howland and his fiancée were awakened about three-thirty this morning by sounds coming from above the bedroom. Howland took a flashlight and his pistol and crept upstairs. Somebody was trying to pry open the window of Brenner's bedroom."

"And the burglar got away?"

"Yep. Fled out of there real fast. When I say out of there, I mean out of the area, not the house. He never entered the building; Howland scared him off before he could get inside."

"Well, you and Marty missed quite a show in Boston this afternoon."

"So I heard. Right out of a soap, eh?"

"It sure was," interrupted Mary. "You know, you guys, Bud Chesterton is really a neat guy."

"Oh really?" I said. "We can tell you think so, Mare, since the two of you were getting pretty cozy over there."

"He wants us to go with him to his plantation in Buff Bay."

"Us, or you?"

"Oh, whatever . . ." she said absently, looking over the buffet spread. How she loves to push my buttons. Joe and I told her about the attempted burglary at Brenner's old apartment building in Back Bay.

"Sometimes I get the feeling that George isn't dead," said

Mary. She had a grin on her face; I knew she was reminiscing about him, this on-the-edge-of-the-law guy with the Peter O'Toole eyes and the wise-guy smirk.

"Hate to disappoint you, but we made a positive ID on the body," I said.

"I know. But only by his face."

"No, Mare," said her brother. "By his fingerprints too. The prints found in Brenner's apartment match the ones on the corpse."

"Well, Doc," boomed a voice behind me, "when are you and Mary coming down to Buff Bay?" I turned to see Bud standing behind me, champagne glass in one hand, Charlena Eames in the other. The guy knew what he liked and went for it; I had to give him that much.

"How about next winter sometime?"

"Sounds good. If not before. And Joe and Marty, you're both welcome too. Joe, remember what I said about the dove shooting there. Where's Lightner—uh, I mean Owen—gone to?"

"He's in the kitchenette, opening more champagne," said his mother.

"Here I am." Lightner came walking in with a tray of full glasses. We relieved him of some of his cargo and walked over to the front window of the suite. It looked down on Boston Garden, a great view, especially considering the early-spring blossoms on many of the trees and shrubs. Too early for the famous swan boats, but the park was gorgeous. I looked over to my left and realized I was probably looking at the rooftop of George Brenner's old apartment on Marlboro Street. Either directly at it or close to it, no more than three blocks away. I asked Joe if he was too busy to walk around to the flat with me after we left this exclusive party.

"You think perhaps I didn't do my job?" His thick eyebrows were raised in a challenge.

"I'd just like to look at it," I suggested, oozing humility. If you push Joe on certain things, his Latin blood gets riled. I have also observed this unseemly tendency in his elder sibling on infrequent occasions. Like twice a week.

"I'd love to come along," said Marty. "I'm dying to see that place, after all I've heard about George."

"Me too," said the elder sibling.

So we informed our gracious hosts of our departure.

"Owen, would you please get our guests' coats?" said Chesterton.

"Yes, Father," he replied, and was off to the bedroom. Mary and Marty watched him, smiling big smiles. I have to admit I liked the sound of it.

We walked out of the Ritz under the elaborate canopy, past the elaborate doorman, and turned left on Arlington Street. The Boston Garden was to our right. The Boston Garden park, not to be confused with the Boston Garden amphitheater in the North End where the Celtics play. Hey, I know it's confusing. The whole city was designed to be confusing, and thus keep visitors to a minimum. There's a certain xenophobic tendency in New England, and in its capital city, this is how it manifests itself. But now we were walking toward the sole place in Boston that had been logically laid out: Back Bay.

Back Bay is that strip of landfill along the Charles River completed in the early 1800s when the city needed more room. They filled in the side of what was then Boston "neck" and gave the city those straight streets and gracious Georgian homes, now mostly divided up into upper-bracket condos and apartments. The cross streets are named in alphabetical fashion: Arlington, Berkeley, Clarendon, Dartmouth, Exeter, Fairfield, Gloucester, and Hereford. Brilliant! During the Regency, the Boston city fathers, in a rare fit of logic, probably sought the assistance of a city planner (no doubt of German extraction) from the Midwest. But enjoy it while you can, folks, because outside Back Bay the insanity starts again: dead ends, "rotaries," streets with changing names, streets that appear and disappear, streets that curl in upon themselves for the perverse joy of it—Boston is a labyrinth even the Minotaur couldn't fathom.

We walked past Commonwealth Avenue, and the next inter-

section was Arlington and Marlboro. Turned left, up a little
ways, and bingo, we were knocking at George's old digs.

"Gee, what a pretty doorway," said Mary, running her hands
along the lustrous enamel and looking up at the Georgian fan
window above. It's almost like—oh, hello."

"Hi. Who are you?" said Luscious Louise, Jim Howland's
fiancée.

Her name wasn't really Luscious Louise, of course; it was
simply Louise. But I thought I'd throw in the Luscious because
it fit.

"I'm Mary. His wife." She pointed at me.

"Ohhh," said Louise with a big, big smile, looking at me out
of the corners of her lovely green eyes. Deep green eyes with
strong, dark eyebrows and long lashes. She was wearing sweats.
They looked great on her, which is difficult. "I was wondering
who was lucky enough to have her mitts on that cute little
sucker—"

Mary tried to smile, but it went hard. Her lips formed a tight,
straight, severe line. The eyes bright.

So long, Louise; nice knowing you . . .

Joe, with the savvy born of years living with his sister,
stepped between the two women, created a diversion by intro-
ducing Marty, and then said: "Would you and Jim mind if we
stopped in for a second?"

"Jim's not here. Does that make any difference?"

"Some. But since we're in the area—"

"Sure! C'mon inside—"

We took a short tour of the house. I was amazed at how much
I remembered from the first visit, and also how many details I
had overlooked. My strongest impression upon returning was
that the place seemed noticeably sloppier, but had a more
relaxed ambience. We headed upstairs. Louise let us go, saying
if we wanted anything to holler.

Inside George's old bedroom—which looked exactly the same
as on my first visit—Joe walked over to the window and pointed
to the cracked putty and broken pane in the lower left corner

where the would-be burglar had attempted to break in.

"He knew the tricks, that's for sure," he said. "He criss-crossed the glass with strips of plastic tape before he broke it. Probably hit it with a small pry bar wrapped in a rag. Break a window that way and all you hear is a soft thud. No crack of glass or tinkle of broken pieces falling."

"The tape's gone," said Marty.

"Lab took it. They got two or three great fingerprints off it too."

I looked out the window. "Did you see that the sloper antenna's been cut outside?"

Joe looked out the window and saw the stiff remnants of the heavy-gauge wire sticking out from the building like half a pair of giant cat whiskers. The rest of the antenna, the end attached to the tree in back, was dangling in a curled heap. "You think he saw the antenna and was going after the radio?"

"Probably. Because why did he pick this window, rather than the one directly over the lower roof there?"

"Yeah. Either he knew the house or the antenna tipped him that there was a valuable piece of equipment in here."

"Uh-huh. But do thieves steal shortwave receivers? Aren't they more into things easier to fence, like stereos and televisions?"

"A thief with a two-hundred-a-day crack habit will steal whatever he can, Doc. *However* he can. Even in broad daylight, which is when most of your big-city burglaries now occur. But I think this guy knew something, either about the house or its occupants. Let me get Louise up here."

Louise studied the window and the broken antenna wire. "You know something? I don't think Jim noticed that cut wire. But he did mention that he's usually out of town at this time, either in Seattle at the home office, or else on a sales trip up and down the East Coast. Nobody knows his schedule better than I do, but I guess I forgot about that until he reminded me."

"So you're saying that whoever tried to break in here might have thought that the house was unoccupied?"

She nodded, biting her upper lip slightly and gazing nervously at the window. "I hope that after we're married we'll live somewhere else," she said.

Being the nice guy that I am, I was about to suggest Concord. But something made me hold back.

"Well, I think it's a local thief," said Joe. "All my experience points to that. A local thief with an expensive habit."

"So who gets this fancy radio?" asked Mary, leaning over and peering at the Grundig receiver. "I bet Charlie wants it, don't you, Charlie? Charlie never has enough toys."

"I guess Sarah will inherit it, unless we find a will that says otherwise," said Marty.

"Yeah. Or the DEA boys could claim it too," said Joe. "So Doc, I wouldn't get your hopes up."

"It's not that big a deal to me," I said, lying through my teeth. We went back downstairs and said good-bye to Louise, who promised to get in touch if she or Jim thought of anything that might prove helpful. We walked down the street to where we'd parked Mary's car, and Joe made the mistake of pointing out the bar down the street.

"*Heroes?*" said Marty. "Is that the gay bar you took Doc into, Joe? And the bar where George Brenner spent his last days?"

When he said that it was, the two women instantly decided they had to see it. *Had* to. Even the most reasoned of arguments were useless against this wish, including the obvious observation that we would hardly be welcome.

"C'mon, honey," cooed Marty. "You do have that snapshot you wanted to show the bartender there, remember?"

"Yeah, that's true enough," said Joe, his voice vague, fumbling in the inside breast pocket of his sport coat. "I guess we could just peek in. . . ."

So the die was cast. Joe held the heavy, varnished door for us as we trooped inside. The bar, noisy with the babble of patrons when we entered, fell silent in a hurry. Fifty pairs of eyes scanned us, then looked elsewhere.

"Great," I said to Mary under my breath. "Just great."

We sat in a booth near the front door. I saw Ken the bartender

walking the length of the bar in our direction, a blank look on
his face. He came over to us and nodded politely, from a distance, as we introduced our wives. A faint sheen of perspiration
was forming on his forehead and chin. *Delighted* to see us. We
did our best to ignore the hostility and maintain our noncha-
lance and dignity. Is this what black people and Hispanics must
put up with daily? I thought about this as Ken went to get four
drafts. Maybe that's one reason so many blacks are plagued with
high blood pressure.

"What's wrong, Charlie?"

"Nothing."

"You think it was a mistake to come here."

"Yep."

"Well, there's a guy at the bar waving at us. He a friend of
yours I should know about?"

She was pushing my buttons again. I had a hunch that somehow, the cause of this was Louise. I looked up and saw the man
in the gray windbreaker who looked like Kirk Douglas. What
was his name? Don; that was it. Joe fished out the envelope from
his coat and opened it. Out came four prints. He told me they
were copies; the original print was impounded as evidence, and
these were his "walking around" copies. Don came over to the
booth and pulled a bentwood chair up alongside. He straddled
it, with his forearms resting on the chair back. Joe slipped a
print over to him and he ID'd the picture immediately, remark-
ing that the T-shirt was a dead giveaway.

"Ever see the black kid who's sitting with him?" Joe asked.
Don shook his head, saying that George had come into Heroes
alone every time.

"He ever make a contact here? You know, pick up somebody
or get picked up?"

"Not that I remember, but let's get Ken over here and ask
him."

Ken confirmed the ID and, like Don, had never laid eyes on
Reggie. Likewise, he could not recollect any liaison formed in
the bar between George and another patron.

"There he is," said Joe in a low voice, looking dead at me.

"Right behind my head, Doc, third from the end at the bar. The kid with the perpetual shot and beer. Remember?"

"Yeah," I said, spotting the young man who'd been diagnosed HIV positive and, having been disowned by his family, had come to Boston to live.

"Who is he?" said Marty. "He looks awfully young to be in here."

We told her. Her face curled in sadness and rage. "Abandoned? His own mother and father *abandoned* him when they found out?"

"Oh, Jesus . . ." whispered Mary, staring at the kid. Just like that, her eyes filled up with tears.

Somebody had nudged the kid; he turned around and looked at the two women looking at him, then turned back, hunching down over his drink. I thought I saw him shiver a little. Joe drained the last of his draft beer and set the mug down a little too loud.

"Let's go, everybody."

The two of us stood up and fastened our coats. The women stayed put, frozen, their wet eyes fixed on the kid's back. Joe stared down at his wife, holding her coat. He looked at me out of the corner of his eye.

"Knew this was a bad idea . . ." he whispered.

Marty's husky voice spoke: "Joe, we just can't leave him here to drink himself to death."

"You can't save him," Joe said. His eyes were sad, and I knew why. We finally got them on their feet, wrapped in coats, and led them outside. They weren't saying much. Halfway down the block, Marty turned and went back. We all watched her walk back to Heroes and go inside. Then Mary followed her, walking more slowly, head erect, perfectly poised, except when she raised her hand up to her face now and then. And there we were, standing outside in the cold, waiting for them to come out.

We waited out there for over ten minutes. Joe was rocking up and down on his toes, his hands stuffed in his trench-coat pockets, flapping the lapels in and out, as if he were learning to fly. He always does this when he's impatient.

Finally the two better halves emerged, grim-faced. "Let's go, you guys," said Marty in her deep contralto, walking right past us in a fast clip.

"What happened?" asked Joe.

"He told us to fuck off," Mary said, wiping her eyes.

We got into the car and drove to Joe's, where we had a quiet, almost somber, supper. I can't recall what we ate; it was that grim. We went to sleep in the guest bedroom. Sometime in the middle of the night I was awakened by Mary clinging to me and shaking. I held her until the shaking and shivering subsided a bit, and felt her wet tears roll down my chest.

"It's just so . . . hard, Charlie. Life can be such a *bitch* sometimes."

"I know, babe," I said, rubbing her back.

"I mean, first we have this great thing at the courthouse, and then the party afterward where . . . where Owen gets to be Bud's son . . . it was so great. . . ."

"I know. . . ."

"And then to go into that bar and see this other kid . . . this poor *kid* who's dying all alone in a strange place and . . . and . . ."

She cried about ten or fifteen minutes, then I felt the tension leave her body.

"It's just that life is so crazy, Charlie." She sighed. "It can be so damned *pointless* sometimes."

I held her close and rubbed her back softly until she fell asleep.

TWENTY-THREE

Mary and I got up at 5:30 that next morning at Joe's. I needed to be in my office by mid-morning for a patient, and I had to go over some cases before then. Mary was in a much better frame of mind. I knew a good breakfast would help even more. She decided to surprise Joe and Marty, and pay them back for their hospitality, by making her buttermilk pancakes. These infamous flapjacks are thinner and chewier than the usual variety—almost like crepes—and are laced with a dollop or two of rum in the batter. Makes them light and aromatic.

They were a hit, especially with Joe, who's loved them for thirty years. Joe was positively chipper, and hummed to himself as he shoveled in pie-shaped portions of a tall stack of pancakes. Marty asked him what he had to be so damn happy about. I studied her face again and saw the reddish eyes and puffy cheeks. She clearly had not recovered from seeing that poor sick, angry kid in the bar.

Joe reached over and squeezed her hand.

"Steady, kid. I know how you feel about that boy. It's a damn shame, and even more so that there's not much we can do about it. But, looking on the bright side—and one must look on the bright side in my line of work, or one eventually swallows one's gun—"

"*Joey!*"

"It's true, children," he said in a serious voice, holding up a finger. "Now, as I was saying about the bright side. I think . . ."

There was a profound silence while Joe sipped scalding coffee. He was still holding up his index finger, like a lecturing professor about to make a point.

"I *think* that this business about George Brenner is winding down. In fact—and I may be going out on a limb here—I'm pretty sure it's all over."

"What do you mean, Joey?" Mary asked. "We haven't found the killer. We've got three dead guys, for crissakes: George, Reggie, and Jonathan Randolph . . . no four, including that murdered Rastafarian who was wearing the T-shirt that seems to be all the rage these days."

Clearly, his sister did not share the sanguine view.

"I admit at the outset I don't have all the answers," Joe said, taking his fork and cutting another wedge off the giant stack of dripping flapjacks, "but we now know that Owen Lightner and Bud Chesterton are in the clear, correct?"

We all nodded.

"So that simplifies things a great deal. Also, since Reggie was gunned down, and since we found the incriminating light signal in his room, it's reasonably safe to assume that he was into more than gardening at the Chesterton mansion, correct?"

We nodded again.

"So as I see it, the tale might go something like this: there was a drug ring operating out of the Chesterton house. Doc's all but proved that. No, he has in fact proved it. The primary movers in this drug ring were George Brenner and Jonathan Randolph. The connection to the Chesterton place was secured through Reggie Westley, whom Brenner met on a trip to Jamaica, probably to buy ganja, or set up a contact. He met Reggie, they fell in love, had their picture taken together at a nightclub, the whole bit—"

"And it was through Reggie that George got the key to the house," I said. "Those special Chubbs keys that can't be duplicated—"

"Right. It also explains, Doc and Mary, why Jonathan Randolph invited you down to this house for that bogus house-warming party."

"It wasn't bogus," said Mary. "It was a real party."

"It was bogus in the sense that it was put on for one reason only: to provide you as witnesses to the shooting—which was set up—and thus provide an airtight alibi for Randolph."

"You mean that if he was at home throwing a party, he'd have witnesses aplenty to clear him," I said.

Joe nodded. "But speaking of witnesses, who better than a doctor and a nurse to hear a prearranged shot, fired just as they walk by the murder scene?"

"And that's the mysterious second shot, the one Karl Pirsch is convinced was fired for their benefit," said Marty. "Kevin did say it would prove to be pivotal."

"And indeed, it has," said Joe, wiping his mouth with a napkin and refilling his coffee mug. "Now, who fired this shot? Who crouched in that chilly house, over that body that was already shot dead hours, perhaps days previously?"

"You got us going, Joey. Who?"

Her brother shrugged his massive shoulders. "Don't know. And it probably doesn't matter. The dead Jamaican might do for starters, but . . . it's almost immaterial. Because if Randolph killed his partner, George, then, sooner or later he knew he would have to kill Reggie too. And he did. Then his luck ran out and the rival gang got to him. This is the big drug ring, ladies and gentlemen. The big drug ring with the nasty habit of bumping people off the old-fashioned way: with sawed-off shotguns and slit throats."

"The bunch they call the Purple Gang?"

"Yep. It's what I think, anyway. And know what? We ain't never gonna get 'em. Know why? Because they're all back in Jamaica by now, or scattered to the far winds. But the point is this: the circle is closed now. All who *should* be dead, *are* dead. See?"

"Hmm," mused Marty. "Randolph betrays partner George and has him murdered in a way that absolutely clears himself.

He also kills Reggie before the kid can blow the whistle. And finally, the rival gang takes out him and his Jamaican hit man. Makes sense, in a gruesome way. Nobody left."

"What about the guy with the golden retriever?" Mary asked. Leave it to her to throw in the monkey wrench. . . .

"He was never part of it," I said. "That's my theory."

"I disagree," said Joe. "And Mary has a good point. I think he was part of it. I think he was the lookout. He was watching both of you after you heard the shot. To see if you were going to streak back to the house and phone the cops. If so, he would have warned the guy in the house to scoot, and fast. But you did no such thing; you went ahead with your walk, giving the gunman time to get into his sedan and get away."

"Well, I doubt that the killer was the Rastafarian we saw dead in the beach cabin," I said. "On Osterville's Wianno Beach in the middle of winter, a black guy sporting two-foot dreadlocks is hardly inconspicuous."

"What about Yellow Bird?" Marty asked. "What does that mean?"

"We're working on that," said Joe.

Mary and I got up to leave. She and Marty hugged. As we put our coats on I turned to Joe. "What you say mostly makes sense. But if Randolph went so far to put himself in the clear with that elaborate alibi, then why did he disappear so soon after George's body was discovered?"

"Who knows? For one thing, I think he expected the body to be found much sooner than it was. And then, he might have sensed the Purple Gang closing in on him and decided to split the scene."

"Yeah, but not fast enough."

"But not fast enough."

"One other thing, Joe. You said there were some pretty good prints taken from the tape that was used on the window of George's apartment."

"You mean in that burglary attempt? Yeah, we got one good thumbprint, that's all. I'm sure somebody is comparing it to those of known burglars even as we speak."

"Well, you might ask Karl if he plans to compare it with the lone print found in the red Chevy sedan that Mary saw the day of the murder."

"The car we found abandoned at the airport? Sure. I think he'll do that anyway. Why?"

"Just curious. *Arrivederla*."

ack in Concord, I didn't get through with my patient until just before noon. In the P.M. I had another patient and hospital rounds as well, but I thought I'd go home for lunch anyway. I knew Mary wasn't fully recovered from seeing that doomed kid in the bar. How did I know? Because I wasn't fully recovered, either. Having kids of your own does that to you—opens up a whole new portion of life you never knew was there. The whole cosmos changes. It's not a big change; I mean it can't be greater than sixty percent.

But it turned out Mary was in no need of cheering up. When I entered the hallway, she came running out to meet me, a big grin on her face.

"Charlie! Guess what? In the midst of all this tragedy, something good finally happened!"

"Really? Moe Abramson's been committed?"

"Charlie, listen: two days ago, Sarah Brenner got a really great surprise in the mail. C'mon, she's out in the kitchen now; she can't wait to show you—"

Mary dragged me into the kitchen on the double. There was Sarah, who came running at me, beaming. She held up a sheet of paper in front of her, almost as an offering. It was typed words on a sheet of paper. Not a letter. Some kind of note. I took it from her and read:

DEAR SARAH: I KNEW GEORGE FOR A LONG TIME. HE WASN'T A BAD GUY AND HE LOVED YOU, EVEN TO THE END. HERE IS SOMETHING HE TOLD ME TO SEND IF HE DIED.

A FRIEND

I looked up at her.

"Doc, it was a bank check for thirty thousand dollars!" squealed Sarah.

"Wow. That's a lot of walking-around money from an anonymous 'friend.'"

"I don't think it was the 'friend's' money, Charlie," Mary said. "The note says that George always loved Sarah and that he set aside some money for her in the event he died."

"Right, so you mean it was really from George, but indirectly. Just a cashier's check, Sarah? Not from an insurance company or anything?"

"No. And it cleared right away. No hassle. I put most of it in CDs. The rest is mine to do whatever I want with."

I picked up the letter again. Southworth watermark. I felt it between my fingers and ran it against my cheek. Stiff with a lot of texture. It was heavyweight bond, high cotton. Very good paper. Typed all in capital letters on one of those ultramodern electronic typewriters that prints with a daisy wheel. Joe said the crime labs were having fits with those; they leave no telltale 'signature' in the message the way old-fashioned typewriters do, such as old ribbon, misplaced striking bars, clogged *O*s and so on. Still, it was important.

"Joe should see this, Sarah."

"Why? I want to keep it . . . for obvious reasons," she said, taking it from me and hugging it to her breast. I could understand its almost religious significance to her. This letter from a close friend of George's witnessing his love for her. The love that never died. No wonder poor Sarah Brenner wanted to keep it. Trouble was, I didn't believe that note. I don't know why; I just didn't. But tell that to Sarah, wearing her first smile in months? No way.

"He'll give it back," I said. "I just think it might be helpful in finding out who killed him."

"Let it go, Charlie. Can't you see Joe's right? We'll probably never find out who killed George. That person is probably in Jamaica right now, part of a big drug gang. And what difference would it make anyway? It won't bring him back."

Sarah handed me the note. "Be sure to give it back."

"We will. What about the check? What bank was it drawn on?"

"I don't remember."

"Oh Sarah—"

"Oh wait, the Shawmut, I think. Is that the one with the Indian?"

I nodded.

"That's it, then. There was the stylized Blue Indian on the left. The amount was typed in with one of those red-ink machines with the checkered effect? Know what I mean?"

"Yes. Where did you cash it?"

"At my bank: Coolidge's in Brighton."

"And they didn't question it?"

"No, not at all. Of course I really didn't *cash* it, Doc. Like I said, I put most of it into CDs, and the rest into savings and checking accounts."

"Oh, that's right. And I assume they were CDs that Coolidge issues?"

"Sure."

"Well, that explains why it was so easy. Still, a bank check, with the proper ID, is as good as cash. Mary, I'm going to call Joe."

But he beat me to it; I picked up a ringing phone. Joe said:

"I'll be a son of bitch."

"Sometimes," I agreed.

"Doc, how'd you know?"

"That you can be a son of a bitch?"

"How'd you know about those fingerprints? Remember, you asked me to check on the two lone prints?"

"One on George's window, the other on the dash of the red rental car."

"Well, guess what? They match. So how'd you know?"

I thought about this for a second. I realized with a start that I didn't know how I knew. Just as I didn't know how I knew the note was somehow bogus—I just had a strong hunch. I told him this.

"Well, this is an interesting development. For one thing, it means that whoever killed Brenner is still alive, and in Boston. Your coked-up friend Jonathan Randolph wasn't the killer."

"Not only that, it may also explain the motive. The killer wants something George had. Let's say that that something was what he killed George for. But after the murder, he still can't lay his hands on it. It's not where he thought it was, or where George told him it was. So in desperation, he tries George's house."

"Bingo! That's what Karl and Kevin and I figured too. Trouble is, it took the three of us twenty minutes."

"I have a steel-trap mind."

"You too, eh? Must be catching."

"And I also have some news, and new evidence."

I met Joe at his office; it was after three when I finally got there.

"Guess what?" he said, flopping down in his stinky old swivel chair. "We found out that *Yellow Bird* is a bar in Port Antonio, Jamaica."

"Great," I said. "So what have you gotten from this lead?"

"Frankly, not much. We've got the local cops down there interviewing the bartender. He recognized both George and Reggie in the photo we sent down. But otherwise, not much else."

"I thought it would be more of a lead than that, Joe. Why else would the killer go to all the trouble of removing that T-shirt from George's body."

He shrugged, growling. "Hell if I know. Probably just wanted to keep the Jamaican connection out of it. Hey, you hungry? I haven't had lunch yet." We decided to hop over to the Greek's for a late lunch. We went up to the counter and ordered our coffee and subs, then sat in the back left booth. It was covered in pink vinyl. The place had that typical "sub shop" aroma: garlic, frying beef, melting cheese, and oregano. There were four of us: Joe and I, Kevin O'Hearn, and Karl Pirsch. Joe leaned over and said: "Nice going on those prints, Doc. Karl would have found the match anyway, but your suggestion was, uh, timely, to say the least."

"How did you know?" Karl asked me, unfolding his paper napkin and smoothing it out perfectly on the Formica. I answered that I wasn't sure; I simply had a hunch.

"We ran the prints through the FBI's wire in Washington," said Joe. "We came up with what looks like a make."

"It looks like a make, but it is not," said Karl.

"C'mon, Karl, Mike Blandik worked in prints and R and I for three years and he says that it—"

"Mr. Blandik left that position," snapped Pirsch. "If you will recall, Joe, the transfer was requested by Major Mahaffey. That says something about his expertise in this field, wouldn't you say?"

"Well, we almost found a make," growled Kevin.

"No," said Joe, glaring at Pirsch, "it's closer to say we found an 'almost make.' A very near match. A close enough match so that some experts would say it's a make."

"It wasn't a twelve-point make," said Pirsch. "But I admit it is very close. No doubt other experts less fussy than I might say it was a make. Remember, we hadn't much to go on: just two prints. It was hard enough matching the thumbprint from the window with the fingerprint on the car, let alone try to mate them with a set of prints that are twelve years old at the very least. So I say it's not a make."

All eyes bored into Pirsch. It didn't faze him in the slightest. He glared back at us like a Panzer tank commander storming through the Ardennes Forest, crushing all the trees in his path.

"Besides," he continued, "Mr. Roy Harris hasn't been seen by law enforcement in some time."

"Who's Roy Harris?" I asked.

"The name belonging to the prints that almost matched the

pair we have. We turned them up in Washington, of course, with the FBI."

"And you don't think this Roy Harris was the killer here in Boston?"

"No, I do not. Highly unlikely. Roy Harris was last arrested in November of 1978, in Kansas City, Missouri. The charge was mail fraud. Hardly a violent crime. I say, therefore, that the chances of him being the man we want are slim indeed. Also there is the possibility that Mr. Harris, if he remained a career criminal, is now dead."

The subs arrived and a hush fell upon the table. Joe had ordered a small (that's right: *small*) veal provolone. He bit into it, squinting in ecstasy, while marinara sauce oozed out the sides of the sandwich from the pressure. Joe's got a mouth like a car crusher anyway. Karl looked on in horror. He had been picking fastidiously at his lukewarm coleslaw while he sipped black coffee, pausing constantly to wipe his hands and mouth with the napkin. Not exactly your fun lunch. No wonder he's so thin.

"So with that, all we do is assume that the killer is alive and somewhere around here," said Joe. "Still, we've got an all-points bulletin out for Mr. Roy Harris, for what it's worth."

"Which is, I think, nothing," snapped Pirsch.

"So let's discuss the mysterious note and check that Sarah got yesterday," continued Joe. "Shit, I wish she'd come to us before she cashed it—"

"We'll have it traced down by tomorrow morning," said Kevin, "and locate the clerk who wrote it, too."

"What have you found on the note so far, Karl?" Joe asked.

Pirsch put down his fork, wiped his mouth and hands, took a small sip of coffee, cleared his throat, sat up straighter, and spoke.

"Typed on an electronic typewriter, probable make Towa. Carbon vinyl ribbon . . . nothing unusual in the residues. Paper is high-rag Southworth twenty-five-pound bond, but not the kind sold as standard typewriter paper. That's all on the paper and ink."

"Not much to go on," I said.

"The interesting part is what has been absorbed *into* the paper," he said, dabbing his mouth again. "In very minute quantities, of course."

"Well?" asked Kevin, leaning over.

"Mineral oil, lanolin, coconut oil, and fragrance. So, any guesses as to its identity?"

We thought for a few seconds.

"Suntan lotion!"

"Correct, O'Hearn," said Karl. "Which made me think of Jamaica again."

"But the envelope was postmarked from Boston," said Joe.

"Yes. But the sender could have been from anywhere. And since it is still spring up here in New England, I would bet that he is from somewhere to the south."

"You certain it's a he?"

Pirsch shook his head, a thin smile playing on his lips.

"But I didn't mention the envelope. It was standard issue. The kind sold in five-and-tens and the supermarkets. The address was typed on the same typewriter, though."

"Why the mismatch?" asked Joe. "Why the expensive paper in the cheap envelope?"

Pirsch held up his finger and cleared his throat softly. I noticed he was much less doctrinaire and formidable when he was away from his lab. Much more laid-back. Almost normal, in fact . . .

"I have a theory in that regard. It is as follows: whoever sent the message had expensive stationery. I have no idea if it was company stationery or personalized. But I do believe the message was typed on a second-page sheet, a blank sheet, of that stationery set. The other two elements, the first page of the stationery set bearing the letterhead and the envelope which no doubt bore a similar logo, or return address at least, were not used for obvious reasons."

"So, to avoid detection, he bought a box of plain-Jane envelopes and used one of those," said O'Hearn, pouring cream into his coffee mug. "That makes me think the guy wrote the message first, using whatever blank paper he could find. Which means maybe he wrote it at home or in his office."

"Yeah, that's good," mused Joe, giving his jowls a wipe and destroying two napkins in the process. "Trouble is, what home? What office?"

Silence for a minute.

"What's wrong, Doc? I know that look on your face and it tells me something's bothering you."

"You do. It is. Thing is, George Brenner had no close friends. Even his wife, who still loves him, scarcely knew him."

"So?"

"So who the hell is this old-time buddy who's sending his widow thirty grand, eh? Just out of the blue like that? I don't believe it."

Joe held up two fingers. "I keep telling you, Doc: George had two lives. Maybe even two identities." He grabbed one finger. "You and Mary and Sarah saw one of these." He grabbed the other finger. "Reggie, and all the other nancy boys in Jamaica or in Europe or Mexico or Fire Island or P-Town or wherever the hell else they went: those guys saw this one."

"And the two never crossed."

"And the two never crossed."

"Then what side did Jim Howland see?"

He grabbed finger number one. "The first one. The guy you knew as George Brenner."

"Then what side did Kenny the bartender and all those other guys in Heroes, which side did they see?"

He grabbed the second digit. "The other one, of course. The gay one. Hell, Doc, a lot of them stay in the closet. They stay there for good reasons."

"So you say there is a good friend, maybe even a lover, of George's that's sending his widow thirty grand," I said.

"Sure."

"And assuming he's a lover, he's not the least jealous or resentful that George had a wife? He's so delighted he'll send her all that money without a thought of what he could get for himself with it?"

Joe was frowning now. I saw his big brown paw heading for the stubble. "Yeah. See what you mean . . ."

"So, Doc. What is your thinking?" asked Karl.

"My feeling is the note and the check are some kind of hoax. We know the murderer is still around. He's looking for something George had. I say the murderer probably sent this to Sarah, possibly for some kind of setup."

"Well, the check's not a hoax; Sarah cashed it, for chrissakes," observed Kevin. "And what sort of setup do you mean? And where would the murderer get thirty grand?"

"Who knows?" said Joe, leaning back in exasperation. "We don't even know who the fuck he *is*."

"We know he's rich, and we know he might have important stationery," I said.

"The note says George instructed that the money be sent," said Pirsch. "That could mean that whoever sent the note was in his employ, and did this as the performance of duty, not out of friendship."

Leave it to a German to think about orders and duty, I thought. But he had a point. Maybe George Brenner was a big shot—far richer than we had even dreamed—who headed a big organization. He would have every detail spelled out in his will, to be executed by the company's faithful. If this were true, then thirty grand was simply a little toss of largess to an ex-wife he'd found amusing.

"That's not bad, Karl," said Joe. "I have to admit it."

"But he'd have to be rich. Really rich," said O'Hearn. "As rich as our friend Northrop Chesterton."

"Pinky," I said. They stared at me. "His girlfriend Charlena nicknamed him Pinky."

Joe stared back at me. "Him again! I swear, this thing's a regular Möbius strip. Jesus, when we find the right kingpin, the whole thing's gonna come together like gangbusters. I can feel it."

"What's a Möbius strip?" asked Kevin.

"It's like an endless strip, that goes around and around."

"Like a fan belt?"

"Uh . . . no. It's attached to both sides, so if you start on one side, you'll end up on the other one."

Kevin stared at him, bending a plastic straw.

"What I mean is, if a bunch of ants were walking around this endless belt? Well, if they walked far enough, soon they'd be on the other side of the belt too, then back to the first side again. Kinda like going through a wall. A whole new dimension?"

Kevin continued to stare at him. He used up the first plastic straw and grabbed another one.

"Okay, put it this way. You ever see one of those Escher prints? No? Well, anyway, on one of 'em he has these ants marching along this Möbius strip, and—"

"Joe, maybe we better go now."

"Hang on, Doc. I was just—"

"I don't wanna know that bad, Joe. I don't give a rat's ass what a Möbius strip is."

Karl Pirsch looked at his watch. "*Ach du lieber!* It's after four!"

That did it; we got up and left.

TWENTY-FIVE

Joe and I left the Greek's and headed straight for his place. The sky was clouding over and looking heavy and dark. As soon as we stepped over the threshold Joe poured me a dose of Johnny Walker and told me to cheer up. I walked out onto the terrace and looked in the coop. No birds. Good. Looked up at the ever-darkening sky and went back inside.

Joe was in his kitchen, standing between the twenty-foot-long, solid end-grain Ash butcher-block counter and the brushed stainless-steel Jenn-Air range. He had wrapped himself in a red, white, and green apron. Out of the Bose speakers came opera. It was Italian, but not *Aïda*. Maybe *La Traviata* or something. For me, a little opera goes a long way. Joe was placing a huge cast-iron pot on the stove. It was a Dutch oven, the biggest made anywhere, I'm sure. Its inside surface was black, slick, and smooth. When you stuck your head inside and sniffed, you smelled garlic.

"Gonna make a batch of meat sauce," he said, holding a bottle of Colavita extra-virgin olive oil over the pot and letting it gurgle a long, long time. He pours olive oil the way he pours booze.

I helped him scalp and crush two bulbs of garlic. That's *bulbs*, not cloves. The Brindellis measure garlic in bulbs. Then we chopped up four big onions and set them into the hot oil with the garlic. This is my favorite aroma in the world (except, of course, for stables and puppy breath, which have always been way up there). Smelling that big pot, I got an instant saliva rush.

Listening to the kettle sizzle and pop, I poured another Johnny Walker and thought about Joe's optimistic appraisal of the situation: his conviction that this case had burned itself out, dead as a brushfire blown by the wind back into its own dark path.

I wasn't so optimistic. One reason is that I'm a born pessimist. I'm glad; it's better to be a pessimist. For one thing, we're generally prepared. Optimists, riding on a smile and a shoe-shine (often not much else), find themselves in the soup a lot of the time. Of this I am convinced: Nothing gets more people into deeper shit quicker than blind optimism. The most horrific recent example is Vietnam.

"That's another thing," I said, snipping the parsley bunch Joe had handed to me. "The killer tried to burglarize George's house. He probably knew the house because he knew George. At least it looks that way. So if he knew the house, why did he try that bedroom window instead of the two bigger ones that were lower? They were all equally hidden from the street."

"I dunno. But I bet he had a pretty good reason. This guy seems like a pro."

He took two huge lengths of sweet Italian sausage and drew a knife along the casing. This he stripped off, pulling the sausage meat with his fingertips and forming it into little balls, which he dropped into the hot oil.

"Who do you think sent Sarah the check?" I asked. "Level with me."

"I'll level with you: I don't have the faintest clue. But either it's as Karl says, and George Brenner commanded a big establishment, or else it's a setup from the Purple Gang. They sent her the thirty grand—which is a drop in the bucket to them. Next, they could send her a series of similar notes, each one gaining more and more of her confidence. Maybe they would even include some password in these letters, telling her, you know, to disregard any other notes not having this password."

"And?"

"And so eventually she will get one telling her, under utmost secrecy, to go alone to a certain place at a certain time to get the rest of George's posthumous gift."

"And she'll go there, not telling a soul," I said in almost a whisper.

"Right, and then they'll kill her."

"But why?"

"Because that's how those third-world people think, Doc. They kill not only the rival, but his family too. Kids or no kids. That's just the way it's done nowadays. Stinky, huh? Take that ground chuck and add it now, okay? That pork's been in there enough to get a good head start—"

I took the five pounds of ground chuck from the refrigerator and slid it into the mixture. Joe used a heavy steel spatula to cut it into pieces and stir it in. The kitchen was beginning to smell very good now.

"So you agree the note and the check are suspect?"

"Yeah. But they could be genuine too. My advice to Sarah Brenner would be to spend the money fast and be very cautious. Since you'll no doubt see her before I do, that's what I'd tell her. Doc, some of the tomatoes that you and Mary grew in Concord are in that upper cabinet. Can you get out three jars?"

I did this, and when the meat turned from pink to light gray, Joe popped open the canned tomatoes, put them briefly though the food processor, and dumped them in. Meanwhile, I had put lots of basil, oregano, rosemary, and fennel seed into his antique pharmacist's mortar, and mashed them up with a pestle the size of a small baseball bat.

"Jeez, that aroma . . ." mused Joe. "Time to open some red—"

He uncorked some Valpolicella while I opened four mason jars of homemade tomato sauce.

"So you think that other than the possible danger to Sarah, this case is closed?" I asked.

"I wouldn't tell that to Major Mahaffey, but yeah, I think that's a fair assessment."

"I don't."

"So? Hey, you got any more of those nasty cigars? If so, let's smoke 'em now, while Marty's away."

I went into Joe's study where I'd left my cigar case, slipped out two of those black torpedoes, and returned to the kitchen. Joe was grating Parmesan cheese into the pot. The mixture had thickened, and the bubbles burst out of the top, making sounds like a carpet beater hitting a wet rug. Looked like one of those lava fields in Hawaii. Sure smelled better, though. Joe finished with the cheese, then added the last of the tomato sauce. He leaned wearily up against the kitchen wall, looking at his masterpiece.

"When will this be ready?" I asked.

"In two days. You remember that, don't you? Let it simmer for another two hours over real low heat. I'm preheating the oven now at four-fifty. When it's done simmering, I'll turn off the oven and slide the covered pot in there overnight. Then let it stand all day tomorrow and tomorrow night."

"And then?"

"And then we'll have the world's best sauce Bolognese, and freeze the rest. Hey, I gotta go take a leak. Can you cut that cigar for me?"

I cut both cigars, putting Joe's in the ashtray. I lighted mine and gazed out the big glass doors at the falling light—*l'heure bleue*, that romantic dusk time so loved by the French. But then my reverie was shattered, and fear took its place.

There, on the white kitchen wall inches from my face, was a huge bloody handprint. Joe had cut himself.

"Hey, Joe!" I called, "you okay?"

I got a muffled reply to the effect that he'd performed this particular bodily function a million times in his life and didn't need any help. But it was sweet of me to ask.

I looked at the handprint again. Tomato sauce; I should have spotted it instantly. What made me think of blood? I knew: this whole bloody business of two former acquaintances turning up with cut throats or bullets in them, that's what.

"Look what you left here on the wall, Joe. That's why I asked if you were okay."

"Well, I'm fine," he said, "just sloppy. Hey, where do you want to go eat tonight?" He got a paper towel, wet it under the faucet, and swiped the handprint away in a flash. "I kinda feel like Italian tonight."

"You kinda look like Italian tonight. Yeah, I'm up for it. Joe Tecce's?"

"Let's try the Charles; it's closer and quieter. I need a nice quiet dinner to soothe my friggin' nerves."

He approached the simmering caldron of meat sauce, humming along with the aria coming over the speakers high on the walls. He lifted the lid and poured the bottle of red he'd opened into it, stirring slowly, sniffing and sighing. Then he lighted his cigar, poured booze, and followed me into the study.

I sat down in a Queen Anne chair that was covered in red Chinese silk and cost a thousand dollars. It was almost too pretty to sit on. During the years Joe was living alone, he had no family except for Mary and me. So he spent his spare time and money on the apartment. The opera disc finished, and Joe turned on WBUR. A string quartet moaned and chirped pleasantly. Then thunder rolled overhead, and soon rain thumped on the windows. I dozed.

But only by his face.

I woke up and blinked at the illuminated gun cabinet. French Circassian walnut, blued steel, gold inlays, and chromed receivers stared back at me.

But only by his face. Who had said that? What was this voice in my head? *If you build it, he will come.* . . . Oh, get off it, Adams. You're exhausted and wrought up over all this. You finally calm down and go over to Joe's—just the two of you, no pressure—and you have two drinks and bingo! You're out.

"But only by his face."

"Huh? Oh, you're awake. I was asleep too, for a while. Bushed, aren't we? What's that you just said?"

"But only by his face."

"What's it mean?"

"I just now remembered; it was driving me crazy. Mary said it. I remember now what she was talking about; she was describing how we identified the body found in the Chesterton mansion as George Brenner."

"Uh-huh. And then you said, if I recall, that we'd identified him, and so did his wife, Sarah. And that should be proof enough."

"Right! And then Mary said, yes, we did ID the body as George, but *only by his face*."

"Right. And then, to settle the matter, I reminded her that we also ID'd the victim as George by the fingerprints in George's own house."

"Oh, that's right," I said.

"And know what else? Remember when you and I first went upstairs with Howland? There was a hairbrush on George's dresser. Well, we took samples of that hair and it matched perfectly with that on the corpse. So you want to go to the Charles now? It's almost six-thirty."

"Hadn't we better call Concord? See what the women are up to? They're probably missing the hell out of us. Probably worried stiff."

"I already called, just a few minutes before you woke up. Guess what? You're wrong, pal. They're not missing us one bit. In fact one of the three—I won't mention her name—even had the brilliant and tasteful idea of driving up to the Golden Banana on Route One and seeing the Chippendales. Know who they are? The hunky guys in tuxedos who strip for female audiences?"

I cleared my throat and placed my fingertips gently together in the manner of Mr. Sherlock Holmes, the world's foremost consulting detective.

"And which of the three, pray tell, might she be?"

"Hint: we're both related to her."

"That's hardly a surprise. Did they like it?"

"That's just it; they didn't go."

"Mary was bluffing, Joe. To get to us. I knew it."

"Yeah. But also, they said Sarah's acting weird. Marty told

me Mary doesn't like the way she's acting one bit. Says she's afraid Sarah's on the edge of a breakdown, or in it already."

"Why now? You'd think she's been through the worst of it."

"Apparently she's got herself convinced that it was George himself who sent her that check. From beyond the grave, or something. She claims she knows he's not dead."

"See? I told you there was something wrong with that note, Joe: a ghost wrote it."

As I said this the image of a red handprint flashed in my mind. Then I saw Joe's big brown hand holding the wet paper towel, swishing it back and forth, washing off his own handprint. That's when it came together, and I knew that Sarah was right.

I got up, stretched, and walked out into the hallway. Joe was at the front closet, getting out our trench coats.

"George Brenner is alive," I said as I took my coat.

"What?"

"Sarah's hunch is right: George sent her that check himself."

"Oh, bullshit."

"Know what else? He's also the killer."

"Don't do this to me, Doc. Not now. Not before dinner."

"Speaking of which: I'm having the Flounder Tuscany. What about you?"

TWENTY-SIX

Twenty-four hours later I was standing in front of the fireplace in my study in Concord, looking down into the flames, and sometimes out the window to watch the heaviest rain I'd seen since leaving the Midwest.

Behind me, sitting in chairs and couches around the room, were Mary, Marty, Joe, Kevin O'Hearn, and Karl Pirsch. Sarah Brenner was conspicuous by her absence. Moe was with her over in his office at the Concord Professional Building, just a door down from my office. A flash, then a roll of thunder that ran away and away and away.

It was a dark and stormy night. I turned to face them and said: "I suppose you're wondering why I called you all here tonight. . . ."

"Cut the shit, Charlie," said a familiar voice. "We wanna know all about it. So spill."

I told them. The two women held their hands to their mouths and breathed in fast, going "*hhhhUHHHH!*"

Karl and Joe and Kevin sat there and didn't move a muscle. They looked dumber than Larry, Curly, and Moe. Reason: they all knew because Joe and I had been down at Ten Ten all day, checking out the Adams hypothesis. After we scrutinized the evidence, it seemed to be holding up pretty well.

"If George isn't dead, Charlie, then who was that we identified . . . that Sarah identified?"

"His name was Wendel Haynes," said Joe, reading from a slip of paper he'd pulled from his coat. "He was a remittance man who lived in Jamaica. He happened to look a lot like George Brenner. Enough to pass for his twin brother."

"What's a remittance man?" asked Mary.

"It's a disgraced son or heir who is shipped off to a foreign land and paid an allowance by his rich relatives to never come back," I said. "It seems that poor Wendel Haynes, a known homosexual and heavy drinker, was a remittance man of the first order."

"How did you guys find all this out?" asked Marty.

"Simple," Joe grunted. "So simple it's embarrassing. We called Jamaica and asked questions. Once we started figuring the victim was a double, then things fell into place quickly. Our third or fourth phone call got us to the town of Port Antonio. Talking to the authorities in this little burg, we hit the bull's-eye. Somehow, somewhere, George Brenner ran into this near double, Wendel Haynes. Probably in Jamaica, since that's where Haynes, born in Poole-Dorset, England, was exiled to."

"What had he done that was so bad?" asked Marty. "Was he too open about his homosexuality?"

"What we got was, he was brought up on charges of molesting children. Whether it's true or not, he was definitely told to stay away from his family. You can imagine the effect this kind of thing would have on a person—"

"His parents used their influence and money to get him off lightly," I added, "with the payback being he never showed his face in England again. This explains why I thought George was British after I completed the forensic work: Haynes had a classic British mouth."

"So George met Wendel in Jamaica—" said Mary, tapping her foot. "They fall in love, or what?"

"Nope," said her brother, wagging his head slowly. "Because, as you and Doc suspected, George was not gay. Not in the slightest. Any interest he showed in Wendel was strictly selfish: to kill him and use him as proof that George Brenner was *dead*. And then the Purple Gang, other drug lords, and God knows who else, could quit chasing him."

"How did they end up in Chesterton's beach house in the dead of winter?" asked Marty.

Joe turned and looked at his wife. "The connection was Reggie. You remember that when Bud Chesterton first discussed Reggie with us, before we'd even laid eyes on him, he told us that Reggie was very depressed because he and his boyfriend had split. Remember that? Well, that boyfriend was Wendel Haynes."

"Who told you all this?" asked Mary.

"The bartender at the Yellow Bird in Port Antonio."

"You said he didn't tell you diddly-squat, Charlie. Isn't that right, Marty?" Marty nodded in agreement.

"That guy didn't, it's true," said Joe. "The first bartender we called was the night guy. But turns out it was the guy on the day shift, when the place wasn't jammed, that really got to know Wendel and his depressing life."

"So how did they get to the beach house in January?"

"We've been wondering too," I said. "We think Wendel got the Chubbs key from Reggie. The most likely reason is the drug drop at the house. My theory is that Wendel went to the house in the winter as a matter of routine. Perhaps it was his job to signal the drops when Reggie was staying on Chesterton's plantation, and safe with an airtight alibi."

"Yes, I think that fits pretty well," said Marty.

"So somehow George tagged up with Wendel and accompanied him to the house, where he shot him," said Joe. "But Doc's theory is especially good, Mary, because it explains the second shot you guys heard—the one fired through the mattress. See, George killed Wendel and removed the telltale black T-shirt with *Yellow Bird* on the front. He couldn't leave it on the corpse; it would give police the connection to Wendel's true identity."

"He shot this guy Wendel when we were standing outside, Charlie?"

"No; he shot him before we got there. I'm sure he checked the beach before he drew out the revolver; he killed Wendel in secrecy. He then had time to remove Wendel's jacket and the incriminating T-shirt, put on the beige dress shirt, cut the fake bullet hole in it, and so on."

"When do we come in?" asked Mary.

"Right about now," said Joe. "Doc and I figure that within an hour or two of Wendel Haynes's murder, George and Jonathan Randolph got in touch by phone. We're not sure who called whom, but you can bet they talked and George was alerted that you and Doc were soon to depart for your little beach walk. In fact, to give himself enough lead time, he even went over to the telescope at the far end of the bedroom and peered through it until he saw you coming."

"And so he fires a second shot to *alert* us, Joey? Because he *knows* us, for crying out loud? I don't—"

"Listen, Mary," said Joe. "We've assumed from the start that the murderer knew you, since you both knew the victim and since he obviously fired the shot knowing you were right outside. Doc finally put the two together and figured out the only logical answer: the victim and murderer were the *same guy*. Figuratively speaking, of course . . ."

Mary half closed her eyes and said: "He fired a second shot so Charlie and I would stop and notice. Then later, we could ID the body. . . ."

"Right! Which is exactly what you did. Down to the button. Hey, I'd like to meet this guy. George Brenner, you are one slick dude."

Mary wasn't sold; she was sitting on the couch, leaning back with her eyes still half-shut and her arms crossed. Body language for refusal. "So what about the fingerprints, Joey? The ones in George's house matched the ones on the guy in the drawer. You told Charlie that yourself just the other day. And I know you can't fake fingerprints."

"What set this whole thing off was when Doc saw me wiping down the kitchen wall after I'd smudged a handprint of tomato sauce on it. . . . Doc, you tell 'em."

"Seeing Joe wash away one of his own fingerprints made me think of the real reason George Brenner had his apartment professionally cleaned a month before he died. It was to erase his fingerprints entirely from the place. Early on, he probably wiped down all his personal possessions, and those in the kitchen. Perhaps he took to wearing light cotton gloves when he stayed there alone. Finally, he called in a gang of cleaners to scrub the whole place inside out, top to bottom. The cleaners wrapped the job up completely. All George had to do next was invite Wendel up for a visit, saying he'd loan him the apartment for a week."

"And so," said Marty in her throaty, steady voice, "Wendel Haynes spent that week installing his fingerprints all over the apartment."

"Yep," said Joe, "He even left his hair on George's clean hairbrush . . . that is, when he wasn't down at Heroes bar swilling rum drinks and showing off his T-shirt to Kenny and the guys."

"I must say," I said, "that it wasn't just Joe's swiping his print off the wall that set me thinking. One thing, Karl, a big thing, was your observation of the mysterious second shot. Kevin, you said yourself it would prove pivotal, and it did."

"Uh-huh, I did. And you wanna know why? Because I'm brilliant, that's what," he said over his glass of malt. "One of these days I might even be ready for the Möbius strip."

"But the main thing that kept gnawing at me the whole time was the notion of the two Georges. It just didn't seem plausible. I mean, Mary and I knew the guy long enough to get a sense of him. One of the Georges fit this pattern exactly: the guy Jim Howland described as his roommate. More especially, the way Louise Howland-to-be described him."

"Oh Louise, huh?" came a voice. Wonder whose?

"I'm surprised she's bright enough to remember," continued Mary. "Of course, since it involved a *man* . . ."

"Actually, Mary, she struck me as very bright."

There it was: a harmless little comment. A mere observation to clear up a minor misconception regarding Ms. Louise's intelligence. And since it is sexist to assume, as Mary did, that an attractive—okay, let's tell the truth: *knockout*—woman must be stupid, then the clarification is certainly more than justified. Right? Well intended and totally innocent, right?

Wrong. Mary wheeled her gaze on me like the Fourth Armored Division. "Oh, *is* she now?" she said in a quick, quiet voice. Staccato and full of passion, like a distant machine gun. She turned and sat down fast. The ax would fall. Mary would not forget this, and sooner or later—probably later to prolong the agonizing wait—Yours Truly was going to get it.

I could almost hear the cement mixer, grinding away. . . .

"What he means is, Mary . . . is that, uh . . ." said Joe, trying to come to my rescue. Just then there came a peal of chimes; someone was at the front door.

"Gee, I wonder who that could be on a night like this?" I said. "Who could possibly be out on such a night?" Not waiting for an answer, I hotfooted it out into the hall, across the long stretch of carpet, down the four stairs to the front landing, through the inner door of the front vestibule, and opened the front door.

"Take your time, why don't ya?" said an unfriendly voice. Brian Hannon came inside fast, taking off his dripping Donegal tweed hat and hitting it against his coat to knock the water off. "Jeez, raining cats and dogs out there, Doc. Who else is here? Enough cars out front for a funeral."

"Actually, the reverse of a funeral, I guess. A resurrection of sorts. Seems that George Brenner didn't die."

"The friend of yours? Whose body you personally ID'd? C'mon!"

I told him as we walked back to the living room. Everybody in there knew him except Karl Pirsch. Brian listened to the story again, the arguments against it, the evidence for it, and so on, before he said: "Trouble is, you're never going to find the guy. A guy that smart, how the hell do you ever expect to nail him?"

"I don't know. Yet," said Joe, leaning over from his seat on the sofa. "But we will. Northrop Chesterton and company are too tied up in this for Bernie Kirk and his guys to rest. If they can put a dent in it, they will. Even if we fail to."

"Where will you start looking for him?" Brian asked.

"I'm not sure. Probably wait till the DEA or organized-crime unit gives us a tip. Yeah, the guy *is* smart. He's at least a jump ahead of us. *So far . . .*"

"But," intoned Kevin from over his glass of Jameson's, "sooner or later he'll screw up."

"Well, I wouldn't hold my breath," said Brian. "Maybe the best thing is to figure out how to get him on his next drug-buying trip."

"Or maybe at a ham-radio convention or something," said Mary, getting up and heading for the kitchen, saying she was going to make coffee. "The way you guys have been at the whiskey, you're going to need some," she said. Marty followed her. The little gathering broke up at 11:30. Mary talked Marty and Joe into spending the night. Karl and Kevin left in Karl's old diesel Mercedes. I was glad Karl was driving; Kevin sure can put away the booze.

An hour or so later, after we'd cleaned up and bid good night to Joe and Marty as they entered the guest room, I pulled up the covers and snuggled down next to Mary, flank against flank. She snuggled over and put her arm over my chest. Kissed me. I remained frozen. She kissed me again.

"What's wrong, Charlie? Not in the mood?"

"Not that; I was just waiting for the other shoe to drop, so to speak."

"What shoe?"

"Remember, when I was talking about Louise? Jim Howland's fiancée?"

"Oh. *That.*"

"Well, I guess I'm glad it wasn't really a big thing. I see you've forgotten about it."

"So I had. Until now. Thanks for reminding me."

You absolutely, positively cannot win in these things; whichever path you choose turns out to be the wrong one. She said nothing for a second or two, then told me that she'd called Sarah Brenner and told her the news.

"When? You were with me all evening."

"No. Remember we went into the kitchen to make coffee? We called her and told her everything."

"I thought she was with Moe."

"She was home, in her apartment in Brighton. Don't forget, it was after ten."

"I wish you hadn't done that, Mary," I groaned, turning around and resting my cheek against the cool pillow. "You should have at least told us first. We come and tell you this in strict confidence, and you go and—"

"Well, shit, Charlie! Whose business is it if not Sarah's?"

"I know. But suppose he's not alive?"

"What? You and Joey spent the evening convincing us he *is*."

"I . . . I think that's the case. But even if he is alive, he's in danger. He's in danger from fellow criminals on one side and the cops on the other. It's unlikely he'll ever surface again, so it's just painful that you—"

"Dammit, Charlie, if he's really alive, she has a right to know. If anybody does, *she* does!"

"First thing tomorrow, Joe and I are going to track down the guy at Shawmut Bank who wrote that cashier's check George sent to Sarah. That should put us on the track."

"I think my idea is better," she said. "Follow the shortwave-radio thing."

"Yeah, but that's so iffy. How do we know where the next ham-radio convention's going to be? And another thing: how do we know he's still interested in DXing?"

"What's DXing?"

"Long-range listening to foreign countries. It's what most fans like to do, including me and George."

"Well, I say George is still interested. If your thinking is right, Charlie, it was George who tried to break into his own apartment, right?"

I nodded.

"Okay: you asked a while ago why the burglar chose that upper bedroom window when the others low down would do. You said they were both invisible from the alley. I say George picked that window because that's where the radio was. He wanted it back. Didn't you say those Gremlins were expensive?"

"You mean Grundig radios? Yes, they cost a grand."

"Well, maybe he was trying to steal back his radio."

I sat up in bed. Looked over at her.

"And didn't you say that the antenna wire was cut?" she added.

I kept looking at her. Genius and beauty all in one.

"So what I was also thinking, Charlie, is that if he couldn't get his old radio back, then he'd buy a new one, right?"

I nodded in silence.

"Well, I've never seen those radios for sale in a store. Have you?"

"No; you have to buy them from special suppliers and mail-order houses."

"Okay, so I'm thinking on the chance George tries to buy another Gremlin—"

"Grundig."

"Grundig, we could get Joe to contact these special dealers and ask for a list of the people and the places where they'd sent these high-ticket items, and then you'd have a start on where to look for him."

I kissed her on the back of the neck. "Incredible. A great idea. But I don't think we should tell Joe or Marty about it just now."

"Why not?"

"Because you've got Sarah involved now, and I want to talk to her next, before we say or do anything else, okay?"

"Fine. I won't tell a soul about my brilliant idea."

"It is brilliant. No question about it."

"Pretty smart, eh?"

"As I said, Mare, incredible."

"But not as smart as Louise whazitz," she said, kicking the backs of her heels into my legs as if spurring a horse.

"Not quite. And not as young or sexy, either. But hey! You're still okay in my book, babe."

There! That would get her. I closed my eyes and pretended to sleep. All was quiet on her side of the bed. That meant she was finally mature enough to accept an occasional barb without craving instant revenge. It also meant that maybe she wouldn't be so free with her own barbs from now on. I was truly proud of her progress in this regard. Feeling relieved and happy, I fell asleep.

jumped out of bed, screaming. Somebody had set me on fire.

No, wait, I stopped at the foot of the bed and tried to wake up. I was wet and cold. Somebody had dunked me in ice water. Now, who could have done that? I was just figuring out who'd be low-down enough to pull a sneak attack on a sleeping person when she flew out the door and downstairs. I know that laugh anywhere.

I met Joe in the hallway. He was gaping at my soaked and shivering body.

"Holy shit, Doc! I've heard of wet dreams, but *this*—"

"Can you believe it? She threw a whole bucket of ice water on me when I was asleep in the middle of the night. You believe it?"

"Mary? Oh yeah, I believe it. Remember what happened to me when I hid her Bobby Rydell record? I believe it instantly. But I also believe you did something to piss her off."

"A harmless little comment," I said, going into the john and grabbing a towel.

"I didn't say it had to be a *big* thing. . . ."

"Where is she? She leave the house or what?"

He peered out the bathroom window that overlooks the back of the house. "I think she's out in the cabin, Doc. And if I were you, I'd leave it alone. At least you know it's over now. She's gotten rid of it. Better that way than having her hold it inside and letting it ferment. *Whew!*"

"Whose side are you on, anyway?" I asked.

"Hers. Don't forget, she's my sister."

He stood there in the dark hallway, silent for a few seconds.

"Always remember two things they used to say about us, Doc. One: a family member's a family member. And two: don't ever mess with anybody from south of Naples. See you tomorrow, guy."

He lurched off to bed. I turned off the bathroom light and leaned into the open window, peering down into the darkness. I could see a light coming from the cabin window out in back. Then it went out, and I heard a window slide up.

"Good night, Charleeeey!"

Before I could think of a nasty rejoinder, the window slammed down. Then all I could hear were the spring peepers.

I knocked at the cabin door. It was 7:30 the next morning; I had an appointment with my first patient in an hour; I had not slept well on Mary's vacant side of the bed; and I was generally not in a good mood. However, considering Mary's astute suggestion about the radio the previous evening (before the fireworks), I was willing to make peace. I carried the olive branch in one hand, as they say.

"Go away."

"Mary, open up."

"Go away and leave us alone."

"Us? Who's us?"

"Haven't had time to catch his name . . ."

"Mary, c'mon; I've got to talk with you before I leave."

"Tell me through the door."

"Get in touch with Sarah and invite her over for tonight. We'll discuss how we want to handle this thing. Remember: don't tell Joe and Marty anything yet."

"Where are you going?"

"I'm going inside to have coffee and breakfast. Then I'm

going to work. Are you sorry about last night?"

"Nope."

"Okay, but don't say I didn't try," I said. In my other hand, the one not holding the olive branch, I had my revenge. My own version of fireworks. I silently pushed a carpenter's awl into the log side of the cabin and stretched the piece of monofilament line across the doorway a foot above the threshold. I pushed a second awl in on the other side to hold it in place, and then fastened a small smoke bomb "popper" to the line, right at the trigger assembly, just the way Laitis Roantis had shown me. Totally harmless, but it should wake her up. Teach her that any untoward action on her part would elicit an immediate reaction from my quarter. That's the way the British and Israelis have learned to deal with terrorists. So be it.

"I should be back here between four and five, Mary. See if you can't have Sarah here by then."

Then I went off to work. All morning long, as I studied X rays, extracted third molars and other problem teeth, made a mock-up for a mandibular resection the following week, and so on, I expected at any minute a frantic and seething phone call from Mary, full of bile and ill humor, deriding me for my little stunt with the popper. But none came.

I returned home to see Sarah's cream-yellow Chevy parked in the turnaround next to Mary's Audi. Inside, the two women were sipping sherry and chatting in Mary's workshop, or "atelier," as she calls it. Mary was wearing a coarse canvas apron over jeans and a sweater. The apron was covered with brownish-gray smudges of potter's clay and streaks of old dried glaze. Her hair was tied up in a blue bandanna. Her work clothes. She looked good, though. Usually does, and that's a fact. I was somewhat surprised that she was showing no aftereffects of the smoke bomb. Usually things like that really upset her. Sarah came up and hugged me, whispered urgently in my ear.

"Oh Doc, is it really true? You think it's really true? I'm so scared about this thing. I . . . I don't know why."

I sat down next to her. "I think it's probably true, Sarah. Probably, but not definitely. And even if it is, there's no guarantee of George's well-being . . . or of finding him."

"If it's so uncertain, then why are you against telling Joe my radio idea?" asked Mary, flexing and unflexing her brown hands and watching the dried clay come off in powder and tiny light flakes.

"Because if Joe thinks about the radio trace, he'll put it into action, involving the bureaucracies of the state police, the FBI, Bernie Kirk and his henchmen at the DA's office, and everybody else in law enforcement east of the Mississippi. And maybe west of it."

Sarah looked down at the floor and said softly: "And what if we find him, Doc? What then?"

I shrugged. "We'll play that by ear, I guess. But we always have to remember that no matter how fond we were of the George Brenner we knew, he's killed a man. Killed him in cold blood to cover his disappearance. We can never forget that."

"No, he didn't," said Sarah. "I knew him that well. George wasn't mean or violent."

Mary sighed. "I know how you feel, hon. But he's got a point; we've got to be careful. Do you think he'd harm us, Charlie?"

I shrugged again. "I'm going to talk to Laitis in the next day or two, see what he says about all this. We may want to take him along."

"Along where?" asked Sarah.

"To wherever George is hiding out, of course."

"How are you going to find that out if the police can't?" she persisted.

"I've got a plan. It's got maybe a fifty-fifty chance of working. If and when I find out anything, I'll let you know. Meantime, keep this to yourselves, okay?"

"Fine, Charlie," said Mary, jumping down off the worktable where she had been sitting. She took off the apron and bandanna and smoothed her hair down with her hands. "Sarah and I are going shopping. She wants to spend some of that money George sent her. You *do* think he's the one that sent the check, don't you?"

"Either that, or had someone else do it. Joe's looking into that;

we should know something by tomorrow, maybe earlier."

The women left then, taking Sarah's car. I walked from the workroom and into the kitchen, where I ground some beans and set the coffeemaker in motion. Then I went into my study and flicked on the big brass student lamp with the green glass shade, reached into one of my file drawers, and drew out a stack of magazines and catalogs dealing with shortwave radios. There were frequency directories, back issues of *Monitoring Times* and the *World Radio and TV Handbook,* and several catalogs. These were what I was after. Soon I had the names and locations of the major supply houses in the East. There were only four big ones:

> Gilfer Shortwave, Park Ridge, NJ
> Electronic Equipment Bank, Vienna, VA
> Grove Electronics, Brasstown, NC
> Universal Shortwave Radio, Reynoldsburg, OH

Looking through these catalogs, I noticed that Grove did not carry Grundig, so that let them out. Of the remaining three, I started with the one in Ohio, figuring that I would try my rather unlikely story on the place least likely for George to have picked. My story was roughly this: I had ordered a Grundig Satellit 650 almost three weeks ago and it had not arrived yet. I did my best to sound annoyed and concerned, but not hostile enough to put the clerk off.

"And what is your name, sir?" he asked.

"Harris. Roy Harris."

Over the phone I heard the faint clicking and tapping of computer keys. It went on for a while.

"Sir, I'm sorry, but I can't seem to find your name in our computer. Are you sure you ordered the Grundig from us?"

"Actually, now that you mention it, I'm not sure. My secretary handled the transaction. I barely even remember signing the damn check, know what I mean?"

"Yes, sir. Have you asked her for details about the order?"

"That's the problem. See, she's on vacation in Europe with

her new husband and I don't know how to get in touch with her. I'm just hoping if there was a screw-up, that my radio isn't lying around in a warehouse somewhere, or that somebody's pilfered it, you know?"

"That's extremely unlikely. We ship UPS, and they're usually reliable."

"But what you're saying, since my name isn't in your computer as having placed the order, that maybe she ordered from another place."

"That's correct."

I thanked him and hung up. Roy Harris was, of course, the name that Karl Pirsch had found when searching the two errant fingerprints: the one in the red Chevy rental car and its mate found on the bedroom window of George's apartment. He personally didn't think the prints were a match, but it was very close. Other people thought it was a make. I knew it was a long shot, but it was all I had. If this name failed to turn up anything, then I'd go to Joe with Mary's idea and have him use the office at Ten Ten to officially contact the suppliers and request customer orders for all Grundig 650s shipped within the past month. I knew there wouldn't be that many. Then we'd go down all the lists and check the names one by one. And that, in turn, assumed that George had indeed ordered another radio. For now, I was trying my long-shot hunch.

The next place was Gilfer, in New Jersey. I expected this to be the one since it's located in the Northeast. But alas, they, like Universal, did not have Roy Harris's name in their computer as a customer. Finally, I tried the Electronic Equipment Bank, referred to as "EEB," located on the outskirts of Washington, D.C. I expected to strike out. Instead, I struck pay dirt.

"Why, yes, Mr. Harris, we have you down as placing your order on May second. You should have received it by now."

"Well, it hasn't arrived. You see, my secretary handled this for me and now she's in Europe. I'm wondering if she had it sent to my summer home at the beach, or—"

"Oh, here's the problem; it wasn't sent UPS. Sometimes we get a request to deliver to a post-office box, and of course UPS, being a private carrier, can't deliver there."

"I'll be a son of a gun! So that's what happened. Now if I could just find out which P.O. box we're talking about. You see, we have branch offices in—"

"I'm showing an address here. . . ."

"You are?"

"Uh-huh. Here it is. It says box number 212, Murrells Inlet, South Carolina. Does that sound right?"

"No. Sure, we've got an office there, but why did she sent it *there* I'd like to know. . . ."

"I'm sure I can't help you on that, Mr. Harris. All I know is that we sent it parcel post, heavily insured, to Murrells Inlet, to be left until called for."

"Well, it's a relief to know it's *somewhere*, at least. Thanks for your time, I appreciate it."

As I hung up the phone and wrote down the address I felt the surge of adrenaline. I love that feeling. Love it. It's what makes living at the tail end of the twentieth century bearable. I got up from my desk to fetch the road atlas when the phone rang.

"Charlie, I forgot to mention this before we left. Did you find your package from Woodcrafters Supply?"

"No. Guess what? I found out—"

"I really don't have time to talk; I think I put that package in your workshop."

"I found out where George is."

"You're kidding!"

"Don't tell Sarah yet. I've got to think about this."

"Maybe you better not get that package just yet. I've got—"

"I've gotta run; I'm going to call Laitis first, then make some plans. Bye."

I opened the road atlas to South Carolina and scanned the coastline of that pie-shaped state until I found Murrells Inlet. It appeared to be a small coastal town midway between the larger ones of Myrtle Beach to the north and Georgetown to the south. It certainly didn't seem a likely place for the suave, dapper, and urbane George Brenner to be hanging out. Of course, that's probably why he picked it. And also, he was now Roy

Harris, not George Brenner. No doubt, in his new persona, he was wearing one of those adjustable trucker hats with a "Bass Buster" logo on the front. Maybe he had a double-wide trailer home and a "bassin' machine" fiberglass skiff with pedestal seats and a fish Lok-A-Tor sonar rig. Or perhaps he'd taken up bowling, or pitching horseshoes. . . .

I grabbed another book, the *Webster's Geographical Dictionary*, to look up Murrells Inlet. Not listed. Yeah. Way to go, George; perfect hideout.

I called the Boylston Street Y and asked for Mr. Roantis. The phone person said he was giving a class in kick fighting. I left a message for him to come out to Concord for dinner, drained the last of my now lukewarm coffee, and started for the front door.

But then I remembered the package Mary mentioned. I was certain it was the German rabbeting plane I'd ordered. And she'd even been considerate enough to put it down on the workbench.

I hopped down into the basement with a light heart. I'd solved the puzzle and gotten my new plane. It was one of those all-too-rare moments when everything seemed to be going just right.

As I walked through the door to the workroom I felt a slight tug on my right leg at mid-shin. At the same instant came a loud bang and a flash that made me jump straight in the air. The room was full of red smoke. When it cleared, and I had finished coughing and my heart had almost returned to normal, I could see the package sitting where she said it would be. Bait for the trap. I coughed again. My left ear was still ringing.

Cautiously, I approached the package. Fastened to its top with tape was a note:

Dear Charlie, here's some food for thought:

"Fools never perceive when they are ill-timed or ill-placed."
—Lord Chesterfield, 1749

"Never mess with anybody from south of Naples."
—Brindelli, 1989

"All right," I muttered to myself as I trudged back upstairs to wash my eyes out. "That's the way you want it, Mare. That's the way it's gonna be. *Total war.*"

TWENTY-EIGHT

Roantis and I sat in deep leather chairs facing each other in front of the fireplace in my study. It was well into May, but the night was cold, so there was a small fire purring and lapping at our feet. Roantis gazed into it, silent. He loves fires more than anybody I've ever met. He loves them the way men who work close to the soil love them. Or warriors who fight and hide in distant lands, far from civilization, love them. Roantis is a little of both. Mostly, I think he's part caveman, a relic of the Pleistocene, like the rhino, the bison, or the musk ox.

"So if you find him down dere . . . what den?" grunted Roantis. His Lithuanian accent gets more pronounced late at night. Or when he drinks. Since both factors were now operative, I was getting a double dose.

"Talk to him."

He shook his head slowly against the soft, shiny back of the chair. He raised the whiskey glass and sipped. "Nahhhh. C'mon, Doc. You remember anyting I teach you?"

His eyes crinkled up at the corners. The hands that held the thick crystal glass had giant bulbous knuckles, red and shiny from trauma oft-repeated. The eyes gray and bright. Sometimes a bit blue, sometimes greenish, depending on the light, or the circumstance, or the state of his dubious karma, or God knows what.

"Slip under his wire before he knows what's going on," I said in a monotone. I wasn't buying any of this stuff. For him, maybe. For me, no. But Roantis brightened.

"Good. That's good."

"Next question?"

"But wait. How do you do it?"

"What?"

"Slip under da wire. Eh?"

"What I figure is, I'll watch the post office down at Murrells Inlet. See who comes and goes. Tomorrow, Joe will probably have a rough description of George from the bank teller who sold him the cashier's check at the Shawmut. So we'll know what he looks like. I'm assuming he's changed his appearance."

"How do you know he sent the check?"

"We're pretty sure he sent it."

"Not sure. Pretty sure. What if he had someone do it for him?"

It was a good question. I shrugged.

"Maybe I better come along," he said.

"No. The fewer people down there the better."

"Since when you know so much about it?"

"Look, if you go, it will look suspicious."

"You mean Mary will find out?"

"Mary's going. Mary, George's wife Sarah, and Yours Truly."

"Two out of three ain't bad . . ."

"When I say look suspicious, I mean we don't want Joe to get wind of this little excursion."

"Why not?"

"Because if he knows, he'll be duty-bound to notify the law down in South Carolina. It's his ass if he doesn't. And don't forget, two people he loves are down there: me and his sister."

"One out of two ain't—"

"Look, Laitis, I hope you see why we have to do this on the sneak."

"An' I hope *you* see that George, or Roy Harris, or whatever, killed a guy. Murdered him. I hope you keep it in mind."

"Sarah doesn't think her husband killed anybody. She doesn't think he's capable of it."

Roantis sighed and rolled his eyes. Just then Suzzanne Roantis came in and informed us that dinner was ready. She's ten years younger than Roantis and looks a helluva lot better. But then, it figures: she hasn't spent her life sneaking through jungle swamps, living on hearts of palm (that's hearts of palm *tree*), slugs, and snake meat. She doesn't throw opponents around in gyms, pound shot-filled leather bags for hours on end, and hang out in rough bars for comic relief. She eats sensibly and does her best to see that Laitis does too . . . when he's home. Otherwise, his diet (whenever I've been with him, which is too often) seems to consist primarily of Camel cigarettes, rare meat, and straight whiskey. That he remains alive and breathing is a perverse wonder of nature. But then again, he's probably got the caveman constitution as well as the prehistoric mind-set.

With a grunt and a groan, Roantis eased himself up out of the deep leather chair and followed me into the kitchen. Smelled great in there. Mary and Suzzanne had made chicken fajitas on scalding cast-iron plates. We ate the sizzling meat, wrapped in cheese and wheat-flour tortillas with salsa and sour cream. We washed it down with Corona beer, ice-cold.

Suzzanne's maiden name was Murzicki; her father was a Polish immigrant who worked as a fireman in Boston and died nine years ago. Her mother had died a decade earlier. All the family Suzzanne had was bound up in the short, stocky, gnarled Lithuanian soldier of fortune. No wonder her eyes sometimes had a weary look.

"Well, what did you guys decide?" asked Mary. I told her my plan. Laitis held up his hand, a pained expression on his creased features.

"Doc, don't do this. This man, who you say is your long-lost friend, has gone to a lot of trouble making people tink he's dead. He even killed to make it look good. He won't want to be found out . . . even by his ex-wife."

"Hate to say it, Charlie, but Laitis is right," said Mary softly, looking down into her plate. I knew she was correct; trying to track George down was a stupid idea. So stupid only a lame-brained idiot would even attempt it.

Which meant that I, as the self-proclaimed lamebrained idiot, would have to do it on my own, on the sneak.

So to get the help I needed, I huddled with Roantis again the next day in his office in the Boylston Street Y for two hours. The first thing he instructed me to do was get a stout cardboard box large and strong enough to hold the necessary items. Then I bought a ticket for a night flight to Charleston, via Atlanta. The man on the phone asked if I wanted a round-trip ticket. I declined, perhaps because I had no idea how long this caper would take, or when I would return. Assuming, of course, I did return.

DEAR MARY: GONE FISHING WITH BRADY FOR A FEW DAYS. WILL
CALL SOON.

LOVE, C

I taped the note to the kitchen table on my way out. Just by chance, a few feet away on the butcher block, were some bro-chures from fishing lodges in Montana, where Brady Coyne spends every day of the year he can afford, and then some. Whether they would lend credence to my flimsy story I couldn't tell, but I was ready to try anything. I trudged out the back way with a heavy heart. I carried only two bags: a canvas grip packed with blue jeans, shorts, bathing suit, beach towels, compact binoculars, tropical-weight sport coat and pants, running shoes, and other items in one hand, and my canvas briefcase slung on my shoulder. It contained the newspaper article in the *Globe* that first mentioned the murder in the Chesterton beach house, several maps, sunglasses, a camera, and pipes and cigars.

On Laitis's recommendation, I had made reservations for the motel beforehand. I chose a small motel called the Smugglers' Den for its location. It was in the town of Surfside, which was near Murrells Inlet. I called them and explained that an important package was due for me there and could they please hold it. They said no problem. I then called an overnight air-freight company and sent the package to myself, the same cardboard box (the size of two shoe boxes) that Laitis instructed me to get.

Contained within, carefully wrapped in crumpled newspaper, was a Smith & Wesson Model 66 stainless-steel .357 Magnum with a four-inch barrel. Although I'd had this revolver for some time, using it for target and silhouette shooting at the local gun club, I had previously always taken my Browning automatic for personal protection. But Roantis maintained that the .357 Magnum was a more powerful stopper than the nine-millimeter Browning. So he had convinced me. He also loaned me a Bianchi nylon shoulder holster for this gun, which would allow me to wear the piece underneath a lightweight sport coat. Along with the revolver and holster were a box of cartridges tipped with 125-grain, semijacketed hollow-point bullets and two speed loaders. These speed loaders are special cartridge holders containing six fresh rounds, enabling me to reload the six-shot weapon in seconds.

If this weren't enough, I also tucked in another item that came highly recommended by Mr. Roantis: a Japanese-style fighting knife known as Tanto. This cute device, made by an outfit on the West Coast called Cold Steel, is a big, nasty knife with a gently curved, single-edged blade tipped with a chisel point. The blade is shot-blasted, producing a dull finish that will not reflect light. The handle grip is checkered "Kraton" hard rubber. The heavy brass pommel on the handle end is designed to crush skulls. The chisel point is guaranteed to pierce Kevlar bullet-proof vests, car doors, wooden door frames, and a lot of other tough stuff while remaining sharp enough for shaving. I wasn't going to use it for my face. Hell, I hoped I'd never need to touch it.

Sending this little CARE package via the courier, of course, was to get around the security checks at Logan Airport. Leave it to Laitis; he's got more answers to these unique problems than the Boy Scout Handbook. Which set me to thinking.

Maybe he could write his own version of that famous compendium. It might be called the Bad Boy's Handbook. And inside, instead of exhorting the reader to be Clean, Honest, Reverent, Brave, Loyal, Trustworthy, Courteous, and so forth, there would be chapters on how to become Shifty, Lethal, Nasty, Sneaky, Vengeful, and Cruel.

Two hours later I was sitting in an easy chair in the private airline club at Logan Airport, watching the planes. I sipped Johnny Walker Red on ice with a splash of soda. Out over the ocean the sky was navy blue, turning gradually lighter until it glowed gold in the west. A clear sky; the flight should be pleasant. This whole business started just like this, I thought: in late evening with a scotch in your hand, looking at the sky. Just about three months ago when you and Joe were out on his roof, looking at those damn pigeons. Well, at least one good thing has come out of all this, I thought. We talked Joe into ditching those damn birds. . . .

I left my chair by the window and went over to a wall phone, where I punched in Roantis's number.

"Don't you think Mary's gonna be mad?" he said when I told him my departure was imminent.

"Yeah, well, it'll serve her right. Did I tell you about the smoke bomb?"

"Yep. You tried to scare her with it, but it seems she beat you to it."

"Yeah, well—"

"I think maybe you should quit while you're ahead."

"Listen, I'll be down there by around midnight, in a rented car. You got the name of the place? The Smugglers' Den?"

"Uh-huh. Do me a favor. Promise you won't do anyting but look and listen for the first two days, okay?"

"That's all I planned to do anyway. Just go down there and hang out . . . see what's up. There's a chance, you know, that this Roy Harris is really just Roy Harris; that he isn't really George Brenner reincarnated."

"I wouldn't bet on it. You sent the equipment?"

"Yep. It should be there already. I'm using the Smith, as you recommended."

"Good. That loading gives you a one-shot stop capability. You sent the Tanto as well?"

"Yes, Laitis."

"Dat's good. Dat's a honey—"

"It's just lovely. Listen: I'll call Mary tomorrow evening and set everything straight. Then I'll call you and fill you in."

"I wouldn't sneak off like this on Mary, Doc. You know how she can be."

"I am extremely aware of how she can be, Laitis. That's why I have to do it this way. You've been around her enough to know that."

"When she finds out, don't include me. Don't mention my name."

I knew the reason for this last request. Laitis Roantis, former officer in the French Foreign Legion, leader of the Daisy Ducks Recon Team, veteran of Dien Bien Phu and a hundred other grisly, blood-soaked campaigns, was afraid of nothing. Except my wife.

With this reassuring caveat echoing in my head, I went by the complimentary snack bar and spread some cheddar cheese and horseradish mix on pretzels, took them back to my chair, and ordered a Beck's. Roantis was right; it wouldn't take Mary long to see right through the phony note about fishing with Brady Coyne. Having talked with Brady within the past week about a plantation quail hunt in Georgia, I knew he was in town, his nose glued to the grindstone. One call from her would blow my frail cover. Aw, hell, as soon as she read the note she'd know. Who was I kidding? *Whom* was I kidding?

I went back for another helping of pretzels and cheese dip. Good thing Moe wasn't around to see this; he'd have a stroke just watching. Last time I was over at his trailer he was eating some kind of alfalfa concentrate. Smelled like horse poop and had enough fiber in it to make three of those hairy door mats. . . .

Thing is, this war with Mary all started when I mentioned

that Louise was smart as well as gorgeous. That was it. Bingo. The pebble that rolled and started three other pebbles, which moved the rock, which tumbled and fell against three or four bigger rocks, which loosened the boulder on the cliff, and so on. Why do people who are supposed to be in love get into these stupid feuds? I thought about it and came up with the answer: because they're supposed to be in love.

The sensible thing would be to call her and explain everything. Or maybe just go back home. I looked at my watch; it was a little after seven. I could be home in an hour. Sure, she'd be mad, but we could clear the air, then settle things up later on tonight. That was an attractive thought. What was she thinking now? I'd give a whole bunch of money for a machine that would tell me, at any given moment, what Mary Brindelli Adams was thinking. A whole bunch.

I drained the last of the beer and felt the warm glow, the thin veil of cozy insulation that the booze threw over me. Somehow it lacked its usual appeal. I kept thinking about Mary and what she was thinking. I was still turning it around and around in my head when they called my flight to Atlanta and I went down the corridor. What to do? I could still go home. . . .

I stopped in thought, looking ahead to the security checkpoint. People were placing their bags on the endless rubber belt and walking through the electronic scanner. Then it hit me: I *had* to go. I had no choice but to go down there, if only to retrieve my gun and knife. That's five hundred bucks' worth of hardware sitting down there in that motel lobby, dummy. Damn right you're going!

That's it, Adams, go down there and scout out the scene. Reconnoiter the beach. Don't do anything rash; keep your word to Roantis that you'll just check the place out. Mainly, see if your hunch was correct; see if the guy down there really is George. Then come back and make up. *Perfect.*

It was so perfect I ordered another beer as we gained cruising altitude. Then they dimmed the cabin lights. I heard vague whispers and distant laughter in the dark cabin. I pushed my seat back, leaned toward the window, and saw tiny specks and blotches of white light far below, crawling past my field of vision. The engines made a soothing, whining, sigh.

I slept.

stepped out of the Charleston airport and a wave of warm, wet air hit me. The smell of flowers and summer rain. At the car-rental agency I picked up my light blue sedan, a Chevy Corsica, and found my way out of the usual airport maze of merging and diverging expressways. I headed north on Highway 17. The people at the car-rental counter told me that this coast road runs along the water and swamps of the low country all the way up to North Carolina and the Outer Banks. My headlights picked up the pretty trees along each side of the road, tall cypress trees and round, squatty oaks, which showed their swaying gray Spanish moss even in the dark. Most of the stretch of road was picturesque, if a bit monotonous. But I was pleasantly surprised at the lack of billboards and other junk along this divided highway.

That is, until I approached the Myrtle Beach area. The welcome signs euphemistically referred to this stretch of the road as the "Grand Strand." Beginning at the town of Garden City, which is right before Surfside, roadside signs and clutter proliferated. Most were ads for touristy sorts of attractions: miniature golf, fireworks emporia, exotic zoos, "theme" restaurants, and so on. Surfside seemed right in the heart of this flotsam and jetsam; when I left Highway 17 and turned onto Business 17, the first thing I saw was a grotesque miniature-golf course with a huge pink concrete octopus in its center. Next to him (her? it?) was a giant white shark, and behind these two, camels, giraffes, and an elephant with a water fountain in its upraised trunk. It was just after midnight, but the whole place remained spot-lighted, just for effect.

I was tired, and could do without it. It took me another twenty minutes to locate the Smugglers' Den, which was off the main road in the south part of Surfside, right next to Garden City. Actually, for being so close to all the roadside trash, it was a pretty nice place, a sprawling white stucco motel with a red tile roof and a mock-Spanish courtyard in the center. There were real palm trees in that courtyard. I was a bit surprised to see them in South Carolina, but that's because I was a new-comer; turns out they're all over the low country.

The Smugglers' owner, Don Lineberry, was a heavyset bald man wearing glasses with thick lenses and black frames. He wore a bathrobe, which meant he'd been waiting up for my late arrival.

"Here's your package, Dr. Adams. Wow, sure is heavy, isn't it?" I detected a hint of suspicion in his voice. Man arrives late at night to pick up a weighty package he could have brought with him.

"Surgical equipment can be very heavy, and expensive. Can't carry the cutting tools on the plane due to regulations, and I sure as hell don't trust the baggage handlers. Do you?"

"Hey, you're right! Got to admit that package had me think-ing for a bit."

"I hope my room is ready, Don. I'm pretty beat."

"Plum tuckered, are you? Well you got your choice, doctor. We're not very full right now. The winter folks left in April, and next month the summer people start to drift in. But this is slack time, and I've got several free rooms. I thought you might like the one on the end, in back. It's one of the few rooms with two doors: one opens onto the courtyard, one directly onto the beach. It's a deluxe, but I'll let you have it for the regular rate."

"Done," I said, hefting my baggage and the cardboard box and heading to my room. Once there, I stripped, took a long hot shower, and hopped into bed. The phone was on the bedside table within my reach. I thought of calling Mary, but decided I was too strung out to make much sense or negotiate in verbal fencing. The whole thing could wait. I opened the seaside window all the way and heard the boom of surf close by. All I needed; I fell asleep real fast.

Next morning I woke up to the sound of sea gulls fussing and fighting outside. I thought for a minute I was down at the Breakers, on Cape Cod. But a glance outside at the spiky palmetto leaves and six huge brown pelicans flying in formation told me otherwise. I put on my swim trunks and walked out onto the beach. It was a fabulous beach, as wide and long as Nauset Beach on the Cape, with big rollers that rose slowly, growing to resemble green ships' hulls, shiny and wet, then crashing in a flurry of spray and foam. I got brave and waded out to just above my ankles. It was the warmest seawater I had ever experienced. I dived in and swam for thirty minutes, got wonderfully refreshed and full of energy, then went back inside to shower and dress. I put on loose cotton beach pants, a knit shirt, and tennis shoes. Time to take a look around.

I took the revolver, now loaded, and the Tanto in the canvas shoulder bag and drove out to Highway 17, then turned south to Murrells Inlet. I had to ask directions twice, but found the post office just off the road, a modern low building that resembled so many others, made of yellow brick with a lot of glass. I guessed it was built in the sixties or seventies. Outside, on the trim lawn, the South Carolina state flag fluttered on one side and the Stars and Stripes on the other. The state flag was unique: a blue palm tree on a white field. I discovered later that South Carolina calls itself the Palmetto State.

I watched the building for several minutes. It was just after 8:30, and there were no customers yet. I ambled inside and pretended to look through the massive zip-code directory while I scanned the boxes along the far wall. Number 212 was near the end of the wall, about as high as my knee. Third up from the bottom and fourth from the end; I could remember that. I closed the monstrous government directory—what did it weigh, twenty pounds?—and sauntered over to the mailboxes. I got my first disappointment: they didn't have glass fronts like the old-style boxes; they were solid, polished steel doors. No way to tell if number 212 had any mail inside. But since the door of the building and its entire front wall were glass, I could see inside the building easily from anywhere in front, so I had some luck, anyway.

Then I thought of something else: if I couldn't tell if there was mail inside the boxes, then neither could any of the box holders. Therefore, George would have to approach his box and open it. That was good. I left the building and headed back to the car, looking for a place to wait and watch without being as conspicuous as the Jolly Green Giant. I looked up and saw I was in luck.

Most of Highway 17 was commercialized. The area around Surfside, as I had already observed, was raucous with capitalism. Farther south, toward the towns of Litchfield and Pawley's Island, the shops were fewer and different. Less fireworks, miniature golf, and fast food, and no places with giant lettering on the windows that said ALL ITEMS INSIDE $1 OR LESS! Instead, there were boutiques and pricey gift shops. Almost directly across the road from the P.O. was a small colony of such stores sitting under spreading oak trees. The complex was called Sawgrass Shoppes. The name was painted on a wooden sign with latticework around its base and what I presumed was sawgrass growing in front of the lattice. I hopped into the Chevy and cruised over there to check it out. I parked and walked around under those oaks whose great black branches spread out from their mammoth trunks forty feet in each direction. Swaying from the massive gnarled limbs were beards of gray-tan Spanish moss that gave the place a drowsy, gothic appearance.

"Frankly, my dear, I don't give a damn," I muttered, and walked to the shops.

There were four stores: the one closest to the road featured designer beachwear and fancy sweatshirts. Behind it and left was a gift shop specializing in duck decoys, locally made net hammocks from Pawley's Island, African style "Gullah" baskets, and stained-glass-window decorations. Behind and to the right was a store that sold cards, posters, those multicolored wind socks, and kites. Finally, toward the road on the other side of the big sign was a snack bar called Small Pleasures that specialized in giant ice-cream cones and other sweets. There were decks and benches outside surrounding a duck pond where the customers could sit. There actually were ducks in there too. Mallards and what appeared to be green-wing teal. This was perfect. I got a whiff of strong coffee from the sweet shop and realized I hadn't eaten. If Mary had been along, we would have found this place twenty minutes earlier by the coffee aroma alone. I walked into the snack shop.

I got a bagful of homemade muffins and doughnuts and a Styrofoam cup of strong coffee that was almost a foot high. One of the waitresses, a tall, leggy, brown-eyed blonde in a ponytail, made me look twice, and want to look a third time. I stopped at the beachwear shop and bought a wide straw hat, the kind with the low, flat crown and the wide brim. A straw gambler's hat. As I sipped the coffee on the deck I put on my dark glasses and the straw hat. This would hide my face, but still, I might look silly sitting out there all morning doing nothing. Then I remembered that the card-and-poster shop also sold books. I ambled back there and browsed through the titles. Tons of Louis L'Amour. Not a great writer, but a good storyteller, and a master historian. There were eight titles there and I'd read them all. Take about an hour each, and some cynics claim not much longer for Louis to write them. The books are short and simple, with rather flat characters. But he does know the country of the Wild West, and how to describe it perfectly. Also, in his books the hero's options are dramatically simple, and the bad guys always lose in the end. If only real life were that clearly defined.

A book cover two shelves down caught my eye. I realized I was looking at the face of Peter O'Toole, i.e., the face of George Brenner. Behind the face sailed Chinese junks and Polynesian canoes. A steamer loomed far off on the horizon, trailing a plume of dark smoke. The book was Joseph Conrad's *Lord Jim*.

O'Toole's face was on the cover because he had starred in the movie version of the book. I bought this book and went back to my corner of the bench and settled down. Soon I was munching, reading, sipping coffee, and watching the low government building across the road.

At the P.O., people came and went all morning. I saw a lot of them check their mailboxes, but nobody went over and bent down in front of the low box three up from the bottom and four from the end. And after two hours of sitting there, I realized just how uncomfortable a wooden bench can be. Sure, winos practically live on them, but remember: *they're loaded*.

The only rather nice thing that I noticed during my initial stakeout—and I'm sure it was purely chance—was that the leggy, brown-eyed blond waitress seemed to be watching me. I say it was chance because I'm all too familiar with the middle-aged male fantasy that attractive younger women are looking at him. But in this case, I think it really was true. Twice I happened to look around in the direction of Small Pleasures, and both times I caught her looking dead at me. Both times she turned quickly away and returned to work.

And so did I, scanning that post office across Highway 17. By 11:30 I'd had enough. How do those private eyes stand it, sitting in darkened cars for hours, waiting to see if Mr. X and Ms. Y get it on in a motel room? No way was I sitting there all day. I wanted to go swimming; both the temperature and humidity were high now, and climbing fast. Get me to the water. I looked down at the book; I was only on page 80, but focused my attention on it, which was hard in the heat.

After a few minutes I raised my eyes to see somebody inside the post office. A figure was bending down right exactly in front of box number 212. My heart started doing the shimmy-shake.

The person stood up quickly, turned, and walked toward the door. My heart resumed to normal; it was a black woman wearing a white pant suit of lightweight material. She also had on a white hat and dark glasses, so it was hard to tell anything else about her appearance. But it was a good bet that she hadn't been collecting mail from number 212. Maybe the next one over, or the one just above or below it, but not *it*. She opened the glass door of the P.O. and walked out, getting into a nondescript tan sedan of some Japanese make, either Nissan or Toyota, and headed south on the coast road. I had a rather unpleasant realization: it was just possible that George, alias Roy Harris, being the cagey sort, checked his mailbox only once a week . . . perhaps even less often than that.

This thought proved to be the final straw; I packed up my meager belongings and split, driving the Chevy back up Highway 17 into Surfside and the Smugglers' Den Motel. I changed back into my swim gear, hid the Smith, the Tanto, and the other funsies under the mattress, and swam for half an hour. The water was impossibly warm; at least seventy-eight or -nine. Nobody appreciates warm water as much as someone who spent his childhood as a skinny kid trying to swim in Lake Michigan. I got out, stretched and flexed, set the zero of my watch bezel on the minute hand (which told me it was 12:42), and began a slow run up the hard-packed wet sand of the water's edge. I headed south, keeping my eyes on a huge building, or complex of buildings, that rose wide and tall, ghostlike and hazy, on the southern horizon.

Running barefoot on packed sand, almost naked, with the sea air blowing around you with all that warmth and aroma is a heady experience. It's also murder on the feet; I can do it only because I've spent years building up the proud tissue on the balls of my feet. I ran for thirty minutes, which, at my slow pace, is just over three miles. But the big building in the distance didn't look much closer, which meant it was far, far away. And very big. I finally reached the spot fifty minutes later. The buildings were condos and rental units called Litchfield by the Sea. They seemed to be first-class abodes, and each had a spacious balcony. Fast shadows made the sun blink; I looked up to see eight huge birds just over my head. More brown pelicans, flying in formation, like geese, except they were more massive. They flapped once or twice, then glided on wings as motionless as a turkey vulture's. I hung around there for ten minutes, resting and watching kids and their parents flying fancy cloth kites with long streamers. Then I began the second eight-mile leg back to Surfside. This is a long run, but I thought I could handle it if I ran ten-minute miles.

I didn't even come close. After a total of less than ten miles I slowed to a fast walk and then walked-jogged the rest of the way back. I hadn't figured the heat and humidity into the equation and was dizzy and light-headed all the way back. A cheap, midday high. Lucky thing my motel had a bright red tile roof or I would have missed it. I had covered a lot of beach, all of it lined with cottages, rental units, hotels, condos and such in varying degrees of density.

I jumped in the water again and swam for a while to cool down. Running at midday wasn't too bright. I had to keep remembering that South Carolina was nine hundred miles south of Boston. I toweled off in the room and was about to crash when I noticed that the little red light on my telephone was winking silently at me. I called the front desk.

"You had a call, Dr. Adams," said Don Lineberry. "A Mr. Roweeder . . . uh, Rowdonta . . . uh—"

"Roantis. Thanks."

"What kind of name is that, anyway?"

"Lithuanian."

"Oh yeah? Hey, aren't they the ones giving the Rooskies all that trouble?"

"Yep. Have been for some time; they seem to be born that way. Anyone else call?"

He said no; I called Laitis at work.

"Shit's gonna hit the fan, Doc. Mary knew right away you din't go fishing."

"I figured she would."

"Maybe she's gonna have Joe track you down."

"You didn't tell her."

"Nah. You can trust me."

"Good. And Joe can't use his position to find me, either; it's not official police business."

"Who says? Finding a killer?"

He had a point; it was only a matter of time before the dy-

namic duo of the Brindelli Kids would put all the pieces together. But I figured I still had a couple days. Still, I felt regret,
and guilt.

"It was a mean thing I did," I said. "It was impulsive and
immature. I'm going to call her. The sooner the better, looks
like. I know she's mad enough to kill me."

"Wrong. She's sad. She tol' me she must have really hurt you.
She said the ice water and the smoke bomb, maybe they were
too much."

"That's real good to hear, Laitis. Thanks for being my
friend."

"Aw, you got me all broke up."

"Look, you jerk—"

"So what have you found?"

"Nothing. I waited all morning watching the damn post office and didn't see anybody."

"Well, don't give up."

"Anything new up there? What about the guy who bought
the bank check for Sarah Brenner? Did Joe get that description
yet?"

"Oh yeah, and you're not gonna believe it. Ha!"

"It was George, wasn't it?"

"Nope. Turns out I was right, Doc. Not him."

"Maybe he was wearing a disguise. Listen, Laitis, you don't
know this guy. He's a tricky one."

"I don't tink it coulda been him, Doc. Know why? It was a
woman."

"You're kidding."

"Nope. And it couldn'ta been him wearing a wig, either."

"You sure?"

"Pretty sure, yeah. Guy at the bank said she was black."

"**W**ell, I'm glad we're having this talk, Charlie," said Mary. "It's good to hear your voice and know you're okay."

Her voice sounded calm. Too calm. It sounded soft and loving. Too soft and loving. Reminded me of those old westerns in which the three remaining cavalry scouts are hiding in the cacti at the water hole, surrounded by a thousand wild-eyed, screaming Comanches. Suddenly the chief, the guy with the most feathers in his cap, rears up on his paint and shouts "Ooooooo-hiyeee!" and gallops off, with all his warriors following. Then all is quiet; the birds return and resume singing. The two young scouts leave the hiding place, jumping for joy that the "injuns" have gone. Given up. But the third scout, the grizzled old veteran of scores of these campaigns, counts his remaining rounds, saving one for himself, and whispers the Our Father. He knows better; he's been around.

Well, that was the feeling I was getting in the back of my mind, talking with the Boss long distance from my room at the Smugglers' Den that evening.

"You're not, uh, mad?" I ventured.

"Of course I'm mad. Wouldn't you be? It's just that I also realize that I helped precipitate this. I had a long talk with Joe and he agreed. By the way, where are you staying?"

"I'm not telling yet."

"Be careful, Charlie. The ice is getting thinner by the second."

"I know; it's a risk I'll have to take. So, I love you too, Mare, and I'll call tomorrow night."

"Don't go yet, Charlie; let's talk this out."

"Talk about what? I told you I'm not telling you exactly where I am, so you and Joe can forget coming down here and screwing up—"

"We'd never do that."

"*Ha!*"

"So you haven't seen anybody at this post-office box yet?"

"No," I lied. No sense worrying her.

"Then I say if you strike out again tomorrow, it's time to come home."

"That's probably what I'll do."

"You know Joe's very upset; you've put him in an extremely awkward position, second-guessing him. By the way, you'll be interested in knowing that the person who wrote that cashier's check to Sarah wasn't George; it was a woman. A black woman, the guy said."

"I know; Laitis told me."

"He called you already?"

"Uh-huh."

"So then he knows where you are."

"Uh, no. I called him, actually." There she goes again, I thought, my hand starting to tremble on the receiver. Good old Mare—can't keep a damn thing from her.

"The bank clerk told Joe she talked with an English accent."

"Oh really? Jamaican, perhaps?"

"That's what Joe's thinking, yes."

"Well, I gotta go. Don't worry about me."

"Not so fast; I've got to tell you what's new with the boys."

So we chatted for another five minutes or so about Jack and Tony and what they were up to. Then we said good-bye, wishing each other well and reaffirming our love. It was a nice call, and I was very glad I'd made it.

Still, as I left the Smugglers' Den to search for a restaurant for dinner, a cool wind sprang up and hit my cheek. A squall was brewing. Somehow the image of those poor, surrounded cavalry scouts wouldn't leave my mind. . . .

Next morning I repeated my sunrise dip in the ocean. I was growing more and more fond of this wide beach and the warm water. Back at the Sawgrass Shoppes, I bought more coffee and muffins and set up my little stakeout again. The brown-eyed blonde waited on me, looking me in the face when she counted out the change. I returned to that rough wooden bench with *Lord Jim.* I had forgotten my straw gambler's hat. I had scarcely put down the empty coffee cup when I heard a pleasant voice off to my left say: "Would you like another coffee?"

I looked up. There she was, standing close behind me. She was leaning over the back of the bench, her head turned toward me. In the sunlight, her hair and skin were golden. She was wearing a pink waitress dress with a white apron over it. The apron had scallops and bows on it and had the look of a jumper. She wore tennis shoes with no socks. Very wholesome. Somewhere between eighteen and twenty. Nice. Cheered an old man up.

"Sure, if you don't mind getting it," I answered, and resumed watching the building across the street. Yesterday, the woman in the light suit had appeared about 11:30. It was now almost ten.

"Here you are," said the Young Thing, whose name, I read from her tag, was Ellen.

"Thanks, Ellen," I said, digging in my pocket. But she waved me off, saying refills were free.

"I came out here because there's not much else to do inside," she said. "Mind if I sit down?"

She sat on my bench, but at the far end of it. Was this a come-on? Don't flatter yourself, Adams.

"Not many customers today?" I asked, closing the book and looking across the street again.

"Nope. This is a slow time. In fact, this is my last day; they just told me."

Her eyes fell; it seemed this announcement was an unwelcome surprise to Ms. Ellen of the Good Looks. I told her that was too bad. She agreed, especially since she and her girlfriend had to pay the rent on their little two-room unit up in North Myrtle. Her girlfriend, Linda, worked at Weird Willard's Fireworks World.

"She getting laid off too?"

"Not that I know of. That business is pretty steady, I guess. But here, they've got two other waitresses, who have been here longer, so I was the first to go. Now I don't know what I'll do. Can I ask you a question?"

"Sure."

"Are you a cop or something?"

"No. Why do you ask?"

"Because you're always looking over at the post office."

"So? There's no law against that."

"C'mon; you're always looking over there; every time a car pulls into the lot, you're watching it like a hawk."

I said nothing.

"You're trying to find somebody; I know it."

"Where are you from, Ellen?"

"Charlottesville. Charlottesville, Virginia."

"That's a great place. Is your family affiliated with the University of Virginia?"

She nodded. "My father teaches English there. He looks—"

I turned to her, waiting for her to finish. "He looks . . . *what*?"

"Nothing. Can I see this book?" Without waiting for an answer, she reached out and took the paperback, sliding over toward me at the same time. "*Lord Jim*. I've never read it, but my father says it's great. His specialty is British lit. Conrad was Polish, but he wrote in English."

"That's right. Beautiful English."

"What's this book about?"

"About an idealistic young seaman who betrays his future by an act of cowardice. An act of self-preservation, really, that any of us might have done at the time. The bad part was, it was interpreted by society as an act of cowardice. And so, there he was: the act followed him everywhere around the globe; he could not escape his past. Finally, he redeems himself by leading a settlement of villagers in a remote outpost in the Pacific."

She flipped through the pages. "If you know the story, why are you reading it?"

"It's a book you can read twice. I haven't read it in over twenty years." I took the book from her. Our hands touched briefly. I turned it over, showing her the cover. "But really, I suppose I was drawn to it because I knew a man who reminds me a little of Peter O'Toole, and also a little of Jim."

"You mean he committed an act of cowardice?"

"Worse than that."

"What?"

"I can't say now. But anyway, we always had the feeling that he wasn't a bad man. But it turns out he's probably very bad. We think the, uh, business he was in led him gradually into a life of fear and hiding."

"You said we had a feeling. Who's we?"

"My wife and I."

A pause.

"You have a wife."

"Yes."

"Well, that figures. . . ."

Somehow, in that brief instant, I felt she was disappointed. And somehow, I felt enormously sorry for her.

"This man you knew; he's the person you're watching for, isn't he?"

"No," I said.

"Ha. I bet he is."

Just then a tan sedan pulled into the lot across the street. I checked my watch: 10:10. The driver's door opened and the woman got out. She was tall and dark, with an African-style turban on her head in the shape of an upside-down flowerpot. I suppose it resembled a fez, except it was of bright fabric. She wore a caftan robe to match. West African, probably. Ashanti, or something like that. Without thinking, I took the compact binoculars from my canvas satchel and brought them up to my eyes.

"Well? Is she the one?" Ellen asked.

"I think so," I answered without thinking as I turned the center knob, bringing her into focus.

"I see her every day."

"You do?" I looked over at Ellen, who crossed her tan legs and leaned back on the bench, laying her arm along its back. Her left hand was behind me. She could have touched my shoulder.

"Uh-huh. She always comes in the middle of the morning. She comes from down near Litchfield, I think."

"How long has she been doing this?" I asked, watching the woman through the binoculars as she entered the building and walked straight to the bank of post-office boxes.

"As long as I've worked here, which is almost two months. She's one of the regular ones."

The woman bent down in front of the boxes. She remained thus for several seconds, then stood up. For a second or two I could see that one of the boxes had its door open. Third from the bottom and fourth from the end. Hot damn. The woman had pulled her dark glasses up so they were resting on her head, like a World War I aviator's goggles. The face seemed familiar. Where had I seen it before? The image was coming to me from far away, through the glass door of the building, and had bright sunlight in between. Tough. Before I could study her face, she had replaced the glasses, put the envelopes into her shoulder bag, and turned and shut the door to the little box. She came out of the building and down the walk to the parking lot.

Suddenly she stopped, staring. I realized, with a tinge of panic, that she was looking straight at me.

"Uh-oh!" Ellen giggled. "She's looking at you—"

Without thinking, I lowered the field glasses as the woman turned away and headed for the car. As she got in I saw her glance back at us. By then I was busy pointing to the branches of a neighboring oak tree, holding the binoculars up near my face, as if we were bird-watching. The tan car left the lot and headed north.

"That's not the way she usually goes," said Ellen. "She usually goes the other direction."

"Dammit!"

"What's wrong? She saw you?"

"Not only that, she saw me looking at her with *these*," I said, putting down the glasses. "She caught me spying."

"Who is she?"

"I don't know. In a way, she looks familiar, but I'm just not sure."

"If she's a stranger, why are you spying on her?"

Cute as she was, the kid was starting to annoy me. Then I knew why: she was asking good questions. Questions that couldn't be shoved under the rug.

"I'm afraid that's confidential."

She said nothing. Just sat there, swivelling the ball of her right foot back and forth in the gravel. I kept watching the road and the trees, angry at myself. All the time I felt her staring at me. She didn't believe me. Not for a second.

"You're some kind of detective, aren't you?" she said.

"Nah. Do I look like a detective?"

The words seemed to reverberate among the trees. I picked up the book again.

"So you're not a detective? A policeman?"

"No. I'm a doctor, an oral surgeon."

"No kidding. My father's a doctor, but not a medical doctor. He looks just like you. You could be twin brothers. Isn't that amazing?"

"I guess. And maybe we are twin brothers."

She smiled. "Where are you from?"

"The Midwest originally. Now I live in New England, outside Boston."

"Hey! My father's from the Midwest too! Ever hear of Fort Wayne?"

I nodded.

"What's your name?"

"Charles Adams. People call me Doc."

"I'll call you Charlie."

"Uh, maybe you better call me Doc."

"How come? Am I too young?"

"No, it's just that only one person calls me Charlie. My wife, Mary."

"Oh. Is she here with you?"

"No; she's up in Massachusetts."

"Well, then, Charlie, I don't see any harm in it, do you?"

"Well, I—"

"Hey! Let me get you another coffee," she said, and was up and gone. I kept watching the post office, but somehow my attention had slipped a wee bit.

She came back with another cup of steaming, holding it out to me.

"Any luck, Charlie?"

"No." I took the cup and she sat down right next to me. Our shoulders were brushing.

"I can't stay long; the lunch crowd will be coming soon."

Good, I thought.

"He's letting me do pretty much what I want my last day," she continued. "I think he feels kind of guilty letting me go. How long do you plan to keep watching?"

"I don't know. As long as it takes, I guess."

"Know what I think? I think that woman suspects you're watching her. I could tell by the way she acted."

"I think you're right, Ellen." I sighed. "I'm too conspicuous here, anyway. I mean, I just can't keep on sitting here, reading *Lord Jim*. . . ."

"I know . . . but *I* could."

"What?"

"Why don't you let me do your watching for you? Now that my job's over I have the time. Besides, people are accustomed to seeing me here; they won't suspect anything's up."

I leaned over in thought, resting my chin on my hands, staring across the road. Actually, it was a damn good idea. And it would free me up to scout around more. Ellen was smart as well as attractive.

"What do you think, Charlie?"

"It sounds like a good idea, but I'm hesitant. For one thing, there's a chance of danger. I don't know how great the chance or how great the danger, but it's there."

"You mean these people are dangerous?"

"At least one of them is; he murdered a man."

"Oh, wow!" she said, her eyes lighting up. "This is scary, huh?"

"Kind of."

"Ooooooooo," she sighed, leaning close to my face, her deep brown eyes alight with excitement. "Don't you just . . . doesn't it just give you goose bumps!"

"No, it doesn't. I don't think it's anything to be excited or happy about, either."

"I didn't mean that, Charlie," she whispered. "It's just that . . . well, it *is* exciting. I've had a sheltered life. You know, growing up a prof's kid in a university town. I've never really had to . . . face things."

"Same here," I said. It was out before I even thought about it. I considered her idea again. What harm could she possibly be in, sitting here along a busy highway outside a restaurant?

"Ellen, can I trust you?"

"Uh-huh. You sure can. Cross my heart and hope to die," she said.

"I'm going to tell you a rather amazing story. I trust you'll keep it to yourself. If you don't, you could be in hot water. Not from me, you understand, but from these other people."

"I won't tell."

I believed her. I told her, in very condensed form, the strange account of George Brenner, the murder in the beach mansion, the midnight slaying of Reggie Westley near the old windmill, the flashing-light signals to the boats offshore, and so on. I took out the article that the *Globe* had run, showing her the photo of Chesterton's beach mansion. I even mentioned Charlena Eames. Ellen was spellbound; she couldn't hide her excitement.

"So what do you think, Charlie? Can I stay here and watch?"

"Uh . . . yes. It's worth a try, at least. What I want to do is follow that woman after she leaves the building. If you stay here and pretend you're working, I can go down the road and find a pay phone. I'll call you here and give you the number. Then, when you see her, call me and I'll hop in my car and try to follow her as she drives by. I want to pay you for your time too. What are you getting here at the snack shop?"

"Three seventy-five an hour, plus tips."

I almost gagged. How could anybody live on that? I told her I would pay her five bucks per for sitting on her duff watching. Her eyes just lit up; she stood there, beaming up at me.

"You mean it?"

I nodded. Then she reached over and hugged me. Hugged me hard. Felt great.

"Can I use the binoculars?"

"Are you kidding? They'll give you away in a second. Wear your waitress uniform too, if it's okay with your boss. And maybe you shouldn't sit here and gawk across the road like I did. I sure didn't fool you; I doubt if that lady was fooled, either."

"Does she know you're after her?"

"I'm not after her; I'm after the man I told you about. I don't know if they think anybody's after them. Except I'm wondering what that woman's thinking right now."

This was nothing new. I was always trying to figure out what various females were thinking. A sideline of mine.

"You said they're dangerous. Would they hurt me?"

She had me there. I sat back down and thought about it. Unlikely as it was, what if something did happen to Ellen? How could I live with myself? What would I tell her parents?

"Yes, they're dangerous, Ellen. I see no reason why they would harm you here, but . . . the potential is there. The more I think about it, the more I think we should forget it."

"No way! Five an hour is too good. All I'm doing is watching out of the corner of my eye. And I'm going to do it now, anyway, because I'm curious. And a deal's a deal, Charlie. So that's that!" she said, sitting down again fast, crossing her arms, and flipping her head up and down in a definitive nod.

It was a dowager's gesture; it looked cute as hell when she did it. Her blond ponytail flipped up and she heaved her chest and closed her brown eyes as she sat down. I saw how beautifully tan her legs were. How tight and smooth her skin was all over. . . .

Of course, this had nothing to do with why I was giving in. The kid needed money, and I needed the mobility. Simple as that. And there were other good reasons, too. Given time to think, I had no doubt I could come up with five, or even six.

"Okay, Ellen. You win. A deal's a deal."

THIRTY-ONE

I handed Ellen a fiver, pay for her first hour that she'd just spent with me, and told her I'd call her from down the road when I'd located a phone. I looked at the highway; cars and trucks hummed along it. I didn't know if the woman driving the tan sedan was going to double back, but a hunch told me she would. And since Highway 17 seemed to be the only reasonable road through this low, swampy country, she would probably take it when she turned around. So I got into my car and scooted. In the rearview mirror I saw the lovely, leggy Ellen lean over and blow me a big kiss. All I needed right now. And dammit, here I was again: up to my hindmost in reptiles.

About a mile and a half south of the Sawgrass Shoppes I spotted a phone that was perfect: on the right-hand side of the road, near a gas station but not bordering it, and also near a picnic bench that sat under a small, rounded, bushy tree. I hopped out and called the Small Pleasures sweet shop, giving Ellen the number.

"Ellen, listen: if time is short, just let this phone ring once and hang up," I instructed her. "I'll know that it means she's on her way down this road."

"What if I've got something to say? Or to see if you're all right?"

"I'll be all right."

"I'm kind of worried about you already."

"Don't be."

"Mr. Baxter is mad."

"Mr. Baxter?"

"The owner of this place. One: he saw you giving me money. I'm sure he thinks it was for something else. Two: he doesn't like the idea of his store becoming a spy hangout, you know?"

I sighed into the receiver. How did I ever meet this person? *Why* did I ever meet this person?

"Look, explain that you're just doing this for today—just until you sight her."

"You said you'd keep me on until the job was finished. That's exactly what you said."

"Okay; just don't tell Baxter that."

"Is it safe where you are?"

"It's fine."

"Where exactly are you?"

"About a mile or so down the road, near a picnic table. Now, listen—"

"I know where it is. Is it under a chinaberry tree?"

"I guess so," I said, turning around and looking up at the branches. "But that doesn't—"

"That's where I used to call my boyfriend from, just before we broke up. I hate that place now."

"Ellen, have you seen her?"

"I don't think you should wait there, Charlie. It's bad luck, you know? Can't you go a little further down the road and see if you can find another—"

"Ellen! Has she driven by?"

"No! I'll tell you if I see her. What do you think I am, a space cadet or what?"

"Space cadet?"

"Dr. Adams? Do you know why I came over to talk to you this morning?"

"You asked if I wanted more coffee."

She giggled close into the phone. "Oh, c'mon. You're the space cadet now. I mean *really*. Why I *really* came over."

I said nothing, trying to figure out what the hell she was getting at. And why she was picking now, of all times, to talk about it.

"It's because you remind me of my dad."

"You already told me that."

"You know what? I'm missing him right now. He's gone away from me."

There was a deep sadness in her voice. My hand tensed on the receiver.

"What happened? Is he all right?" I asked.

"Well, I guess *he* is. But I'm sure not. See—and this is easier to say over the phone, that's why I'm telling you now—my mom died four years ago. When that happened, my father and I got really close. But now he's . . . now he's—"

I heard her throat tighten up, she was squealing and coughing . . . crying. Poor kid. And she had chosen me to unload on.

"He's married this . . . this *bitch* who doesn't want me around . . . and so I hardly ever *see* him anymore . . . not like the old days when . . . when . . ."

She was crying in earnest now. I tried to soothe her, but it made it worse, made her open up like a burst dam.

"And so, when I saw you, I just thought how much I'd like to talk to you and—"

"Ellen, I hate to interrupt, but are you watching the road? Are you looking for that woman in the tan—"

"Yes. *Yes, I am . . . Dr. Adams . . . sir!*"

She slammed the phone down. Almost broke my eardrum. Now, what was that all about? I wandered over to the picnic table and sat down on the end of a bench, staring at the road. I looked up at the chinaberry tree and recalled a photograph of Dorothea Lange's, showing a black tenant farmer in the south holding on to a leashed hog that had wrapped the rope around a tree that was a dead ringer for this one. The picture's title: "Under the Chinaberry Tree." How did Ellen know its identity? She was smart, that's why. And I had hurt her just now.

I dropped coins in the box and dialed Small Pleasures again. I had to wait awhile before she came on.

"I'm sorry, Ellen. I didn't mean to sound like that."

"I'm so glad you called me back, Charlie. I thought I was going to die. . . ."

"Have you talked with your father about this? It's got to hurt. Couldn't you just ask him—"

"It doesn't do any good, Charlie. He just says, oh, it'll work out. Everything will work out. That's what he says, when I'm just *dying* inside."

"I'm sorry, Ellen. See, I never had a daughter and I don't—"

"I wish you'd come back here. Just to hold me a little. Just for a little time. I don't mean romantically, Charlie, honest! Just hold me a little and—"

"Listen, I'll buy you dinner later on and we'll have plenty of time to talk."

There it was: the words were out of my mouth before I knew it.

"Ohhh, *thanks*, Charlie. I just can't wait."

I hung up and staggered over to the picnic table, where I sat for maybe thirty minutes trying to figure out what the hell was happening.

Then the phone rang. Just once.

I was up and sprinting for the car. In seconds I had the engine running and the Chevy angled so I could watch the road behind me in the rearview mirror. After an eternity, it must have been almost a minute, I saw the tan sedan coming along the road. After it passed, and another car, I eased out behind it. Ellen had done her part well.

"And I never had a daughter," I whispered. "God, what I've missed!"

I followed the tan car for a long time before it slowed in the left lane, then entered the turning area of the divided highway, its left rear blinker flashing. I saw that it was a Toyota Camray. I kept going, of course, intending to turn around at the first chance and follow the car. Thing was, I had to go down the road almost two miles before I could find a gap in the median strip to turn around. I came back the other way wondering if I could remember the place where she had turned. It looked like a small road named Pelican Watch, but I wasn't positive. Same three palm trees growing together near the big high fence, though. Looked like a good shot. So I drove up Pelican Watch Road toward the ocean. It was immediately apparent that Pelican Watch was a development, and a very high-class one at that. What I saw on each side of me as I followed this small gravel road were luxury cottages, all of them set on big stilts a story high. They were huge, beautifully landscaped and maintained, and looked cozy and fun despite their size. Big bucks for these babies; they made most of the summer houses on the Cape look like manufactured homes. This included the Breakers.

Then I thought of another beach house on the Cape.

Nope. These weren't bigger or better than Northrop Chesterton's little hideaway in Osterville. No, sir.

What did that mean, if anything? Two beach houses in this little adventure: the one the original killing was done in and this one . . . somewhere down here. Maybe it didn't mean anything at all. Now, where the hell was the lady in the tan car?

I slowed to a stop along the gravel shoulder, looking at all these deluxe raised cottages. An older couple came walking down the road, each wearing golfer's-style sunshades. They were walking a small white poodle, who was panting, his little pink tongue hanging out. I asked them if they'd seen a tan Toyota.

"Nope. Sorry."

"Can I ask you something? Why are all these houses set up on stilts?"

"Hurricanes," answered the man, taking a cigar with a plastic tip from his breast pocket and lighting it. Above and behind him, a palm tree swayed in the sea breeze, its fronds rasping. "Those tidal surges come a-roaring right through here."

I thanked them and drove on. One thing about those stilts, they made spotting cars easy because the cars were parked right underneath the cottages, with no garage walls to hide them.

I drove at a crawl up the road, checking all the houses. Still no luck. The road ended right near the ocean at a T-intersection. I turned left and prowled around the cottages, driving slowly and taking all the corners I could without appearing too nosy. No tan car. But I did see a place that stuck in my mind, a cottage named the Walrus and the Carpenter. I thought this name, taken from Lewis Carroll's wacky poem (which is set on a beach) was rather clever. The cottage had four of those bright-colored wind socks waving from the eaves.

I went back to the T-intersection and continued down the road, taking me south. There weren't many people outside; too damn hot. They were either inside, spending the heat of midday in air-conditioned comfort, or out over the bluff on the wide beach. I cruised around that cluster of upper-bracket vacation homes for ten minutes. No dice on the car or the lady. How did the car disappear? Another twenty yards and I had the answer: straight in front of me was Highway 17.

This development had two entrances. Both of them led out to the main drag. All she had to do was turn in, take a right, and follow this curving road right back out, doubling back on me.

Feeling skunked, I drove back to Small Pleasures. Mr. Baxter was waiting for me.

"She's gone. I sent her home. And I told her she couldn't hang around here spying on citizens. You ask me, feller, you shouldn't ask a young girl to do your dirty work for you."

"You're right. Absolutely right, Mr. Baxter. It was a stupid idea."

I turned and began walking back to the car. Somehow this softened him. He followed me to the car. "Just a second; you don't have to rush off. Are you really a doctor?"

"Yes. A surgeon. I live up near Boston."

"Well, mind if I ask why a surgeon is goin' around snoopin' on people this far from home?"

"I'm not going to answer that question," I said after a few seconds' thought, "because I'm not sure I know the answer."

He watched me climb inside, then leaned in the driver's window, scratching the side of his jaw, sticking his finger in his ear. "You Yankees shore kill me. Y'all wouldn'ta won the war if yuh had to rely on yore brains."

As a sometime student of the Civil War, I saw no reason to

dispute this. I was aware of the South's superior military leadership and battle tactics. The North won the war simply because we had ten times the industry, twelve times the rail capacity, and four times the population of the Confederacy. So? This was my fault?

"Ellen says your intentions were honorable," Mr. Baxter offered. He was about sixty, lean with a little potbelly and granny glasses. He wore a Sam Snead–style straw hat with a bright band. He pulled out a pack of Winstons and fired one up. I assured him that my intentions were indeed honorable, but that there still might have been danger involved, so it was perhaps best that it was over.

As I drove back to the motel I couldn't help feeling relieved. It seemed all poor Ellen was looking for was a little surrogate fathering. But there were undertones about it that had made me uneasy, not the least of which was the potential for violence if and when we located our quarry.

Assuming that our spur-of-the-moment dinner engagement was likewise canceled, I went into my motel room, turned the air-conditioning up all the way, and fell onto the bed. The "white noise" from the cooler unit, coupled with the boom of surf outside, made me fall asleep fast.

The phone by my bed woke me up. It was probably Roantis.

"Hi, Charlie, it's me."

"Mary! How did you get this number?"

"It's me silly. Ellen."

I almost dropped the phone.

"Have you forgotten all about me already?"

"Uh, no. Of course not."

"I'm calling to remind you that we're going to dinner tonight. I've got a real special place picked out."

"Ellen, I don't think we better do that."

"C'mon, you promised."

"Well, I've been thinking, and—"

"Is this how you keep commitments?"

We went around and around on this until she talked me into it. It took a while for her to persuade me. Twelve or thirteen seconds, at least. Just call me Iron Will Adams.

"By the way, how did you get my number, Ellen?"

"You told me where you were staying, remember?"

"No. But then, I don't remember much these days. I'm over the hill, you know."

"No, you're not; you're just fine. Listen: I know a real nice cozy seafood restaurant down near Surfside. I'll be down at your place in an hour, okay?"

"Ellen, what's your last name?"

"Findlay. Ellen Findlay."

I rubbed my eyes and looked at my watch: 6:15. I'd slept longer than intended.

"Okay, meet me here at seven."

At five of, a soft knock came at my door. I tightened up all over. Couldn't help it. I opened the door and let her in. She was wearing a pink jumpsuit of some light material, a string of small pearls around her neck, and a pair of white heels. She wore some makeup now, not too much. Just the right amount. And she'd let her hair out; it fell all around her shoulders in waves of gold. And she smelled great. She carried a blue-and-white beach bag slung on her shoulder. She went over to the bed and dropped it there, then came back and looked out the window at the beach. As she leaned over to peek at the ocean I noticed that this jumpsuit had apparently been applied with a spray gun. If she looked fetching before, in her waitress clothes, she was now enough to give this old guy the triple fantods.

This is a mistake, Adams! said a voice.

"Gosh, what a lovely view," she purred, sitting down in a chair and tossing her hair back. "I could get used to this place."

"I . . . I don't know about this, Ellen," I said, fumbling for my car keys. "I tried to tell you on the phone. See, the thing is, I'm worried about—"

"It'll be fine; you'll love this place," she said, sidestepping the issue. "Trust me."

There were a lot of seafood joints along the road. One that sticks in my memory is Drunken Jack's, a restaurant with a big carved drunken sailor out front, drinking rum out of a bottle.

I could skip it. At Ellen's direction we drove on and turned off the main road, then down a curving gravel lane up to a cottage-style place right on the water, surrounded with big oaks and swaying Spanish moss. As we walked up the wide, creaky wooden stairs onto the veranda Ellen explained that the restaurant was a converted house. The place was called Esmeralda, and it was gorgeous. We were told there would be a thirty-minute wait for a table, so we sat on old wicker chairs outside on the veranda, on the sea side, and watched the evening come.

The sky was getting deep, dark blue on the horizon; the setting sun's rays were golden red on the beach, and the western sky, out over the blowing palm trees, was glowing. Strings of brown pelicans drifted silently above the shoreline while tiny sandpipers scampered in the breaking waves. I was sipping on a martini. Ellen was having a whiskey sour. They hadn't asked for her ID card, and this surprised me. Ancient ceiling fans swirled above our heads. I smelled lilac and honeysuckle and warm sea wind. And Ellen Findlay.

I heard a faint pop up the beach and turned to see a ball of silver light and a puff of gray smoke.

"Fireworks," said Ellen softly. "Every beach has signs saying they're illegal, but every night you can watch those skyrockets going off all night long." Another plume of smoke spiraled its way into the air above the sand, and another pop, another ball of flame, this one orange. The sparkles fell earthward. I liked this. I liked it a lot. I took another sip.

"Well, did you find out where she lives?" she asked.

"Who?"

"C'mon, Charlie: the woman in the tan car. I was so upset earlier I forgot to ask you."

"No, I didn't; she gave me the slip in a development she turned into."

"Well, where do you want me to watch tomorrow? Mr. Baxter said he doesn't want me watching from the shop."

"I don't know, Ellen. Maybe there's no more spying for you to do."

"C'mon, Charlie; you said I could. You said you'd pay me five dollars an hour. And I need the money. I have an assistantship next year, but grad school's expensive."

"What are you studying?"

"Psychology. I'm going to get my Ph.D. and become a counselor."

"I have a good friend who's in that business. He's crazy."

"Well, I'm not. Now isn't there *anything* I can do for you?"

Looking at her sitting there in the evening light, smelling the perfume coming off her, I could think of several things.

"I'll pay you five an hour if there's anything to be done. Problem is, Ellen, I don't think there's anything right now."

She shifted in her chair, trying to hide her disappointment.

"So, how many times a week do you work out?"

"Four. How did you know I work out?"

"Come on. It's real obvious," she said.

I looked out at the darkening ocean and shook my head slowly. Two days ago I was up in Massachusetts with Mary, being an oral surgeon and a respectable member of the community. At least, as respectable as I ever get, which is about eighty percent. Then what happens? I get a wild hair and go down to South Carolina. Next thing I know I'm having dinner with a girl who could be my daughter, and she's calling me Charlie. I realized I was feeling a trifle light-headed. Must be the martini. But then again, it could be the sea breeze, the sunset, and this young woman. I glanced around and saw that many of the patrons in the bar were staring at us. The men were grinning, their wives were frowning. Somehow this didn't bother me.

Careful Adams! You can be a real knucklehead at times! said the voice in my head again. Funny thing about that voice, though; it was getting fainter and fainter. . . .

The headwaiter approached and informed us our table was ready. We followed him inside and he put us in a booth next to a picture window. It was dark in there and lighted with candles in hurricane lamps. I had blackened mahimahi; she had lobster. The food was great. We split a bottle of chenin blanc with the meal. After dinner we had Irish coffees. About that time they started playing live music out back on an outdoor dance floor. Ellen stood up and grabbed my hand.

"C'mon," she said, leading me toward the music. "This is why I picked this place."

It was a dance floor out under the oaks. The huge trees were illuminated by spotlights pointing straight up. The effect was, well, romantic. I just can't think of another word for it. A five-piece band, dressed in white dinner jackets and sitting under a gazebo, was playing 1930s dance tunes. But the music wasn't loud and brassy; it was cool and cozy. A dozen or so white- and blue-haired couples were out there, sliding around on that open-air dance floor. I'm not much into the dance thing, but Ellen was pretty insistent. Soon we were swaying together in the near dark. She was up against me, and pretty soon put her arms around my neck.

"I love this, Charlie. I just love it," she whispered.

At the end of the dance I raised my head and half turned, ready to walk off the floor. But she reached up and caught my head, holding it down, and kissed me on the cheek.

"Thank you," she said in a throaty voice.

As we walked off the dance floor I had a sudden vision of Mary. I saw her standing among these oldsters in the crowd, looking at us with tears in her eyes. That did it. I knew what I had to do.

"Why so *soon*?" said Ellen, pouting as I put her into my car. "I mean, it's only nine-thirty, Charlie. What's the deal, huh?"

"The deal is, I just can't . . . can't stay out with you."

"You feel guilty?"

"Yes. Very. It was one thing to have you on the lookout for me. It's entirely another to go out to dinner and then dance together. That's a date. And it's wrong."

"Am I tempting you?" She said it in a whisper so low and throaty I could scarcely hear it.

"Yes, you are. And how."

"Thank God for that, at least. I was hoping we could go swimming later on."

"No way."

We pulled into the lot at the Smugglers' Den. I had the routine all planned out, and there would be no deviation. I got out of the driver's door, walked around, and helped her out. Then I walked her directly to her car and put her inside, and grabbed her hand. Pumped it twice.

"So this is it?"

"Yes," I answered. "I had a nice time, Ellen."

"I had a wonderful time, Charlie, and I'll see you soon."

Her eyes were slightly wet. She backed out of the parking slot fast, squealing her tires in anger. She stopped at the road, waiting for a break in traffic. I saw the window come down.

"You'll see me again, Charlie," she promised. "I won't forget tonight . . . and neither will you." She cranked the window back and drove away, heading for North Myrtle Beach. I heaved a big sigh of relief. Was it also disappointment? No; for once in my stupid life I had done the right thing. Even Moe would be proud of me. What would Mary think?

I shuddered. She must never, ever know.

THIRTY-TWO

Next morning, all I could think about was the close shave I'd had with Ellen. It was killing me. I went for a dip in the ocean, trying to drive out the twin demons of guilt and lust with strenuous exercise. I think it worked. Kind of.

I called home three times. No answer. I wondered where Mary was. I tried Joe and Marty's apartment. No answer. Perhaps the three of them had gone down to the Breakers for a breather. Positive this was the answer, I dialed the cottage and got no answer. I had the funny feeling that something was brewing up in Massachusetts.

It was now past ten, and time for me to resume watching the post office, or perhaps hang out under the chinaberry tree and wait for Madame X in the tan Toyota. As I was getting ready to leave the motel room I noticed Ellen's blue-and-white beach bag on the floor. She'd forgotten it. I picked it up and unzipped it. I smelled suntan lotion. Inside was a small makeup kit and a bikini bathing suit. It was made of lightweight tank material, colored hot pink with lime-green neon stripes. There was maybe enough material in the whole outfit for a large hanky. I shuddered; if she had come back to the room and squiggled into that flimsy thing, there's no telling what would have happened. On my way through the lobby I told Don Lineberry to tell any female caller that I checked out.

"Back up to Massachusetts, you mean?"

"Just tell her I'm gone."

"Whatever you say, doctor."

"If she comes by, can you give her this?" I asked, holding up the beach bag she'd left behind.

"I'd rather not keep things for other people, if you don't mind. They tend to walk away."

"I understand. I'll drop it off where she used to work."

Half an hour later, at 10:30, I was sitting with my straw beach hat and sunglasses on a small concrete bench next door to the P.O. at Murrells Inlet. I avoided Small Pleasures for obvious reasons, not the least of which was that the woman had seen me there across the highway, gaping at her.

At 11:15 I saw a young man with long hair wearing a billed fisherman's cap go inside the building and lean down in front of George's box. For a while I was unsure if he was after the box I was watching, but as he walked out of the building I caught another glimpse of him and a bell went off inside my head. Damned if he didn't look a lot like that guy on the beach in Osterville. The one throwing the Frisbee for the golden retriever.

I waited until his silver sedan was almost out of sight, heading south on Highway 17, before I pulled out in the Chevy and followed. When he turned left onto Pelican Watch Road—the same place that the woman had turned into earlier—I was fairly certain he was the same man Paul Keegan and I failed to outrun up on Cape Cod. Once again I drove on by the road, doubled back, and turned into the development, scouting the cottages for his car. No dice. Where the hell were they hiding all these cars? It was hot now, and I was disgusted. I gave up the chase for the time being and headed north, deciding it was time to see Myrtle Beach.

Shortly past noon I was walking along the boardwalk of Myrtle Beach. I suppose at one time the place was meant to rival Atlantic City. In tackiness, it sure came close. The wide beach—

that ran, as far as I could tell, for scores of miles with scarcely a break—was bordered on its back side by sloping bluffs that were covered with beach grass, scrub oak, sumac, and similar stuff. At the top of this bluff, sixty or seventy feet above the beach, was a paved walkway that constituted the boardwalk. On the inland side of this roadway, facing the ocean, was a line of boutiques, theaters, souvenir shops, fireworks stores, smut shops, videogame parlors, music stores and so on, and on. But the view from the big piers was impressive. These piers were set up on tall pilings, like the ones on Malibu Beach. They seemed to be spaced along the Grand Strand every quarter mile or so. I walked out on one and leaned on the railing, looking south. The beach and the people and the piers and sea gulls and pelicans and the rippling kites seemed to go on forever. The air was misty now, with a light fog. It made the place look ethereal, dreamlike.

I watched the surfers riding their "bungy" boards along the big swells. All the surfers had their boards tied to their wrists by long plastic lines. While convenient, I thought this might be unsafe, since a board caught in a heavy current, or lodged against a piling deep down, could drown its owner. But apparently not. The riders fell into the soup in spider forms of tan limbs and bright suits. Milliseconds later the bright bungy boards would pop out of the surf like Trident missiles, then the surfers would sputter to the surface, shouting and whooping and waving their slick arms. Far up the beach came more faint pops and smoke puffs—the ever-present fireworks.

Speaking of fireworks, I wondered what would have happened if by some chance Mary found out about Ellen, brief and innocent as it was. I shuddered. Then I thought of Ellen again. Couldn't help it. Why had she been attracted to me? Because I remind her of her father, I theorized. A man for whom she has strong Oedipal feelings. Forbidden feelings, which she was transferring to me. "Well, you're better off away from it!" I whispered to myself.

As if a sign from on high, a sea gull glided over to the pier railing, landed on the wooden board in a flurry of wing beats, and waddled to within six feet of me. He leaned over and blinked his yellow eyes at me and screamed. Scolding me.

"Take it easy, pal," I said. "I'm behaving myself." He wasn't convinced, and kept yonking at me. Maybe I was standing on his turf. I left the pier, musing on the nature of women, undoubtedly the most fascinating, and dangerous, things on earth, and walked along the boardwalk, looking for a present for Mary. Frankly, the selection wasn't all that hot: T-shirts with gross pictures on them, and even grosser words. Beach hats. Fake jewelry, tacky souvenirs, and so on. One window did catch my eye, however. I found myself staring at a very sexy-looking teddy. I pictured Mary wearing it. Nice. Then my mind's eye pictured Ellen wearing it. Total, nonstop knockout. I closed my eyes and squeezed the bridge of my nose to clear my head. Pictured Mary wearing it again. Good. Mary is gorgeous anyway. Nobody can fill out a pair of undies or a French-cut bra like she can. I looked up at the name of the store. It was called Under Cover. The name seemed appropriate. I went inside.

"Now this outfit we call the Temptress," said the lady wearing lavender eye shadow and glossy purple lipstick. She was somewhere between fifty and sixty, with a lot of miles on her. Still, I liked her leather miniskirt. It was appropriate in this kind of shop, I thought. "I'll hold the briefs up for you. As you can see," she continued, "it's a sheer fabric—"

She held the panties up. I could see her clearly through them. And if they accidentally fell from her grasp, they'd take ninety seconds to reach the countertop.

"Yeah, I can see that," I said. "Give me two in size six, white and black."

"Size six?" she said, eyeing my wedding band.

"Yes, they're for my wife."

"Right." She winked a big, slow wink at me. "As if your wife wears a size six . . ."

"She does, actually."

"Well, then you're a lucky man."

"I know."

I walked out of the lingerie store and headed for the car,

which was parked in the big lot at the end of the strand. I couldn't wait to see Mary in these new undies, but I felt a little funny carrying the sack around. It was bright pink plastic and had pictures of scantily clad women all over it. When I got to the car and had opened the doors to let it cool, I noticed Ellen's beach bag again. I stuffed the lingerie bag inside it; it made a handy way to carry the goods back to the motel without announcing the contents to the world.

I drove back to the motel for a run and a swim. I needed some limbering up. I took my canvas rucksack and Ellen's beach bag inside with me. I took the Smith and the Tanto fighting knife and stuffed them underneath the mattress. I wondered what to do with that damn beach bag. I could find out where Ellen lived and drop it off, but that was trouble; I'd rather not know where she lived. Probably the best thing was to take it back to Small Pleasures and leave it with Mr. Baxter. For the time being I stowed it underneath the chair next to the back door.

I went running first, making my way down the beach in a slow trot, thirty minutes down and thirty minutes back, which was about seven miles. I was running barefoot, with nothing but shorts on, so when I finished the run, I jumped right into the ocean and swam and played in the big rolling breakers for another forty minutes. It's amazing how tired you can get fighting all that big water. I have never seen another beach with water so warm and comfortable. I finished the swim with a dip in the motel pool to rinse the brine off, then went inside, dried off, and lay down on the bed in the cool of the air-conditioning. I dozed off and woke much later than I expected. Looking out the window, I saw it was early evening. You're getting old, Adams, I thought.

Then the phone rang. Funny, thinking back, I'm sure I had an uneasy feeling before I even picked it up. . . .

"Charlie, it's me."

"Mary?"

"Who else?"

"How? How did you get this number?"

"I got your number by keeping you on the phone a little

longer during our conversation the other night. And Joe traced the call."

"You want me to come home?"

"No. I want you to tell me what room you're in, dunderhead. I'm out here in the lobby with Joe."

"Where?"

"In the lobby of this place. The Smugglers' Den. Listen, sweetie, I'm sorry I was so rough on you. I'm sure I can make it up, okay? Now, tell me the room and I'll be there in two seconds. How's that sound?"

THIRTY-THREE

A knock on the door. "Charlie?"

I went and opened it. Mary was standing there, smiling. Looking great in a light pink dress and her long hair pulled back. I hugged and kissed her. She put her hands on my arms and shoved me away, looking at me at arm's length the way a doctor examines a patient.

"Hey, are you ever tan! What have you been doing down here, lounging by the pool all day or what?"

"I've been scouting for our old friend, George. In my spare time I've been running the beach. You won't believe how great the water is down here. Where's Joe?"

"He's with Marty, driving up the highway looking for another motel. The manager here says this place just got filled up." She looked at her watch. "Hey, it's almost six; don't you want to go out to dinner with us?"

"Sure. Just let me shave and get dressed—"

She followed me into the room and sat down in the window chair.

"Nice place. So, I take it that George Brenner, a.k.a. Roy Harris, is nearby?"

I nodded. "He's up the beach, I think. In a plush beach house. Doesn't that strike you as odd, Mary? That this whole business begins and ends at beach houses?"

"I guess so. You know, Charlie, I'm still a bit chagrined that you just took off like that. And don't think I believed any of that shit about you and Brady going fishing, either."

"When's Joe due back here?" I said, changing the subject.

"In about thirty minutes. The manager, what's his name?"

"Don Lineberry."

"Uh-huh, well, he called a place up the road for Joe. He knows he can get a room. I plan on staying here with you, chum. That is, if you haven't coerced some young thing to shack up with you already."

"Ha! Very funny!" I said, feeling my knees begin to tremble. Then I remembered something. Ever so cautiously, I sneaked a look downward. There, on the carpet right underneath the chair Mary was sitting in, was Ellen's beach bag.

My blood went cold.

"Charlie? Are you okay?"

"Yep . . ." I mumbled.

"You look pale all of a sudden. And you're twitching."

"I'm fine; never felt better. Hey, Mary, maybe you'd like to go wait for Joe out by the pool. Sit underneath those palm trees and—"

"I'm fine right here. Now go into the john and shave and get dressed, will you? You know Joey; when he comes back, he'll be hungry."

"Well, there are plenty of good seafood joints all along this road," I said nonchalantly. Oh God, to get out of this room and into the lobby . . .

I went into the john and closed the door. I ran the electric razor over my face quickly. Not only was this faster than a blade shave, but safer. The way my hands were trembling, I'd bleed to death in no time if I used a real razor. All was quiet in the room. I hoped she was looking out the window. So far, Mary hadn't noticed the bag. Maybe there was hope. Please, God, don't let her notice it. *Please.*

"C'mon, Charlie, let's go. I'm hungry; we haven't had anything to eat since the snack on the plane."

"I'm moving as fast as I can." Boy, was that an understatement. As I stood before the sink I promised God that if Mary didn't discover the beach bag, I would join a monastery. One of those isolated clifftop ones in Macedonia where they send food up to you once a month in a basket on a rope and pulley.

I heard footsteps from beyond the door; Mary was walking around the room!

I would also shave my head, wear a hair shirt, and spend all my waking hours praying on my knees in a cold stone chapel....

I heard Mary sit down in the chair again. There was hope. I was rounding a nasty corner, but I saw a glint of daylight through the thorns. If my luck held, it would be clear sailing once I got her out of the room and into the hallway, walking to the lobby to meet Joe. Almost there . . . almost there . . .

"Who is Ellen Findlay?" came a voice from the bedroom.

My heart gave three mighty thumps and stopped. I was probably going to die now. Just as well. The john door opened, and I turned and saw Mary holding the blue-and-white beach bag, looking at the name tag affixed to the handle. All was lost. So close to safety . . . I looked heavenward—

"She's . . . she's, uh . . ."

Mary walked back over to the bed and unzipped the bag. She was pawing inside it.

"What the hell is this, Charlie?"

I came into the room and reached for the bag. She pulled away and spun around, still looking inside. I heard the crinkle of the pink plastic bag as she pulled it free. She held up the bag, looking at the semidressed women on it. *"Under Cover?"* Would you like to explain this?"

"This, uh, person, was helping me watch the post office. She accidentally left her bag here. . . ."

"What was she doing in here? Speak up, Charlie! *It better be good.* And this person, this Ellen Findlay. For your sake, she had better be over fifty, fat, and homely. Do I make myself clear?"

"Perfectly."

She reached into the bag, extracted a pair of panties, and let them fall. They began their slow, silky descent to the floor. She held the bag over the bed and shook it upside down. Out fell the two sheer sleep outfits, a garter belt, a peek-a-boo bra, three pairs of nylons, a bustier, a merry widow, and two sheer teddies.

She turned and looked at me. On her face was a look of bewilderment and deep hurt. Oh God.

"They're for you, Mary. Honest."

She flung the bag down. "Don't lie to me, Charlie! It's bad enough—"

I moved to comfort her and explain everything. How could this happen? Things couldn't possibly get any worse.

There came a knocking at the door.

"Who's that?"

"I have no idea," I said, moving toward it. But Mary intercepted me and got there first. I knew she suspected something. She tried the door, saw that it was locked, almost broke the hardware getting it unfastened, and flung it open. There, in ultra-brief cutoff jeans and a tight cotton jersey, stood Ellen Findlay. She had obviously spent the day sunbathing. Her golden skin was set off by her golden hair that cascaded in waves down along her shoulders.

"Charlie? I came by for my beach bag that I left here the other night."

"Charlie?" gasped Mary. "You called him *Charlie*?"

"That's his name, isn't it? So, hey, what's the deal, lady? And who the hell are *you*, anyway?"

THIRTY-FOUR

Joe met me out on the beach at 8:20 as the sun was getting low in the sky. The red sky looked the same as it had the previous night. But instead of being gorgeous, it was now a bloody wound in the western horizon. What a difference a day makes. Life sure is funny.

In fact, life is a regular riot.

I was standing barefoot on the wet, hard-packed sand, ready to start my second run of the day. It was now way past time for drinks and dinner. But—surprise, surprise—we weren't going out to eat at one of those Grand Strand seafood joints. Why? Because Mary was telling Joe she wanted to divorce me. Right now.

"You've got to admit, Doc, it doesn't look good. You run off to the beach to locate George Brenner. So we follow you down here—"

"By sheer trickery, Joe," I said, leaning into a stretch, "Mary kept me on the phone so you could use your law enforcement authority to have the call traced. She admitted it. Well?"

"True. We did so in the interests of family unity. What a laugh that turned out to be. We arrive on the scene to find you shacked up with a twenty-two-year-old woman, a girl just a few years shy of jailbait."

"I was not shacked up with her. Now, listen: I'm going for

a run to get all these bad chemicals out of me."

"That's another thing: Mary says that whenever trouble looms, you always run."

"Right. The same way I 'ran' down here to find George. She's just trying to push my buttons again. Tell her it's better than fighting. I have been unjustly accused, and it's making me angry. Now, listen, I'll make you a deal."

"No deals on this."

"Oh yes; hear me out. When you have a pair of suspects, what's your usual interrogation procedure?"

"We separate them as soon as possible. Put them in different rooms, then interview them one at a time to see if their stories match. If they don't, we examine the discrepancies to see what they might mean."

"Right. Now, do that with Ellen and me; that's all I'm asking."

"What if she doesn't agree?"

"Tell her it'll get Mary off her ass. She'll agree."

"So what are you going to do, run down the beach?"

"Yes. You see those big buildings way in the distance?"

He squinted into the darkening horizon. "You aren't going to run all the way down there, are you?"

"Yes, and back again. Along the way I'm going to be on the lookout for that silver car I mentioned. See if I can spot it parked under one of those beachside villas, okay? So if I don't come back within, say, three hours, call out the guard. Meantime, why don't you and the women go out and get some seafood?"

"I think just Marty and I will go; Mary doesn't feel like eating."

I looked down at the sand and tried to draw patterns in it with my big toe. "I can understand that, and I'm sorry. I never claimed it was the smartest thing I've done."

"It sure as hell *wasn't*."

"Does Sarah Brenner know you came down here?"

"You kidding? Nobody knows we came down here. Mary didn't even tell Moe. And I didn't tell anybody at work except

Kevin. Lucky it's the weekend. We've got to wrap this thing up tomorrow and get back Sunday. So you see why this Don Juan bullshit has us a little rattled."

I looked out to sea for comfort and found none. "Well, it's a good thing Sarah didn't come with you; there's no telling what we'll find down here, but I've got a feeling it wouldn't make her happy. Ever since she got that check in the mail she's had this romantic notion that if she can locate George, they'll get back together again, happily ever after."

Joe shook his head. "That's not in the cards. No way. I guess it's best we just sneaked down here without telling anyone."

"How much authority do you have here in South Carolina?"

"Zip. I'm a state cop for Massachusetts. Period. As far as we're concerned, I'm a bystander."

"You bring your Beretta?"

"Oh yeah. An off-duty cop is permitted that. Now tell me: where do you think he's holed up?"

I explained as best I could, saying I hadn't located the cottage, but I was pretty sure of the general location.

"Okay, Doc. Tomorrow, if things calm down a bit, we'll check it out. If we think we've got a line on him, I can get in touch with the locals and we'll flush him out. Meantime, I think—hey, here comes your loved one. Now, please, no fisticuffs—"

I looked up to see Mary walking toward us. She was stamping her bare feet down hard on the sand as she walked; she had been crying again. It was devastating to see the hurt on her face. That was what so surprised me about her reaction. Expecting anger, I was surprised and shocked to see the pain I had caused. And I had not meant to.

"I'm sorry, Mare. I told you that before. And remember: I never even kissed her."

"Oh, spare me. What do you want, the fucking *Victoria Cross*?"

"So what should I do? Kneel down on the sand and commit hari-kari?"

"It would be a nice start."

She started sniffling again.

"Here's what's going to happen," growled Joe in his official police tone. He rarely uses it, especially with family. But when he does, everybody listens. "Mary and Marty and I are going to have cocktails, then go out to eat. Then I'll interview Ellen. When you get back from your run, Doc, I'll interview you. If your stories match and it appears you're correct, then as far as I'm concerned, that settles the matter."

"Well, it won't for me!" said Mary.

"Oh yes, it *will*," said Joe, stomping off. Good old Joe; you can always count on him when the chips are down. And I'll say this for him too: he seemed to have come a long way with his sister since those Bobby Rydell days.

Mary and Joe walked off to find Marty. I squinted into the southern horizon and began my run, starting slowly and breathing deeply from the start to get ahead of oxygen debt. That's the secret.

Thirty minutes later I was in full swing and feeling better already. My body and mind felt much more relaxed; nothing gets rid of excess adrenaline like prolonged aerobic exercise. I knew Joe would smooth over things because he believed my story initially, and conversations with Ellen would confirm it. Then, when we got back home, I would make it up to Mary.

I didn't make it to the condos, and no wonder: I had already run ten miles earlier that day. In bare feet, on the sand. My legs were knotty and weak. I sat down on the sand and rested as the light began to fall, getting drinks of water every few minutes at a nearby spigot. The beach down here was almost deserted. No kiddies with kites. No fishermen casting bright plugs into the surf. A few couples lounging on their terraces after dinner, that was about it. I looked at my watch. It was past nine. The sun had disappeared over the palmettos on the landward side of the beach. In about twenty more minutes it would be dark. I started back, aware that my legs had tightened up even more during my rest. Two miles into the homeward leg, my right knee began to ache. I slowed to a trot, then a brisk walk, then back to the trot. Then I noticed that I had an open blister on my left foot. Great. Resigned to walking back, I limped another half mile until something over the sea berm caught my eye in the falling light.

It was a cottage with three of those brightly colored windsock pennants flying off its upper deck. I wanted to get closer, so I went to the beach stairs and climbed them, then walked along the raised wooden walkway that led from the beach over the low bluffs, or berms, to the roads beyond. It was dark on the other side of the sea berm; the trees hung over the roads and blocked the glow from the west. The cottage with the three wind socks looked familiar. When I got closer, I knew why. It was the cottage called the Walrus and the Carpenter. I remembered it from my scouting earlier. Therefore, I was near Pelican Watch Road, the same development in South Litchfield that I had followed the tan car into.

For ten minutes I walked along the gravel roads, working the kink out of my knee. When that didn't work, I sat down on the side of the road on the cool sand and massaged it. The blister was nasty, and hurt like blazes. I stretched my legs out and just sat. The sea breeze was blowing through those coastal pines. Nightjars called in hollowy echoes. I smelled more sweet flowers: gardenias and lilacs. The air was dark blue now, and wisps of silvery clouds were drifting overhead, almost invisible until you stared awhile. All I could think about was Mary.

I kept telling myself that the thing with Ellen was innocent. It was accidental, brief, platonic. It was innocent. And therefore I was wrongly accused.

I thought about this. I could fit most of the first part in the cubbyhole. The part about the thing with Ellen being innocent, at the start at least. Accidental and . . . not exactly accidental. Unplanned is better. Innocent and accidental. Pretty much. But the part about being wrongly accused didn't fit in. Didn't wash. I wasn't wrongly accused; I was wrong. Wrong at least for giving a misleading impression. Not only to Mary, which was obvious and hurtful, but to the world. The worst part was, I was pretending to be somebody I wasn't. . . .

I stood up, walked on another block, and sat down again. Daylight was gone; the only illumination came from house lights and those monstrous blue-vapor overhead horrors, bright as flashbulbs that won't wink out, every hundred yards or so. I heard the pad of feet and saw a dog waddling toward me in the dark. I smooched at it, and it crept up to me, sighed, and leaned its head over to be petted. Looked to me like a fat setter. I petted it and felt the long setter coat between my fingers. It sighed again and sat down. I petted the dog, talking soft nonsense to it. It wagged its tail at me and licked my hand.

How can some people not love dogs? *How?* Answer me that.

The breeze picked up and a clump of nearby palmettos made a scraggly, raspy sound as the spiky fronds flapped together. The plants were only a few feet away, but I could scarcely see them. Next, I smelled broiling chicken and my salivary glands had a convulsion. I realized I hadn't eaten since my snack with Ellen at two. Mug of coffee and a stale, sugary doughnut. Then all the emotional strain, and the running on top of it. No wonder I didn't feel so hot. But mostly it was guilt. Guilt in droves. I stood up in the darkness, realized my eyes had accustomed themselves to it, and followed the very dim pale path of crushed rock before me. It hurt to walk, and I took it slow. The dog at my side turned up a side street and I followed. We walked down a hedgerow and around a broad curve before I realized the pooch was going home. I stopped and did an about-face, ready to return to the beach and resume my run, when I heard chimes.

It was the sound of a giant music box, far away.

Tum . . . ta tum *ta ta ta* tum, *TA TUM!*

A pause, then the tune played again:

Tum . . . ta tum *ta ta ta* tum, *TA TUM!*

I walked toward the sound. It was not coming from far away; it was coming softly from close by. I walked between the giant stilts of a raised beach cottage. The sound seemed to be coming from directly over my head now. I knew what those chimes were.

They were the "interval" melody of Deutsche Welle, the German national world-service radio. I cocked my ears, and soon heard the booming, guttural voice of the announcer coming all the way from Cologne, West Germany.

"This is the world service of Deutsche Welle, the voice of Germany. The time is now one hour, seventeen minutes, Coordinated Universal Time. . . ."

Tum . . . ta tum *ta ta ta* tum, *TA TUM*!

I looked at my watch again: 9:17. He was reading Greenwich time, of course, the time used by all world-band transmitters, which was five hours ahead of ours. But only four hours now, because we were on daylight savings time, having set our clocks ahead an hour. I walked softly now, a spook among the large vertical beams. Then I saw it.

Toward the back end of the cottage was the wire I was looking for: a thin, sloping cable descending at a forty-five-degree angle from the top of the cottage roof and fastened to a tree forty feet away. I looked closer in the dark and saw the two coil condensers affixed at strategic points along the antenna. A DXer's "sloper" antenna. The dog was now walking placidly up the front stairs to the cottage. As he climbed the stairway he walked into the pool of light thrown by the small bulb over the cottage's front door, and I finally got a good look at him.

The dog wasn't a fat Irish setter.

It was a golden retriever.

I walked slowly on underneath the cottage, toward the far end of it, and peeked around a thicket of bushes and palmettos. There, cleverly hidden from all roads, was a silver sedan.

"Who are you and what do you want?"

The voice was a rich female contralto. I turned to see a woman standing behind me. She held a dark object in each of her hands. Two guns? She took a step toward me. She was the black woman we'd been watching at the post office. I was sure of it. I thought the thing in her hand was indeed a gun. And what about my weapons? The Smith & Wesson and the Tanto fighting knife? Left behind at the last minute. This is your own fault, Adams.

"Who are you? What do you want?"

I decided to level with her.

"I'm looking for an old friend of mine. George Brenner. I think now he's calling himself Roy Harris."

"Who are you?"

"My friends call me Doc. I knew George when he was living with Sarah up in Massachusetts. Also, I think I've seen you before. Where would that have been?"

"I'm asking *you* the questions." Her voice had the Jamaican lilt to it.

"I know who you are; I saw your picture in Chesterton's mansion, with the other household staff. You're Anne Rawlings, Margaret Chesterton's personal maid."

"Don't talk; just walk in front of me up the stairs."

"Is George up there?"

"Just walk."

I began walking toward the stairway, and remembered Rule Number One.

Roantis is always stressing Rule Number One: if they've got you covered, make your move *before* it's too late. Before they've got you chained to the old bed frame with the electric wires hooked to it. Just before I put my right foot on the first stair, I ducked and pivoted, beginning my swing. I caught Ms. Rawlings on the jaw, and she staggered back. I hit her again in her stomach. It was a very hard stomach. Then she raised up her right hand. I saw what looked like a thin gun in it. I was getting ready to duck when she moved her arm up next to my shoulder. Just before she touched me with that little black tube I heard the high whine of a capacitor charging. Sounded just like a strobe flash unit charging up.

She tapped me with the black gizmo and a bolt of lightning hit my shoulder and ran all through me. I collapsed on the ground just as I heard the screen door open overhead. From the same direction, almost directly above me, came the metallic *clink-clank* of an automatic pistol being cocked.

"Who is it, Anne?" said a vaguely familiar whisper.

"A man who says he knows you. A man named Doc."

"I'll be damned. I'll send Henry down to bring him up. Meantime, if he moves, shoot him."

It was George, all right. But he didn't seem all that glad to see me.

realized I was lying on my side, my right cheekbone grinding into the dry pine needles that covered the ground. I couldn't move my arms or legs, but my eyes could look about. Anne Rawlings, personal maid of Margaret Chesterton, had been a sentry below the house. She'd used a stun gun on me, and I was temporarily paralyzed. I saw the stairway above me. The screen door opened and a man descended the stairs, turned at the bottom, and walked to where I was lying under the cottage. He was big and dark. He lifted me in his arms and carried me fast up the stairs, as if carrying a baby back to his crib. When he sat me down in the dark room in a soft chair, I got scared. I suppose it hadn't had time to hit me before.

The big man backed off.

"Anne, draw the curtains, please," said the familiar voice. The curtains closed and a light at the far end of the room glowed brighter and brighter. The man standing next to it was the same height and build as George Brenner, but there the resemblance ended. This man had thinning dark hair and a mustache. He turned the rheostat of the light up further. Then I saw the familiar jawline and facial features of the man I had known in Concord. George Brenner, his dapper old self, was now dressed in a khaki safari coat and pleated pants. He casually reached inside his coat pocket and drew out a small pocket automatic pistol.

"Well, Doc Adams. I guess I'm not altogether surprised you showed up here. Larry, my assistant who's been keeping watch for me up in Massachusetts, has been telling me about your activities regarding this . . . business."

I was regaining feeling and motor control in my limbs now. I tried to stretch out my legs and half succeeded. The carpet was plush beige. The place seemed very expensively furnished.

"Henry, go outside and keep watch, will you? The others could be nearer than we think."

The big man went for the front door, taking a big .45 from his coat as he did so. I got a good look at Henry now that the light was turned up. He was bald, tall, and very muscular. Must have been a body builder or boxer. His skin was dark, but not the rich brown of most black people. Instead it was dark, smoke gray. The same color as the old government pistol with the dull bluing that he held in his monstrous hand. The color of stale coffee when you add milk to it. The big man went out the front door without a sound. I wasn't sorry to see him go.

"How did you find me here, Doc?"

I told him.

"Ah, the radio! You remembered the radio thing."

"You got me going on it, in case you don't remember."

"Who else knows I'm here?"

I told him a whole lot of people, including Lieutenant Detective Joseph Brindelli, who was waiting in a motel room not two miles away. I added that if I didn't return soon, he and a bunch of other cops were coming looking for me. I advised him to act accordingly.

"Turn myself in? You're kidding, of course."

"It won't take them long to find you, George. Or is it Roy now?"

"I have a lot of names. But my friends always call me George. If you haven't guessed, the reason I left no ID on the corpse found in Pinky Chesterton's house was because I knew then, as now, that I may have further need of George Brenner sometime in the future. Anne, is the lady still awake?"

The maid nodded.

"Please tell her to get her things together immediately. I'm afraid we'll be vacating the premises within the hour."

"She says she's plenty tired of moving, sah."

"I haven't time to argue; tell her to get cracking, will you?"

Anne Rawlings disappeared through the darkened doorway, and he turned to me. "I have other things to worry about than the police, Doc. Maybe your stumbling across us is just what we needed; if you hadn't come, we might have been trapped. You didn't happen to see a brown van in the area, did you?"

"Yes," I lied. "Out toward Highway 17, before I came up this road."

He glanced toward the front door and at the windows.

"Who are you expecting? The guys in the brown van? The Purple Gang?"

He froze and turned slowly toward me, crouching in fear.

"Who told you about them?"

"The police up north. By the way, the Purple Gang got a hold of our mutual friend, Jonathan Randolph. We found him in a beach shed with his throat cut. Did your young pal Larry tell you about that?"

The change that came over him was palpable. His legs seemed to grow weak; he grappled for the nearest chair and half collapsed into it. He ran his hand through his dyed hair and sighed. The other hand, the one holding the pistol, was beginning to tremble.

"So that was it. So *that's* what happened—"

"You've got lookouts posted, George, and the lights are low in here. Are you hiding? Are you expecting them here any minute?"

"Never mind."

"You murdered a man to fake your own death; that surprised me, George."

"I didn't kill him . . . myself," he said, lighting a cigarette and exhaling a huge cloud of bluish smoke in the semidark room.

"It was a damned clever idea. Randolph's, not mine. But it was my idea, not his, to have you and Mary on the beach to witness the killing. A mistake, though, because you obviously saw through it. What went wrong?"

"We found evidence of the two shots you fired: one to kill Wendel Haynes, the second to alert us as we passed the house. Nobody could explain the second shot. So it became our main lead."

He muttered something I couldn't understand. The golden retriever got up off the carpet and went to the door, wagging his tail and whining. I heard people coming up the stairs. Tried to count the steps again. Eight or nine. Maybe only seven? Two people came inside, a man and a woman. The man was young, maybe thirty years old, thin, with long brown hair. I knew him: this was Larry, the same guy Paul Keegan and I couldn't catch on the beach. The guy who'd checked George's mailbox this morning. The dog jumped up and put his paws on the young man's chest, whining and licking him on the wrists.

But it was the woman with him I was watching closely. She had glided in on Larry's arm in a drug-induced fog. Except for the lamp George had turned up, the room remained dark. I doubt the lady saw me. Even if she did, I doubt she was able to make any connection between the man in running clothes sitting in the dark and the guy who came to her housewarming four months previous.

No—I doubt if Michelle Randolph, the pretty, perky, former Kilgore Rangerette, even recognized me. I decided to jog her memory.

"Hello, Michelle. Glad to see you're on vacation too. Sorry about what happened to Jonathan."

She turned slowly, as if moving underwater.

"Whaaah?"

"I said, 'I'm sorry about what happened to your husband,' Michelle. You remember your husband, don't you?"

"Huuhhhh?"

"Your husband, Jonathan? The radiologist who sold drugs. I'm Doc Adams, Michelle. Remember?"

"Hey!" she said in a slur, taking two quick sidesteps to gain her balance. "Hey . . . yeah!"

"Well, I'm sorry that the Purple Gang killed Jonathan. Left him in a shed with his throat cut. Sorry about that."

"Shut up, Doc," said George.

I turned to face him. "George? Isn't this the kid who we saw with the dog on the beach? Was he the lookout while you killed Wendel?"

The kid looked at me, his long curls flopping around his neck. It was a big neck, however, and well muscled. I had a hunch this guy was another enforcer. Then the kid spoke, in a low, gravelly voice.

"He didn't kill him; Henry killed him. I was there to make sure Henry got away."

"Then how did you leave your fingerprints on the telescope and the rented car, George?" I asked. I saw him gulp once, and the hand holding the automatic twitched more violently.

"It was before . . ." he said weakly. "It must have been earlier."

"Careless of you, old boy," I said, mocking him. In my desperation I was trying my damnedest to throw these people off center—to set them against each other if I could.

"And as a final touch, leaving a print on your old apartment windowpane when you tried to steal your radio back, that was terribly careless. A real doozy if you ask me. If you hadn't left that third fingerprint, George, we wouldn't have put the pieces together. And you'd be safe."

He stared at the carpet, flipping the small automatic up and down, as if in time with some dance tune in his head. I could tell he was still impressed with himself. George Brenner had never really grown up.

"We're safe *now*," said a woman's voice, coming from the bedroom. I had a hunch who it belonged to, but I didn't say anything. Larry and Michelle went over to the far end of the room and sat together on a couch in the dark. I could scarcely see them. They whispered together for a few seconds, then I heard Michelle's muffled sobbing. Was it for her murdered husband? Somehow I doubted it. I turned back to George.

"So how did you come across your near double, Wendel Haynes?" I asked. I could move my limbs much better now. I kept flexing them, getting ready to spring out of the chair and . . . something, before it was too late.

"Through me," said the voice again. A tall dark woman entered the room, dressed in black slacks and a black cotton sweater. Dark brown hair, but not as dark as Mary's. Slender, sexy. A stunner. I had seen her picture twice before: the mysterious Margaret Chesterton, estranged wife of Northrop. Whereabouts unknown . . . until now.

"Why did you come in here?" George blurted. "I didn't want him to see—"

"You didn't want Doc Adams to see me? Why not? He seems to have figured out everything else. Hello, Doc Adams. I've heard a lot about you."

She flipped her head around, sending the long hair swirling around her head like a shampoo commercial. She kept smiling and clutching at herself in a very self-satisfied way. She tapped her feet and moved her hands nervously, restlessly. I would bet that Michelle wasn't the only person who was high on drugs. Margaret was laced with something. Speed perhaps. More likely coke. With the line of business her lover, George, was into, it would be easy enough to get.

"Come on, darling. Why don't you tell the good doctor how one day in Jamaica last year, when you were busy trying to set up a distribution network in the States, a skinny fag named Reggie Westley came up and embraced you in the marketplace at Port Antonio, down by the docks, trying to kiss you and moaning for you to come back to him?"

George Brenner arched his left eyebrow and smirked. There it was again: the Peter O'Toole look, even through the latest disguise.

"Yes, that's how it happened, Doc. And I confess I was puzzled and outraged. I struck him across the face and threw him on the ground. He kept coming back to me, trying to put his skinny arms around my neck. Drunk, whining, sissified. It was disgusting. It wasn't until later, when my punches sobered him up a bit, that he finally realized I was not his lover, Wendel, but a look-alike stranger."

"But then you knew you had your man, your substitute corpse."

"No, not then," said Margaret. "It wasn't until later that the idea came to us. My Anne knew Reggie pretty well. She also knew he was running a drug business out of the beach house in Osterville. His partner was Wendel. She kept this secret to protect him, but once I decided to leave Bud and go with George, she came with me and told us all about it."

"So somehow you lured Wendel to come up to Boston with you," I said, looking at George. "It must have been right after he and Reggie broke up. You let him live in your apartment long enough to leave his fingerprints all over the place. Then you took him down to Osterville so he could show you Reggie's end of the operation. You used Margaret's key to unlock the house, and once you got him inside, the rest was easy. But you had to take off that incriminating T-shirt first. The one with the Yellow Bird on it."

"Wendel didn't really care whether he lived or died by that time," said George softly. Margaret sat down next to him on the arm of the chair. "He knew he was sick and dying. He couldn't stand Reggie anymore, with his crying and whining . . . he was sick of the whole thing."

"So he was glad when your thug Henry put a bullet into him," I said.

"He wasn't glad or sad," hissed Margaret. "If you want the truth, he didn't have time to think about it. It was like putting a rabid dog to sleep."

I turned to the front door. Maybe they saw the anxiety on my face.

"Where were you, Margaret, when this happened?"

"In Mexico."

"Yes, to give yourself an airtight alibi. But you knew what happened there, didn't you? You knew because you helped plan it. You helped George devise a way to lure Wendel Haynes up to Boston. You knew everything would go like clockwork, as long as Reggie didn't put the pieces together and recognize his old lover on the floor of the bedroom, which he wouldn't do because he wasn't coming back up to the Cape until April."

"Correct. We knew Lightner would be there, but he had never laid eyes on Haynes."

"But you suggested that it be done in your estranged husband's beach house, didn't you, Margaret? You knew that finding a body in there would all but ruin him. Right?"

"Maybe." She said it with a smirk. I decided I didn't like Margaret Chesterton at all.

"You have no idea what a first-class son of a bitch Northrop Chesterton is, Dr. Adams."

"I rather like the guy myself," I said, turning my head back to the front door. As far as I could tell, it was a screen door on an aluminum frame. The heavy glass door was pulled all the way back, probably so the occupants could hear approaching vehicles. Like maybe a brown van. The stairway beyond the door was straight and wide. There were between seven and ten steps. . . .

"Anne felt sorry for Reggie, but she really didn't care for him. And she hated Wendel Haynes with a passion, didn't you, Anne?"

The woman, who had been standing in the shadow of the doorway, spoke. "Haynes corrupted Reggie, Miss Margaret. He used the boy for his own pleasure and his own profit."

"So then George came along and put all the pieces together," I said.

"Let's just say I was in the process of dissociating myself from certain lines of business and looking for new opportunities," said George. "A key part to this was having, uh, certain parties think I was dead."

"You decided to take over Reggie's drug business on the Cape. Is that why you enlisted the help of Jonathan Randolph?"

"You know," he said, drawing in his breath and placing his finger along his lips, "the interesting thing is, Jon and I met in Texas quite a while ago. It was only after your name came up that I began to figure out a way to die and get away with it."

"Who was on the Cape first, you or George?"

"I was, of course. On the Cape and in Gloucester too. The only competition, in a serious way, I had was with this group . . . the ones you call the Purple Gang. Tell me. . . ." He jerked his finger nervously, flicked his eyebrow up. "What do you know of them?"

He was trying like the devil to maintain his cool. But he was scared. Scared as hell, and it didn't take a genius to see it.

"They killed your partner, Jonathan Randolph. And in a gruesome way. They're partial to sawed-off twelve-gauges and tommy guns, and they don't mess around. By the way, did they kill Reggie . . . or did you?"

"Not me," he said, leaning back in the chair with a sigh. I saw both his hands begin to shake. I looked at the front door again, then back to them. I wondered where Henry was, the big bad man with the big bad gun. I also wondered what they had in mind for me. Did they plan to kill me, or did they sense it was too late for that? All I knew was, the more I could tell them about their own plans, the more they would realize that their secrets were already out—that their best plan now was simply to run while they still had a chance.

I thought I'd try something else. Try to throw a little spin on things.

"George, your former wife, Sarah, told me before I left that if I should find you, to be sure to give you her thanks, and her love. She's most grateful for that thirty thousand dollars you sent her last week."

Margaret snapped her head around at George. "Thirty thousand? What thirty thousand? Was that the same thirty thousand I gave you two weeks ago?"

"Could be," I said, as if making idle conversation. "Anyway, it really tickled Sarah. She said if—"

"Shut up, asshole!" she screamed at me.

It seemed Margaret Chesterton and I were not destined to be chums.

"I don't know what he's talking about," George said.

"It was a check, issued to Sarah," I said. "Anne herself bought it and probably mailed it. I know because the police asked the bank teller in Boston, didn't they, Anne?"

The maid shrank back against the wall, denying it. Then she admitted it, pleading that George had absolutely *promised* her that her missus would never find out. Margaret exploded, right on cue. I figured I was maybe three big steps from the door at the top of the stairs. If I could only find a way to get a three-second head start before George shot me. But even if I did, there was Henry, the monster lurking below. How was I ever going to get past him? George managed to quiet the women and turned his back to me, very angry now. I realized I had probably sealed my own doom by that last little stunt. Still, it felt good pissing Margaret off.

"Tell me more about what happened to Randolph," said George, trying to change the subject. But it was more than that; he was worried, and anxious to find out.

"We discovered the signal system you devised with Reggie's slide projector. One night we flashed it into the dark and got flashes in return. Next day, with the help of the map Reggie had taped under his desk, we found our mutual friend and an unknown Jamaican dead in a beach shack filled with fresh Jamaican grass. About two million worth. The Jamaican was never identified."

George's gun slipped from his hand. He fumbled and grabbed it again before I had a chance to move. He stared at me, wide-eyed. I saw the two women staring at me too. They were all scared.

"Anne, call Henry up here," said Margaret. The woman went out the front door and down the steps, moving fast. I think she was glad to get out of there. I tried to count the steps without making it obvious.

"When was this?" asked George.

"Two days after Reggie was killed. But you know that; you killed Reggie. Gunned him down with a shotgun on Route Six, just below Eastham."

"No, we didn't—we weren't even up there. You say a shot-gun?"

"That's what the police told me," I said.

I thought I counted nine steps as Anne Rawlings went down to the beach to find Henry.

George jumped up now from the couch. "Get your things; we're leaving," he snapped. Larry rose from the couch and dragged Michelle to her feet; they disappeared through another door in the dark. Margaret didn't move. "I won't have time to pack all—"

"Take what you can grab in the next five minutes. *Now.*"

"What about him?" she asked, waving her hand at me.

"We'll take him with us . . . or let Henry handle him."

I felt the dark, numbing, electric bolt of panic run through me. I tasted copper in my tingling mouth. Things moved slowly now, as if in a bad, bad dream. George and Margaret were moving underwater, I felt adrenaline surge through me, leaving me weak and giddy. . . .

Mary! I thought. *Mary! Mary! I'm so sorry!*

Somebody was coming up the stairs now fast, with a light tread. Anne Rawlings came into the room and said in a hoarse whisper: "Henry says he sees lights through the trees. They might be here."

Almost before she was out with these words, the big man came inside, moving fast and quiet. He made a series of hand signs to Anne. I realized then he was mute. Anne made some signs back and said: "He says they're close now!"

"Tell him to take the doctor into the other bedroom," said George, following Margaret into the far hall.

Anne made some signs to Henry, and he turned to me.

He walked to me with blank eyes, his smoke-colored, shaved head looming high over me. I saw his hand move slickly inside his coat. I was dead meat.

Then I remembered Roantis's Rule Number One. . . .

held up my hand in a silent plea. I was very, very afraid.

The man stopped, watching me as I struggled to get out of the chair.

I knew my body was fine now, but I pretended otherwise. Make your enemy think you're helpless, says Roantis, and get his guard down. I'm sure the giant thought I was harmless as a butterfly as he looked down at me struggling to get to my feet, obviously scared out of my wits.

That part I wasn't faking. I saw Anne Rawlings looking at us from across the room. George and Margaret had gone into the master bedroom. I pushed down on the arms of the chair, making my bare feet flop. I stared down at them, but let my eyes come up. I fixed my gaze at a point eight inches below Henry's belt buckle and curled the toes of my left foot tight.

He came a step closer now, which put him about six feet away. I pushed myself off the seat of the chair, into a crouch.

His hand moved further inside his beach coat, grabbing the gun. He probably wouldn't shoot me, but he could swat me with it and knock me cold. Then it was all over; they'd strangle me in the bedroom and make their getaway.

Help me, Mary!

I came up and forward fast, swinging my left leg in a kick as far, high, and hard as I could.

The arch of my naked foot caught Henry right in the groin. I felt a terrific concussion with my foot, but no pain. Adrenaline does that.

Mute that he was, I heard him squeal as I ran for the door. Just before I left my feet and began my headlong leap, I heard the thunk of the .45 hitting the floor as the big man dropped it in agony. I dived right through the screen, hands out in front of me, and braced them for a landing on the stairway. After hitting the bottom step with my hands, I ducked into a roll. I rolled over twice and onto my feet, just the way Laitis had taught me to recover from a fall, and sprinted for the dark trees beyond. A series of explosions boomed out behind me, and I knew Henry was in the doorway, gunning for me. I fought my way through a sea of palmettos, found an open space, and kept running until a sharp, deep pain in my left wrist made me look down, then grab it.

I was faint with fear and pain as I realized I had broken it. Sharp bones projected through my skin, and my hand was on all wrong. My right hand, holding the injury, grew wet and slippery very fast. Groaning, I headed for another thicket, then groped through the brush in a crouch. Finally, I stopped and peered back.

A rectangle of bright light showed me the door was open. A woman was standing in the doorway, silhouetted. That would be Anne Rawlings. But I also saw the snaky bright lines of car headlights flickering through the palms. Maybe it was more than one vehicle; I couldn't tell. Then came a sound like a bear crashing through the woods, and I knew Henry was headed my way.

It was safe to assume he was not in a good mood.

I went another fifty yards or so, until I could hear the surf. I crouched in the bush again, waiting in the lee of the berm that separated the beach from the land. Then I heard something that puzzled me. It sounded like more explosions, coming from the cottages and trees. I was so beat I had no way of knowing if the sounds were real or imagined. I noticed that my wrist had stopped throbbing; the ache seemed to go away. At first I thought this was good news, but then I realized I was going into shock. The body makes its own anesthesia. Trouble is, shock can kill you. I shivered in the sea wind. I was too tired to be afraid. My thoughts refused to go in a straight line. I had trouble remembering where I was. . . .

I woke up fast: again came the sound of heavy footsteps and the crashing of brush and limbs, coming in my direction. How was he able to follow me in the dark? Could he see my blood trail? My teeth chattering, I stood up and moved on. Christ, I could barely walk. I staggered like a drunk. Then I saw the golden retriever out of the corner of my eye. The dog was leading him straight to me.

I realized my best hope was to cross the sea berm and get into the water. That way, the dog couldn't track me and the waves would hide me. If I didn't die first. God, I was tired. . . .

I staggered up the sand hill and fell down its far side, sliding down the sandy bank on my chest. I couldn't seem to keep my eyes open and managed to curl up underneath a sumac bush for a little nap. Just a little one . . .

I woke up with the cold wind blowing on me. I heard the jingle of the dog's collar, coming closer fast, and knew I had to make a run for the water. I got up, fell down, and made myself get up again. The wind was strong now and the sea was high. How long had I been passed out? Five minutes? Half an hour? Not long . . . it just seemed like an eternity. I staggered in a crouch toward the water. Sixty yards to go. Fifty . . . thirty-five . . .

There was a mean buzz off my right ear, followed by a shot. I ran the rest of the way, not looking back, zigging and zagging, falling into the ocean. And that woke me up. All I could think of were Satchel Paige's words of wisdom: Don't look back, something might be gaining on you. . . . Don't look back, something might—

Two more shots. I had no idea where the slugs went. I was waist-deep now and went under, swimming as far as I could before surfacing again. The waves crashed over me, the noise and spray providing good cover. The night was cloudy and dark. I knew Henry couldn't see me.

But I saw him, pacing up and down the beach, the big gun cradled in his hand. I began working my way northward, up the beach toward Surfside. It would only take me two days to get there. . . .

Another figure, dark against the pale beach sand, came running toward the big man. I saw her dress fan out behind her as she ran. She was shouting something, but I couldn't understand it. She ran up to Henry and threw her arms around him, crying and saying something over and over that sounded like go . . . go . . . go. . . .

She pointed back toward the cottage twice, jumping in agitation. Then two sparks of light appeared from behind the sea berm. Then another joined the first two. They came onto the beach, elongated in pencil-thin beams that swept back and forth. I saw Henry drop to one knee. Saw the pistol in his hand buck skyward, spurting flame in the dark. Anne Rawlings was screaming, holding her hands up to her face, jumping up and down in fright. The flashlights stopped then, and I saw three figures spread out and move toward us. Then the couple at the water's edge was caught in the light.

I saw a ball of flame as big as a beach ball and heard the crashing boom of a twelve-gauge from the approaching men. Henry flew backward, landing in the surf. Anne Rawlings, still screaming, turned and ran down the beach. The second shotgun blast caught her in mid-stride, and she crumpled like a blasted rabbit.

I kept only my eyes and the top of my head above the waves, jumping up quickly now and then for air. The sea wind howled in my ears.

I moved farther out into the dark water, wide-awake now and running on desperation. I moved northward, slowly, slowly, keeping my head down in the waves. I was an invisible witness to this double murder. The men scurried down to the victims, talking urgently in Spanish. I heard the word *muerte* more than once. Dead. You bet your ass they're dead, I thought. I wasn't sorry.

Ten minutes or so after I'd seen the flashlights go back over the berm, I hauled myself out of the surf, numb, and shaking awfully with cold. I walked along the wet dark sand, clutching my shattered wrist with my right hand, moaning to myself. The moaning kept me going. I knew if I didn't get warm soon, and get treatment, I might die. These thoughts were secondary, however. What was in the forefront of my thoughts was what I was saying, calling over and over again:

"Mary! . . . Mary! . . . *Mary, help me!*"

Then, over the basso boom of the surf, I heard a quiet *pop* up the beach. I looked up and saw the bloodred, drooping spark trails of a skyrocket in the distance. With the little strength I had remaining, I made myself head for it. As I drew closer I saw a golden flicker on the sand: a beach fire ringed with partying teenagers.

I reached the fire staggering and shaking like a lunatic. The kids almost ran away when they saw me. Then, to the startled gaze of the partying teenagers, I fell in a heap, shivering in the fire's warm glow, still calling Mary's name.

THIRTY-SEVEN

Almost five weeks later Mary and I were sitting out on the porch of the Breakers. She had just finished peeling the potatoes for a big caldron of her clam chowder. I was fiddling with one of my two new toys. I punched in the selector for nineteen-meter band. In seconds I was listening to the BBC.

"Football scores: Nottingham three, Chelmsford Cross zero, Leeds six, Birmingham four . . ."

Mary came in, watching me fiddle with the big Grundig. She crossed her arms and shrugged.

"Bells and Whistles Adams. That's you, Charlie. Aren't you glad Sarah gave you that?"

"Uh-huh. Particularly since Laitis still hasn't returned my ICOM receiver. Spends every spare second listening to the news from Eastern Europe. As usual, the Lithuanians are giving Mother Russia more trouble than all the other places combined. . . ."

"More power to 'em," she said, then turned and looked up the hill to the gravel parking area just above the cottage. To look at my Big New Toy. The wine-red Subaru XT sport coupe crouched there on its oversized, speed-rated radials. Looked as if it were about to leap. Is that why the Brits named their famous car the Jaguar? Boy, I sure loved this new toy. Zero to sixty in eight seconds. Turn on a dime. Four-wheel drive to make it go anywhere my old Scout could go. Only much, much faster. It was almost enough to make me think about selling my Beemer bike.

Almost . . .

"Charlie, it's two-thirty. Joe and Marty are due at three, and the Chestertons are coming at five. If you're going for a run, I suggest you do it now."

I regarded the heavy cast on my left wrist. Running with it was a pain. Perhaps I would just take a long sauna bath instead.

What had happened in the intervening time since I collapsed on the beach that night down in South Carolina? Plenty.

1. The next morning, as I was undergoing surgery for my compound wrist fracture, the police found not only the bodies of Henry the Mute and Anne Rawlings on the beach, but those of Michelle Randolph and Long-Haired Larry in the living room of the beach house. All were killed by close-range shotgun blasts of buckshot, as was the late Margaret Chesterton, who was found slumped on the bed in the master bedroom of the rented cottage. They never found George. And a curious thing was this: the M.E. found a contusion on Margaret's head inflicted before death. Joe speculated, from visiting the crime scene firsthand, that George had knocked her cold with his pistol when they entered the room, letting her fall on the bed while he escaped the premises, probably by the bedroom window, before the Purple Gang closed in on his cohorts.

2. Pinky Chesterton and Charlena Eames had gotten engaged. Since this was to result in what is called a "mixed marriage" (of course it's a mixed marriage, said Mary: male and female), Bud was persuaded to give up his ambitions for the statehouse. He didn't seem to mind. Not only that, he seemed relieved.

3. Their son, Owen Lightner Chesterton, had become captain of Jamaica's posh Buff Bay Polo Club. We had been invited down to watch him play in November, as guests at Shooter's

Hill for as long as we liked. Joe and Marty were coming too. Joe said he might even take a few of his prize Italian double guns for a go at doves.

4. Our two sons, Jack and Tony, were settled in at the Cape for the summer. They were spending a lot of time hanging around with Owen, who was teaching them reggae music, the fine points of soccer, and the fundamentals of English-style horsemanship.

5. James Howland and Luscious Louise—excuse me, make that simply *Louise*—were getting married in three weeks. Time to be buying a lot of wedding presents, Mary said.

6. Ellen Findlay returned to Charlottesville, Virginia, to mend fences with her dad. She was planning on returning to graduate school. Mary said she wanted to give her a going-away present: a one-way ticket to Pago Pago.

7. The last of Joe's pigeons pulled up stakes and flew the coop. Praise the Lord for small favors. Amen. Would that Moe Abramson's ugly fish would take a similar hike, but you can't have everything.

8. Sarah Brenner disappeared right after we returned to Concord. She came over to our house for dinner and presented me with George's old Grundig. She did not seem overly concerned with what had happened on the beaches of South Carolina the previous week. Moreover, she had a vague, detached aura about her we found unsettling. Next day she was gone, leaving a vacant apartment and no forwarding address. Joe found out she'd applied for a passport. Mary said, "Do you suppose the two of them . . . ?" But later she said no, Sarah had more brains than that. But personally, I have my doubts. George was a slick customer. I still picture him with that Peter O'Toole smirk, the raised eyebrow, and the heavy-lidded eyes. With him, anything that happened wouldn't surprise me.

9. Roantis gave me hell when I returned to Boston, saying that what had saved me was *not* Rule Number One. Rule Number One, he reminded me sternly, is: *Always carry your gun and knife.*

10. I got a cryptic telegram from Holland just the other day.

It read as follows: HENRY WASN'T GOING TO DO YOU IN, OLD BOY, JUST TIE YOU UP AND GIVE US TIME. I WOULDN'T DO THAT TO AN OLD CHUM. S SENDS HER BEST. CHEERS: GB.

11. Finally, and most important, was what was happening right now. Mary Brindelli Adams, the Knockout of Knockouts, was sitting in that certain way, with the sea breeze blowing through her hair. The way she was smiling to herself and tilting her head. The way she was touching her neck when she talked to me . . .

She got up and came over and sat on my lap. She turned off the shortwave and snuggled up close.

"You were calling my name when they found you on the beach, Charlie," she whispered. "You weren't calling that bimbo's name, or Louise's name. But my name . . ."

"Couldn't remember them."

"Don't push your luck, pal."

"I love you, Mary."

"I know," she said, and kissed me again.

As I was easing her down onto the grass mat of the porch a big herring gull flashed past, almost touching the screens.

But he didn't scold me!

ABE-8816